# By B. S. H. Garcia

The Heart of Quinaria

Novels
Of Thieves and Shadows
Of Love and Loss (forthcoming)

Novelettes/Novellas
From the Ashes
From the Depths

From the Ashes is free to my mailing list subscribers at bshgarcia.com/subscribe*

OF
THIEVES
AND
SHADOWS

Of Thieves and Shadows

The Heart of Quinaria: Volume One

B. S. H. Garcia

Lost Relic Publishing

Cover design and illustration by Jeff Brown Graphics

Interior design by B. S. H. Garcia

Map and interior illustrations by Jared Garcia

First edition: June 2023

ISBN 979-8-9867208-3-8 (hardback)

ISBN 979-8-9867208-0-7 (paperback)

ISBN 979-8-9867208-1-4 (ebook)

www.bshgarcia.com

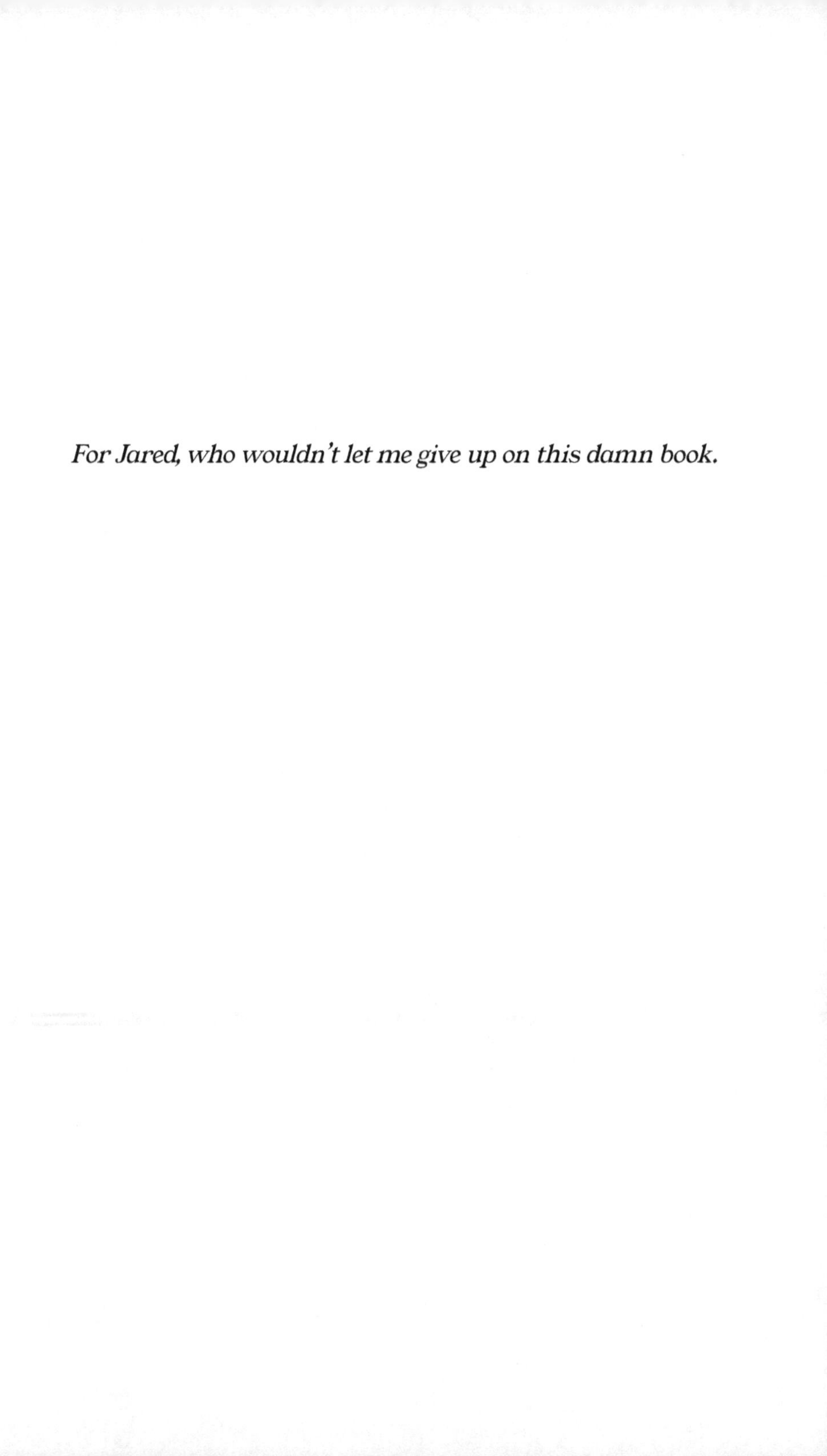

For Jared, who wouldn't let me give up on this damn book.

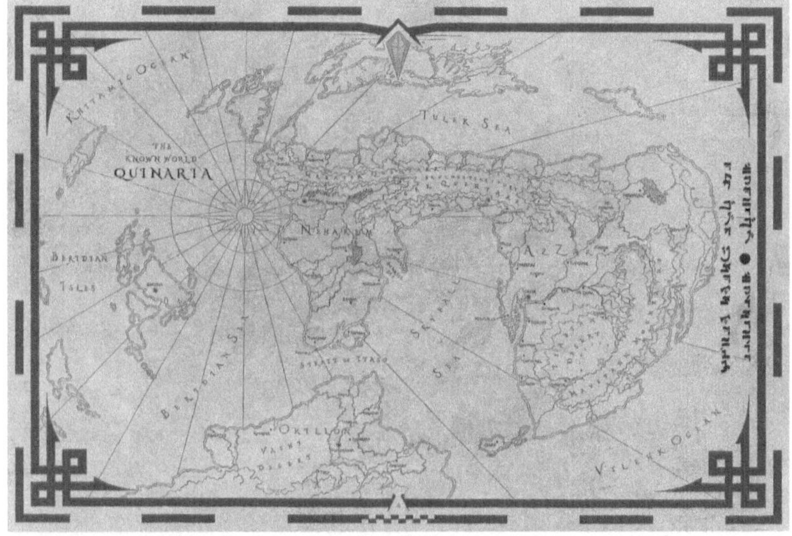

Please visit bshgarcia.com/map for a scalable, full-sized PNG.

I **highly recommend** pulling this up on my website so you can reference it at your leisure while reading. Otherwise, the following two pages offer a zoomed in version that is easier to read.

Thank you!

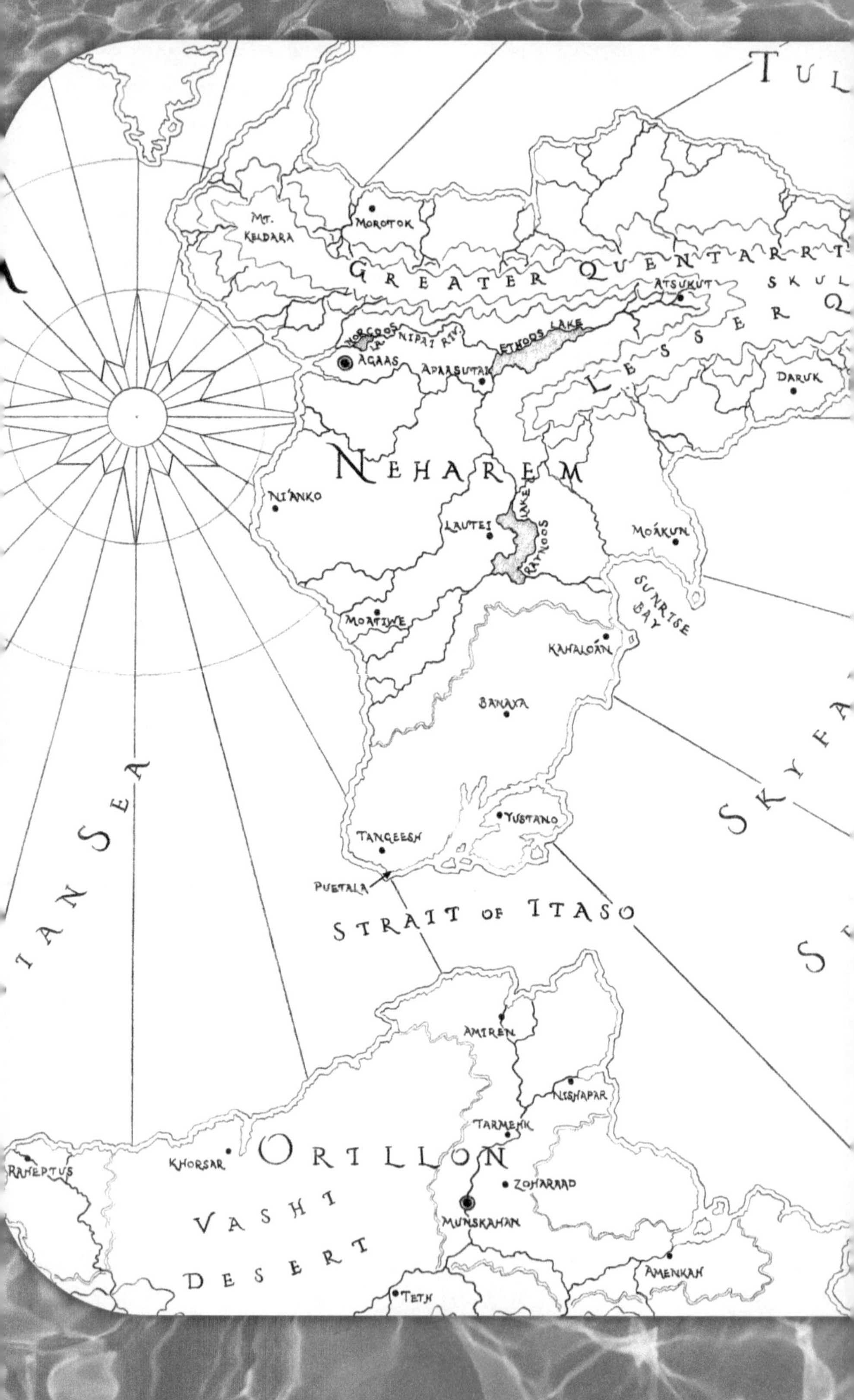

TUL
GREATER QUENTARRT
SKUL
ATSUKUT
LESSER Q
MT. KELDARA
MOROTOK
NORCOOS LA
NIPAT RIV
ETHOOS LAKE
AGAAS
APAASUTAK
DARUK
NEHAREM
NI'ANKO
LAUTEI
LAKE
RAYNOOS
MOÁKUN
SUNRISE BAY
MOATIWE
KAHALOÁN
BANAXA
SKYFA
IAN SEA
YUSTANO
TANGEESH
PUETALA
STRAIT OF ITASO
S
AMIREN
NISHAPAR
TARMEHK
ORILLON
KHORSAR
RANEPTUS
ZOHARAAD
VASHI
MUNSKAHAN
DESERT
AMENKAH
TETH

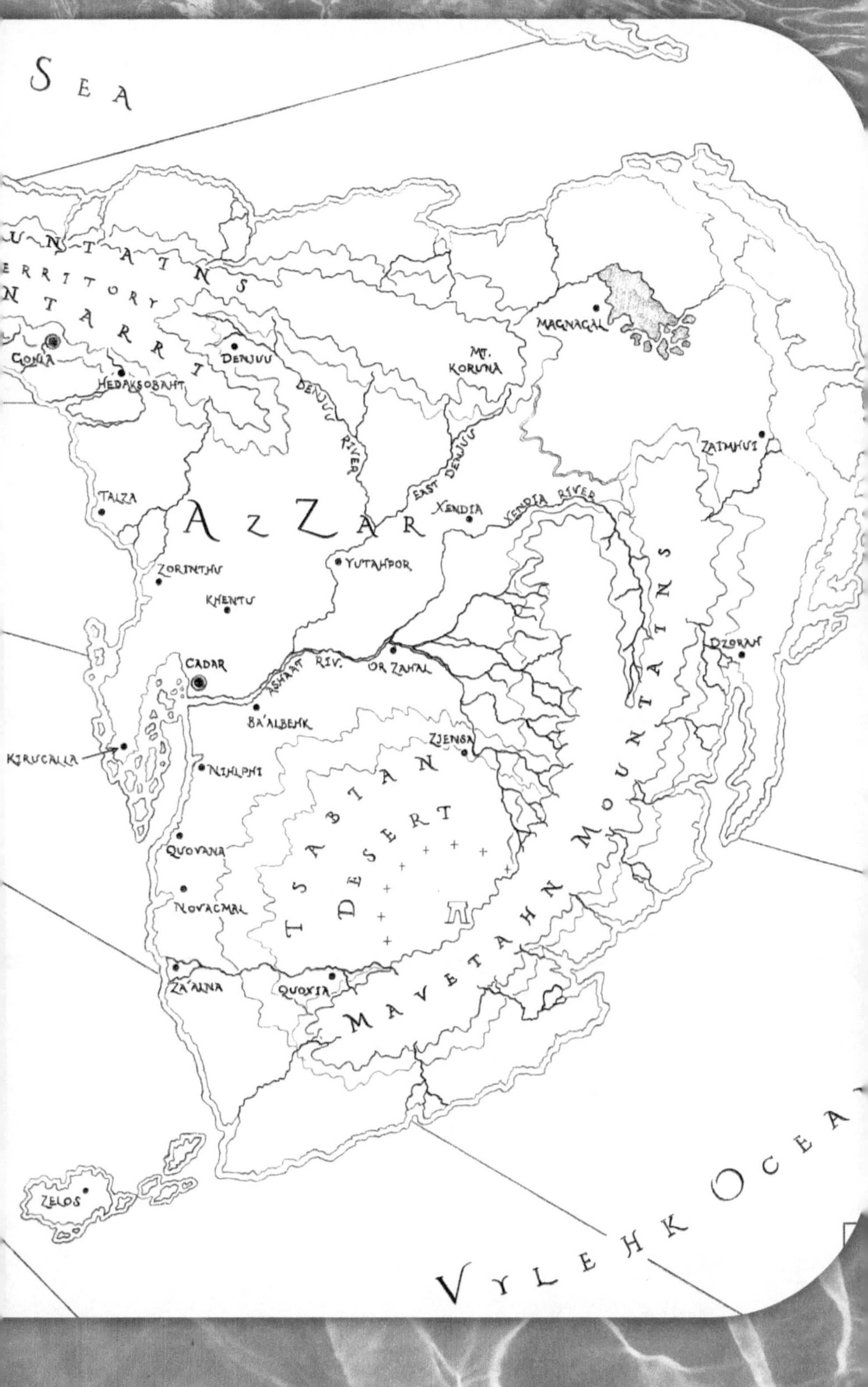

SEA
MOUNTAINS
TERRITORY
NTARRI
GONA
HEDAKSOBAHT
DENJUU
MT. KORUNA
MAGNAGAL
ZAIMHUI
TALZA
AzZar
XENDIA
XENDIA RIVER
ZORINTHU
YUTAHPOR
KHENTU
DZORAN
CADAR
ASHAAT RIV.
OR ZAHAL
BA'ALBEHK
ZJENSA
KIRUCALLA
NIHLPHI
TSABIAN DESERT
QUOVANA
MAVETAHN MOUNTAINS
NOVACMAL
ZA'ANA
QUOXIA
ZELOS
VYLEHK OCEAN
DENJUU RIVER
EAST DENJUU

CONTENTS

One of the first conditions of happiness is that the link between man and nature shall not be bro–ken.

—Leo Tolstoy

Whoever fights monsters should see to it that in the process he does not become a monster. And if you gaze long enough into an abyss, the abyss will gaze back into you.

— Friedrich Nietzsche, *Beyond Good and Evil*

PROLOGUE

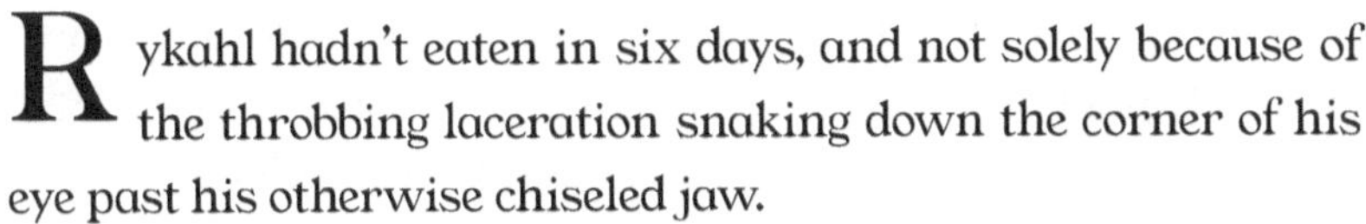

R ykahl hadn't eaten in six days, and not solely because of the throbbing laceration snaking down the corner of his eye past his otherwise chiseled jaw.

The plate of food before him—a steak cut and formed into a pyre atop roasted vegetables garnished with some flower the kitchen deemed edible—lay untouched and steaming, his knife planted in the middle. He drove it in further until the pottery cracked from pressure and the blade struck the table beneath. Father wouldn't be pleased. He cherished the family heirlooms so.

Satisfied, Rykahl caught the skirt of a servant girl and motioned for her to remove his plate. The palace's newest head cook undoubtedly paced in the kitchen, awaiting word of his satisfaction. Pity. They were running out of cooks.

"Husband, is everything alright?" His wife's voice, shrill as a hatchling, spoiled the moment. He clenched his jaw and welcomed the tension throbbing from his teeth down his throat. "If tonight's meal doesn't please you, we should let the kitchen know."

"Aren't you quite done with your meal, my dear? And the children too, yes?" Rykahl pushed away from the table, honeyed wine in hand, and leaned against the wall. His gaze lingered on their unfinished dinner plates. "On with you. I've a visit to prepare for."

They answered him with the sound of chairs sliding against marble.

Wide-eyed and silent, his youngest three scurried by with heads bowed and limbs hidden in a sea of silk the same blood-red shade of the dining room walls. They flocked to their mother like the frightened poultry they were, heeding her whispers before she turned them over to the maidservant.

His wife shuffled toward him and stopped half a body's length away. She never drew closer. No need. Three boys were enough to put the concern of heirs out of his father's mind, and if tonight went as planned, they'd become obsolete. She tugged on her gemmed necklace, exposing a jutting collarbone, lips parted for whatever plea she'd rehearsed.

Rykahl held a finger to her lips. "Your beauty wanes swiftly as of late. I'd advise against tainting what's left of your redeemable qualities by meddling in matters you can't fathom."

A servant gasped. The corner of Rykahl's mouth lifted.

Hair veiled his wife's eyes as she lowered her head like a hound caught stealing from the butcher. "I didn't intend to displease you. I thought with your father's condition, this might not be a good night—"

"That's why I don't leave the thinking to you. One can only imagine our nation's downfall, were you left to *think* on it."

The harpist in the corner plucked a sour note, severing the melancholy tune he played variations of every evening during dinner. A cause for celebration. Rykahl finished the rest of his wine and hurled the cup at the harpist, who ducked before it smacked the wall behind his head. The servants froze. Plates stacked in one's hands. Dirty rags in another's. Clearly, they needed motivation.

Rykahl snatched his wife's drink and finished it in one gulp. The cup rolled off the table and clinked on the ground as he marched toward the harpist.

"Best melody you've played in ages, minstrel. Let's ensure the good performance continues." Rykahl seized a sword from the armor display. "Move aside unless you want to sink with your ship."

Mouth agape, the harpist melted into the star-shaped leaves of the potted plants and watched silently as Rykahl hacked at the instrument until it was no more than kindling.

"Now out. All of you, out," Rykahl screamed at the gawkers. "Haven't you work to do? If not, I relieve you of your duties for the evening. Go home to your miserable shacks and breathe deeply of your naivety. It's the gods' only gift to your kind."

Everyone swarmed the door, lips undoubtedly burning with gossip that would spread like a plague. All but his eldest, Ryman. He lurked in the corner, face angled toward a wall of portraits displaying the ruling lineage of Zal Drusa. The lad stood before the newest and largest addition: a portrait of Rykahl himself, albeit painted in poor imitation of his beauty, though everyone assured him the opposite.

Rykahl touched his son's arm. "You know my displeasure is never directed at you."

"Of course, Eudna." Ryman's tone dripped with apathy. He traced a finger over the portrait. "And when do I get mine?"

Rykahl's nostrils flared. "You know we don't commission them until your rule is official."

"Hasn't stopped you. You commissioned this moons ago, far before Hal-eudna fell prey to whatever illness beset him." Ryman met his gaze, sun-colored eyes contrasting his silvered skin with features so like Rykahl's it haunted him.

Rykahl huffed and walked through the curtains separating the dining room from the balcony. Tepid air laced with sweet blossoms embraced him, a welcome reprieve from the incense his late Ireena insisted on contaminating every room of the palace with. He couldn't bear to part with it. Not yet.

Below, the city of Cadar glowed against the darkened sky, illuminated by nevethium crystals housed in the lamps hanging from upturned roofs and tangled in the vines strung across the pathways. Bridges connected a web of islands in the peninsula, and sun-blood trees, their crimson blossoms in full bloom, fenced in each one. Every island had a precise ratio of shops to homes, complete with a bathhouse or garden. Their bridges spilled into gated access ways to the mainland's Sun-blood District where the palace gleamed at the center. Perfectly constructed so one never need set foot in the districts where slaves and commoners roamed about freely. Rykahl avoided such visits at all costs. He rested his arms on the railing and waited for the door to thud shut.

Instead, Ryman joined him. "You've an important meeting tonight."

Never a question with his boy. He'd always seen through facades, even as a child.

"No one else is to be present. You're no exception."

"Your decision, or *hers*?" Ryman drew out the last word and followed it up with a smirk. "I thought I might attend to better prepare myself for such interactions, should the burden of ruling befall me sooner than expected."

"You forget yourself." A warning. The lad knew better.

"Oh, dearest Eudna, we both know I inherited such treasonous thoughts from you."

Rykahl seized his son's collar and pulled him toward the railing until half his weight teetered over the side. "And we both know who prefers action to talk."

Ryman's eyes widened. A flicker of fear passed through them. He pulled free of Rykahl's grip.

"As you wish, Your Excellence." Ryman exaggerated a bow and stormed toward the dining room. He paused at the curtain. "You know, sometimes I'm grateful Eumma's dead. It's a mercy she'll never have to see what you've become."

The door slammed. It echoed in his mind long after.

Rykahl paced until his silks clung to the layer of sweat forming on his skin. He poured himself another glass of wine, even though the previous one sat untouched on the railing. Above, clouds covered the tri-moons, bathing the balcony in darkness. A chill seized his flesh.

There was nothing to fear. The scroll had called to him for a reason, and he could no longer deny Mavet's power. This was the only way to see Az Zar's success far into the future.

"I'm told it's more effective to drink wine than fondle it, but to each their own," a voice purred beside him.

The glass slipped from his hand and smashed onto the stone, spewing droplets down his robes and onto his sandaled feet. He faced his visitor, expression contorted with equal bouts of shock and irritation. "For Mavet's sake, Karliah. Would it trouble you to announce your presence from the door?"

"What kind of advisor would I be if I didn't encourage our future emperor to be wary of his surroundings?"

"The theatrics aren't necessary." Rykahl eyed her robe. It enveloped her slender frame, exposing nothing but her lips and chin. "I sent the servants home for the night, and my guards know to keep this perimeter clear."

"Don't be so naïve. People are only loyal to an end, and that end is their weakness. If you find it, you can purchase it, and suddenly old loyalties may seem misplaced." She pressed her body against his long enough to let her warmth linger. "Come. Sit at the table with me, won't you?" Arm linked in his, she guided him to the dining room.

"I'd rather not sit."

"But you will."

He did.

Karliah flitted about the room, dousing the sconces until the only remaining light emanated from the thumb-sized nevethium crystal hanging around her neck. However small, it still lit half the room. She sat across from him and steepled her fingers.

"The war council chambers offer more privacy," Rykahl suggested.

No reply.

He cleared his throat. "Is your brother—"

"His path no longer aligns with ours."

"It's treason, then." Rykahl touched the scabbed edge of his wound. "Say the word, and I'll have my best bounty hunters bring him in."

Karliah stiffened. "He's no concern of yours. If that changes, I'll be certain to inform you."

"Oh? I'd think he's our greatest concern, given the other night."

"Our greatest concern is ensuring we remain in Mavet's favor."

Rykahl imagined her squirming beneath the robes and drew some satisfaction from it. The only thing of value his father had taught him was to find everyone's pressure points. Especially one's allies. And she'd made the mistake of confiding in him.

"I've carried out everything asked of me, haven't I?" Rykahl folded his arms and leaned back in the chair. "I'd expect he's pleased."

Karliah's lips drew thin. "He's no more pleased by your actions than by the sun rising and setting each day. Both serve their purposes. Nothing more."

"Thank goodness he has you to speak for him since he never cares to communicate such thoughts himself. Without you, I'd have no way to learn of my insignificance."

"Surely, I've helped you learn more about yourself than that."

Rykahl's cheeks flushed. "We don't have all night for your games. Begin the ritual, or I'll have my guards escort you out."

"Patience, dear emperor. It's the holiest of virtues, and one you'd do well to learn." Karliah sauntered into the hallway and shut the door softly behind her.

"And you'd benefit from some chastity," he muttered, reaching for the wine jug.

Crash.

Rykahl jostled awake. "Karliah?"

He forced his numb legs out of the chair. Steadied himself on the table. Felt around blindly until he secured the sword from the harp kindling pile. When his eyes adjusted to the scant moonlight, he ducked behind the plants with an unobstructed view of the door. Eyes narrowed. Breathing stilled. His veins pulsed with life; a welcomed rush long absent.

The door swung open.

Karliah dragged a boy into the room and kicked the door closed behind her. She eyed the sword in Rykahl's hand. "Really?"

"One can never be too careful around you." Rykahl tossed the sword aside and moved to inspect the boy. Unconscious, on the cusp of adulthood, and wearing nothing but a rough spun tunic. That birthmark, though. His stomach lurched as recognition washed over him. The nursemaid's son. "Last time it was a beast."

"Everything in life comes at a cost. A beast best prolongs the soul of another beast. We'd go through countless animals to stay ahead."

The boy stirred.

Karliah delivered a swift kick to his temple. "An infant of our kin would be ideal, but I figured you'd only be able to stomach one of your servants tonight."

The glint of a knife caught Rykahl's eye. "Will it be painless?"

"Is it problematic for you if it isn't?" She drew a satchel from her robes and dumped the contents onto the table: two stakes, a hammer, and a scroll sheathed in a nevethium case. "No need to partake if you're feeling under the weather. You do look a shade grayer than usual." Before Rykahl could reply, she drove a stake into the boy's feet with one stroke. Muffled cries filled the room.

His hands went cold. Sweaty. He retreated to the balcony and wiped them off on his robes as the other stake found its mark with a *thump*. More cries. The grasping claws of guilt tugged at his heart.

"Is this the only way?" he called over his shoulder.

"Do you want this or not?" she hissed.

"Of course, I do."

"Then the way shouldn't matter."

Karliah's voice spilled out of the dining room, no longer in the smooth cadence of Nyrinian. Rykahl resisted the urge to cover his ears. The tongue she uttered now was a rasping, beastly chant that raised the hairs on his neck. It was of another world. One where mortals shouldn't tread.

The chanting ended as abruptly as it began, followed by the *cling* of metal scraping against a sheath.

A cry.

Silence.

Rykahl vomited over the railing. Head spinning, he stumbled into the darkened tomb. The scent of blood filled his nostrils, stung his eyes, and clung to his body like a mist. He bumped into Karliah as she pulled the crystal from her robes, filling the room with a greenish glow once again.

"Brought you a gift." She thrust a slick mound into his hand.

Rykahl gasped and shut his eyes. He'd never seen a human heart, much less held one, but he didn't need to look to confirm his suspicions. It still carried the heat of life, and, considering its owner, was quite large. When he pried his thumb off the mass, blood pulled away from it and clung to his skin. He dry heaved. The heart slipped from his fingers and landed with a *thud*.

Karliah bared her teeth in a predatory smile. "And I thought you loved heart stew." She wiped the blood from her hands onto her robes and gestured to the floor. "Be a kitten and help me with the sigil, won't you?"

The boy's corpse loomed in the shadows behind Rykahl. "Shouldn't we dispose of the offering? I'd rather not have my household discover it."

Karliah offered no response and knelt with a piece of charcoal in hand. She drew a serpentine eye with flames emerging from the bottom and encased it in a diamond. The heart rested in the center. She pricked her finger, then Rykahl's, and smeared their blood onto the heart. He backed away as she unrolled the scroll and resumed chanting. Her body writhed with each moan until a flame shot up from the sigil's outline. Rykahl clutched the back of a chair, eyes transfixed on the scene. The flame ebbed and flowed, dancing with a brilliance to rival the sun, then faded to a sinewy black thick enough to grasp. It swallowed the heart.

Rykahl leaned forward. The chair slipped out from his fingers with a *crash*. He crawled into the protection of its legs as the black sludge formed into a figure foreign to Quinaria.

The creature stood several heads taller than him, cloven hooves giving way to two muscled legs covered in coarse hair. Although its bare torso resembled a human or a nyrian male, its goat-shaped head bore the skeletal snout of a wolf with a spiny mane jutting out beneath curved horns. Bone spikes sprouted from its back. A twine fastened about its horns held the bottom half of its blood-crusted jaw in place, creating a permanent snarl. In one hand, it held a scythe etched with glowing symbols. In the other, a flawless nevethium crystal trapped in a bone lantern. Its pupil-less eyes found Rykahl's.

An angel. A Caman.

Rykahl's insides turned to liquid. He pressed his face to the floor, hands atop his head. Time slowed, forcing him to imagine the worst scenarios possible before the destined one unraveled. The clopping of hooves filled his ears. Sulfuric odor seeped into his ragged breaths, burning his lungs. He peered between his fingers. It was halfway to him. A few steps more. An arm's length away now.

Almost there.

His chest threatened to burst from his heart knocking against it when something sharp, pressure no firmer than a kiss, pierced through his skin and into the bone beneath. Fire ignited across his spine, followed by a frost threatening to break his back, should he flinch. Pain faded into bliss. He shuddered.

Release.

It freed his mind first, smashing old thought patterns and carving pathways to enlightenment with a feeling he could only liken to drawing the first breath fresh from the womb. The euphoria tingled from his head to his toes, igniting every part of him with a strength his mortal soul had never experienced. He rose, happily oblivious to the creature still skulking in the shadows. He tasted the air. Traced the blood as it journeyed through his veins. The world hummed around him, ripe for the picking. Karliah gasped. She, too, had been blessed.

The Caman stalked back to the sigil, pounded its scythe on the floor, and vanished along with the flames.

Rykahl stared into Karliah's glazed eyes. "Did it work? I feel different." Different? No. His skin tingled. The air flowed into his lungs like ice. All the colors in the room magnified.

"Of course, it worked, you fool." She rubbed her neck as she studied the now empty sigil. "I just don't know how often we have to repeat—"

A *crash*. Karliah froze.

Rykahl spun toward the entrance. A soldier hung off a cabinet masked in shadows, a shattered vase beneath the perch. Rykahl cursed and lunged for the sword. He aimed, handle loose in his fingers, but Karliah shoved him as he launched it, causing the blade to miss its target. The soldier fled, footsteps echoing down the hallway. Rykahl screamed and hurried after him, but the soldier was long gone by the time he reached the doorway, and he'd seen to it no guards protected their wing of the palace.

He stormed back to Karliah and slammed his fist on the table. "Why in Mavet's name did you do that? That soldier probably witnessed everything."

Karliah shook her head. "Are you so easily fooled? That was no soldier. Only one person would've dared to come here tonight."

Rykahl drew a slow breath, clenching and unclenching his fist. "I'm going to kill him," he whispered. "He could ruin everything."

"You're the future emperor. Your word stands above all. And if others believe the ravings of one person, what of it?" She grabbed an empty cup and raised it to him in a mock toast. "We'll outlive the rumor. And them."

KONAR

Today was the beginning of the end, at least for Konar. He lingered by the pond, drawing a moment's peace before entering the summit lodge. Wispy-finned fish wriggled through his reflection, popping in and out of view as they swam beneath the fallen leaves, flaming scales mirroring the foliage.

He frowned.

Like all nyrians, his lifelong white hair helped conceal his age, but the wrinkles tugging at his eyes and creasing his forehead suggested his five-hundred-year lifespan was closer to the end than the beginning. His spirit felt older still: a leaf thriving on borrowed time, masked in green and sapping away from the tree of life. With luck, fate would soon lie in his hands no longer.

"Ready?"

Konar jerked his head up. Elaysia stood beside the pond, cloaked in fog and her mother's dress, a foreign moss-colored silk that would've plunged below her belly button had she not layered beneath it dyed fabric of the same color. It accented the green in her right eye and deepened the maroon in her opposite. Now a grown woman, she bore Annalee's narrow frame and Elishon's high cheekbones, but her skin was a violent mixture of both: russet-brown, splotched with cream. The alterations to the gown shrouded her body, but the gradient tint to her pointed ears and the light-skinned patch around her mouth made her parents' coupling undeniable. And her hair—raven locks streaked with nyrian white. A nyman. A body at war. Not all nyrian and human offspring resulted in such dramatic renditions, but Elaysia was why many in Quinaria believed the gods cursed interbreeding. Few nymans were conceived, and fewer drew their first breath.

"For Khiev-Tatamic's sake." Elaysia whipped a sheer shawl off her shoulders and dangled it like a soiled loincloth. "Why do people desire these fabrics? They cling to everything and offer no protection."

Konar rose to meet her. "It's not as if you're going into battle."

"I beg to differ." Elaysia scrunched her face and eyed the summit lodge wearily.

A smirk tugged at Konar's lips. He lifted the beads wrapped sevenfold around his neck. "Ceremonial garments aren't my ideal attire, either. It's all I can do to stand upright in these layers. Or this collar; does it need to rise so far behind my head?" He clucked his tongue. "The founders of Agaas chose aesthetic pleasure over practicality, I fear."

Elaysia thrust her braided hair behind her shoulders with a huff. "I should've worn something Agaasian. I wanted to honor my mother, but I saw the way High Elder Sower looked at me when the ceremony began." She crumpled the shawl in her hand. "He wasn't the only one."

"They understand your respect for your mother's culture." *Even if it is an abomination.* Konar heaved open the door to the summit lodge. Firelight danced on the walls within, lavishing him in warmth. "Besides, your induction went nearly perfectly, and now you can relax. This is the simple part."

"Nearly?" Elaysia hesitated in the threshold. "What do you mean, *nearly?*"

"Ellie, it's nothing to worry about. Just some notes on orating for next time. We can discuss it tomorrow."

Elaysia's brow furrowed. Though her glare penetrated the room, Konar knew it was intended for him. "I'd rather discuss it now."

Konar bowed to the other elders as they entered ahead of the chiefs. "This is hardly the time," he whispered.

Whether inspired by her own fears or newly awakened maturity, Elaysia regained composure and simply muttered, "It never is."

She strode to the head of the gathering table: an oval oaken slab resting directly on the floor and carved with markings symbolizing the twelve tribes of Neharem. The blue and red stormbird of the Apáasutai tribe. A bountiful basket of fish for the Kahaloán. For the Lautei, a buffalo-headed warrior representing Rayanti, god of war—a deity they emulated too strongly for Konar's liking.

Konar glanced around to ensure no one caught wind of the almost-dispute. Satisfied, he sat cross-legged on Elaysia's right. The chiefs trickled in, examining their new high chieftain with scrutiny as they took their seats. Elaysia stared off, taut-lipped and seething.

"Greet them," Konar urged. "They expect to be acknowledged as they enter."

"I'm aware." Elaysia scooted her cushion away from him, enough that he alone would notice, and forced a smile at Chief Arkuun of the Apáasutai. The elderly nyrian placed his right fist over his heart in greeting, then gave Konar a knowing look when Elaysia's attention drifted elsewhere.

The temperature of the summit lodge rose as bodies crammed around the table. From the heavy furs and stoic expressions of the northerners to the brightly patterned tunics and lackadaisical stances of the coastal tribes, the chiefs and their representatives were as diverse as their languages. Vibrant and neutral skin tones. Shaved heads and flowing manes. Bare skin and torsos covered in tattoos. Straight shoulders and slouched ones. Besides ancient hereditary ties and allegiance to the high chieftain, the only thing they had in common was the clear nyrian dominance in the room. With their pointed ears, icy hair, and luminescent eyes, Konar's race was hard to miss. Even the human-dominant tribes rarely appointed one of their own over the longevity of a nyrian.

Elaysia fidgeted beside Konar, readjusting her dress to narrow the slits even though she wore leggings beneath. He reached a hand to still her, but she shirked away and signaled the cooks to bring forth platters of corn and bean salads, smoked salmon, roasted venison, steamed squash, and fried bread with honey. Pitchers of mineral-rich water and spiced wine were plentiful. Before the meal began, everyone filled their wooden cups or drinking horns and held them high while reciting the blessing reserved for the gathering of the tribes:

> Khiev-Tatamic, Great Spirit,
> whose voice makes the wind,
> whose tears nourish the soil,
> whose breath gives life to the
> races of land, water, and sky,

> Let us live in peace, make our
> eyes ever behold your gifts,
> teach our hands to respect
> all you have created, and qui-

et our spirits that we might
hear your voice.

We ask wisdom for your high
chieftain, and for all your
people, that we may understand the essence of your
world, that you might show
us the lessons you have hidden for us in every plant,
beast, mineral, and person.

May we never take more
than we need, neglect our
stewardship, or kill without
reason, and may we draw
from your strength, not to
conquer our kin, but to fight
our greatest enemy: our–
selves.

We ask all this with open
hearts, so that when this life
fades as the fading sunset,
our spirits may greet yours
without shame.

Konar crumbled herbs into the boiling pot before him and asked Khiev-Tatamic and Chai'Tik, The Daughter, for guidance as Neharem entered a new era. When the mixture cooled, he took a sip and passed it around the table. The chiefs drank, offering prayers to the deities and spirits worshiped by their tribes until the pot ended its journey with Elaysia, marking the beginning of the feast. Chatter spread like wildfire as everyone helped themselves to food straight from the serving platters. Konar abstained, preferring to circle the room and evaluate the reactions of others while they feasted. Smiles adorned most of their faces, but he caught snippets of skeptical conversations when his back was turned.

"What's the consensus on my least redeemable quality?" Elaysia asked—a little too loudly—when he returned to his cushion. "Besides my mother's blood, of course. Let's not go with the obvious."

"Are you a child?" Konar clenched his fists, painfully aware of the eyes she'd drawn. "We've far greater concerns to contend with than your insecurities."

"Like the council's archaic views on commerce?"

"Elaysia." Konar gritted his teeth while he refilled his pipe with kinawa leaves.

As the food dwindled and drink flowed, lighthearted conversation gave way to current affairs—a transition that made Konar wary of joining the discussion. He puffed his pipe, relishing in its mind-altering peace until Orandus, the stocky chief of the Moákun and one of the few human leaders, pounded on the table.

"Many of you know trade with Az Zar has been demanding as of late," Orandus said, his gruff voice quieting the remaining whispers in the room. "I fear the Moákun won't be able to satisfy their demands much longer."

Chief Raenais of the Kahaloán propped her bony elbows on the table and rested her chin on her fists. "I've had similar concerns, old friend. What have they asked of you?"

Konar drew deeply from his pipe. The Moákun shared the eastern border with the Kahaloán. Both were key to maintaining trade with Az Zar, and therefore, peace.

Orandus rubbed his jaw. "They want more than double our agreement last Sowing Moons, and my tribe can't sustain it alone. Boats take time, and quality wood is harder and harder to find. They're also decreasing the rate of exchange for the rest of the tribes' goods. But more importantly"—he gestured to the giant, green crystal nestled in the center of the table—"they claim the last nevethium shipment got lost at sea, whether ravaged by storms or pirates or whatever other excuses they've conjured, and my crew never returned. We've since ceased all exports, including anything provided by other tribes, but before I embarked for the holy city, I received a message detailing the alleged debt we've amassed."

The room erupted in murmurs. At the heart of the trade alliance was nevethium, Quinaria's most precious resource. Found underground and in the water, the crystals were the essence of life, influencing the health and prosperity of everything from air to plants to people. When extracted sustainably, nevethium provided renewable light and heat, and its mere presence promoted wellbeing and healing. The tribes of Neharem had learned to take just enough to maintain the health of the land while still reaping the benefits. Other nations weren't so benevolent. They sought dominance over the natural world instead of harmony, and progress and luxury were to be achieved at any cost. Az Zar's sophisticated industry and Orillon's vast deserts were proof.

Konar leaned in toward Elaysia and whispered, "This is the primary concern of the chiefs, so please handle it with poise."

Rajar, chief of the Lautei, caught wind of the exchange. He cleared his throat and strode around the table, looking down his beak of a nose at the others. "My heart is with your people, Orandus. Neharem will be indistinguishable from the barren lands of the east and south, should we sacrifice any more crystals. These are treacherous times. One can't help but wonder if we should entrust them to a High Chieftain who's scarcely seen twenty-one Gathering Moons." He reached a muscular, brown arm around Orandus's shoulders as if they shared a secret. "She contributed little more than a few words during the feast, and now she's dumbfounded by our most urgent affairs. Concerning, no?"

Konar glared at Rajar. "Perhaps she's gathering her thoughts before speaking. Some of us would do well to heed such wisdom."

That earned a few chuckles. Konar nudged Elaysia to seize the moment. She ignored him and twisted her vine-shaped bracelet in silence, gaze locked onto the headdresses of past high chieftains adorning the walls.

"Pondering is only helpful when it leads to action," Rajar growled.

Elaysia faced Rajar. "Last I checked, the trade alliance with Az Zar wasn't the concern of the Lautei."

The chief's upper lip curled. "It is now. A strained relationship with Az Zar affects all the tribes, and I fear you're doing little in the way of offering us comfort." A few chiefs and elders murmured in agreement. "If the high chieftain sees fit, I can arrange a solution with my warriors and the Banaxa. You need only speak the words."

Konar shook his head. Rajar's solutions tended to be violent.

"Agaas will address all concerns and supply you with information as it comes to us," Elaysia said through clenched teeth. "In the meantime, we encourage everyone to use imported goods sparingly and cease nevethium mining, effective immediately."

"But how will they be addressed, Moonrider?" Rajar leaned against a wooden column and traced his fingers around the indentations. "I hope your relations with Az Zar are superior to your father's. Or do you plan to offer your life as well?"

Konar slammed his hands down on the table. "That's enough." He marched over to Rajar. The chief was tall, but Konar had enough height to look down on him. "You will address our high chieftain by her proper title and refrain from speaking ill of Elishon Moonrider. Though"—he lowered his voice—"I daresay I'd enjoy correcting you if not."

"My humblest apologies, High Elder Lightfoot, and to you, my exquisite High Chieftain." Rajar swept his hand in a mock bowing motion, then sauntered back to the table and wedged himself in between the Lautei elders. "But I'm surely not the only one wondering if you plan to avenge the murder of your parents. This pretense of peace has gone on long enough."

"Shut up and let the rest of us speak," roared Gibrund, chief of the pale-skinned Daruk. Bits of food fell from his mouth and onto his beard as he spoke. "I grow tired of your constant blabbering, Rajar, but you have a point. High Chieftain, will Az Zar be dealt with?"

Elaysia froze. "I... they..."

Before Konar could interject, the Ni'anko chief Kelsia, a dark blue nyrian beauty with golden tattoos on her face, flitted over to

Gibrund and placed a delicate hand on his arm. "She struggles to make the plan simple enough for you to digest, my friend."

Gibrund rubbed his blind eye in irritation. The burly nyrian grabbed a wine pitcher, finished its contents in one long gulp, then glared at Kelsia while everyone held a collective breath.

He burst into laughter. Wine flew out of his nose and landed in front of a disgruntled Rajar, sending half the room into an uproar.

Konar grabbed Elaysia's shoulders amid the spectacle. "What are you doing? We prepared for these questions."

"It's not my fault." Her tone was blind to discretion. "You heard what he said about me. About my family."

"And you're reacting exactly how he wants you to. Do you want to be unseated?"

"It doesn't matter." She slumped in her cushion. "They made up their minds about me long before the ceremony."

"So, change their minds."

"Maybe I don't care."

"Maybe you don't deserve this."

The heat left her eyes for a fleeting moment, widening at the blow. She finished her wine and poured another cup, gaze never leaving him. "I never have, remember? Might as well enjoy a few pleasures on my way out."

"Fine. Let the wolves ravage you."

Konar fought the urge to snatch her wine cup as she drained it. He'd tried to set an example by abstaining from the liquid poison, but Elaysia often did the opposite of his advice. A recipe for destruction.

"Thank you, Chief Kelsia, for that much-appreciated respite," Rajar called over the dying laughter. "No doubt we're all in need of it as the hour draws late. However, our high chieftain, may she reign eternally, has yet to answer our questions or apologize for her incompetence."

"You want an apology?" Elaysia lurched to her feet, cup in hand. "I'm sorry I'm not my father, I'm sorry I'm not my brother, and I'm sorry I'm the half-bred daughter of an Az Zarian human, but last I checked, that's not outlawed here." She took a step back and spat. "Not yet."

The flutists stopped playing.

Konar attuned to everyone breathing, judging, waiting. A controlled demeanor was key to success in the delicate governance of Neharem, and Elaysia had all but shattered the chiefs' confidence. Tribal law had required them to wait until she reached the age of leadership after her parents' deaths, but now she entered a trial period that could rule the years of his work obsolete.

Rajar, evidently bent on hurrying that outcome along, clapped loud and slow. "Quite a performance. I was expecting a typical Agaasian feast, but who would've anticipated the added benefit of theatrics?" His face darkened. "Moonrider, you've moments to debrief me on your plan before I leave this hall. I'd hate to return later under unfortunate circumstances."

Veiled as it was, Konar caught the threat.

But what could he say? If he reprimanded Rajar, they'd see her as weak.

And if he answered on her behalf? Just as destructive. They'd assume her incapable of leading.

Well, he had to try. Everything depended on this moment. One misstep would undo years of preparation, all hopes of setting the past right lost in a sea of talking heads concerned only with satisfying their personal grievances. He couldn't permanently retire if Elaysia's leadership skills floundered even more than her late father's.

The darkness beckoned him, its release close enough to taste but forever out of his grasp.

He cleared his throat "My chiefs—"

Boom.

The summit lodge rattled with a sound like concentrated thunder.

Kelsia gripped the table. "Do you normally get groundshakes in Agaas?"

Konar shook his head. "Not in my lifetime."

Boom.

Another rattle.

The chiefs scattered from the table. Before anyone reached the door, Zavik burst into the room, face as red as his hair.

"One of the living trees was attacked. There's a billow of smoke like..." Zavik paused in disbelief. "I don't know. I've never seen its like. People are in danger."

Elaysia pushed through the crowd. "Show me."

Zavik led her from the room. The council turned to Konar.

"Please, join your people in the guest lofts," he said. "I don't want to put anyone in unnecessary danger. We'll reconvene once we've neutralized the threat. May Chai'Tik protect us."

Konar strode from the room, keenly aware of the relief washing over him despite the circumstance. The distraction would give Elaysia time to prepare an apology and response. For him to prepare it. He could still carry on as intended and wash his hands of Agaas for good.

The gods worked in mysterious ways.

ZAVIK

Zavik darted through the platforms of Agaas, trying (and failing) to avoid visualizing what it would be like to fall hundreds of feet.

When he'd first arrived as a child, the concept of an interconnected village in the trees, suspended by decks and bridges, filled his throat with bile and his mind with nightmares. A recurring vision entailed mushrooms growing over his dismantled corpse until they buried the brief life of Zavik Mon Talab into oblivion.

"It's safe," six-year-old Elaysia had told him as he peered over the railing his first day in Agaas, fingers wrapped tight as a merchant's coin purse. "The trees are our friends."

"Do you have any idea how old they are? The city could collapse at any moment." The world spun around him until he lost his balance and fell into Elaysia, sending her into a flood of giggles. He untangled himself from her and backed into the security of the trunk—the furthest he could be from the edge.

To be honest, he was no less terrified now, but this time falling wasn't the only threat. He kept his eyes fixed on the smoke-stained sky as he pounded down the path.

"Which living tree?" Elaysia shouted over the rumble of cries. Normally, he fought to keep up with her, but this evening she trailed him, ceremonial dress making her strides short and uncertain.

"Igtheos," he gasped. "It—"

Elaysia yanked him back before he collided with a group of Tangeesh gawking at the smoke.

"Thanks, High Chieftain," he said, eager to use her new title for the first time.

She glared. "Don't."

"Sorry."

Zavik stopped at the foot of the Igtheos bridge. People swarmed across the rickety decking, tears streaming down their ash-smudged faces as they clutched loved ones. Beyond the bridge, mossy colored smoke seeped from the tree and fused into the dusky sky. The lofts visible from the main path looked mostly intact. Whatever calamity befell the tree had occurred on one of the three lower platforms.

Elaysia disappeared into the crowd. Zavik plowed after her, eyes on the tree, and collided with someone. His seers—the name he'd assigned to the contraption he'd crafted and wore over his eyes to enhance his sight—crashed to the ground. He felt around blindly, cursing and muttering to himself until someone placed them back over his eyes. A woman trembled before him, clutching a whimpering infant. He struggled to his feet and offered her a hand, but she sprang up and pressed herself and the babe against him. Sobs escaped her throat.

Zavik patted her back awkwardly, then held her at arm's length. "I'm so sorry. Are you hurt?"

She wiped some blood off her chin. "We're fine. My neighbors, though…" Tears welled in her eyes, and the infant wailed. "Shh, shh."

"Did you see what happened?"

She shook her head.

"What about before?" Zavik guided her across the bridge as quickly as he could without seeming inconsiderate.

"I was feeding Nadia when the ground shook beneath me. Things crashed around us. We barely got out in time." The child quieted in her arms and looked up at Zavik as if sensing the tension.

Zavik kissed the top of her head. "Speak to the elders. They'll find lodging for you."

The woman nodded, but she didn't release her grip on his arm. Zavik bit his lip. He considered taking her all the way back to the High Tree, but she was safe now. Elaysia wasn't. He pried off her fingers with a sympathetic smile and hurried back across the bridge, trailing a line of watchers with buckets of water on their shoulders.

An anguished moan rose above the other cries. Zavik made his way toward the sound, smoke stinging his lungs as he wove around the remaining evacuees. Elaysia knelt beside a man cradling his face in his hands. Though most would mistake her demeanor as calm, Zavik recognized the tension set deep into her brow. He waited a few feet away until the man trudged to the bridge.

Elaysia beckoned him closer. "The incident occurred on the platform above his. A loft fell on top of his family's and collapsed it. He only survived because he was returning with the evening meal." Her voice broke, and she looked away. "I've never heard of anything like this, Zav. What could cause such destruction?"

Zavik frowned. In Orillon, he'd seen lightbursts imported from Az Zar. The contraptions relied on deconstructed nevethium and lit up the sky with bursts of greenish-yellow light for celebrations. Had they discovered a way to weaponize it? "It reeks of Az Zar," he said finally.

Elaysia rubbed her face. "But why?"

"Your ceremony?" Zavik regretted speaking as soon as the words left his mouth. Elaysia wrapped her arms around herself. "But"—he touched her shoulder—"whoever did it was probably waiting for a distraction to sneak into the holy city. It wasn't *because* of your induction."

It was undoubtedly because of her induction. Given her expression, she wasn't the least bit convinced by his lie, either.

Zavik slouched against the railing. Night had fallen, and across the way, the Hannasah Tree's nevethium heart beamed in response, the smaller crystals in the lofts mimicking it like stars among a moon.

The heart.

He spun back toward the Igtheos. Its heart faced opposite the bridge, but there was no green glow. A sick feeling took hold of his stomach as he raced up the winding ramp to the final platform. He reached its resting place and froze.

"What is it?" Elaysia shouted from below.

Zavik's throat tightened. "It's gone."

"What's gone?"

"The nevethium heart."

"That's not possible."

"It's not like we secure them. Someone cut it out."

"But..." Zavik couldn't make out Elaysia's form in the darkness below, but her voice told him all he needed to know. "What do I tell the council?"

"The truth. They'll find out eventually, anyway."

She didn't reply. Despair hung in the air like a fog. He'd suggested regimented watcher duty for several moon cycles now but received laughs in response. The holy city had never been attacked before. It was impenetrable.

Until it wasn't.

Zavik plodded down the ramp. He traced his fingers over the living tree's gnarled bark, summoning the rest of the memory from his first day in Agaas.

Six-year-old Elaysia ran her hand across the bark as if she petted a small animal. "The trees won't let us fall, you know. If we're good to them, they're good to us."

Zavik reluctantly pressed away from the security of the trunk. "They aren't conscious."

"Maybe your trees back home aren't, but ours are. They talk to me."

"You're crazy."

"Touch him." Her eyes sparkled. Zavik tried not to stare too long at the diamond-shaped patch of cream enclosing her lips. It outlined the bottom half of her nose and trailed down her chin. "Say 'hello.'"

Zavik tapped the tree. "Hello."

Elaysia beamed. "Now you're friends." She tugged on his hand, fingers sticky with sap. "Come on, let's meet another."

Such was the Neharem way. All twelve tribes lived in harmony with the land: ice block shelters and longhouses in the north; huts on the coasts; yurts or tents for the nomadic tribes; soil-covered domes in the south. Though founded long after the rest of Neharem, Agaas emulated tradition and integrated its people directly into the behemoth trees that grew a few thousand feet from the coastline. Of course, stormbirds made the feat possible—if one believed the lore. Villages of its equal wouldn't manifest again in their absence.

Konar's emotionless voice rang through the night long before Zavik reached the main platform. Two women flanked him on either side as he interrogated Elaysia; neither was surprising. Maseeya was Elaysia's surrogate mother and never far from her side, and Jakki rivaled Zavik for the role of Elaysia's closest friend and confidant.

Zavik crept up to the circle. He stiffened as Jakki patted him condescendingly on the back. Others pined over her tattooed midriff and long, golden-brown legs, often exposed in high-slit skirts, but he loathed the attitude simmering beneath her polished exterior.

"Never far from trouble, are you?" he muttered.

"I'm always here to support Elaysia, if that's what you mean," Jakki whispered. She elbowed him to keep quiet.

"... and no one saw anything?" Konar was asking a slump-shouldered Elaysia.

Elaysia shook her head. "Nothing suspicious before the attack."

Jakki threw her waist-length snowy hair behind her shoulders. "I'll head back to the High Tree and see what information I can glean from the survivors." She needlessly shoved Zavik out of the way as she departed.

Elaysia glared at Jakki. Zavik extracted some satisfaction from it.

"It can wait until morning," Elaysia said. "The people need a moment to themselves. They've lost loved ones tonight."

"A moment can sour the memory. I'd rather salt their wounds than lose valuable information." Jakki shrugged and sprinted across the bridge.

"I'll stop her," Zavik offered to Elaysia.

Konar blocked his path. "That won't be necessary. She's right."

Cheeks burning, Zavik returned to Elaysia's side.

"We need to reconvene with the chiefs and elders at once," Konar continued, still eyeing Zavik. "This theft needs to be addressed."

"I don't think they should know these things yet," Maseeya said resolutely, tugging her shawl tighter around her narrow shoulders. "It's just one crystal."

"Just one crystal?" The controlled tone in Konar's voice slipped. "Nevethium hearts have been at the center of all living trees since Agaas was founded. Without it, the tree's stability might be compromised."

"The people are safe. Let it fall if it must." Maseeya folded her arms, and Zavik became painfully aware he observed a conversation he was no longer welcome in.

Recognition flickered over Konar's eyes as if he'd solved a puzzle. His face softened. "You're afraid of them blaming Az Zar."

Maseeya's moon-toned skin paled. "It's not worth starting a war over."

"Hiding it from the council will only give them more cause for war."

"Then you address the chiefs while we tend to the people."

"She needs to lead the gathering."

"So they can blame this on her, too?"

They loomed in the darkness like Apáasutai totems, eye-locked in debate. Two parents vying for a child's loyalty. Zavik was about to suggest a discreet departure when Elaysia brushed past him, triggering a wave of prickles across his skin.

"Come on," she whispered. "I want to explore the lower levels."

"Gladly."

Zavik hurried after Elaysia, looking up as he often did to better process his thoughts. He rounded the bend and slammed into a wall.

At least, it felt like a wall. The impact sent him reeling toward the ground, but someone snatched his tunic before impact. Zavik readjusted his seers. A mountain of a man towered over him. One of the Banaxa, given his scant clothing and intricately scarred chest, the largest tribe in Neharem known for their predominantly human population—all skilled warriors and hunters. Scar Man hadn't loosened his grip on Zavik's tunic yet, either.

Zavik tugged free. "Thanks, and sorry."

Elaysia had disappeared, and Scar Man didn't seem keen on letting him pass. Zavik lurched to the side. Scar Man mirrored him and crossed his tree-trunk arms.

"If we keep letting foreigners into Neharem, things like this"—Scar Man waved his arm in a violent, swooping motion at the smoldering tree—"will happen more."

"Possibly, yes." It was hardly the time to engage in debate.

"People like you without a tribe, you've got nothing to lose." Scar Man grabbed Zavik's collar again, pulling him close enough to smell the warm, soured wine on his breath.

Zavik braced himself for more of Scar Man's wisdom, but then Elaysia appeared beside him and rested her hand on the man's fist. "People like Zavik have everything to lose, brother. He chose this home and doesn't take it for granted."

"My High Chieftain." Scar Man loosened his grip enough for Zavik to step a safe distance away. "The Banaxa will always fight for Neharem. To protect her from evil." He pounded a fist on his chest and marched off.

Zavik attempted to rub the stains off his tunic where Scar Man grabbed it. "Title's already carrying its weight."

Elaysia rolled her eyes. "You're hopeless."

"I like to think I give others hope."

He leaned against a branch the way watchers did off duty. It snapped under his weight, and he slammed into the railing, stomach-first. As he hung there like a hide left to tan, the melody of Elaysia's laughter filled his ears. He grinned, then tightened his expression into feigned irritation before facing her.

"Are you alright?" She traced her gaze over him like a concerned mother, then bent to brush some dirt off his tunic.

He grabbed her hand to stop the fussing. It was cold. He squeezed it and patted her shoulder. "You're doing a good job tonight."

"I guess." She rested her forearms on the railing and her chin atop them. "I wish Konar saw it that way."

Zavik inched close enough that their sleeves touched. "That calloused nyrian has a knack for making people feel small. Don't take it personally. You know he loves you. He just struggles to show it."

"He doesn't even try."

"Well, I do."

Elaysia's eyes widened

Zavik clenched the railing. *Brilliant, Zav. Just brilliant.*

"I do..." Zavik pawed at his face and fumbled for a retraction. "I do see *it*. His love, I mean. It's always easier for someone on the outside to notice, right?" He forced a chuckle and marched ahead, motioning Elaysia to follow. "Let's get on with our investigation, shall we?"

Elaysia followed and spoke no further of the incident, and the burning in his cheeks subsided. Maybe she hadn't noticed. Or didn't care.

Somehow, that was worse.

The Igtheos's lowest platform better resembled kindling than lodging. Nearly a third of its trunk had been torn away and splintered. Even if the missing heart didn't compromise the structure, that would.

Though the smoke dwindled, the scent of charred wood smothered the air, and the rich, burgundy coloring of the few recognizable lofts had transformed into ashen gray. A leg stuck out from the debris like a morbid cairn. A shredded torso there. A hand. Given the condition of the tree, it was unlikely anyone survived, much less remained intact.

Zavik clutched his stomach. "We should go. I don't think anyone's left."

"Wait." Elaysia rushed toward one of the partially intact lofts. Only one wall was missing, and a faint green glowed within. Zavik followed, taking care with his footing as the debris groaned beneath his weight.

Inside, a man rocked on the floor, face smudged with ash. He clutched a small child to his chest. Beside him sat a table with untouched supper. Three place settings. Elaysia touched the man's shoulder, and he startled, gaze darting around as if waking from a dream.

"My High Chieftain. Forgive me; I was putting the little one to bed." He laid the child on a cot. "Can I get you both something? Tea? Yes." He shuffled to the caved in fireplace and fiddled with some mugs. "My mate's not home yet, but she'll be honored to hear the high chieftain stopped by."

Zavik crept toward the child's cot. The girl, no more than five, lay far stiller than children of that age should. Her face was a pallor gray instead of reddish-brown like her father's, and a thin line of blood trailed from the corner of her mouth. Zavik held his breath and pressed his ear to her chest. No heartbeat. He shook his head at Elaysia.

"Be at peace," Zavik whispered. He closed the girl's eyes.

Elaysia touched the father's arm. "Do you know where your mate went? Can you gather some things and follow us to a temporary loft?"

"She's out. Best to wait." The man's hands trembled as he extended a mug to Elaysia.

"Thank you, but I'm alright without. Come with us. We've plenty of tea in the summit lodge."

"I can't. My daughter is sleeping." The man knelt beside the child and hummed a lullaby.

Zavik dug at his cuticle with his forefinger until it drew blood. "I don't think we should force him."

"We can't leave him."

"Let him grieve. I can check on him in a few hours."

Elaysia gave one last look at the child and trudged out.

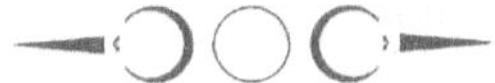

Zavik hurried across the Igtheos bridge, eager to set foot on stable ground. Well, stable for Agaas. It was well past time to sleep, even for him, and the air was filled with harsh winds and the haunting moans of survivors.

"Ellie, come on," he shouted. She lingered on the bridge, gaze lost somewhere in the deep shadows and twisted branches of the woods. "You need to get some rest."

She stormed past him, yanking the twine from her braids as she went. "Rest? I'll be up past dawn dealing with the council. They were already on edge because of lost nevethium shipments. If we confirm Az Zar was behind this, they'll demand justice. From me." She pinched the bridge of her nose. "I don't want to be responsible for people's lives. I never wanted this. Annonitus did."

Zavik swallowed. Though Elaysia's older brother had been dead almost as long as her parents, she still lived in his shadow.

He playfully bumped his shoulder into hers. "I guess the responsibility falls to me."

The corner of her mouth raised. "Not your worst idea. Maybe after a few days with you, they'd want me back."

Zavik chattered the rest of the way to the High Tree. Located at the center of Agaas, it resembled a small village and contained the high chieftain's quarters, multiple outdoor cooking posts, additional housing for family and elders, the summit lodge, visitor quarters, the only library in Neharem, and a giant storage chamber for supplies and weapons. Unlike the other living trees with structures built into and around the trunks, the High Tree's core was cut and smoothed into a platform, leaving the exterior branches to create a natural enclosure. The center of its pavilion contained the largest nevethium heart in Neharem's possession. Had it been taken—assuming stealing a horse-sized crystal could be done discreetly—more than the peoples' hopes would crumble.

Elaysia hesitated outside the summit lodge doors. Her hair tumbled around her shoulders, teasing her collarbone and blowing over a face streaked with sweat and dirt. "How bad do I look?"

Zavik tore his gaze away from her. "Terrible. Absolutely terrible."

"You always know what I need to hear." She bit her lip. "See you in the morning?"

"First thing."

"Wish me luck."

"You never need it."

She rolled her eyes and disappeared into the lodge.

Zavik slammed the door to his loft and plopped down at his desk. Jagged and unleveled, its craftsmanship was lacking, but making something on his own had been better than asking for help and facing the accompanying mockery.

He retrieved a dagger from the folds of his tunic and turned it over in his hands. A lyvium blade. He'd found it at the Igtheos before notifying the others. Native to Az Zar, lyvium was stronger than any other metal, yet light and flexible, making it ideal for weapons—if one could afford it. The sleek hilt was Az Zarian. It was enough for the council to formulate an opinion about the attacker's identity. Convenient. Too convenient.

Zavik frowned and shoved it into the drawer. He'd let Elaysia decide.

ELAYSIA

The chiefs departed the lodge in a storm of whispers, leaving Elaysia and her mentor alone to debrief. While the Apáasutai agreed to shoulder the burden of the homeless—the Igtheos had collapsed the day prior, leaving over two hundred people without lodging—the council was no closer to resolving the other issues.

"The Lautei and Banaxa crave war, thinking it's some glorious endeavor," Konar said as he shoved away his untouched meal. "We're no match for the Az Zarian military."

Elaysia tore off a chunk of flatbread and compressed it between her fingers until it resembled a pebble. "Our warriors have unmatched instinct and love for our land."

Konar shook his head. He lit his pipe, gaze looking askance. "Unless they're lucky enough to be born into wealth or power, The All-Sovereign drafts every firstborn male in Az Zar at the age of six. These boys spend their lives training and become superior soldiers. It's a cruel system, and one we cannot contend with."

"Then we'll keep the peace. Many see the wisdom in your advice, and we don't even know if Az Zar was behind the attack."

"Don't be foolish. Regardless of what we admit to the council, we both know they are. Zavik's little discovery all but confirms it."

Elaysia winced. Zavik had begged her not to tell anyone else about the dagger, but she thought Konar would have insight on how to best locate its owner. Perhaps conversing with chiefs individually or questioning the survivors. Instead, he confiscated it and forbade further discussion.

"As for Rajar"—Konar inhaled the pipe and loosed a cloud of smoke over the table—"he's yearned for war since your parents' murders. Others trickle to his side with every setting sun, aching for revenge. This is the justification they've waited for."

"Konar." Elaysia crushed the bread ball in her palm. "Why didn't you avenge my parents? Were their lives not worth a war?"

"No one's is." Konar leaned back against the wall and shut his eyes. "Go to bed. I've much to think about tonight."

"You always do."

And I've come to a conclusion of my own.

With a final glare, Elaysia marched out of the lodge and slammed the door behind her.

Elaysia grabbed the satchel hidden beneath her cot and filled it with items essential to travel. Maps of Quinaria, both modern and ancient. A skin of wine, another for water. Dried berries, smoked fish wrapped in seaweed, and flatbread. Her grandfather's bone-hilt dagger. Healing herbs she'd borrowed from an unaware Zavik. A well-worn riding cloak.

Someone stirred outside her door. She froze, heart pounding, until the footsteps trickled away. Only watchers. Konar requested more volunteers to patrol after the attack, and Elaysia had grudgingly gone along with his request. It would make tonight's escape problematic but not impossible.

She crept to her chest and yanked out knee-high boots and a forest green tunic. Embroidered with leaves and vines, it was slit at the thigh to make room for leggings and draped down over her crotch and rear for an easier ride. Her ceremonial garments, now exposed, glared out from the bottom of the chest. She closed the lid.

Her fingers trembled as she secured her braids in extra twine. Bow and quiver slung over her shoulder, she gave her loft a final glance, her gaze lingering on her mother's sword hidden beneath a tangle of plants sprawled across the table. The weapon wasn't native to Neharem, and she'd not yet learned to wield it. Maybe she'd have time now. She fastened its sheath to a sash and creaked open the door.

The hallway was dark. No light beneath Maseeya or Konar's doors. Elaysia stepped out, toes landing only, the way she'd mastered for escapades long ago. Outside, the breeze hurled leaves around like a swarm of bats, creating enough commotion for her to slip across the platform to the High Tree's drop off.

She'd lowered herself down the first rung of the ladder when a brusque voice rang out.

"Who goes there?"

Elaysia froze. *For Khiev-Tatamic's sake.*

She climbed back up and found her face inches from an exposed chest. The watcher's towering stature, sharp nose, and ornate, feathered headdress indicated a Lautei warrior. His eyes shifted like a fox on the hunt. Probably one of Rajar's.

He lowered his spear. "It's late to be out, High Chieftain. Unsafe."

"I appreciate your concern, Brother, but I must clear my head. Too much time spent in stuffy rooms, I'm afraid." She fanned her face in mock exasperation. The warrior wasn't convinced. "Khiev-Tatamic keep you." She took a timid step toward the ledge.

The Lautei positioned himself between her and the drop off. "I'll escort you back now. Unless you'd rather me awaken the high elder."

"That won't be necessary." Elaysia retreated, glaring. "I'm thankful for your loyalty to Agaas."

"My loyalty lies with the Lautei."

"How honorable of you. We appreciate you all the same." Elaysia hoped he caught the sarcasm thickening her words as she slunk back inside.

As soon as the loft door closed, she slammed her fists onto her cot. The commotion loosened her necklace from its home in her bosom. She traced her fingers over the stormbird at the end of the leather string and brought it to her lips.

"I'm sorry, Annonitus," she whispered. "It's not my burden to bear. I hope you understand."

She only recalled fragments of her elder brother now. Playful eyes the color of roses at dusk, egging her on in a game of hunter and prey as they tore through the bridges of Agaas while onlookers raised eyebrows. His face twisted in mockery when they received the reprimand later. Gentle hands guiding her first arrow. The day he'd carved her the stormbird.

The day she watched him die.

Elaysia fell back into her pillow, her gaze fastened to the ceiling as if it held the remedy for despair. For all the nights spent begging safe passage to Everworld for Annonitus and her parents, not a word returned to her in meditation. No solace or comfort in her prayers, no whisper of peace carried on the wind. Her only hope lay in the barren valleys of the unknown; if no one could prove it existed, no one could prove it didn't. That's what she told herself when the world grew dark, as it did now. When the voices beckoned her to join them.

She gave the stormbird a squeeze and forced herself up.

The watcher loomed outside her window, blocking the only entrance to her quarters. Konar's loft faced the opposite direction. If she climbed out his window, she could use the Kyas Tree's drop off.

Tomorrow was the final gathering with the chiefs. They'd expect a decision, and either choice would ruin her. Or she could flee, find the freedom that came from abandoning her name, and explore the furthest reaches of Quorath. An uncharted future.

Her future.

Elaysia waited until the watcher paced by her window, then covered the nevethium sconce, dousing the room in darkness. Convinced, he resumed guarding the main entrance. After a few minutes, she crept back into the hall and pressed her ear to Konar's door. He was often in the library late and, given his mood earlier, chances were good. But if not...

"Konar." She knocked softly, her gaze darting down the hallway. "It's me." Another knock.

She opened the door.

It took her eyes a moment to adjust to the darkness. A perfectly made cot, bound scrolls neatly stacked on the table, ceremonial clothes folded on top of the chest, and no Konar.

Elaysia darted to his window before she could change her mind. This time she took the long way around the summit lodge, taking care to stay in the shadows and stopping frequently to check for other watchers. When she reached the Kyas Tree, Zavik's light still glowed in his window. She hesitated outside for a moment, then tore herself away, offering him a blessing from a distance. He'd understand. Or forgive her, at least. He always did.

Elaysia planted her feet on the ground and filled her nostrils with the aroma of sweet moss and musty soil. She glanced up several hundred feet to the platform. No one followed. Most Agaasians relied on the lyvium-infused stairs and ramps for their comings and goings. The ladders were reserved for catastrophes.

And her evening jaunts.

She dashed to the stables where the horses greeted her with snorts and gentle nickers. A cluck of her tongue summoned Baudier, a dapple-gray stallion, who trotted over and placed his forehead on hers. She stroked the strands of hair between his eyes. They never judged, those eyes.

"Hello, friend." The base of his mane wound tightly around her fingers, she climbed up. "One last ride tonight, if you don't mind? As far south as you can." Baudier snorted, leaped over the enclosure, and broke into a gallop. Somehow, he always understood. Most creatures did, given the chance.

The forest flew by in a blur, horse and rider finding footing with ease under the cloudless night sky as Agaas's radiant green hue faded behind them. With luck, the memories would fade along with it. A distant dream of an old, forgotten life.

Drowsy from sleepless nights, Elaysia didn't realize they'd lost the path until they came alongside a brook she'd never seen before. She tugged gently on Baudier's mane until the stallion stopped and allowed her to dismount. A nytak buck drank from the other side of the brook, his scaled hooves sinking into the mud as his antlers, twisted with ivy, shone elegantly in the moonlight. His long, furry tail curled upward in contentment, and Baudier took it as an invitation to drink from the bank opposite him.

"Don't be long. I want to clear Apáasutai territory by sunrise." Elaysia pulled the wineskin out of her satchel. She hesitated, pouch pressed to her lips, imagining Konar's raised eyebrow. "It doesn't matter anymore," she muttered, fishing inside herself for a hint of resolve. "I've no appearance to keep."

Baudier and the nytak jerked their heads up and stared at her, unblinking.

"No one asked you." She slumped against a tree and poured wine into her mouth, relaxing as it warmed her stomach and eased her muscles. Maybe a few minutes of rest would do her good. As long as she stayed awake, it'd be fine.

Elaysia awoke to a half-emptied pouch and the feeling of being watched.

The forest was silent. No mice skittering in the brush. No melody from the crickets. No breeze tousling the leaves. Baudier dozed by the brook, ignorant of the fear constricting her throat.

She crept toward him on hands and knees, breath manifesting in a fog as leaves crackled beneath her weight. The woods never frightened her before, but that was when she was Elaysia Moonrider, the future high chieftain, daughter of Elishon and ward of High Elder Lightfoot. Tonight, she was no one with no backup.

Branches crackled behind her.

She halted. Glanced over her shoulder.

No one.

A small, paranoid laugh escaped her throat. If she couldn't handle one night alone in the woods, what could her future possibly hold? She started for Baudier when a voice like wind rustling through leaves cut through the night.

"Why do you run, daughter of Neharem?"

Elaysia stifled a scream. A face appeared in the tree she'd leaned against. Slowly, as if being carved by an invisible craftsman, the form of a woman grew from the tree, skin the pattern of polished alder with mossy hair coiled down its back. Leaves covered its breasts, and branch-like arms unfurled from its torso with long, twisting fingers. Just below the midriff, its body transformed into the base of a trunk and flowed out like a skirt, branches and leaves woven thick like brush.

Elaysia rubbed her eyes. Still there.

"Khiev-Tatamic keep me," she whispered.

As a child, she adored tales of spirit walkers—the gods and goddesses appointed to govern the natural realms of Quinaria—but now, faced with one, she retrieved the dagger from her hip. The forest goddess didn't move, and she wasn't certain it could. Fireside stories never mentioned practical details like that.

A gust tore through the goddess's leaves as she reached her spindly arms. Elaysia shirked away and sprinted to Baudier. She wrapped her fingers around his mane and prepared to leap up when the stallion bolted.

"Stop," she cried as he galloped away. The goddess advanced, roots upturning the soil. Elaysia clutched her chest to still the thudding. "Please, let me leave in peace."

"If you leave, there will never be peace."

Elaysia ran. She made it to the edge of the clearing only to watch the forest close off her escape. Branches wove into briar patches. Trunks thickened, leaving barely enough space for her hand to slip through. Everywhere she turned, it was the same. A corral of trees.

The ground rumbled beneath her. Dagger leveled, Elaysia approached the goddess. "What do you want from me?"

The goddess's face softened, her sharp, wooden features giving way to curves. "What do you want from yourself?"

Elaysia loosened her grip on the dagger. It wasn't a question she'd pondered. Her whole life had centered on the expectations of others, and the last shred of resilience surviving inside her screamed *run.*

"To prove I'm not fated," she said finally. "My life is my own. I don't know what that looks like yet, but I'd rather face the unknown than keep living a lie."

"But you are fated." The goddess's eyes narrowed. "Nothing can change fate. It is the path bestowed upon you. Destiny, however, is what you do with it."

Elaysia took a step back. "Leading Neharem wasn't supposed to be my fate."

"But it is your destiny." The goddess's roots bubbled the soil beneath Elaysia's boots.

"I'm not ready. I never will be."

"And that is why it must be you."

Elaysia backed against a tree, determined to slice through the forest, if necessary. "Forgive me, goddess, but I refuse to be responsible for anyone ever again. Find yourself another savior."

"Then you leave me no choice."

"What?"

Roots wrapped around Elaysia's legs and pulled her into the ground.

Everything went dark.

Air swam around her. Its warm current cradled her legs and back. She flailed like a beast caught in a trap until her feet scraped against the ground. She fled. The slapping of footsteps drowned out her panting as she barreled through the void, but no matter which way she ran, she found no escape, no light.

Then, blinding light.

It happened so fast Elaysia could scarcely process the scene as it unfolded before her.

Jaws snapping, long and serrated, dripping in blood and splattered with flesh. Hungry. The beast was so hungry. It had dined on a thousand dishes and still craved more. It was a human. No, a nyrian. Then a beast again, form hulking yet emaciated. Bones here. Horns there. Like an adult nytak but also like a ram. She could never see all of it, big as it was. Evasive as it was.

The beast vanished, burned in a firestorm. But the fire was green. The smoke yellow. It ravished Agaas. Neharem. Quinaria. Then floods and ice storms. Barren woods and dried up rivers. The people, how they screamed. Young and old. Ancient and advanced. When was this? What was this?

And then Quinaria screamed. A sound like fire mountains. Like thunder. Like the death of all living things.

Elaysia screamed with it. The light faded.

"Little Fox."

Her father's voice. His nickname for her. She ran toward it.

"Edoja?"

"Find them, Little Fox. The birds will guide your path. Find them before she does. It's Quinaria's only hope."

His voice faded with each word. Elaysia ran and shouted for him until her throat was raw.

He was gone.

She knelt, breathless, and swiped the tears from her eyes. When she opened them again, a light shone on a nest large enough to sleep a grown person, and within it lay eggs the size of bread loaves. Around them, a cliff. An ocean.

Elaysia recognized the shoreline, the way the jagged trees grew out of the cliffsides like bed-ridden hair. Her eyes widened.

The world went black again.

Wooden arms cradled her firm as a cage. She opened her eyes to find herself inches away from the goddess's face.

Elaysia tore herself from its grasp. "Get off me." The echo of her father's voice still lingered. She shook her head to rid herself of it. "What just happened? Why did you show me that?"

The goddess's arms retreated into branches indistinguishable from any other tree. "I did not show you anything. I merely opened your mind to Quinaria's essence—past, present, and future—as you have before. As your blood always has. Have you forgotten?"

"No, I've never experienced anything like that before." She shook her head. It was light, fuzzy, as though caught between sleeping and waking. "I'd remember."

"The mind has a way of burying things one is not ready to grasp, but the spirit always knows."

"Convenient."

The goddess frowned, mouth twisting until it was no longer a mouth at all but a knot in the bark. Her other features faded, becoming one with the wood. "Long have the scrolls been hidden. They want to be found, and they will be. Many search. Few can be trusted."

"What scrolls? And what were those eggs?" Elaysia lunged for the spirit walker, but the tree was already just a tree, all traces of divinity gone.

Fists clenched, she pivoted toward the tree line. The forest had resumed its original state. Dark and looming, but no longer a formidable enclosure. Something rustled within. Elaysia scrambled for her bow, which was propped against the goddess tree with her wineskin. Before she could draw it, Baudier trotted into the clearing, oblivious to his untimely departure.

"Kind of you to return." Elaysia jumped on his back and urged him onward, but he snorted and pawed at the ground. "What? Why heed wine-filled delusions? Let's go."

Miles poured behind her as she fell into rhythm with her steed's gait. The further she rode, the more prominent the vision became. The beast. The destruction. The eggs. All foreign; all madness. But that shoreline. She knew it, and it was close. Wouldn't take more than a few hours' detour.

"Alright, Baudier. One last thing for you."

They raced for Sunset Bay.

Elaysia arrived at the beach amid a downpour. A lone plateau loomed a hundred feet above the water like an ocean tower. If she was to hide something, it would be there. She'd wondered what was at the top for as long as she could remember but never attempted the feat. Although climbing came naturally to her, this climb was a death wish with its sheer face and few footholds. Not to mention she had to swim a few yards out into frigid waters.

"What do you think, boy?" she murmured to Baudier. He whinnied, and Elaysia took that as support. No one else could offer input. No judgement from Konar. No paranoid rationalizing from Zavik. No words of caution from Maseeya.

Wind ripped tears from Elaysia's eyes and tore into her clothes as she trudged through the sand. Though she'd worked up a sweat (mostly from nerves), the waves hit her like a punch to the gut. Her limbs wanted to freeze. Her lips trembled uncontrollably. She forced herself to swim, wave after wave, cramp after cramp, until the rockface loomed above her. Its sharp edges gleamed in the moonlight. She reached a shaky arm to search for a weight-bearing crevice in the stone.

Just like any other climb.

She took a salt-filled breath and pulled herself out of the water.

Her limbs burned, straining, grasping, clinging to the barnacle-covered rock that taunted her life with every reach. When the top beckoned her an arm's length away, she reached to secure her final hold. Her fingers found a groove like a glove. Confident, she transferred her weight to the cliff's edge. It crumbled beneath her fingers. She dangled from one arm, heart thrashing and lips dry. Her free limbs flailed like a baby bird pushed early from the nest. She dug into the ledge with her secured hand. Pain flashed through her arm like lightning as her fingernails separated. Her heartbeat counted down the seconds until her grip would fail.

Three.

Two.

One.

Gathering the last of her strength, she thrust her free arm back to the ledge. A shudder of relief washed over her as she found purchase. She flopped onto the surface. Cheek pressed against the rock's slick skin, bile slipped back down her throat. She laughed hysterically. When she finally raised her head, she found herself surrounded by a handful of trees lucky enough to find livelihood atop the otherwise barren cliff. It took a matter of minutes to investigate the totality of the surface: scant shrubbery, some crumbling rock formations, and no sign of a nest. Rage flared inside her.

She flung a rock and a horde of expletives into the ocean, then sat on the ledge. Her legs dangled, kicking back and forth in the wind.

Wait. Why weren't they banging into the cliffside?

She peered below and found a cutaway in the rock resembling a small cave. Not daring to hope, she lowered herself below the ledge and pulled a shard of nevethium from her tunic to chase away the shadows. Its mossy light poured into every crevice and illuminated a handful of rocks piled together in the back. She dropped inside. The rocks, large as a human or nyrian's head, were perfectly smooth and curved. She ran a finger over one, and it came back coated in a thick layer of grime. Beneath, a shimmering heat as colorful as the sun. It was as if she peered into a mother's womb. And it pulsated.

The eggs from her vision. Stormbird eggs, if her memory of Konar's lectures served her well. One of the Great Beasts of Old, every bit as intelligent as a person, as powerful as a god. And extinct.

Why in Haeshol had the spirit walker led her to them? She couldn't just leave them. Not the single greatest discovery of her lifetime. Besides, her father said they'd guide her. To... something. He'd been a part of the vision. He'd wanted her to find them.

She rested her cheek on the egg, jaw set and tears pooling. She'd have to return to Agaas for help. If anyone knew more about the eggs, it'd be Konar.

"It's decided then," she murmured.

No more running.

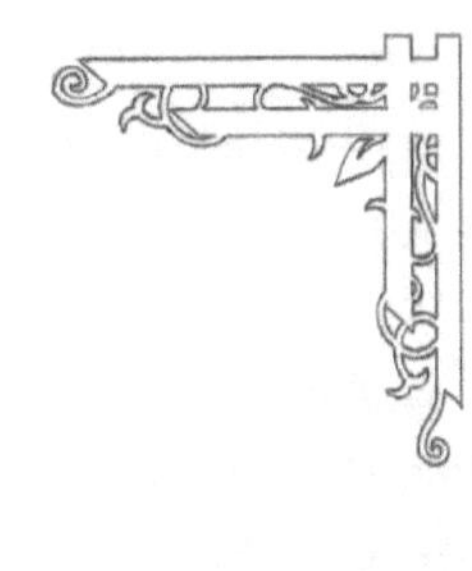

LUMIRA

V oices; close by.

Lumira pulled the hood further down her face, smashing her whiskers. Being beridian wasn't a death sentence in Neharem, but she didn't dare call attention to herself, even during the day. She snaked through the treetop path and pressed up against the smooth siding of a hut just before a family passed. They didn't so much as glance her way. When they were out of earshot, she gave the handle a tug. It opened freely, like the six she'd already looted. The citizens of Agaas didn't seem to understand the concept of lock protection. Though, given her luck so far, it appeared they had little worth protecting.

She opened the lone chest at the foot of the cot and growled as she rummaged through trinkets and heirlooms valuable only to their owner. Worthless. She eased the lid closed and turned to leave, but then a silhouette appeared in the doorway.

"I hope you put up a fight, cat," a woman said coolly in Nyrinian.

Lumira had picked up the ancient nyrian language during her time on the mainland, but she feigned ignorance. The woman stepped into the room, a nyrian lightly clothed in the fabrics of one of the southern tribes with a staff at her side. She looked strong for her kind, but Lumira doubted she'd exert much energy killing her.

"Jakki," someone outside shouted. "What is it?"

The woman called Jakki flashed a dark smile. "A thief."

A man barged inside. He was several inches shorter than Lumira's six-and-a-half-foot frame but thick as a boar. "You've wronged Agaas, and you'll pay." He raised a club.

Lumira's claws extended. She judged the distance to the window and flung herself through the shutters, tumbling onto the pathway below. A handful of onlookers crowded outside the hut. One noticed her and summoned a swarm of scowls and raised fists. She pounced to open the biggest assailant's throat but hesitated when his eyes met hers. An unnecessary kill. Not again. She needed to stay clean.

When he lunged to strike, Lumira flipped over the railing. She landed the twenty-foot drop with ease, never once hesitating as she tore through the winding bridges of the trees. Her escape, a descending staircase, was mere feet away when someone grabbed her throat and slammed her to the ground. Stars filled her vision. She tried to writhe free, but hands yanked on her from every direction. Within moments, they'd bound her.

Lumira snarled as they wrenched away her spear and bag of pilfered nevethium. "I don't want your pathetic belongings. Let me go if you give a damn about your lives. I won't warn you again."

Someone laughed. Lumira squinted until she found the source: the nyrian wench, Jakki.

"Save it for the High Chieftain," Jakki sang in a sickeningly sweet voice. "You've the honor of being her first act of judgment against a criminal. Theft and assault aren't things we take lightly in Agaas. Perhaps worthy of execution?"

Lumira maintained a stoic face.

Jakki shrugged. "Probably not, but we can at least hope for a few months in the cliff holds."

Lumira's ears flattened. "It's been a while since I've had a seaside holiday. Even if the conditions are savage."

Jakki's mouth parted slightly. She pulled her hand back to strike Lumira, but the big nyrian from the hut caught it mid-swing.

"Judgement is the High Chieftain's," he grunted.

"Here's a reasonable one." Lumira stuck her feet toward her larger captor. "Now, if you'd kindly unbind me, I'd be honored to meet your high person."

The nyrian grabbed her like a sack of grain and threw her over his shoulders. Had her fur the ability to reveal her emotions like the pale-skinned Az Zarians, it would've turned a shade of red. She struggled a bit for good measure, not that it mattered.

Her luck, like goods worth stealing in Neharem, was unlikely to turn up.

The palace was not the type of palace Lumira was accustomed to. Not a palace at all, really. The governing of Neharem was conducted in a handful of modest buildings carved out of one of the largest trees in the middle of the city. Save for a few guards pacing about, it was unprotected, ungated, and unsuspecting. Her nostrils flared, hating Agaas more with each passing moment. She should've stayed in Munskahan. Though dangerous, there the drunkards were many and their pockets deep.

The large nyrian dumped her on the ground and sliced the bindings off her feet. "Walk. You try anything, I'll bring you in unconscious."

Lumira skulked through the courtyard. Two guards with long, plaited hair stood at attention in front of a building with a filigreed gable. One eyed her and muttered something that made them both chuckle. She snapped at him as she passed by, earning herself a punch to the gut. Worth it.

Voices fell silent as Lumira walked inside. She ignored the bystanders and basked in the lustrous green hues highlighting the room's many carvings. Battle depictions etched into the walls. Neharem's gods reimagined in the pillars. Stormbirds ingrained in the ceiling. It must've taken many hands over many years to make such detailed beauty from an ordinary wooden canvas.

The room could comfortably host one hundred people, and at least half that many could gather around the massive oak slab in the center. There were no chairs and no throne for their ruler to command from. Lumira's captor shoved her across the room and forced her to kneel before a trio caught up in a spirited discussion.

A dark-skinned nyrian male past his prime regarded her with disdain. She glared back. The other two were human, the eldest Az Zarian with graying dark hair and skin the color of moons. She averted her gaze and touched the arm of the girl next to her. The pointed ears of a nyrian poked out beneath the girl's streaked hair, and her ruddy-brown face was marred with cream around the nose, mouth, and chin. A nyman in the palace?

"We caught this one thieving at the Kyas Tree," her captor said. He bowed like a dog dropping a bone in front of its master.

Jakki thrust her staff into Lumira's side as if she kept a wild beast at bay. "And she tried to kill us, but we stopped her before she harmed anyone."

Lumira gritted her teeth through the pain and imagined nailing Jakki to one of the pillars.

"Enough, Jakki," the elder nyrian said with a voice like thunder. He adjusted his beaded belt and turned to Lumira. "Is what she says true?" His thick cords of white hair were tied back behind perfectly postured shoulders, and he wore the frown of a strict, but fair, man.

"From a certain point of view, High Chieftain." Lumira's Nyrinian must've been rusty because Jakki stifled a laugh.

"I appreciate your formalities, beridian, but I am not the one you need to address." The elder nyrian gestured to the nyman girl.

Lumira snorted, perhaps too audibly. It earned her a kick from her larger captor that sent her to the floor, chin-first.

"Barkas, unless you want to be treated the same, I suggest you leave judgment to my discretion." The girl's voice sounded stronger than Lumira expected, rich with low notes like a honeyed wine.

"Sorry. Honest mistake." Lumira shoved back to her knees as Barkas backed away, face sullen.

The girl locked eyes with Lumira and gestured to the table. "Have a seat."

"High Chieftain." Jakki swooped between them with her ass in Lumira's face. "She's a criminal and should be treated as such."

The girl crossed her arms. "Until I hear all sides of the story, she's a visitor. Now, everyone, leave us."

Jakki huffed and dragged Lumira to the table before filing out of the room with the others.

The elder nyrian lingered. "We have her weapons"—he glared at Lumira—"but beridians fight well without them."

"And she's bound, so I'm not exactly sure what the problem is."

"As you wish." The nyrian muttered something about extra watchers and closed the door behind him.

Lumira suppressed a smirk. With the girl's naivety and a little luck, she'd be sailing to Orillon by nightfall.

The girl poured two cups of wine and slid one across the table. "What's your name?"

"Lumira." No point in lying. Her name didn't carry weight on the mainland.

"Lumira, what?"

"Just Lumira."

The girl blinked, then snapped her fingers in resolution. "Right. They only give you one name on The Isles. Most of our tribes are like that." She traced the rim of her cup with a pale hand and, as though she'd felt Lumira staring, abruptly hid it beneath the table. "What clan do you hail from?"

"Doubt you'd know it."

"Fair enough." The girl retrieved a dagger from her thigh, and Lumira shirked away. "If I wanted to hurt you, do you think I'd wait until we're alone?" She reached out slowly and sliced the bindings.

Lumira rubbed her wrists. She forced herself to take a sip of wine instead of bolting for the door. It was sweet and spiced. "It's good."

"Not as strong as your Moonlight, I'm sure, but I'm glad you like it." The girl took a drink, two-toned eyes fixated on Lumira's ivory and amber-kissed tail. "You must forgive my companions for any hostility. We experienced a devastating attack on one of our living trees last moon cycle and are wary of unfriendly outsiders."

Lumira took another gulp. "Sorry to hear that." Moons be cursed, why hadn't she just stayed in Orillon?

The girl shrugged. "It could always be worse. At least, that's what they tell me."

They sat in silence, sipping their wine.

Lumira had nearly worked up the courage to escape when the girl asked, "So, just Lumira, what brings you to Neharem?"

"Uh…" Lumira chose her words carefully. "Change of scenery. Orillon was getting too hot and dry."

"Why'd you leave The Isles?"

"I'm a free-spirit."

"Sounds exciting."

"It is."

The girl folded her arms, her brow etched heavy with strain beyond her years. "Is there much work in Orillon?"

Lumira closed her eyes and remembered her last job as if it'd happened yesterday: claws extended, slashing into the innards of an innocent man; his pleading eyes and how the light in them faded as his spirit departed; his family cowering in the room she'd locked them in. He'd been a simple man living a simple life who'd let a simple debt grow out of control, and debts weren't taken lightly in Orillon.

She drained her cup. "Some."

The girl rose. If she sensed Lumira's discomfort, she didn't draw attention to it. "I'm afraid I'm not much of a conversation-alist. Can I show you something instead?"

Lumira followed her to a mound of decorative stones nestled in blankets beside a sizeable chunk of nevethium. Likely one of their shrines. The girl retrieved a stone and offered it to Lumira with the gentility of a mother passing off her newborn babe. Its lightness surprised her. Warmth rippled off its iridescent, smooth coat, and she instinctively drew it to her bosom.

"Well," the girl said, watching her closely, "we must deal with the fact you've committed a crime. In the holy city, of all places. I have to punish you, or they'll disrespect me even more."

Lumira flattened her ears and glanced at the door.

The girl grabbed her arm with surprisingly strong fingers. "Don't try it. Jakki's quick, and Konar's probably stationed additional watchers between those doors and the nearest descent."

Lumira ripped her arm free. "Get on with it, then."

The girl knelt beside the shrine and traced her fingers gingerly over one of the stones. "It seems you're already growing attached to that egg in your arms."

Lumira held the stone at arm's length. It *did* look like an egg the more she beheld it, and she couldn't explain the warmth it emitted even after moving away from the nevethium. But she knew better than to trust the word of a stranger.

"It's a stormbird egg." There was no humor in the girl's eyes. No deceit. Crazed or not, she believed it. "Like everyone else, I believed them extinct, gone along with spirit walkers and everything else that fills fireside stories. The circumstances by which I found them, however"—she took a sip of wine—"leave me little room for doubt. I've also had my most trusted advisors look over the few surviving parchments we have, and they describe exactly what you hold in your arms. Are you familiar with the Great Beasts of Old?"

Lumira nodded. Beasts as intelligent as the races of land, lacking spoken language but unmatched in ferocity and strength. It was said stormbirds bonded with a single rider; a kinship, not an ownership. They'd died out well over millennia ago, along with the frost giants of the north, peace on The Isles, and anything else resembling hope.

The girl took a hesitant step closer and adjusted her boldly patterned blanket that masqueraded as a cloak. "Would you like it?"

Lumira's ears perked up. Fake or not, she could pawn it off in Orillon to some populum-high royal on his way between love dens. If it turned out to be real, well... she'd never have to take another job again.

"Seems generous," Lumira said, tail twitching. "Why trust me?"

"You could've easily killed a dozen people today and escaped. But you didn't. Why?"

Lumira extended her claws and retracted them. "Wasn't worth it."

"Or your conscience wouldn't let you." The girl placed her hand on the egg, fingers nearly touching Lumira's. "I know times are hard, especially for an outsider in Orillon, and I don't blame you for the theft. We do what we must to survive. So, in exchange for your crime, all I demand is your time. Fourteen moon cycles of service, and in exchange, you may keep this." The corner of the girl's mouth flicked into a smile. "Call it a contract, if you'd like."

"I'm done with contracts." Lumira set the stone that was supposedly an egg on the floor. "What would you have me do to avoid the cliff holds? Someone in your council need removing? A chief acting unruly?" The girl sat cross-legged on a cushion and sipped her wine as if she hadn't heard. Lumira's blood boiled. "You don't even know me, girl. I've easily lived three of your lifetimes, and I've done things you'd execute me for. Tell me what you want."

"I told you what I want."

"Then I say no."

"Then you serve fourteen moon cycles in the cliff holds." The girl's tone changed from melodic to monotone. "It's so cold and lonely, and some jump to end things before their sentence is complete. I'm sure you're strong enough to last, though."

Lumira closed her eyes to hide her frustration. She'd never clear the city if she ran now, and the mere mention of cliff holds made her shiver.

Fine. She'd play along to amuse the child-chief, at least for a while. If things took a sour turn, she'd sneak away once they trusted her, and if—by some miracle—the egg hatched, she'd make off with fine severance pay, too.

"My claws are yours, gir—High Chieftain." She offered her finest bow.

The girl appeared amused. "It's Elaysia. Come, I'll show you to your new quarters."

DAVIER

S weat collected in Davier's palms and trailed down the nape of his neck. With incense bowls rivaling the temple's and a general lack of windows, the palace was nearly as sweltering as the midday sun back home in Or Zahal. Rugs woven with golden embroidery spilled out from all four entrances into the great hall and connected in the center to form the eye of Mavet. From the second level, hemmed in by a geometric lyvium railing, one could observe the entire tapestry hung across the room, an idyllic landscape of Az Zar in her prime: land lush, rivers rich, and nevethium intact. A chandelier made from the crystals swallowed the ceiling, bathing the room in warm, deep-green hues.

Davier peeled himself off the bench and paced. He'd run through multiple scenarios of why the All-Sovereign requested a private audience with him *now* when he'd been a decorated captain for several years. If his performance in The Skulmor Rebellion had finally been noted, it was about time. A promotion to major would mean better wages, better housing, and hopefully, better missions. Cadar's sterilized streets and religious overtones provided little release aside from the training yards and brothels, and though he frequented the latter for drink, stepping foot into such an establishment was forbidden to active-duty soldiers. It would be a life-threatening reason to be summoned to the palace. Or they might've caught him sending unused rations back to his family. Equally incriminating.

The more Davier thought, the sweatier he grew. Civilian silks, while essential for interacting with the upper-class citizens of Cadar, were more restricting than his uniform and likened him to one of his sisters' dolls.

A bald, nyrian dwarf shuffled into the room, nose in the air and hands clasped atop a ruby pendant running the length of his torso. "I'm to escort you to the veranda," he said nasally in Zarith. He didn't wait for a reply and marched away as though utterly inconvenienced.

The dwarf led Davier down never-ending hallways, each corner revealing another stretch of carpet and an endless array of closed doors. What any one family needed with such space was beyond him, royal or not. And the All-Sovereign had no family.

"It's a fine afternoon," Davier said when he could no longer take the silence. Speaking released some of his pent-up energy, like pouring liquid from an overfull cup.

"Aren't they all." The dwarf quickened his pace.

Davier clenched his fists. The ungrateful wretch was lucky to have a lush position in the palace while most dwarves carried out miserable lives as slaves or entertainers. He probably had a better diet and lodging than most of the military. Life had a cruel way of slathering undeserving people in luck while others, like Davier, nearly died pursuing mediocrity.

The dwarf halted before a double-doored archway. "If you please."

Davier swallowed a scathing remark and heaved a door open. Fresh air and sunlight poured in from the veranda, bending around pillars wrapped in vines and reflecting off a transparent table in the center of the platform. Below, a lush garden filled with exotic plants and the melody of birds. A bowl of cloves, a bottle, and two chalices rested upon the table, and two chairs were angled away as if beckoning one to sit. Davier chewed the inside of his cheek as he abandoned the palace. Too pleasant.

The door groaned behind him. He rushed after the dwarf and wedged his boot between the door and its frame. "His Holiness is coming?"

The dwarf let out an exasperated sigh. "At his leisure. Have a seat, and be sure to suck on some cloves, Captain Zadel. Also,"—he kicked Davier's boot from the doorway—"the All-Sovereign prefers the ancient tongue to Zarith. I hope you can speak it, for your sake."

"I'm a little rusty, but—"

The door slammed shut.

"My training ensured fluency in many tongues," he muttered.

Davier shot the dwarf down with an imaginary arrow, then snagged a handful of cloves off the table. Freshening one's breath was one of the many prerequisites to an audience with the All-Sovereign, and in many ways not the worst. There was the hour soaking in the communal baths, the smearing of oils, abandonment of weapons, and the day's fasting for clarity of soul and mind. A grumble erupted from Davier's stomach as a reminder. He ventured down to the garden for distraction and was immediately drawn to a vibrant, sapphire blue cluster of flowers. Their two-tiered petals looked like the union of a daisy and a lily, and long, golden-brown stamen sprung from the disc florets like tentacles. Not native to Az Zar. Perhaps from The Isles? Rumor had it the All-Sovereign had a penchant for collecting foreign plants. And creatures.

The garden centered on a nevethium statue of the holy man himself. Larger than life, he loomed over his horde, showering them in life-giving auras, so the uprooted foliage flourished no matter the climate. A nytak fawn native to Neharem peeked its head around the statue, then sprinted off.

Davier shook his head. Only in Cadar. Most Az Zar lay infertile and exhausted, but the capital was a seaside paradise where nyrian lands segregated from the lesser races. Clean air. Multiple water supplies. Fertile croplands. Wealthy and groomed citizens with nothing to stress over beside the vintage of their wines and where to purchase land to best suit a second home. The capital knew only abundance. And while he spent much of his off-duty life in Cadar, he was bred in Az Zar's largest human city: Or Zahal. There, dirt eroded the walls, stifled the crops, and suffocated the people. He'd been lucky to be his family's first-born and only son, and luckier still to have risen through the military ranks so swiftly. Az Zar only considered humans worthwhile if they were among the handful born into prestigious bloodlines or those like him who'd made themselves indispensable to the empire.

"Captain Zadel, I presume," a flat voice said in Nyrinian.

Davier spat the cloves out and fell to his knees. "Your Holiness." He kept his head down and up-raised palms extended until the All-Sovereign planted a kiss on his head.

"You may rise. Join me on the veranda."

Davier followed the All-Sovereign up the stairs, struggling to avert his gaze as he'd been taught. The nyrian had ruled for ages—far longer, some believed—than the half-millennium life span of his kind. But looking at him now, bare chest firm and adorned in nothing but a nevethium collar, he scarcely appeared older than Davier. His white hair hung straight and silken down to a skirt of the same color. A golden leaf crown adorned his head. On his feet, gemmed sandals matched the collar. He regarded Davier with a frown and extended a chiseled arm toward the table.

"Sit."

Davier slid into a chair that was obviously designed for discomfort.

The All-Sovereign grabbed the bottle with disdain and dangled it like a dead rodent. "Dalgus," he called out. "I told you to stop placing this tainted water of a wine at my guest table."

The dwarf shuffled over, grumbling, a dark ceramic bottle in hand. He retrieved the rejected bottle and placed the new one on the table. "My apologies, master. I didn't think you'd want to waste the Moonlight on"—he looked sideways at Davier and folded his pudgy arms—"men in your service."

The All-Sovereign shooed him like a fly. "*All* men are in my service, dwarf. Return to your duties at once, lest you find yourself even shorter." Davier looked away to hide his amusement as the All-Sovereign filled both chalices. "Beridian Moonlight?"

Davier hated rejecting anything free, especially imported drink, but it had to be a test. "I appreciate your kindness, but I should refrain."

"It's a poor excuse for a soldier who makes his All-Sovereign drink alone."

Mavet Almighty. "Forgive me, Your—"

"Enough with the formalities. If I wanted that, I would've asked Dalgus to stay with us. I know who I am. You know who you are. If we maintain that knowledge, we'll have no cause for discord."

Davier looked briefly into the All-Sovereign's golden eyes and raised his chalice in a toast. One sip instantly loosened his muscles. He pushed it aside to avoid the temptation of drinking more.

The All-Sovereign swirled the liquid in his chalice. "My responsibilities are many and my time lacking, so I'll get to the point."

Davier held his breath as the All-Sovereign retrieved a parchment from the folds of his skirt and laid it on the table.

"It says here you've shown exemplary service to the empire during The Skulmor Rebellion these past three years."

"I do my best, sir." Davier took another sip—this one celebratory—while the All-Sovereign pored over the parchment. "We've reclaimed several thousand square miles of skulmor land now. My company was commanded to stop after conquering Hedaksobaht, otherwise we could've taken their capital."

"I don't doubt that, Captain. Not at all." The All-Sovereign slid the parchment back into his skirts, then steepled his fingers as he regarded Davier with unblinking, luminous eyes. "You've an impressive record for a human. Are your parents proud?"

"They're honored their son serves the greatest military in Quinaria and know they contribute to the growth of Az Zar and protecting her righteous leader, may he reign forever."

"They train you well, don't they?" The All-Sovereign glided to the railing. "How old are you?"

"Twenty and seven."

He rubbed his jaw, gaze lost in the garden. "That will do."

"Sir?" Davier forced himself to join the All-Sovereign at the railing. Up close, he smelled like blossom oils and spices, as if he were a walking incense stick himself.

"What if I told you there's an opportunity for your promotion to colonel?"

Davier choked on his drink. What kind of joke was this? "Anything Your Holiness asks of me in duty to the empire will be done."

"I'm not asking if you accept your duty." The All-Sovereign rested his hands on Davier's shoulders, squeezing firmly, as a father might. "I'm asking if this is your heart's desire."

Davier lifted his gaze to meet the All-Sovereign's. No human from a low-born family had ever been given such an opportunity, even after years of service and memorizing Mavet's seven books of prosperity. His rank of captain was already a rare achievement.

"My heart desires nothing more," he whispered.

"Good. That's all I wanted to hear." The All-Sovereign withdrew his hands and eased back into a monarchal demeanor. "Az Zar has need of you in the west. I'm afraid our relationship with Neharem has soured."

"Neharem, sir? They've been peaceful for over a thousand years. I thought—"

"If you'd let me finish, perhaps I'd answer your questions before you berate me with them." The All-Sovereign's nostrils flared.

Davier took a step back.

"We've been fair to them always. Generous with our goods and understanding of their rudimentary, pagan ways. Imagine my horror when I learned they've been cheating us precious nevethium in trade agreements."

Davier glanced at the All-Sovereign's statue in the garden and thought of the chandelier, the crystals in his collar, and the general architecture in Cadar dripping in nevethium. Something smelled foul, but he gave the horrified expression expected of him. *Get on with it, you pointy-eared prick.*

"It's true," the All-Sovereign continued, satisfied with his reaction. "Why, the last shipment we received was mostly dyed leather and bead work. They'd layered the tops of the barrels in crystals for appearance. It's not the first time it's happened, and they have no other way besides trade to pay us back since they won't embrace our monetary system."

Davier stiffened his jaw to strengthen his words, but inside, he fought to find the righteous anger the All-Sovereign searched for. "They're unwise to bite the hand that feeds them. How do you intend to correct them?"

The All-Sovereign smiled wide enough to bare nearly all his gleaming teeth. "Oh, dear Captain, we're far beyond that. As if cheating the empire wasn't enough, they now seek war. Not two fortnights ago, they staged an attack on their capital to convince their people to rally against us. And they've elected an infertile half-breed to lead them." He spat the last words, chest flexing. "It's an abomination, a slap in the face to the rightful order set in place by our Lord and Savior, Mavet."

Davier backed against the railing. A fire burned behind the All-Sovereign's eyes. Something fierce. Otherworldly. "I value your confidence in me to share these things."

"Necessity, not confidence." The All-Sovereign drained his chalice and tossed it onto the veranda. "Now, listen closely. I want you to infiltrate Agaas and plant your handsome little face amid their leadership. Learn their plans. Investigate their nevethium stocks. Find potential allies and weaknesses. I want to know everything. But most importantly, I want you to bring that disgrace of a ruler back to Az Zar."

"Wouldn't it be easier to take her out quietly, sir?"

The All-Sovereign glared. "She's more valuable alive for the time being. Besides, it's rumored she's discovered items of great value. Something we thought long extinct. If they exist, they'll be easier to confiscate if she surrenders them unwittingly."

Curiosity tugged at Davier, but he tried to remain in a stance of indifference. "What am I to confiscate, Your Holiness?"

"Stormbird eggs." The All-Sovereign raised his brow at Davier's unmasked bewilderment. "Please, no more questions. If the eggs exist, I want them by any means necessary. They're worth more than your entire miserable city. Do you understand, Captain?"

Davier's skin prickled. A thousand questions swirled in his mind. He bit them back. "I'm the empire's to command."

"Of course, you are. Prepare your things. You leave on the morrow." The All-Sovereign strode into the garden. He lingered by the exotic blue flowers, his back to Davier. "Should you fail, I cannot guarantee your family's safety. The empire always needs extra slaves during trying times." He disappeared into the greenery.

Davier poured himself another glass and forced his thoughts away from his family. It would be fine. Only good could follow such an opportunity. The All-Sovereign chose him because he was the best, and he wouldn't fail. With a colonel's pay, he'd finally have enough aspar to purchase his own boat and plenty of rest days to set out on the voyage he'd always dreamed of. He pictured the Vylehk Ocean to the east, the salt and wind tangling his hair as he sailed away from all who could command him, and smiled.

Only a fool would stand in the way of the Az Zarian Empire. And Davier was no fool.

JAKKI

Jakki didn't complain about the sun beating down on her skin, the dull ache in her ass from days of riding, or the fact she'd hardly slept since departing Agaas. She'd tolerated Elaysia flitting about Neharem with no itinerary in search of Stormriders, her special warriors chosen to bond with the stormbirds. Helped convince Konar to delay the council in taking offensive action. Coordinated supplies for the journey. Mother Itaso, she'd even embraced the validity of the eggs without question—at least publicly.

It wasn't enough, though. Apparently, one needed to steal from the holy city to earn Elaysia's affections. Some turn-the-scoundrel-good complex. It worked for the cat who was, at present, riding in *her* spot beside Elaysia as they giggled like children and shared a wineskin.

Jakki returned her gaze to the orchard they rode alongside. Sugary air lifted off the fruit trees, and in the distance, sunlight deepened the dimples on the hills. Several Tangeesh toiled, skin rich with sun and hair tied back in knotted locks. Predominantly human, the tribe had become so intermingled with their kin in Orillon that she could scarcely tell them apart. A woman waved her silk scarf as they passed. Jakki winked back.

Mardus trotted up, blocking her view of the woman. "A tuross message arrived at the nearby village. It's from Agaas."

The stocky Moákun human was, like Jakki, the offspring of chiefs, but they'd rarely interacted prior to Elaysia's expedition. He wasn't her type, but his dark eyes, thick hair, and broad features made him attractive enough, assuming one could overlook his eternally stoic face and utter lack of personality.

Jakki snatched the parchment from his hands. Tuross messages contained scant space as they had to fit into the waterproof cases strapped to the flying lizards' backs. Both aerial and aquatic, they were the most reliable form of delivery, bred from ancient times when messages needed to transcend water, land, and sky.

"There was a raid on a Morotôk village not two nights past," Mardus blurted before she'd finished reading. "All their nevethium was stolen."

Jakki's anger at the interruption was quickly stifled by the blow of his words. She finished the message, stomach twisting into knots. "I suppose it was only a matter of time after the attack, but that far north? They're the smallest tribe."

Mardus rubbed his jaw, his face scrunched as if someone tasked him with determining the fate of all Neharem. "I'll tell the high chieftain."

Jakki slipped the parchment into her cleavage. "I'll take care of that."

Her jaw ticked as she approached Elaysia and Lumira. Not sentencing the cat to the cliff holds was bad enough, but to reward her with an egg? Even Zavik, ever in agreement with Elaysia, admitted it was a mistake. But their pleas were more likely to stop the sun from rising than to get the high chieftain to admit a mistake.

After Jakki received her consolation egg, which she accepted with a painted-on smile, she'd grudgingly supported Elaysia's decision to travel throughout Neharem to secure Stormriders (there were plenty of capable warriors in Agaas). They'd snagged Yerakai of the Apáasutai first, a lanky nyrian in his prime with ashen-violet skin and the disposition of an ancient elder, then headed east for Mardus. Jakki expressed no opposition to the additions; they were logical choices that gained the support of crucial tribes. Elaysia's plan unraveled soon after, however, and aimless travel commenced. Jakki had offered village after village and name after name, but Elaysia never gave her suggestions a moment's thought before waving them off and insisting they needed *unconventional folk* to *bring strength and diversity to the party*. Said logic led them to the coastal lands of the Ni'anko. Pacifist and undisciplined, the Ni'anko dedicated their lives to the seas, the stars, and self-discovery.

The perfect place to find a warrior.

Grokhion resulted from that deviation, all eight feet of him with his black and orange striped fur and a mane that hung down to his shoulders. He'd been reluctant to join. Like most beridians, he'd come to Neharem looking for escape and chose the Ni'anko for their tranquility. Lumira persuaded him, no doubt seeking the companionship of her kind. Jakki admittedly preferred Grokhion to Lumira. He lacked her abrasive and competitive tendencies.

That was six days ago. Now, they encroached on Neharem's southern border, no closer to securing the final two Stormriders. But this message changed everything. It would force Elaysia to address the raid. More were likely to follow.

Jakki worked her horse in between Elaysia and Lumira, blocking the cat from her view. "High Chieftain, if it pleases you, might we stop for a moment? Mardus received a disturbing tuross message."

Elaysia's smile faded. She pulled her mount to a stop. "Let me see."

Despite herself, Jakki found some satisfaction in the instant sobering of her friend. She pulled her mount close enough that their legs touched and put a hand on Elaysia's shoulder while she read the message. "I know you hoped to find the final Stormriders here, but we've been gone from Agaas nearly two fortnights. Konar's probably struggling to keep the council content, especially with this news. We must turn back."

"One and a half," Lumira butted in.

Jakki clenched her teeth and faced the cat. "I'm sorry?"

"One and a half fortnights since we left Agaas. Approximately." The beridian's sapphire eyes bore into her own. Always challenging.

"How kind of you to keep count." Jakki leaned in close. "It doesn't change the situation."

"I'm sure Elaysia has a plan, if we'd all be patient," Zavik quipped, sunburnt face nearly as red as his hair.

Jakki rolled her eyes. "I'd adjust that headwrap unless you're wanting to return home as a tanned hide."

"Leave him alone." Elaysia glared at her and motioned to the others. "An urgent situation in Agaas demands my attention. We'll leave tomorrow. Lumira and I will ride ahead to secure lodging in Puetala. No need for the rest of you to overwork your horses. We're in for a less than luxurious ride back."

"Not like it was luxurious to begin with," Jakki muttered. She urged her horse forward but kept the gait at a walk, determined to be the last one to arrive.

Puetala, the tribal capital of the Tangeesh, less resembled a village than a budding city. Stalls lined the streets, adorned in vibrant canopies and filled with Orillon luxuries the tribe had recently adopted, such as rare spices and perfumes, ornate rugs, and bountiful silks imported from Az Zar. Merchants bathed Jakki in compliments as she meandered by, one suggesting—in a thick Westmun accent—a beautiful lady deserved to be garbed in the finest silks. Another tried claiming she could smell as good as she looked. Jakki lingered long enough at each stall to tease interest. One merchant didn't call out, however. The dark-skinned woman eyed Jakki from a hammock behind the counter, clad in a heavy jeweled necklace covering her breasts and a thin sash wrapped around her waist. Only a handful of dried herbs and roots were on display. Jakki meandered closer.

The woman swung out of the hammock and leaned against the counter. "She doesn't deserve you."

Jakki tried not to stare as the necklace swayed. "What?"

"She whom you love." She spoke as if she'd known Jakki for years. "She passed by recently with the other."

The hairs on Jakki's neck rose. She gripped the hilt of the dagger strapped to her thigh. "Do I know you?"

"Not yet." The woman scooped a handful of dried leaves from one of her jars. "To loosen the lips and the heart."

"No thanks."

Jakki was ten paces away when an icy hand slipped something into her waistband from behind. She whirled, staff first. No one within striking distance, much less arm's reach. She rushed back to the stall and froze. In it stood an old woman bent over the counter with stick-thin arms.

"Looking for a remedy, m'dear?" the old woman rasped.

"No, I just... did you..." Jakki rubbed her eyes. "Does someone else work with you? A younger woman?"

"I've run this stall by myself since I was twenty and three." The old woman furrowed her brow. "If you're not browsing, on with you."

"I was already leaving."

Jakki ducked behind the next stall and pulled a satchel of dried leaves from her waistband. They didn't appear special, though she didn't recognize them. Something told her to toss them onto the road for some unlucky bastard to find.

She shoved them into her pouch.

Elaysia's laughter carried on the wind, drawing Jakki's attention a few yards away, where she and the cat conversed with a stranger clothed in a headwrap and flowy pants of Orillon make. Jakki shook the chill lurking from her encounter and sauntered toward them. The newcomer was human. Brown-skinned and nearly halfway through her lifespan. Dual belts hung off her exposed midriff, one sheathing a scimitar, and her golden greaves and spaulder showed signs of heavy wear.

"Ladies enjoying yourselves?" Jakki asked as she wedged herself between Elaysia and Lumira.

"Always." Elaysia pulled her in for a side hug, any tension from their earlier encounter gone. She gestured to the woman. "Jak, meet Anahi. She's a spice trader."

Anahi removed a hand from her hips and extended it to Jakki. "Pleasure."

Jakki gripped her hand. "Fighting in the arenas not something you wanted to do long term?"

"You've a trained eye." Anahi pulled her hand away and raised both eyebrows.

"You don't hide it." Jakki knocked her knuckles against Anahi's spaulder. "The plating on your armor is hard to get outside the arenas. You've got scars on your arms. Knotted hair to pull out of your way at a moment's notice."

"I stopped trying to hide a long time ago. All you need is ask." Anahi's Nyrinian was endearingly broken, as if her full lips and dark brown eyes weren't comely enough.

"Anything in particular I should ask about?" Jakki folded her arms and waited for worry to flicker in Anahi's eyes. It didn't.

"Enough with the interrogation." Elaysia elbowed Jakki playfully and gave her a side-eye glance.

"It's fine," Anahi said. "All you need to know is that I left my old life behind in Orillon. Been trying my hand at trading with the Tangeesh for several years. Although, it hasn't gone splendidly." Anahi loosed a hearty laugh and leaned against her stall. "Your high chieftain was entertaining me with stories of Great Beasts and spirit walkers. I must say, I'm intrigued."

"So much for subtlety," Jakki muttered.

Lumira looked up from picking at her claws. "We need seasoned warriors with no ties, and Anahi is one."

"Allegedly." Jakki glared at Lumira. "Like you."

"I'd be happy to prove my worth in combat." Anahi slid her curved sword out of its sheath and gave it a few skillful swings in the air. "Care to test me now?"

"That won't be necessary." Elaysia stepped between them. "Your perspective alone will bring strength to us, and perhaps you'll provide a connection to obtain allies in Orillon, should it become necessary. What do you say?"

Anahi sheathed her sword. "I'm overdue for a new adventure. Give me a day or two to close out my affairs here, then I'm yours."

The Gilded Shore Grotto sat against the ocean, its muggy air rife with scents of roasted boar and toi—a fermented plant drink with fruity undertones—and the ambient harmony of flutes and drums alongside crashing waves. Constructed to satisfy the needs of Orillon traders, it was the only inn in Neharem. Unlikely, though, to be the last.

Despite preceding events, Jakki found herself in good spirits and reclined, drink in hand, beside Elaysia while a light-footed girl of sixteen danced from table to table with ever-flowing pitchers and baskets. The others appeared equally relaxed. Grokhion sang with some merchants in a pleasant and thunderous voice. Lumira and Yerakai tried their hand at a cup-stacking game, their table located dangerously close to where Anahi guided Zavik through various fighting stances. The lesson attracted some onlookers in need of humor. Even Mardus cracked a smirk as Zavik threw a wayward punch that plummeted him into Lumira's tower.

"Jak." Elaysia set her empty mug on the table and leaned against Jakki's shoulder. "You know I couldn't do this without you, right?"

Whether induced by wine or exhaustion, Jakki harnessed a flicker of bravado and twirled one of Elaysia's loose strands between her fingers. "Oh, you could. But it would be a disaster."

A snort escaped Elaysia's mouth. "I won't argue with that." She tugged at her embroidered sleeves, her gaze lost across the room where some patrons dozed in the corner. "I was hoping to ask one more thing of you."

"Fine. Last request." Jakki finished her wine and stretched her arm over the booth backing. And Elaysia's shoulders.

Elaysia took a deep breath and straightened, the way she often did before a speech. "I foresee my duties as high chieftain increasing with urgency, so I've chosen someone to lead in my absence and assist with decision making. I think she'll be perfect for the role."

Jakki's chest swelled. Her eyes traced the curve of Elaysia's lips, the dip in her collarbone, the faint gleam of sweat on her chest. Shit, she needed more wine. "I don't know what to say."

"I was worried you'd say that. But Lumira will be perfect. She's—"

"I'm sorry, what?"

Elaysia shirked away. "Lumira. I was talking about Lumira."

Jakki shut her eyes tightly. Being overlooked for the position was bad enough, but to lose it to an outsider Elaysia barely knew when Jakki had been by her side since she was naught but a toddler? Jakki had moved to Agaas at the age of fifteen (her mother's idea of grooming for her eventual role as chief of the Yustano), and she'd been nothing but loyal since, patiently guiding the girl into the woman she'd become. After all these years, this was the best gratitude Elaysia could show her?

"And what exactly are you asking me for?" Jakki scooted out of the booth. "Seems you've already made up your mind."

Elaysia looked wounded. "Your support."

"Apparently that's not enough for you." Jakki made to leave, but Elaysia caught her hand.

"It's not like that. This is primarily for the sanity of the elders and chiefs so they don't devalue my selection of Stormriders. This will help them respect her. You were the obvious choice, but I want them to see the unique aspects everyone brings."

"Maybe there's nothing to see."

"Jak, please."

"Just don't come groveling to me when that"—Jakki gestured to Lumira and shouted—"criminal betrays you to the highest bidder. I thought you were smarter than this. Fuck."

Jakki stormed past a bewildered, toi-infused Zavik and stomped up the stairs. She kicked open the first guest loft door without bothering to check if it was vacant. A painting crashed to the ground as she slammed the door behind her. Darkness blanketed the room. She fell onto the bed and buried her face in its cushions.

Someone knocked at the door.

She ignored it.

Jakki awoke sometime later to shouting and clapping.

"To Lumira," a voice rang above the rest. "May her sunrises always hold promise."

"And may her sunsets always hold peace," the crowd replied.

She wondered how many the beridian had left.

ZAVIK

The Kahaloán embraced Elaysia's band of weary travelers without question. Chief Raenais herself prepared the meal for their first night's stay, a feast of fish from Skyfall Sea alongside a multitude of vegetables, roasted, pickled, raw, and seasoned—half of which Zavik had never seen. When he thanked Raenais, she cocked her dual-bunned head and said Minara, the goddess of love, would have it no other way; everyone was made to serve each other. While they feasted, Zavik observed the locals meandering about the village as if time didn't exist. Not a disgruntled face in the bunch.

After dinner, Raenais gave them sand-colored dresses and kilts made from local grains while several youths gathered their dirt-crusted clothes for washing. Kahaloán clothes smelled of honey and herbs with a hint of seaweed and had an instant calming effect. As Zavik lay in a net hammock, its movements rocking him to sleep, he decided that, under other circumstances, he would happily remain here.

There was just that small matter of not being near Elaysia.

Zavik awoke the next morning to the commotion of being shaken. Startled, and forgetting his bed was a hammock, he shot out of it and tumbled to the floor, feet twisted in the fabric.

Someone snickered.

He fumbled for his seers. *Jakki.* She'd been in a sour mood the past few days, and Zavik had endeavored to stay out of her way.

"Urgent gathering." She lifted the tent flap. "Elaysia's waiting."

Zavik struggled to untangle his feet from the netting, growing flustered as it wrapped tighter around him with each yank. Jakki would, no doubt, embellish the event to entertain others later at his expense. Tunic rumpled and boots untied, he trudged onto the dewy grass. No sounds greeted him, save for the sloshing of waves and the cries of seahawks. He rubbed his eyes. The village still slept, and the sun hadn't fully risen. He glared at the solitary figure seated at the campfire: Jakki, flashing a smile scarier than her typical scowl.

Zavik folded his arms. "Where's everyone else?"

"Probably enjoying their gullibility-free sleep." Jakki poked at the coals to reawaken them and patted the spot beside her. When Zavik hesitated, she blew air through her lips. "Oh, please. You should be grateful for the attention."

"Is there even any news?"

"Word from a Tangeesh trader."

"And?"

"We really should wait for the others. But if you insist"—she pulled a parchment from between her breasts—"come and get it."

Zavik looked away. "I'm not in the mood."

"Fine." She threw it at him.

He pored over the contents. A small batch of Az Zarian forces made camp on the Orillon coastline near Amiren. Not standard trade practice, but hardly a war proclamation.

"What do you think?"

A small squeak escaped Zavik's throat. *Elaysia.* Her hair hung unfettered, still tousled from sleep and glowing in the morning light. He looked down to hide the blush overwhelming his cheeks. "It's a bit unusual, but they've done nothing wrong yet."

"Some would agree with you." Elaysia nodded toward Jakki. "I think it's suspicious, given recent events. They've never sent soldiers to Orillon outside wartime."

Jakki tore off a chunk of smoked fish and popped it into her mouth. "You have concerns proven by more than a hunch to address back in Agaas. Even the cat agrees."

Elaysia touched Zavik's arm. "But someone could return home while the rest of us travel south. Pacify Konar and the council until we've confirmed the threat in Orillon."

"By someone, she means you," Jakki taunted.

Zavik dug his hands into his pockets. The soldiers were likely little more than protection for some ambassador. But if they weren't, he'd never forgive himself if something happened to Elaysia in his absence. Sure, the others would do their best to protect her, but no one could reason her out of rash decision-making like he could. Besides, he couldn't shake the feeling that half the reason for this Stormrider venture was to avoid duties back home, and now she'd found the perfect excuse to prolong it. She had to stop running. He was almost certain that had been her plan the fateful night she found the eggs, but she'd never admit it. Not even to him.

"I see the logic in it," he said gently, "but it might be risky, going into a potentially dangerous situation with so few of you. And it would be best for you to be the one to share the news. The council will be eager to see you again."

"Oh. I thought you'd..." Elaysia backed away, shaking her head. "Never mind. I appreciate your insight."

Zavik's body sagged. *Run after her. Tell her how great her plan is.*

He didn't. The plan wasn't great.

Zavik trudged to the shore. He heaved a rock into Sunrise Bay, wincing as it plopped a few feet from where he stood. He'd convince her it was a dangerous plan at dinner tonight. A moment alone was all he needed.

The moment never came. Elaysia didn't notice him—or ignored him. Feasting gave way to drinking, drinking to stories, and stories to songs. The night grew old, and he'd all but lost resolve for confrontation when he caught her sneaking away from the fire. No one else seemed to notice, so he stalked after her.

Elaysia took a shortcut across a boulder field, her form graceful as a nytak. It took all Zavik's determination to keep pace as he flailed from one boulder to the next, and he still lost her. When he arrived at the tent they'd assigned her to, it was dark and empty. Impulsively, he walked up to her hammock and grasped the cloak in it, caressing the fabric as he held it close enough to smell her.

"What are you doing in here?"

Zavik's heart raced. For the love of Quinaria, could something work out in his favor, just once? He faced Elaysia.

"I saw you wander off. Couldn't find you, so I came here. I thought you might"—Zavik swallowed. *Might be in a good place to talk with me alone.* "Might be cold. So I, uh... here." He tossed her the cloak.

She caught it in one hand and clutched it to her chest. "You're always a step ahead of me. I don't take it for granted. It's why I trust you to represent me in Agaas."

"About that." He pinched his thumbnails into his fingertips so tightly they went numb. "I was thinking more about your plan. It's a good one, truly. But maybe I should accompany you. I'm from there, after all. I doubt anyone speaks Westmun as fluently as me, and I know no one knows the land like I do." Zavik held his breath. If he couldn't convince her to call off the endeavor, then he was tagging along.

"We have Anahi now. Besides, I thought you swore to never return." A teasing voice. Zavik counted it a victory. Elaysia spread her cloak on the ground near the open tent flap and patted the spot next to her. "Come here. You can see the stars perfectly tonight."

Zavik resisted the urge to run over. He lingered by the edge of the cloak and spent a moment deciding where to lie. Too close to her would be awkward, but too far would make it obvious. Once he calculated an ideal distance, he yawned and reclined slowly. A cool breeze flapped against the tent, carrying the scent of campfire. Drums beat in the distance.

Elaysia rustled beside him. He kept his gaze on the stars, afraid to meet her face. "So..."

"Only you can reason with Konar in my stead, Zav."

Zavik snorted. "History would say otherwise."

She continued as if she hadn't heard him. "He trusts and respects you. He'll listen."

"He's not so easily swayed."

"Are you sure that's not you?"

Zavik folded his arms across his chest, senses heightened to the warmth of her body as the night air set in. He scooted closer. "Maybe a message would suffice?"

"I sent a tuross this afternoon. I doubt he'll respond, though." Elaysia propped herself up on her elbows and implored him with wide, hopeful eyes. "You can explain everything I couldn't convey in the message and join us with reinforcements after."

"Or"—Zavik scooted in front of her—"you send another message tonight restating your decision and demand the reinforcements. You're the high chieftain."

"It's not that simple."

It wasn't. The council would never agree to send warriors without proof of a threat, regardless of how battle-hungry some were. Unsure of how to proceed, Zavik rested his chin on his knees.

Lumira's feline form appeared in the tent's threshold, and Elaysia stood to greet her.

And there went his chance.

"High Chieftain." Lumira brought her fist to her heart. The look in her eyes suggested the formality pained her. "We found a snake-bellied slaver slithering outside the village. I was going to take care of him, but Raenais doesn't want blood spilled on Kahaloán land." She flattened her ears. "He asks for you."

Elaysia traced the hilt of her dagger. "Bring him forth."

The beridian returned with an Az Zarian soldier garbed in black from head to toe, a sheen on his armor, and the Mavist fiery-eyed sigil embroidered on his cowl. His exposed, squinting eyes were the only sign something living existed beneath the layers. Zavik disliked those silver eyes the more he studied them. Lumira had bound the soldier's hands behind his back and retained his sleek swords. The moons decorated one of the hilts, and the sun adorned the other.

"Reveal him," Elaysia said.

"With pleasure." Lumira shoved the soldier to his knees and ripped off the mask.

The man's jawline was everything Zavik's wasn't with its sharp angles, wide chin, and young beard. The last feature was odd. Az Zar required clean-shaven soldiers.

"My lady," the soldier said in a gruff voice.

Lumira dug the tip of a sword into his back, which provoked him to smile, his eyes dancing as if he'd a humorous tale to share.

"Begging your apologies. High Chieftain, correct? An honest mistake. Where I'm from, it's customary to refer to—"

"We don't care about your customs here, slaver." Lumira growled, poking the sword deeper. Zavik silently cheered her on. "High Chieftain, if you want me to silence him, say the word."

Elaysia regarded the man with a stern mouth and lively eyes that didn't beget anger. "Did he assault you?"

Lumira's ears flattened. "No. He voiced his approach."

Elaysia nodded. "Unbind him. He's an ally until proven otherwise."

"An ally." Lumira hesitated, whiskers twitching as she looked from Elaysia to her prisoner. Zavik didn't blame her. Other 'allies' with less-appealing features wouldn't have fared as well. Not that the beridian could complain. Elaysia's judgment was proving credulous. "As you wish."

Lumira sliced through the bonds with a single stroke. The man rubbed his hands, oblivious to the blood dripping from where she'd nicked him. Lumira stationed herself at the entrance.

Elaysia knelt across from the man. "What brings you to Neharem?"

He eyed her with a wolfish grin. "I've journeyed from Az Zar—"

Obviously. Zavik rolled his eyes as the man beguiled them with a tale dripping with lies. When he couldn't listen any longer, he squared his shoulders, clenched his fists, and cleared his throat. Loudly. All eyes fell on him.

Zavik's throat tightened, but he took a dry swallow and spoke. "Fascinating as your journey sounds, you've yet to explain *why* you've come. What are you hiding beneath a captain's garb?"

"Wouldn't you like to know?" The man winked at him.

"Enough." Lumira rested her hands on his shoulders, claws extended. "Name. Now."

The man raised his hands in mock submission. "Zadel. Davier San Zadel."

"And why are you here among the Kahaloán, Davier?" Elaysia asked.

"Like I said, I was out for a sail—"

Lumira crept her claws toward his throat. "Only truth."

Elaysia drew Lumira's venom-tipped claws from Davier's neck. "We know Az Zarian forces landed in Amiren not long ago. Did you travel with them?"

Davier dropped the smirk he'd worn since Lumira removed his mask. "Yes, but I've taken care of them. They were a means to an end. You see, I'm a deserter." He ran a hand through his sandy hair and twisted his face into something reminiscent of remorse. "There are things I've done that give me sleepless nights, and I've taken my leave of the madness."

Zavik reached into his boot for his knife. He'd never used it on a living creature before, but he'd make tonight the first time, if necessary. "Compelling tale, but humans don't rise easily in Az Zar. Captain seems too coveted a rank to throw away for peace of mind."

"And how could you possibly know that? Life back home is more complex than your scrolls tell, scholar. But I've not been entirely honest." Davier locked eyes with Elaysia. "They sent me here to kill you."

Zavik's blood ran cold. He lowered the knife at Davier. "You'll never touch her."

"If I'd meant to do it, you'd have never seen me, and she'd already be dead." Davier narrowed one eye at Zavik and smirked. "Though, I commend your bravery."

Lumira held both blades to Davier's throat and snarled something in Hispen.

"You asked for the truth; I gave it," Davier said calmly as he raised his chin above the blades. "They sent me to do a terrible thing, and my conscience got the better of me. I figured the least I could do was warn you. Maybe I could be of use?"

"And what purpose would you serve?" Elaysia asked.

"I'll be a wanted man in Az Zar now, and as your friend was so kind to mention"—Davier rolled his eyes at Zavik—"there's little opportunity at home for me outside the military. If I swore fealty to you, it might serve as penance for my transgressions and restore my spirit for the next life."

Lumira pressed the blades dangerously close. "Say the word, and I'll gut him where he kneels."

"That won't be necessary." Elaysia waved a reluctant Lumira back and leaned in close to Davier. "Do I have your word? You swear you've deserted and no longer serve the All-Sovereign?"

Zavik's mouth hung open. A thief was one thing, but an assassin? "Ellie," he said, touching her arm. "Be wise about this."

She shook his hand off. "I don't recall asking for your counsel. He's hardly a threat with everyone around."

Zavik backed away. He turned the knife over in his hand—which looked harmless compared to Davier's swords—and tucked it back into his boot, cutting his calf. He cursed under his breath and dabbed at the blood fervently.

Davier bowed. "I swear it, High Chieftain. I swear it to you, your people, and your gods. May they strike me down should I be found false."

Elaysia rose and beckoned Davier to follow. "You'll return with us to the holy city. As an ally," she added, eyeing Lumira. "You may prove useful."

They left the tent, forgetting Zavik still nursed his wound in the corner.

"Brilliant, Zav. Just brilliant," he muttered to himself. "Got what you wished for."

KONAR

K onar drew the blanket tighter around his shoulders to fight the chill seeping through the threadbare fabric. It rarely snowed in Agaas, even during the Resting Moons, but it was cold enough tonight. A vividly clear sky laced with howling, icy wind dampened his bones, stiffening them like a rusted hinge.

A horned owl swooped down, its wings grazing his head before it snatched a mouse from the platform. It melted into the darkness with its kill, returning to gods knew where. Maybe it didn't care, content to ride the winds of uncertainty with each setting sun. Such freedom would never again be offered to Konar. A comforting thought. In time, Elaysia would see it that way, too.

Assuming she returned to fulfill her responsibilities.

He'd rebuked her untimely decision to flit about Neharem searching for Stormriders, especially when they'd yet proven necessary, but she contained every bit of her father's stubbornness and her mother's charm. It didn't bode well for the council's impression of her. A new, albeit shaky, trade pact with Orillon had eased the chiefs' doubts in her absence, but word of the Morotôk nevethium raid unsettled them again. The Lautei and Banaxa were an incident away from raising arms. If the two largest tribes declared war, it would only be a matter of time before chaos ensued. Agaas and the High Chieftain unified the people, but the self-governed tribes of Neharem still operated under rules of their own making.

"Konar? Is that you?"

Konar peered over the edge of the library's single pitch roof. Below waited Maseeya, hair whipping across her face and a blanket wrapped around her sleeping gown. She was never up this early. His stomach knotted, but he refused to assume anything ill had transpired.

"What is it?" he asked, climbing down from his perch.

Maseeya grabbed his arm and yanked him across the platform. "Hurry. Elaysia's come home. I've already gathered everyone in the summit lodge to take refreshment." She halted, her face scrunched as she glanced back at the library. "What were you doing up there? It's freezing."

"Praying." Or something like it. Konar turned Maseeya's face back to him. "How is she? What did she say?"

"She looks well. We've spoken little." Maseeya chewed her lip. "She brought foreigners with her."

"Foreigners?"

"Promise you'll be kind."

Konar hurried around the bend to the summit lodge and barged through the double doors. The warmth from the bustling room washed over him with the scent of smoke and well-traveled bodies. Leftovers from the evening meal were strewn about the table alongside weapons and pitchers of wine, and though fewer than a dozen feasted, the din was comparable to a gathering three times that size. Konar recognized some faces. Yerakai and Mardus he'd known since their births—and bore witness to their parents' births—and he trusted their bloodlines and intentions. The others included another beridian much older and larger than the thief, an Orillon woman covered in golden-flecked tattoos, and a pale man garbed in the uniform of an Az Zarian captain.

Konar drew the pipe from his robes. Apparently, Elaysia had also inherited her father's utter lack of intuition when it came to befriending outsiders. She must've sensed his dismay, for she waited several minutes before trudging over to join him at the fire.

"The eggs haven't hatched," she said, as if that was the best way to begin a conversation after an abrupt and untimely departure.

Konar took a long draw. "Things rarely go as planned." Another draw. "What of your mission to Orillon?"

Elaysia toed the floor with the edge of her boot. "I didn't want to act without the council's blessing."

"How mature of you. I'm sure they'll appreciate the consideration after you explain to them exactly why it is you brought a potential threat into our home."

"You're the one who said not to jump to conclusions." She lowered her voice, though the tone was far from friendly. "He's not a soldier anymore. He wants to help—"

"By revealing the locations of our nevethium stocks to Az Zar?"

Elaysia's eyes flashed. "Is that what you thought of my mother when she arrived?"

Konar didn't reply.

The look Elaysia gave him stung a thousand times worse than anything hateful she could've spewed. She turned to leave, but Konar grabbed her shoulder.

"Don't find yourself so lost in chasing what you want that you lose out on what you have. A nation left in disarray is not becoming of a leader." He nodded toward the table. "You'd be wise to attend to your true allies."

"I'm learning to decipher who they are." She stormed off and slid into a cushion in between the Az Zarian and Lumira.

Konar followed—more out of reputation than interest—and took his customary spot at the far end of the table. Amid the jesting and cheer, Jakki stuck out from the rest, isolated and stabbing at her fish as if she intended to kill it again. And though Zavik plopped beside Konar to chatter about their journey, he often glanced across the table at the Az Zarian, eyes narrowed and lips pulled in.

After the party drained the table's resources, Elaysia walked over to the eggs. She picked one up, not the largest, shiniest, nor most beautiful, but the one that seemed to set the standard for the others, the one that commanded belief, and raised it for everyone to see. The room quieted.

"Something's happening to Quinaria," she said, her voice commanding the confidence Konar had struggled to coax out of her for years. His chest prickled with pride. "My father feared we were on the cusp of irreversible change. That belief led him and my mother on a journey for answers. One that killed them. I have to believe their lives weren't lost in vain. That they were onto something the rest of the world hadn't yet grasped. Or maybe others had, and they wanted my parents silenced."

Elaysia tugged her necklace side to side as she spoke, her gaze never landing on a target. But something in her demeanor had changed. She clung to some newfound resolve, and despite its source, Konar, for a moment, felt he'd done something right.

"The last thing my father told me was we, whether my family or Neharem, were meant to find *them*. I'm certain now he meant the Prophets' Scrolls."

Murmurs fell over the room. Konar's throat tightened.

"I have little to go on besides my parents' last destination: Az Zar. I think now, after what's happened, we've no choice but to assume they intend ill." She set the egg back in the nest and faced the table, shoulders squared and gaze intense. "I want to take a small group of warriors across Skyfall Sea and continue in my parents' stead."

Konar fought to keep most of his thoughts to himself. All but one. "We cannot move against Az Zar without justifiable cause."

Elaysia reached for a glass of wine. "Even if they aren't behind the raids, they were to blame for my parents' murders. That alone should've been avenged long ago. Perhaps under different leadership, it would've been."

All eyes fell on Konar. He held his tongue. There were times to defend one's actions, to list the heavily weighed pros and cons, explain the deep-seeded factors few were privy to.

This was not one of them.

"There's cause," the Az Zarian interjected casually. "I'm not well-informed on most of the All-Sovereign's schemes, but the terms he sent me under were not of the friendly, peace-affirming sort."

Konar faced the soldier. "I'm sorry, and you are?"

"Captain Zadel. But you can call me Davier." He winked and extended his hand in greeting.

Konar refused it.

Before anyone else could offer input, two watchers burst in. Between them, another Az Zarian soldier, this one far lower-ranking than Davier with a smooth, pale face accented by dark hair and eyes like Maseeya's. He couldn't have been more than eighteen.

Konar glared at Davier. "Friend of yours?"

"Never seen him." Davier folded his arms, brow furrowed.

"He announced himself and handed over his weapons," one watcher said. "Must've been following your party. He won't state his purpose. Only that he wants an audience with the high chieftain."

Elaysia motioned the watchers to release the boy. "Let him speak."

The boy fell to the floor and held his open palms up to Elaysia. "Empress of Neharem, I'm Xaren Le Solah, former soldier of Az Zar and enslaved to the All-Sovereign, and I've come to swear fealty to you."

"Quite the change of heart spreading through your ranks." Though similar thoughts formulated in Konar's mind, it was Jakki who voiced them. "Were you sent to kill her, too? Backup in case Lord Captain the Golden here"—she jabbed a thumb toward Davier—"failed?"

Maseeya gasped.

Xaren's gaze lingered on Davier with an unmistakable blink of confusion. "A task of that nature would never be assigned to me, nor would I take it. I left because the Lord Priestess murdered some of my fellow soldiers."

Davier's face sobered. "You have proof?"

"The Lord Priestess requested five escorts from our squadron for one of her pilgrimages to Dzorah. They never returned because of an alleged bandit attack, but she's holed up in Cadar without a scratch. Somehow, she's the only one who survived."

Davier flicked the wooden splint he'd picked his teeth with. "So?"

A tinge of pink dusted Xaren's cheeks. "She murdered them, sacrificed them, tested new weapons on them, something." He uttered something in Zarith, then raised his voice. "This isn't the first time something like this happened. They were all human. Expendable. You've heard the stories about what goes on there."

"That's all they are, kid. Stories."

Xaren planted his palms on the table, nostrils flaring. "I was assigned to nevethium acquisition and development. Soldiers in our unit go missing all the time, especially when *she's* involved. There's a lot they don't tell us. If you're not suspicious, you're either blind or in on it."

Elaysia rested a hand on Xaren's shoulder. "Enough. I trust you both have good intentions. One doesn't need a reason to leave tyranny, only the eyes to see its oppression. Xaren, you're welcome in Agaas. There's much you can share to aid our cause."

Xaren bowed. "My bow is yours, my lady."

"Good. Let's regroup tomorrow." Elaysia heaved a door open. "Come. Maseeya's prepared lofts for you all."

Konar stayed long after the room emptied. He'd planned for countless perilous scenarios, but not a repeat of Elishon's mistakes. Not after everything he'd done to keep Elaysia from that fate. But life often ventured down the one path he hadn't expected, happy to drag him along, kicking and screaming.

So be it. He'd molded worse situations into optimal outcomes. War had yet to be declared. The Az Zarians could go missing. That left one problem.

Or eight, to be exact.

Konar stood outside Elaysia's loft, balancing a bowl of corn porridge in one hand and a tray of steaming mugs in the other. He'd stayed up all night forming a convincing argument against her plan. Now, to test it. He adjusted his grip and tapped on the door. No answer. He knocked again, longer and louder.

"Ellie." He pressed his face against the wood. "I've brought food to break your fast."

A muffled reply came from within. "I'm not hungry."

"You, who can scarcely go a few hours without eating, turn down a hot meal? I think not."

The door cracked open. Elaysia still wore her travel-weathered tunic from the night before, and despite the dark circles beneath her eyes, she surrendered a soft smile. "It better be delicious."

Konar stepped into the organized chaos that was her loft: plants sprawling over every surface; maps and paintings masking the walls; heirlooms and artifacts tucked into the remaining nooks and crannies. It was a wonder she ever found a place to sleep. She'd nestled the eggs in a blanket on her cot and patted a spot next to them for Konar to sit. They ate and talked about things that didn't matter, but he enjoyed the normalcy, however fleeting it was.

When both food and pleasantries ran out, Konar cleared his throat and moved to stand by the window. "About last night—"

"It's alright." She drew her knees to her chest. "I know I left you in a precarious position with the council, and for that, I'm sorry. I promise I'll make things right."

"That will be hard to do if you insist on this absurd mission to Az Zar where you'll find yourself in the company of thieves and shadows." Konar winced. That was *not* how he intended to begin the conversation. "Forgive me, I—"

"What did my father tell you before he left?" Elaysia clenched her necklace and fixed her fiery gaze on him.

Konar sipped his tea. "I can't recall. It was a rather stressful time."

Elaysia paced the little space in the room, wringing her hands. "I know he wanted you to go to Orillon. I couldn't sleep the night before they left, and I heard you two arguing in your loft. What was that about?" She joined him at the window. "Why Orillon, Konar?"

Konar reached for his pipe, then thought better of it. "I've tried to protect you. Your father's choices were—"

"Stop." Elaysia rubbed her face. Her eyes were moist, whether from irritation or sorrow, he knew not. "Stop protecting me. I know you're not telling me everything. Keep your secrets if you want, but know it won't change my decision."

Her tone exuded conviction. Konar dropped to the cot and folded his hands in his lap. Perhaps a little truth was warranted. Just enough.

"Your father believed one of the Prophets' Scrolls rests in Orillon. He wanted me to investigate while he and your mother stirred up trouble in Az Zar."

"Why didn't you go?"

"Elishon was..." Konar rubbed his jaw. *Delusional* came to mind, though that would only worsen his position. "Averse to reason during his final days. He spoke of visions, rarely slept—I don't think he was well. Not to mention his source of information was less than trustworthy."

Elaysia sat beside him, some of her venom displaced by curiosity. "It's said the scrolls contain the knowledge of gods. He must've felt something terrible was coming to seek such power."

"The Prophets were a fanatic sect, Ellie. It's a myth. Nothing more."

"Like the stormbird eggs."

Konar gripped the smooth railing of her cot, forcing his fingers to relax one by one. "If they're genuine, they're long fossilized by now, so I hope you have alternative plans for the little war party you've amassed."

He grimaced as the lie left his lips. The eggs carried an undeniable warmth reserved for living beings. Wishing them away wouldn't help now. He'd all the time necessary to dispose of them while Elaysia traveled the nation. All the excuses to relieve the watchers of their duty. All the sleepless nights when no one would've noticed him slipping away. And now, sitting abed with his doom, a familiar vibration tingled in his spine. The room was quiet enough to hear the skittering of squirrels on the rooftop.

No, he prayed. *Not now, please.*

A cracking sound akin to small twigs snapping filled the room as a jagged line formed in the largest of the eggs. A small beak broke through the shell. Its eyes were closed, and its white down was plastered to its head, wet with the waters of birth. Elaysia gasped and rushed to the creature, cooing sounds falling from her lips.

Konar retreated into the shadows.

There'd be no dissuading her now.

DAVIER

Atuross shattered Davier's hopes for a simple mission. The message sent from the northernmost tribe claimed there was another nevethium raid, only this time, they had a culprit: skulmor. Elaysia's newly amassed Stormriders set out to investigate, stormbirds in tow. Davier volunteered to stay in Agaas with the hatchlings, but Elaysia insisted they needed to bond with their riders. But he'd accompany them, wouldn't he? They could use his knowledge of the wolven race. Of course, he'd replied, cursing inwardly. What was a little more time with the skulmor? He had to keep Elaysia and the hatchlings in sight, even if it meant traversing the Greater Quentarri Mountains and venturing into the frozen landscape of Morotôk territory, where the people were scarce and the villages more so.

Davier freed a hand from his cocoon of fur pelts to scratch his beard. Haggard as it was, he appreciated its warmth. Though the sun glared off the snowbanks at its highest point of the day, it only served to obstruct one's vision. The evenings fared worse; the locals' dome-shaped huts made of sod and ice blocks offered little protection from the night's frosted death. But the mornings he enjoyed. Something about the crackling fire and not being crammed alongside strangers reeking of sweat and blood. And the quiet. Few woke before the sunrise. This morning, however, a woman plodded from the direction of the ice holes, bloody harpoon in one hand while the other balanced a seal one-third her size on her shoulders.

"Would you like some help?" Davier offered.

She uttered something in the Morotôk tongue and marched past without so much as a glance.

He shrugged and turned back to the fire. "Charming people," he muttered to the stormbird who'd perched beside him on the log. "Which one are you? Xaren's? I can't believe that colt was entrusted with one instead of me."

The stormbird cocked its head.

Davier's face softened. At a fortnight old, they stood the size of nursling wolf pups. They screeched loudly and often, especially at feeding time, and loved flapping their little wings to no avail. Hardly a threat. But some believed otherwise.

"If the stories are true," he said, reaching to stroke its snow-white down, "you're something fearsome to behold. A summoner of thunder and a wielder of lightning. The ruler of beasts. In you lie the thoughts of a man and the power of a god. But all I see is another trophy for the All-Sovereign's garden."

The stormbird sunk its beak into his glove. Davier shook it into the snow. "You little shit."

"Bonding, I see."

Davier grimaced. It hadn't taken him long to pin down the deep notes in Elaysia's voice or the way Nyrinian sounded like it was made for her tongue. He set the disgruntled creature back on the log with as much care as he could muster. "Just prepping him for battle."

Elaysia scooped up the rogue stormbird, who melted into her arms. She wore furs bundled up around her face and had strapped paddles the locals used for snow travel to her boots. "You could freeze out here, poor thing. Why'd you wander so far from Yerakai?"

Mardus emerged from one of the ice huts and marched over to the fire. He stopped to loom above Davier, dark brows scrunched together. "You're up early. You always are."

Davier shrugged. "Light sleeper."

"He's bonding with the birds," Elaysia teased. "Isn't that helpful of him?"

"Since you're up and *bonding*, you can help prep their meal." Mardus retrieved several fish from the sack on his shoulder and dropped them at his feet.

Davier sized up the Moákun as he cut the fish into smaller bits. Strong, but he'd defeated stronger. And he bore the eyes of an honorable man. It would be his undoing.

Mardus shifted, and the sun caught his golden plate earrings, creating a flash of light that forced Davier to avert his gaze. As if anyone wanted to stare long at him, anyway. Davier had met friendlier skulmor.

Elaysia sat next to him on the log, close enough that their furs touched. "Here. The chief swears this will warm even a desert dweller's blood." She offered him a horn filled with steaming water and an herb compote, letting her hand linger on his longer than necessary.

Davier found the curve of her lips and allowed his mind to wander. He'd expected Elaysia to be the grotesque nyman that the All-Sovereign warned him about, but her clashing features didn't make him writhe with revulsion. Quite the opposite. Not the most beautiful woman he'd ever laid eyes on, but she was unique. She carried the fire of a wild mare and reeked of naivety. Both would fade with time.

He nodded his thanks and lifted the horn to his mouth. It smelled of char. Bitter notes tinged his tongue. "Not sure it's worth the warmth."

"If you can't handle it…" Elaysia tugged it away from him, eyes dancing.

Davier held firm. He pulled her in closer. "There's little I can't handle."

"Handle this," a new voice said.

Someone tackled Davier from behind, sending him reeling forward. The steaming liquid jumped out of the horn and onto his face. He whirled around. "What the fuck?!"

Two cat eyes peered out at him from beneath a hood. Lumira. It wasn't the first time she'd crept up on padded feet to startle him. He almost regretted his comment about beridians being unrightfully lauded as hunters. However, each time she proved her point, she treated him a little better the rest of the day. A little.

"So much for the third time being the charm," she sneered. "Do they teach you anything at your academy besides how to kiss royal ass?"

Davier wiped his face with a gloved hand. "Are we done now? I don't want to keep watching my back in what should be friendly company."

"Poor slaver. I can't imagine what that's like. Oh, wait." She flattened her ears as she stroked her stormbird, a larger female with gray eyes. It butted its head against hers and chirped.

Mardus snatched the fish Davier had sliced up and fed the pieces to his red-eyed female. "If they keep growing at this rate, they'll be the size of a horse in a year. Keera will be the largest, I think."

"Hopefully she's more charming than you," Davier muttered.

Mardus ignored him.

Chatter announced the rest of the party as they trickled in to take seats by the fire. The seal-carrying Morotôk woman trailed behind them hauling a sack. She dumped its contents onto the snow: dried fish, raw slabs of what presumably was seal, a pile of organs, and a jar of pungent sauce. Grokhion thanked her, earning himself a hint of a smile from the wind-dried woman before she plodded back to one of the ice huts. He snatched up a dried fish, which looked like a mere bite in his paws, and plunged it into the sauce.

"Fermented oil." Grokhion dropped the fish into his mouth and licked the grease off his lips. Sensing Davier's gaze, he dipped another and offered it. "You won't taste anything like it."

Davier wrinkled his nose. If it assaulted his senses from a distance, he didn't dare venture closer. "I'm not hungry."

Grokhion shrugged and inhaled it.

"Is there anything else?" Davier whispered to Elaysia as the others dug in.

She stopped mid-chew. "This is a fresh kill. They honor us by sharing their best meat."

"I meant no offense. I just didn't see any cooked portions."

"The Morotôk sometimes eat it raw, or they ferment it along with the oils. They left it untouched so we can have our preference." She thrust a sharpened stick into his hands. "For cooking."

"Thanks." Davier stabbed the cleanest cut of meat and moved closer to the fire. "Better than the rations we're used to. Right, Xaren?"

The boy acknowledged him with a scowl before returning to his conversation with Yerakai.

Little shit.

Davier had hoped the ex-soldier was another spy, but a few private conversations proved the boy's newfound allegiance was genuine. He'd avoided Davier since, distancing himself from distasteful association. No matter. Brute force wasn't an option for the time being, so having an extra ally would do little to aid him. Davier pressed on alone, documenting the number of their warriors, the quality of their weapons, and assessing their nevethium stock, which, from what he'd seen, they'd only mined a fraction of.

He bit into the hunk of charred seal. Gamey and fishy with a texture not entirely unlike steak. Somewhat palatable.

Davier had only taken two bites when Jakki started kicking snow over the fire. The others moaned.

"What?" she said, hands on her hips. "We need to leave now if we want to reach the village by sundown. Chief Amkah said she'll watch the stormbirds so we can move faster."

"What about the sleighs?" Davier asked. Their horses hadn't made it far into Morotôk territory, and they'd relied on their hosts' generosity to bear them between long stretches on reindeer-drawn sleighs.

Jakki rolled her eyes and gave Davier a look that suggested sub-par intelligence on his part. "They won't go near that village. They believe the skulmor are cursed; they've defiled that place and evil spirits roam about freely. Sort of like where you're from." She strutted toward the huts, white hair spilling out of her hood like ocean spray.

At first, Davier thought she'd been inclined toward him in a teasing, aggressive way. He'd only risked being with a nyrian once—humans couldn't even enter nyrian whorehouses in Az Zar—but she was a tempting deviation, provided there was no offspring. That fantasy shattered a week ago when he awoke in the night to her tangled in another woman's bedroll. Subtle as they were, it was hard to ignore the soft panting and moaning in an ice hut packed to the brim. Or his arousal at the spectacle.

Elaysia squeezed his arm. "Don't worry about her. She'll come around."

Davier shoved more seal into his mouth. It didn't matter if she did.

It would all be over soon enough.

They were two-thirds of the way to the village when the storm hit. The wind howled like a mourner, hurling icy gusts of snow that ripped through their furs and blurred their vision. Some in the party begged to stop and wait out the storm. Davier didn't dare let them. To stop would mean to rest, and in a blizzard, rest meant death.

When Davier could no longer see more than a foot away, he tied a rope from each member of the party to the next to ensure they lost no one. Lumira volunteered him to lead. He didn't complain. Arms extended and hood pulled down as far as it would go, he plodded forward blindly until he ran into an ice wall.

"I think I found a hut," he shouted into the storm. "Is this the village?"

"Should be. It's the only one around here," Elaysia called back. "Be careful. We don't know if any skulmor remain."

"I'm severing my line so I can assess the area faster. I'd tell the others to do the same."

"If you think it's a good idea."

Would I suggest it otherwise? Davier wasn't staying out in the blizzard any longer than required, and if any skulmor still lingered, they'd be holed up inside.

He cut the rope and worked his way around the wall until it opened into a tunneled entrance. Unlike the previous villages, ice made up the entire structure. The tunnel spilled into a darkened room. He retrieved the nevethium necklace Elaysia loaned him, spilling its light against the ice like crystalline moss. The space was fit to house four people and contained a pile of furs, a spear, a table covered in knives and frozen meat, and a barren firepit. Abandoned. No sign of blood or struggle. He eased his hands off his hilts and sat on the furs, immediately regretting it. Their caress beckoned him down, tempting him to sleep. A few moments wouldn't hurt. He lay back into the warm embrace.

Davier awoke to the crunching of snow. Elaysia ducked inside, Lumira on her tail. Dammit, how long had he slept?

Lumira folded her arms, ears pinned back. "Got your hands full, eh?"

Elaysia failed to mask a smirk.

"All good here." Davier sat up and inspected the furs. "I thought I saw a bloodstain. Turns out it's nothing."

"Uh-huh."

The rest of the party trudged in, eyebrows and eyelashes crusted with snow. They looked tattered and wind-burned, but none had seen battle.

Davier cracked his knuckles beneath his gloves. "Have we found anything?"

Elaysia shook her head. "It's deserted. Just a few bodies buried in the snow. One warrior and two elders. The first"—she rubbed her neck and looked down at her boots—"gutted and covered in bite marks. The others' throats were torn out."

"Skulmor," Lumira interjected.

Davier touched the scar on the back of his neck. "I'm no stranger to their work." Skulmor could stand on two legs like beridians, but they preferred to move on all fours and fought with the strength of five men. Men with fangs.

Jakki shoved between them to get to the firepit. "Excellent observation, cat. Don't know how we would've come to that conclusion without you." Lumira and Davier exchanged glances while Jakki knelt to kindle a flame. "They're long gone, and most of the Morotôk escaped safely. Worthless journey."

Elaysia opened her mouth to reply, but all that came out was a cloud of breath.

While everyone made to bunk down for the night, Yerakai unrolled a map atop the furs. The parchment looked like it might crumble at any moment. Davier rolled his eyes. Neharem relied too heavily on myth, and what little existed of their written accounts wouldn't last much longer. *Like her people.* The thought brought him a twinge of guilt. He ignored it.

"I don't understand," Yerakai said, face buried in the map. His voice had a commanding presence despite being gentle, and the room quieted. "The skulmor have been peaceful for ages."

"Peaceful?" Jakki snorted.

"They never attack us and keep to their lands." He threaded his fingers and stared down the tunnel into the storm. "What would provoke them to such sudden aggression?"

Mardus refastened his dark bun as he eyed Davier and Xaren. "I might have a guess."

"You've guessed wrong." Davier's hand twitched for the blades nestled against his back. He'd no patience left for veiled threats. "Look, I was there. They hardly fought back when we reclaimed our lands, and they've never invaded Az Zar in retaliation."

"Then you've pushed them here," Grokhion said, stroking his whiskers.

"Our—Az Zar's war with the skulmor started years ago. Why would they become hostile now?"

"They've never cared about nevethium," Xaren added. He didn't look up as he spoke, content to draw patterns on the packed snow floor.

"So why take it?" Davier asked.

Anahi stopped passing out the evening meal—more dried fish—to interject. "They know it has value. Perhaps lust for power has finally gotten the better of our barbaric brethren."

"Skulmor don't want power."

Grokhion chuckled. "Everyone wants power, no matter what they say. It's the gods' curse on all who walk Quinaria." He folded his arms and leaned his head against the wall as if he intended to sleep.

Yerakai rolled up the map. "If that's the case, the Morotôk would be the perfect target, even though the Daruk and Atsukut are closer. They aren't as well protected and are spread apart in isolated villages."

Davier shoved a fish into his mouth to keep his opinions at bay. If the skulmor sought Neharem's nevethium, someone, or something, drove them to it. They'd been crippled during the rebellion. The All-Sovereign made them agree to countless terms, most of which Davier knew nothing about.

This could very well be one of them.

Later that night, they all lay together with skins piled to keep warm, Grokhion and Lumira bookending since their fur could handle the exposure. Rested from his preemptive doze, Davier lay awake, imagining life as a colonel, only this time it wasn't a dream. He felt the cushions in his new living quarters and the crisp uniform pressed against his skin. Tasted the women who'd flock to him. Returned nods to respectable nyrians in Cadar who had ignored him before. Heard the sincerity in his father's voice as he exclaimed how proud he was of his only son.

Davier did dream that night, but not of Cadar or of his new life. He dreamed of skulmor crashing into the hut and tearing out their throats while they slept. He dreamed of the All-Sovereign. Of screeching stormbirds. The stench of blood.

And Elaysia.

ELAYSIA

Self-governed tribes and the ability to supplant unsuitable leaders set Neharem apart from the rest of Quinaria, but today Elaysia understood why some rulers opted for total control. After debriefing the council on potential threats Az Zar posed to their nevethium and sovereignty—one she'd spent the better part of two days preparing sans Konar—she cast her token, worth two votes as high chieftain. Agaas stood in favor of sending both ambassadors and scouting parties east. Chief Rajar surprised her by placing his token beside hers. The Banaxa, Daruk, and Atsukut also supported the offensive advantage, but then it unraveled.

"Discrepancies over shipments don't amount to war declarations," scoffed Chief Arkuun, wrinkled face melting into a patronizing smile.

"Your parents worked hard to maintain peace," offered Chief Kelsia. "Why disrupt it?"

Others echoed similar concerns. Jakki and Mardus's efforts to influence their parents fell on deaf ears; there'd been no backing from Chief Jattai or Chief Orandus. The obvious signs of Az Zarian handiwork only made them more apprehensive. The vote tallied eight to six in favor of remaining on the defensive, despite the increasing number of nevethium raids. Any proactive action now would be out of favor with the council.

If they wanted to force her into her father's footsteps, she was well on her way.

"They made up their minds before I even opened my mouth," Elaysia told Zavik after the last chief left the summit lodge. He'd waited outside for the gathering to conclude and just slipped in to join her at the table.

Zavik's lips parted to speak, then he closed them and nodded. Since her return from Morotôk lands, he'd lingered closer than normal, prodding her with questions and offering constant input. But he knew when to simply listen, when she needed to unbridle her rage or else burst. No one deserved such a friend.

"They could've at least pretended to hear me out instead of insulting me by having separate conversations while I outlined my proposal," she continued. "They're scared and using my inexperience as an excuse. It'll be ages before they convene again." She crumpled onto the table. Novitae festivities were underway to celebrate the story of creation, and it'd taken persuasion on Konar's part to gather them all for her proposal.

Zavik patted her arm awkwardly. "If they're too close-minded to see the brilliance in your plan, we're better off without them."

"Except we're not." Elaysia untied the leather strip holding one of her braids and worked her fingers through the tangles. "I can't blame them. Their concerns are valid. But I can't deny what I know to be the right course of action either. How can we ignore such blatant acts of war?"

"By putting on our ceremonial outfits and indulging in some well-earned comforts." Zavik nudged her toward the door, almost giddy. "I hear there's a celebration brewing."

Ceremonial drums pounded through Agaas like a heartbeat. Waves of people crowded the paths, sloshing drinking horns and wooden cups as they danced and sang their way to the Ritual Tree in a sweaty herd. It smelled of campfire and wine, and the ground rumbled with footsteps.

Elaysia hesitated outside the summit lodge. Large gatherings could only be tolerated with a good bit of drink in hand, and given the circumstances, tonight was more daunting than ever.

"I'm not sure I'm in the mood for revelry," she said.

"I'm inclined to agree." Zavik shook the curls out of his face. His eyes appeared remarkably green in the late afternoon cloud cover. Large and innocent as a child's, but skeptical. Always skeptical. "But the council wouldn't approve of your absence."

Elaysia rubbed her eyes with her palms. "Fine. Keep me company while I prepare?"

"I'm not sure." He cleaned his seers with the edge of his cloak, feigning disinterest. "Quite busy, at present."

"As if." Elaysia shouldered him and led the way around a cluster of blue-skinned Moatiwe, their ice-white eyes hot on her back as they passed.

Zavik looked back, face scrunched. "Do they ever speak?"

"Rarely, if their chief shares any resemblance." Elaysia stole across the platform, sticking to the outskirts as if she intended another evening escapade, and waited outside her loft for Zavik to catch up. Somehow, he'd trapped a leaf in his hair on the brief journey between buildings. She plucked it. "Saving this for later?"

Zavik blushed. "Salads, teas, experiments. The options are endless."

Elaysia brushed past him with a smirk. Inside, an ambient green glow warmed the room. Roused by the creak of the door, Onitus stirred in his makeshift blanket nest and opened his beak in anticipation. Elaysia tossed him a strip of raw venison and set to mixing a pot of paint. She drew a thick line under her eyes and across her nose, then added a row of small dots beneath it. Zavik's stare bore into her from behind.

"What now, Zav?"

"Why the white? Isn't that for mourning?"

"It's also the color of peace."

Zavik folded his arms, but a grin crept up his cheeks. "So, you can mourn their decision while implying you're at peace with it?"

"Damn, you're good."

He raised his chin ever so slightly. Elaysia motioned for him to turn around while she shrugged out of her woolen council cloak and into a fitted nytak skin dress decorated with fringe and beads. She tugged the sleeves to cover the white patches on her forearm. It was nothing the people didn't know, but Davier…

Why in Haeshol did she even care? This was hardly the time for romance, and there were plenty of capable partners in Agaas to ease any sense of loneliness. She traced her fingers across her collarbone, still feeling naked in the wide neckline.

Oh well. Nothing a little wine and the setting sun couldn't cure.

She plopped on her cot beside a shut-eyed Zavik and bent down to wedge her feet into nytak-hide boots. "Coast is clear."

"You look wonderf—I mean, you always look… This, it's just very, um…" Zavik's voice trailed off, his face pink with embarrassment. He abruptly turned to stroke Onitus's head. "Annalee's handiwork?"

Elaysia nodded. The hairs on her neck rose at the mention of her mother's name. She motioned to the door. "Shall we?"

"Of course. I just don't know what in Quinaria I'll wear." Zavik placed a hand on his chest and widened his eyes. "Stay in my brown tunic or rush back to my loft to don my green?"

"You can always borrow something of mine." She stuck out her tongue and handed him Onitus. "Let's get this over with."

The sky grew dark with streaks of purple, pink, and red running like blood through water. A blanket of fog kept most of the chill from the air, though the cold would've been welcome among the heat generated by the dense gathering of bodies. Nevethium poles lined the pathways like green firebugs in the night. The crowd stretched through the High Tree courtyard, continuing through the gate and descending the ramp to the lower levels.

"Maybe we should take a different—"

Elaysia froze as a hand covered her eyes. Onitus squalled, and she ripped the fingers off in time to watch the stormbird clamp down on them.

"Mavet Almighty." Davier wrenched his hand away, furrowing his brow as he wiped blood on his trousers. "Your guard bird grows ferocious."

"Only when he perceives threats." Elaysia glared to suppress her rousing pleasure in his presence. He'd changed out of his uniform in favor of a less-incriminating tunic of white canvas that exposed part of his chest, but he'd kept his Az Zarian pants and boots. He had the decency to leave his weapons in the loft he shared with Xaren and Grokhion. The visible ones, at least. "Will you be attending our festivities?"

Davier offered an exaggerated bow. "My first pagan celebration? Wouldn't miss it."

Zavik muttered something unintelligible from where he brooded a few steps away.

Under the guise of passing Onitus off to him, Elaysia leaned toward Zavik's ear and whispered, "At least pretend to tolerate him, will you? We need his insight on Az Zar."

Zavik huffed, but he accepted Onitus and fell into step behind her.

Davier offered his arm. "If you care to humor me in some of my ways while I indulge in yours?"

Elaysia adjusted her sleeve to mask the point where her skin collided with itself. Davier didn't appear repulsed. Quite the opposite. Not that she cared. She just needed a drink to remember that. She hooked her arm in his and smashed the butterflies that dared to stir her stomach. His body radiated warmth.

Davier's gaze occasionally drifted over her while they walked. After the third or fourth pass, Elaysia stiffened and said, "Something on your mind, Captain?"

Davier looked affronted—all in show, of course. "A thousand pardons. I was simply admiring your dress. Wasn't aware you had some to rival our own." He gestured to the crowd rushing around them like spawning salmon. "Half your women seem to prefer trousers or naught but their skin."

"Let that be your first lesson in underestimating us." Elaysia kept her gaze forward as heat bloomed throughout her body. "Is skin so rare in Az Zar?"

"It's considered sinful for women to show too much flesh outside the marriage bed."

"You might want to shut your eyes tonight, then."

Davier winked. "I'm not a staunch supporter of the rules."

The closeness of his body suddenly alarmed her, as if she stood naked before the world. She pulled away as they approached an older woman passing out hand pies, and she grabbed two. They smelled like the anderberries that grew at the edge of the forest near the coastline: sugary and salty, and one of her favorites.

She shoved one into Davier's hand. "An Agaasian delicacy."

He made a show of the first bite, but his pretentiousness soon melted into bliss. "Shit, that's good." He inhaled the rest and licked his fingers. "What did the council think of your proposal?"

Elaysia took a bite. She hardly tasted the juices as they trickled down her throat. "They weren't overly fond of the parts they listened to."

"No one is eager for war," Zavik added. He sidled up beside Elaysia and scowled at Davier. "Given your country's reputation, we can't count on peaceful negotiations."

Davier pulled up abruptly. "Strong words for someone who has the appearance of an Az Zarian. Unless you claim Daruk blood, which I find unlikely."

Elaysia could practically see the steam coming out of Zavik's ears. Instead of waiting for him to rally a comeback, she wandered toward the Ritual Tree. The bridge leading up to it was the largest in Agaas, arched with supports built into the platforms below and wide enough to accommodate multitudes of people crossing at once for celebrations like Novitae. Elaysia tossed a final glance toward her still-squabbling companions, then darted across. The air smelled of smoke, drink, and sweat, no scent overpowering the other, creating a strangely alluring medley. A green-skinned Ni'anko danced by wearing nothing but wooden jewelry and a wrap around her waist. She tossed her half-shaved head of hair back and forth to the beat, nearly colliding with Elaysia, then offered a carved bead and a blessing when she recognized her High Chieftain. Elaysia clutched it in her palm. Perhaps some people believed in her after all.

"Something I said?"

Elaysia spun to face an amused Davier. Zavik ran up to join them, panting as he dodged some children caught in a game of tag.

"Sorry," she shouted over the music, "didn't want your debate to cost us a good view. This way."

The Ritual Tree was alive with a roaring fire, its flames rising higher than the summit lodge and stretching wider than the gathering table. Like the High Tree, it had long ago been cleared at the thickest part of its trunk to accommodate large gatherings, and a variety of logs, furs, and skins were laid out around the central fire pit for spectators. Elaysia selected a pile of furs reserved for chiefs and their families. Normally, she hated sitting so close, but there was no avoiding it now.

The crowd quieted as dancers encircled the flames, ushered in by a chorus of flutes and additional drums. Zavik took the spot on Elaysia's right and passed a disgruntled Onitus to her. She ran her fingers over his feathers, marveling at the softness of the baby down. He twisted his head around and chirped.

"This seat taken?" Davier's lips brushed her ear as he spoke. It was probably because the drums made it hard to hear, but it didn't make the proximity of his mouth any less real. Nor did it stop the tingling sensation on her flesh.

"Yes." Elaysia squirmed and tried to focus on the flames. "But I'll make an exception."

Davier plopped beside her and pointed to a tall dancer cloaked in sparkling robes with a nevethium-tipped staff. "Who's the glamorous fellow?"

"Khiev-Tatamic," Zavik interjected crossly. "Maker of gods and conqueror of the stars."

"I was asking the expert," Davier said, nudging Elaysia.

Zavik bristled. "I *am* an expert."

Elaysia bit back a smirk. "He is."

"By all means, continue." Davier shot Zavik a mocking look and returned his attention to the performers. "Better narrate the whole thing to be safe. I'm fairly uneducated when it comes to pagan religions."

Zavik cleared his throat, seemingly unaffected by Davier's sarcasm. "Khiev-Tatamic loved Quorath more than all his other worlds combined because he fell in love with its guardian moons: four sisters with whom he shared"—Zavik's nose wrinkled—"relations, unbeknownst to the others. They had a lot of children, who had a lot of children. Gods. Demigods. Whatever you want to call them. His favorites were his firstborns, bore from different sisters. His son, Mavet, and a daughter, Chai'Tik. Eventually, all the gods grew tired of living alone in Quorath, so Khiev-Tatamic created Vysilliam, the first of the races, for them to rule over."

"Our glowing-eyed and pointy-eared narcissistic friends," Davier said.

"The myrem and shaktar were Vysilliam, too." Zavik rolled his eyes as more costumed dancers poured into the center in a colorful parade. "Together, the Vysilliam made a trinity of sky, water, and land. For many years, they lived in peace, and death only summoned those who'd reached the end of their natural life."

Davier snorted. "A nice thought, but we're all inclined to violence."

The flutes struck an ominous tone as a performer adorned with a nytak's skull and antlers skulked onto the stage. He wore ragged robes, and beneath those, a real ribcage. Children hid their faces in their mothers' breasts when he lunged at the audience, growling and hissing. Elaysia stiffened.

"Mavet," Zavik said. "He grows bored with the Vysilliam and demands Khiev-Tatamic to create new people to govern, ones with competitive natures and unsettled spirits."

"Can't say I blame him. Who'd want a world filled with passive servants?" Davier motioned to a man passing around drinking horns.

Zavik continued as if Davier hadn't interrupted. "Khiev-Tatamic complied and created two new races: humans and beridians. For a time, they satisfied Mavet's curiosity."

"Lucky us." Davier took a swig of wine and offered some to Zavik.

"Stop interrupting," Zavik hissed. "We're already causing unrest." He looked worriedly at the handful of people glaring in their direction. Still, he grudgingly accepted the wine from Davier. "Thanks, though."

Davier shrugged. "Don't mention it." His eyes found Elaysia's. A rush emanated from her chest, up her neck, and down her arms. "Why are all the dancers running around like that? With the scarfs?"

"It represents time passing," she said. "Khiev-Tatamic leaves to oversee his other worlds, and unrest breaks out among his offspring. Mavet amasses a following, both from his realm and ours, and entices a human to commit the first murder."

"Humans ruining everything, eh? Sounds like the storytelling of a nyrian." Davier pulled the skin away from Zavik and offered it to Elaysia.

She took a sip, then another, her body releasing inhibitions like falling leaves. Cyan's anderberry wine, dark and thick as blood, the closest thing Neharem had to Beridian Moonlight. The old Apáasutai swore by his recipe—and just about everything else.

"Chai'Tik learns of her brother's plotting," Zavik said as Jak-ki, adorned in a great bearskin, danced into the fray, every bit as tall and powerful as the goddess she represented. "She creates the skulmor, intending them for her warriors, but Mavet steals the skulmor's hearts and leaves them void of love."

Domesticated wolves tore into the clearing, snarling, and Davier startled. "Oh, they have hearts," he said, quick to disguise his discomfort. "I've held one beating in my hands."

"And then the Caman appear in Quinaria and wreak havoc." Zavik pointed to dark, hooded figures lurking in the back. "Some say they're gods and goddesses loyal to him. Others say they're his mortal slaves. There are always six, and it's said they can fool the wisest of people."

Davier covered his mouth with his hand in feigned surprise. "Surely not a scholar like yourself."

Zavik glared. "I'm done."

"No problem. Even I know this part of the story." Davier reclined, bracing himself with his arms. He used his chin to gesture to the skirmish reenacted before them, a blur of bodies colliding. "War breaks out, and when all seems lost for us lesser-beings, the siblings battle in the stars until Chai'Tik delivers a final blow by sending Mavet's mother to her death."

"It cost her own life as well. She hurled herself and the moon-mother into Quinaria, and the impact created a crater, revealing nevethium. Kind of important." Zavik pushed his seers back up the bridge of his nose. "In Mavet's sadness, he's easily overtaken by those loyal to Chai'Tik."

"And your great god?" Davier asked. "Where was he?"

"He's not my god." Zavik said. Then, as if suddenly aware Elaysia was present, added, "Khiev-Tatamic kept his distance. He was too torn between his offspring to intervene."

Davier shook his head. "Seems like a coward to me."

Elaysia chewed her lips. It was a part of the story she struggled with herself. Sure, unconditional love was admirable, but to refuse to address any wrongdoings at the cost of a world?

"He did return once more to transfer his life essence to his children," Zavik added. "He resurrected Chai'Tik's spirit and placed it in a single-formed vessel. Most believe it's something akin to a bear. He also restricted Mavet's powers and banished him to Haeshol."

"A mistake. You should never leave an enemy alive." Davier cracked his knuckles. Something told Elaysia he'd experienced the fallout of such a mistake.

"In some cases, I'd agree," Zavik muttered, eyeing Davier.

The ceremony ended with a unified cry and a moment of silence. People rose to dance with the performers, and Jakki motioned for Elaysia to join her at the center where she'd soon amass an audience of admirers. Bronze skin shimmering in the firelight, she never missed a beat and drew people to her like moths around a flame. Elaysia shook her head. If Jakki's beauty alone didn't give one cause for self-doubt, dancing next to her was enough to arouse feelings of inferiority. Elaysia was no exception. She handed Onitus to Zavik and grabbed Davier's arm.

"Come." She guided him away from the commotion. "I know a better place to watch."

They retrieved more drink and climbed atop a loft that served as a storage chamber. Elaysia let the wine wash away any lingering anxiety as Davier lay down and propped himself up with an elbow. Zavik climbed up behind them and cleared his throat to make his presence known.

Davier leaned in close, a smirk playing on his lips. "You know, you *are* the high chieftain."

"I didn't know." Elaysia hid her face with her drink. Her head spun, and words piled up on her tongue like a dam ready to burst.

"Right." Davier lowered the drinking horn from her face and brushed her hair behind her ear. "That means you can do what you want without seeking approval. Your people seem loyal to you, and you've got your Stormriders." He raised his horn to hers, eyes twinkling "And me."

"Some might argue you're our downfall."

Davier playfully tugged at her horn. "That's it. No more wine for you."

Elaysia tossed the rest back and lay down beside him, eyes on the stars as her body melted into the ground. "You're serious, aren't you? Go to Az Zar without the council's consent?"

"Why not? You've many able warriors in Agaas right now. It's the perfect time to recruit. I don't believe in coincidences."

Elaysia nibbled on her thumbnail. He was right, and the festivities would continue for several days. "And we could slip away without causing a commotion," she murmured.

"Until they realize we've left." Zavik's voice startled her. She'd forgotten he was there. He wore a furrowed brow and thinly drawn lips. "You'll have a greater upset on your hands than if you'd made your decision known. If we're going to go, we should be upfront about it. They might disagree, but they'll respect you."

Davier shrugged. "In my experience, it's better to ask forgiveness than permission."

"He's right, Zav." Elaysia pushed herself up to face her grimacing friend. "Someone will try to stop us. Especially when they learn where I intend to send you."

"Me?" His face softened, and she brushed the hair out of his eyes.

"Yes, I have a special request if you'll hear it. You're the only one I can entrust this to."

"Anything," he replied. "I'll do anything."

JAKKI

Damn north.

Though Jakki opted for a thick, fur-lined hood and wrapped her neck twice over, she couldn't escape the numbing cold set deep into her bones, much less scratch any itches through all the layers. Daruk territory was arguably better than the suffocating snowdrifts and blinding blizzards of the Morotôk lands, but that was comparing rotten fruit to rotten meat. What the northern tribes found pleasurable in their hostile landscapes was beyond her. Isolation? They weren't the most sociable people and cared little for art and dance. Or love. Duty was the way of the north. Duty and survival, and the latter was being threatened now.

When word of a skulmor attack on a Daruk village arrived amid Novitae festivities, she'd hoped it was an anomaly like the Morotôk incident. It turned out to be a recurring nightmare. They'd visited four villages now, and all but one had suffered. The skulmor wreaked so much havoc on the last that they'd converted their longhouse into a recovery chamber for the wounded. At another, the surviving adults hardly spoke, and the children cowered behind the smithy's anvil when she tried to coax them over. Nevethium was the target of the raids, the destruction of property and lives a bonus to the invaders.

While the journey proved necessary, it didn't lessen the sting of being subjected to cleanup while Elaysia embarked on an investigative mission to Az Zar with her new favorites. They shouldn't have split up. Going into enemy territory required more than the two dozen or so warriors Elaysia set out with, but Davier weakened her judgment, and Lumira encouraged spontaneity. Bad combination. Jakki said as much when they parted ways, earning herself eye rolls and pursed-lipped nods for a goodbye. So be it. They deserved each other.

Jakki stopped beside a river to watch the water slither over the rocks and crash back into itself. She knelt and brought some to her lips. Icy and pure. Perhaps the freshest she'd ever tasted. Siren stirred in the pack behind her, peeping a downy white head through the opening as she chirped in interest.

"Want some, girl?" Jakki cupped water in her palm and offered it to the stormbird.

Yerakai descended the ridge ahead, voice carrying the unmistakable burden of anguish. "*Endei,*" he called again. An Apáasutai warning. *Bad omen.*

Jakki hurried across a log to meet him, motioning to Mardus and Anahi to follow along with the twenty warriors Elaysia entrusted to her. "Brother," she said, stepping over the craggy rocks leading from the riverbed, "what did you find?"

Yerakai waited until Jakki drew within arm's reach. A shadow not entirely cast by the thick-knitted pine trees hung over his face. "The entire village"—he covered his mouth with a fist—"they've passed on to Everworld."

A lump formed in Jakki's throat. "May Khiev-Tatamic keep them by the light of eternal moons." She bowed her head, and the others echoed their condolences. A stormbird cried out. "We still need to examine the village."

"And prepare the dead in the way of their people," Yerakai added.

"Which is?" Jakki hadn't bothered to learn the various death rituals of all twelve tribes and their many varying sects. She could barely keep up with her own.

Mardus wrinkled his forehead. "I believe they cleanse their shells with Rash-Yaanah's fire to ensure safe passage."

Jakki nodded. "Let's get this over with."

From a distance, the village looked like any other Daruk settlement. Livestock enclosed in wooden pens. Small family homes with thatched, pointed roofs. A smithy. Stables. A central longhouse in the middle. As she drew closer, however, the illusion faded. No ale-infused shouts from the longhouse. No smoke rising from the holes cut into the roofs. No children scurrying about with play weapons or herbs from the garden. Not a single body, nor a dog's bark. Even the wind held its breath as if sensing misfortune.

The entire village.

The severity of the carnage hit Jakki like a blow to the stomach. She grasped Yerakai's sleeve. "Where are the bodies?"

He wouldn't meet her gaze. "The longhouse."

Jakki sprinted down the fern-covered hillside, hood flapping behind her. Siren screeched in protest. Yerakai called out, but she didn't stop to wait for him or the others. No one could outrun her.

She cleared the outlying fence with a clean vault. Mud pulled at her boots as she tore down the abandoned path leading to the longhouse. She hesitated at the threshold. The doors were ajar, revealing a yawning darkness. The stench of rot and bowels permeated the room, triggering her gag reflexes.

Jakki forced herself inside, staff at the ready, the light from her nevethium pendant guiding her path. Empty chairs lined in furs. Pelts on the walls. Dried herbs and fish hanging from the ceiling. Decomposing meat on the plates. Shields and weapons piled beside the door. They'd been celebrating. Unarmed. No doubt intoxicated.

As if sensing the doom, Siren quieted and sank into the pack. A shadow loomed ahead. Jakki tensed with each step. She removed her necklace and held the crystal up to reveal the shadow's secrets.

Her legs buckled. She fell to her knees, bracing herself with her hands.

Heads. At least one hundred. Lifeless, severed, and stacked in a mound. No discrimination in age or sex.

Painted above the heads, a message in blood:

They fought well.

Jakki retched.

Footsteps pattered into the room. Mardus knelt beside her and buried his face in his hands. "The Daughter have mercy."

A hand rested on her shoulder. "I tried to warn you." Yerakai's voice.

White heat coiled in Jakki's chest. She threw off his hand and hurried to inspect the message. "This can't be skulmor. They can barely speak Nyrinian, much less write it. And since when do they decapitate?"

Yerakai ran a hand through his long, silken strands. "I was puzzled, too, but the bodies are stacked out back. Blatant bite marks, and they've been disemboweled."

"Filthy dogs." Mardus threw a chair across the room. It splintered against the wall, and his stormbird screeched. "They'll pay for what they've done."

"In time, Brother." Jakki brought her fist to her chest and bowed to the massacred. "Yerakai, what of their nevethium?"

Yerakai ran long fingers over his stormbird's head protruding from his pack. "Nothing yet. The others are scouring the village."

"They won't find any." Jakki's throat tightened. "Burn this tomb to the ground and choose some homes to shelter in tonight." She drew Siren out of her pack and handed her to Yerakai.

"Where are you going?" he asked.

"I need air."

Jakki ducked outside and found Anahi lurking on the porch. She hurried on before the outsider could berate her with questions. Beyond the village lay a small wood that divided Daruk and skulmor territory. It would do.

The woods were as quiet as the village, save for her breathing and the snapping of twigs beneath her feet. If there was a trail, it eluded her. Trees grew clustered, forcing her to use her hand as a shield to protect her face from stray foliage. She failed to block a branch. It struck her across the cheek and grazed her eye.

"You fucking animals," she screamed, "these people did nothing to you." Arm trembling, she ripped the branch off the tree and smacked it against the trunk until it broke.

When her rage abated, she noticed a gap in the trees ahead. She dropped the branch and stumbled into a clearing. It was smaller than the village and predominantly filled by a pond with a few rocks jutting above the waterline. They bore unfamiliar markings. Shapes carved cruelly.

Jakki sat beside the pond, ignoring the dampness seeping into her leather pants. The cold tightened the skin on her fingers as she pulled out the leaves the mystery woman had given her back in Tangeesh lands. What had she said? Something about loosening the mind and the lips?

Haeshol, why not?

Jakki ground some with a stone and retrieved a pipe from her pack. It took a moment, but she got a spark with her flint and breathed deeply. Richer than kinawa and fruitier. She didn't feel much of anything, though. Maybe a little relaxed. With a frown, she emptied the pipe and closed her eyes.

A vision entered her mind, one she'd been subjected to before: Elaysia on a boat with Davier's arms wrapped around her waist. Wind pushing them closer together. The beridian thief at their side, making jokes about Jakki being sent to the northlands to follow worthless leads.

She slammed her fist on the ground. "I hope you're enjoying your pleasure sail. Turns out you sent me into the fray. Your people are dying, and you can't stick around to face it. I'm tired of covering for your ass. I'm done, Ellie. Done."

"Not becoming of a friend, is it? To cast you aside so carelessly?" a quivering voice said.

Jakki jumped to her feet, staff in hand. Her pulse quickened as she scanned the trees. It had gotten dark so fast. Had she lay down that long? A cackle rose behind her. She whirled to face the pond.

A creature huddled atop one of the carved stones, surrounded by a golden-green glow. His hair and beard, all tangled and stuck with twigs, ran long and gray past his wrinkled stomach. A loincloth covered his midsection, and antlers that appeared more organic than ornamental sprouted from his head. But those eyes. White eyes, glowing far brighter than any nyrian's. The source of the golden-green glow was a crudely carved staff with a gem nestled in the top. It radiated beyond the span of nevethium and hummed like a distant swarm of bees.

"Captivating, isn't it?" the creature-man said. "Come, have a look."

Jakki slipped off her boots and stepped into the pond. The water was warm, the slime slick beneath her feet. Accusations piled in her head, but a question screamed louder still. "What is that crystal?"

"It's what nevethium could be. Like most things in life, its potential is often"—he looked up at the sky, fondling the crystal—"wasted."

Jakki lowered her staff. "Who are you? I doubt you're a friend of the Daruk."

"Would that I was, my child." Another cackle. "Alas, my lord has not willed it."

"What lord?"

"It's of no concern to you." He twisted his beard around his fingers, coils wrapping tighter and tighter. "You've more pressing questions. They circle you like ravager birds honing for the kill. One might think you'd want answers to those instead?"

Jakki glowered. "It's of no concern to you, either."

"No matter. You're not worth fretting over." He waved his hand and looked beyond her to the woods.

Jakki's pulse quickened. She shoved through the water until she stood face-to-face with the creature. He was a little taller than a dwarf, though his spindly limbs were thin enough to snap. He reeked of unfulfilled cravings, like the monster from fireside stories who always hungered and thirsted no matter what it consumed.

"Listen, you decrepit little bastard. I'm the daughter of Jattai Rain-Bringer, Chief of the Yustano, and I'm next in line to lead my people. I'm worth ten warriors and dozens of whatever you are."

He clucked his tongue against the roof of his mouth. "Next in line to be chief is a promise, nothing more." Mock sadness settled into his face. "You're just a warrior, then? But a strikingly good one, I'm sure, despite not having seen battle."

Jakki tightened her grip on the staff. Two seconds, and she could end this creature. A swift crack over the head. But she wouldn't let him go so easily.

"A damned good warrior, thank you. My time as leader will come, and I'm honored to serve my people as needed in the meantime."

"Serve indeed. You'll have that mastered, at least."

Jakki raised her staff. It took every ounce of her strength to resist swinging it. "If you want to live, I suggest you explain who you are and what you're doing in Daruk territory."

"Whatever's the matter?" His eyes widened. "You act as though some calamity befell them."

Maybe he needed more convincing. Jakki slipped a dagger from her hip held it to his throat. "Are you with the skulmor? Az Zar? Who sent you? Tell me now."

"Neither. I'm solitary. Prefer the quiet life. I stumbled upon the village the same way you did." He stretched his boney arms, ignorant to the blade at his throat, loose skin flopping as he moved. "Though, I may know a way you can avenge them."

"Besides slaughtering every wolf that crosses my path?"

"There are better ways to avenge and find the answers you seek, though they require no shortage of sacrifice."

Jakki lowered her dagger. Unnerving as he was, there was little to suggest the old man–creature had any hand in the massacre. "What sacrifice?"

He held a finger to his lips.

"Do you speak for the gods?"

"Not your gods." He gestured to the water where a corked jar floated beside the rock. Had it been there the whole time? "Destiny is an ambitious creature. Who knows what she wills? Your potential is limitless as long as you don't let anyone..." He paused, eyes dimming until they were nothing but black holes. "And I mean *anyone*, stand in your way." He folded into himself, fading and shrinking until he disappeared.

Jakki swiped the air around the rock where he'd perched, but her hand glided through the space as if he'd never existed. *What in Haeshol?* She waded through the pond to check behind all the rocks and even investigated the outlying trees before giving up. As she slipped her boots on, something in the pond caught her eye. The jar. She pulled it in with her staff and loosened the cork. A small, bound parchment rested within. Fingers twitching, she untied the twine.

"Jakki, is that you?"

Jakki gasped and spun to meet the intruder, shoving the parchment behind her as she turned. Anahi. Her spirited stormbird, Corvax, perched on her shoulder. Of course, it would be her.

"What do you want?"

Anahi's face glowed in the firelight radiating from her torch. "You've been gone for hours. Yerakai was worried." She evaluated the clearing through narrowed eyes. "Have you met trouble?"

"No."

"Mhmm." Anahi regarded her for a moment, hands on her hips, then strode from the clearing. "You should return to the village and get some rest before we head back to Agaas tomorrow. Siren's been screaming for you."

Jakki gripped the parchment. She refused to accept defeat, not with so many questions left unanswered. "We're continuing east in the morning."

Anahi halted. "Elaysia said to investigate Daruk lands and report back to her."

"Elaysia didn't know what we'd find." Jakki planted her staff in the ground as Anahi turned, face fixed in a scowl.

"You have no right to rebel against the high chieftain's wishes."

"I have *every* right." Jakki closed the gap between them. Corvax shrieked, plumage rising. "As the leader of this party in the high chieftain's absence, I'm in command. Not Yerakai. Not you."

Anahi's mouth hardened. "I respect your decision."

Her voice suggested she didn't.

Jakki ran her tongue across the front of her teeth as Anahi disappeared into the woods. The parchment danced in her hands, daring her to look. Maybe it was an overdue blessing from the gods. If not, maybe it was time she made her own destiny.

She unraveled the parchment.

LUMIRA

Wind slammed into Lumira's back. She anchored her claws to the deck and let it bend her like a sail. Seahawks chortled above, swooping low now and again to scrounge for fish stupid enough to swim near the surface. One was. Its luminous scales shimmered in the sunlight, begging to be plucked from the watery oasis. A seahawk barreled down in a swift torrent. It disappeared beneath the waves.

Three. Two. One.

The seahawk burst from the sea, fish imprisoned in its talons. It spiraled into the air, shaking water from its wings, soaring higher and further until it vanished into the horizon. Nothing but water for miles.

Lumira relaxed into the sweet rhythm only the waves could bring. With clear skies and a strong wind at her back to compensate for the novice crew, today felt like sailing around her native isles. She never anticipated a botched job in Agaas would result in food, shelter, and a prize. Even if she was in the service of an unseasoned ruler, it was better than raiding homes or completing contracts for people who didn't want blood on their hands. Perhaps the moon goddesses hadn't given up on her after all.

"Twenty-three," she purred, nudging an embittered Xaren. "And it's been what, a quarter day?" She snatched a raw fish from the crate between them and tore off its head. "I told you, seahawks will *always* be superior fishers to whatever contraptions your people create."

Xaren waved her off, one hand still clutching the railing. Despite constant exposure to the sun, his face had regressed a shade paler since departing the Moákun bay. If he wasn't clinging to the rail for comfort, he was grabbing onto it while puking up supper for the fish. The rest of the crew didn't fare much better. Except for Grokhion, a Moákun seafarer, and Davier—the latter she regretfully admitted took to the sea like a beridian—Elaysia's band of warriors could scarcely contain their stomachs, much less sail. Of all the Neharem people, she'd enlisted the worst seafarers. Maybe the in-landers were dumber, more prone to risk-taking. No matter. They didn't require a large vessel to transport their twenty-something warriors. Four skilled sailors, along with some well-directed apprentices, easily navigated the Moákun catamaran.

Xaren adjusted his wide-brimmed hat. "You can't compare their fishing techniques to ours. They're beasts."

"And you aren't? What of your bird?" She eyed the tiny black stormbird, aptly named Shadow, hiding between his legs with its talons wedged into his boots.

Xaren folded his arms. "He's special."

"Aren't we all." Lumira rolled her eyes and stroked Anadu's silver down feathers. Humans like Xaren had little to offer over conventional beasts, especially by lifespan. She'd outlive the boy by double.

"What's that supposed to mean?"

Lumira ignored him. "Az Zarians are a special breed, isn't that right, slaver?" She directed the comment toward Davier who, at present, lay slumped against the base of a mast with a rag over his face.

"And don't you forget it." Davier lifted his hand in an obscene gesture before falling back into whatever alcohol-induced slumber he wallowed in.

He hadn't endured a day sober since joining their company, and based on the empty wineskins and bottles stacked beside him, he held his drink as well as some beridians. Hardly surprising. The better someone performed, the more they had to lose, and the more destructive tendencies they developed. His war trauma probably didn't help either. She carried enough of those demons around herself to understand the desire to silence them by any means necessary. Still, despite his debauchery, he accomplished his duties with unmatched skill and only indulged when they were completed. So far, at least. That said nothing of his intentions, which could range from bedding the high chieftain to some foreign usurping plot. Probably both.

Lumira sauntered by Davier on her way to Elaysia and paused to deliver a swift kick to his leg. Following her lead, Anadu clipped the same spot with her beak. The stormbird held her head high and hopped toward Lumira, an act she rewarded with a raw fish.

Davier tore off the rag to reveal a reddened face. "It's funny while she's small, but—"

"It'll be even funnier when she's grown." Lumira flicked her tail and hurried away before he could get another word in.

Onitus, Elaysia's solemn stormbird, perched on a plank between the dual prows, still enough to appear as one of the seahawk carvings that adorned them. Anadu flapped her flightless wings and hopped up beside him without a sound.

Elaysia leaned against the starboard railing, gaze lost in the water, oblivious to Lumira's approach. Hair tumbled behind the girl in a flurry of black and white waves broken up by the occasional braided section. She wore a high collared tunic patterned in the bold reds and blues of the Apáasutai, though the cut was not theirs. Some Agaasian interpretation, then. The fitted fabric gave the girl some illusion of curves while providing coverage of her skin.

Lumira leaned back against the railing and faced Elaysia. "Still want to make port in Cadar? Not sure the convenience is worth the risk."

Elaysia shrugged, her fingers tracing the worn bits in the wood. "We aren't at war. We haven't even accused them of anything. I expect to be treated as ambassadors."

Lumira bit back the snarky remark brewing on her tongue. "I'd expect the worst, especially with these moon-cursed birds. They're a liability."

In truth, she'd grown fond of little Anadu's feisty spirit. No reason to sell her bird when there were plenty more for the taking. Could they breed? Shouldn't be a reason not. She'd have to save that question for her next encounter with Elaysia's bugged-eyed scholar, Zavik. If he survived his mission to Orillon.

Elaysia shook her head. "I refuse to sneak into Az Zar like I'm plotting something."

"But aren't we?"

Elaysia made a sound that was half snort, half laugh. "Plotting's a strong word."

"So is prison."

"You said we shouldn't give them any reason to think our arrival's suspicious. Hence the trading boat?"

"And that translated into serving us up on a platter in their most heavily guarded city? They'll seize the stormbirds as soon as we dock and throw us in prison."

Elaysia's eyes widened. "They wouldn't dare."

"Based on what happened to your parents, they most certainly would."

A thousand emotions danced across Elaysia's face. She whistled Onitus down from the prow and stormed to moons-knew-where; the boat wasn't that big.

Lumira slowly extended and retracted her claws. If the girl couldn't take some learned advice from an ally, she'd suffer a far worse fate when an enemy caught her wallowing in the mire of poor decision-making. She didn't wish her ill; Elaysia was likeable enough for a mainlander. But if her ship started sinking, literally or figuratively, Lumira wasn't going down with it.

A cry pierced her thoughts.

Lumira looked to the watcher's perch. The warrior on post was from one of the northern tribes. Maybe Atsukut, given the woman's massive frame and brightly dyed furs. Lumira hadn't bothered learning all their names.

"A ship due east," the woman shouted again. "Looks like they're in trouble."

Lumira flattened her ears and squinted toward the Atsukut's claim. A ship bobbed in the distance, smoke billowing above it. Flames licked at the sails.

"We should help them," Elaysia said, motioning the others to attention. "Xaren, do we have supplies to spare for their wounded?"

The boy pried himself off the deck to investigate. Between his over-sized tunic and wobbly steps, he looked like a toddler exploring the confines of an unfamiliar room.

"Some," he said, after concluding his inspection and closing the trapdoor.

Davier roused from his stupor with a yawn. "If anyone's asking, I think we should stay our course." He joined Elaysia's side and regarded the horizon with indifference. "We're less than a day from the Az Zarian coastline. Someone will come for them."

Elaysia's brow furrowed. "We can't abandon someone in need. Besides, it could be one of ours."

The fur on Lumira's spine rose. Something was off. "It's ablaze as if they were recently attacked, but there's not another ship in sight." She looked to the crew for support. "No one finds that odd?"

Grokhion rubbed his whiskers. "The fire could've been an accident. Or no one's left alive to put out the flames."

"Convenient it's only burning the sails and not the rest of the ship," she muttered.

If anyone heard, they didn't acknowledge her concern, much less echo it.

She leaned against the railing and hoped that maybe, just this once, she was wrong.

An upturned flag cut through the smoke. The symbol, three waxing moons and the outline of a fish, was of Nishapar, one of Orillon's coastal cities. The fully battened sails, however, were not of Orillon make. The ship was larger than the Moákun catamaran, though not by much, and offered little in the way of storage beneath the deck. Char covered the masts, and one was close to snapping. Nets hung off the side. No passengers or crew. At least visible.

"Take the stormbirds below," Elaysia commanded Jörd, a petite Daruk human and one of the few names Lumira had been forced to retain because she was always a few feet away from the high chieftain, eyes shifting like a watch dog. "Just in case."

Davier assisted Lumira with the sail. "Someone's attacked a fishing boat and left its sails aflame as a warning. Makes sense." He rolled his eyes.

"Unquestionably." She yanked one of his swords from its sheath and inspected the blade before tossing it to him. "Just in case"—she nodded toward Elaysia—"if you're wanting to prove your loyalty."

Davier gave the blade a few skillful swings before sheathing it again. "It'd be an honor, my lady." He spoke with disdain. Lumira found herself fond of him in the way one might have a favorite fly.

By the time they drew close enough to lower the plank, most of the smoke and all the flames had dissipated. Lumira brushed her claws against the bone beading of her necklace and counted the five arrowheads adorning it. Three for the moons. One for the dead. One for the living. Today, she'd remain the latter.

Grokhion volunteered to board first. His face was calm like the sky above, but his hand twitched ever so slightly toward the double-bit war axe slung across his back. It was nearly as tall as Elaysia, edges sharp and gleaming. Only a beridian would recognize that the symbols on the handle signified his role back on the isles—she hadn't yet asked how long ago he'd left his life as a weaponsmith. *Belzaith* was the axe's name. She had asked that. It meant underworld spirit in their native tongue. Fitting.

Lumira grabbed her spear, sinking her fingers into the subtle indents from years of wielding it, and hurried after him with Davier and five warriors on her tail. Her hackles rose as soon as she leaped onto the ship. The sails were in shambles, but the deck was pristine. No blood. No weapons. No sign of struggle.

Trap.

Lumira raised a hand to halt Elaysia, who'd already made it halfway across the plank. "High Chieftain, don't come—"

A scream pierced the silence.

Lumira spun toward the sound. Aboard the ruined ship, a Neharem warrior grasped at a blood-stained blade protruding from his stomach. Behind him, a man with a red sash wrapped around his head twisted the blade and yanked it out. The warrior crumpled into himself. With a second blade unsheathed, the killer charged toward Grokhion. The great beridian brought his axe down in an arc on the assailant's shoulder, severing his torso in a swift, bloodied strike. Lumira rushed to block entry to their ship, claws and spear readied. She scoured the deck. Two armed humans crawled out from a trapdoor like rats scrabbling out of a grain shed. Others emerged from the captain's quarters.

"Slaver, on your left," she shouted to Davier, but he'd already lunged toward the one nearest, who appeared to contain traces of giant's blood.

Another enemy climbed out of the trapdoor, then three more, all dually armed in Az Zarian fashion and charging ahead like boars on the hunt. One made for Davier, who still dodged the giant man's barbed flail. Lumira launched her spear. It sailed clean through the Az Zarian's neck and stuck to the mast, pinning him like herbs left out to dry. In the chaos, Davier dove between the giant man's legs, slashing him behind the knees. The giant toppled. Davier opened his throat.

Lumira snatched a sword from her kill and sank her claws into the deck, whiskers twitching. Someone was behind her. She waited until the hairs in her ears tingled, then swung around, sword first. The blade lodged in her enemy's neck with a *crack*. She wriggled it up and down as the man's eyes faded from anguish to emptiness. Cheap blade. His gasping slowed. Arms went limp. She let him fall, the sword still lodged in his neck.

Tongue pressed against her teeth, she prowled forward. The sound of clinging metal and shouts from the wounded and dying filled the air as Neharem's warriors collided with twice as many enemies pouring out the trapdoor like a colony of ants. Despite the sun's rays, a chill seized her body.

Grokhion caught her attention and tossed her a new blade. Together they raced into the fray, a pair of predators on the hunt. The only time disdain for her kind benefited her was in battle. She was the beast they wanted her to be. The beast they feared.

One of the scum alerted his comrades as they approached, but they'd little time to ready themselves before Grokhion and Lumira descended. A woman challenged her first, every bit as bold as the men. Lumira parried two attacks and locked her blade with her enemy's, then twisted until she disarmed the woman. A quick slice severed the woman's hands from her wrists. Claws to the throat finished the job.

A girthy human ran at her, cursing and foaming like a madman. When he came within arm's reach, she leaped onto the railing, dodging his blow. Another hop landed her behind him. She opened his throat. One of his counterparts watched from several feet away. Lumira held his gaze while licking blood from her paws. The tip of her tongue tingled and sent a shiver down her spine. Whether caused by the blood or the fear in her enemy's eyes, she didn't know. It didn't matter.

A roar rose above the commotion. Grokhion. His face twisted in anguish as he pulled a knife from his back. The assailant scrambled away, only to meet a swift end with a blow to the head from a Neharem club.

Lumira rushed toward her kin, heart racing.

"Behind you," Grokhion cried, motioning for her to duck.

She dropped. A blade cut through the air where her head had been. Before she could strike, an arrow pierced her enemy's skull. He stiffened and fell sideways like a chopped tree. His breathing stopped. She drew a claw across his throat to be certain.

Lumira looked to their ship. Xaren crouched in the watcher's perch, stringing another arrow. The lad had a purpose, after all. She raised a hand in thanks and hurried toward what remained of the skirmish, dodging hacked and arrow-ridden bodies and the expanding pools of blood. She wrenched her spear free from the mast and drove it into someone's stomach.

Neharem's warriors soon surrounded the last enemy. Lumira lowered her spear and moved in closer to examine the catch. A human, at least halfway through his lifespan, with broader features and tanner skin than most of the Az Zarians she'd had the pleasure of meeting. He wore a canvas vest exposing a bare chest slick with sweat. She wrinkled her nose. Nasty trait humans and nyrians had.

Grokhion lowered *Belzaith* to the man's throat. "Drop your weapons. You don't have to die like the rest of your crew."

Davier translated. The man tossed his blades aside. He kneeled and pushed his neck against the axe head, upraised hands revealing an inner wrist tattoo of a flaming ship.

Pirate. Likely from the Zelos Islands off the southwestern coast of Az Zar. Explained the lack of honor in battle. He shouted something derogatory in Zarith, given the tone, and spat. Phlegm landed on Grokhion's feet. The great beridian used the edge of his axe to clean it off without so much as a hint of irritation.

Elaysia broke through the circle, eyes wide. Lumira doubted the girl had seen much bloodshed before today—if any. What surprised her, however, was the wave of relief that washed over her upon seeing the high chieftain in good health.

Lumira shook it off and elbowed Davier. "What did he say?"

Davier sheathed his blades behind his back and chuckled. "I don't think you want to know."

Lumira kicked the man in the stomach. He doubled over, laughing through the pain. She kicked him again. And again. He coughed up blood and said something vulgar, eyes burning as he took her in. No need for Davier's translation; she'd seen that look enough. She pressed the tip of her spear into his neck.

Elaysia grabbed her wrist. "Stop. We need to learn why they lured us over and attacked."

Lumira scowled. "Why? They're pirates. They attacked because that's what they do."

Elaysia's face hardened.

"Fine, do it your way." Lumira backed to the edge of the circle, teeth clenched. Prisoners were never a good idea.

"Uki." Elaysia beckoned a gold-skinned nyrian from the southern tribes. "Help him up."

Uki knelt and extended her arm. The pirate elbowed her in the face. He yanked a knife from his trousers and pressed it to her throat. Spittle flew from his mouth as he screamed at Elaysia in Zarith. Lumira backed further away, twisting her spear in her fingers.

Davier placed himself between the pirate and Elaysia. "He says he's going to kill her unless we back off and leave him to his ship. I don't think it's an idle threat."

Elaysia looked frantically between her warrior and the pirate. "Do as he says."

The others backed away. Lumira hurled her spear.

It pierced the pirate's head and pinned him to the deck. Uki lurched to her feet. She gave Lumira a nod of respect, then rushed to Elaysia's side.

Davier gave the corpse a condescending pat. "Enjoy the afterlife, friend." Then, to the others he said, "Not Az Zarian.

Purely, anyway. We sometimes hire off-landers for dirty work or purchase their goods at discounted rates. Might be some loot left on board."

Elaysia tore her gaze away from the pirate and ordered everyone to search. Everyone but Lumira. The high chieftain pulled her aside.

"Why did you do that? You could've killed her."

Lumira's tail twitched. "I *saved* her. I knew what I was doing. I've been in far hairier situations than you can imagine."

"But you didn't listen to me. The others will think you don't respect me." Elaysia ran a hand around her throat and paced.

"A good leader doesn't command obedience. She encourages free thinking."

Elaysia halted. The corner of her mouth raised. "You're making that up."

"Maybe. It sounds good, though, doesn't it? If you command a mindless army of drones, how are you any different from the All-Sovereign?"

"I..." Elaysia's words faded as Davier sauntered over. "Another time."

Davier dangled a parchment in front of them, white teeth flashing. "Got our answers."

"And?" Lumira reached for the parchment, but Davier yanked it away at the last moment.

"Give it here." Elaysia stuck out her hand, smirk growing into a full grin.

Davier planted a kiss in her palm first, then the parchment.

Ugh. Lumira snatched the parchment from Elaysia and unraveled it. Zarith. *Moons be cursed.* She shoved it back in his face. "What. Does. It. Say?"

Davier's expression sobered. "It's a contract from Cadar. They've been paying pirates from Zelos to intercept Neharem shipments. Not sure who commissioned it. It's just signed, *a friend of the empire.*"

Elaysia crossed her arms. "Orandus was right."

Lumira didn't know who Orandus was, nor did she care. If Az Zar was already targeting Neharem, their visit to the capital would be a surprise, and not a good one.

"High Chieftain," she said, yanking her spear free from the deck and the pirate's head. "If you care to hear any more free-thinking, Xaren's mentioned a better place than Cadar to make port."

ZAVIK

Z avik leaned against a pile of wool rugs and pored over the map for the thousandth time. He'd marked half a dozen potential locations for the Shaktar Caverns—all well-educated guesses born of ample research—but none were promising enough to storm recklessly into the desert. Not yet. If anyone could offer insight on a place with less viability than a fireside story, it'd be Lanston. However, finding him amid the squall of Munskahan's marketplace proved challenging thus far. Zavik sighed and tucked the map away as a merchant rounded the corner of the stall he'd taken shelter in. He marched up to Zavik, scowling.

"I'm gonna let you in on a little secret," the broad-chested man said in Westmun.

"Oh. Alright." Zavik hadn't spoken Westmun in years, but the trills and throatiness of it came back to him with ease.

The merchant swept a hand over his wares. "Stalls are for bartering and trading."

"I'm aware of how—"

"I don't think you are." The merchant leaned in close. The stench of curdled cheese rolled off his breath. "I could've finished two lamb legs in the time you've loitered here, and not once have you browsed my stock."

Zavik adjusted his seers. He debated telling the merchant he looked capable of eating lamb legs faster than most, then thought better of it. "Sorry. I needed some shade to gather my thoughts, and I didn't see anyone shopping here."

The merchant's eyes bulged.

For goodness' sake, Zav. Might as well have told him to piss off.

"So, of course," Zavik stammered, "I said to myself, 'what better stall to visit than one with such luxurious goods and—'"

The merchant pressed a bloated finger to Zavik's chest and shoved him back into the boiling street of the marketplace. "And don't come back."

Zavik muttered an apology as he donned his hood and rejoined the throng of shoppers. They swarmed the stalls like flies, drawn to the pulsating cloth tents stuffed with grilled meats, bold silks, golden spices, and finely potted incense.

Someone slammed into him. A basket of figs skittered across the street. The woman carrying them cursed and swatted him away when he tried to help, so he drew the hood tighter around his face and fled.

Heat rippled off the stone path in waves, thick and sticky, scented with the oddly comforting combination of manure and spiced fruit. Munskahan might've doubled its population in twenty years, but it still smelled the same. Ahead, another street intersected the main thoroughfare. Zavik hesitated at the crossroads. He recalled his younger self, blistered and chap-lipped, dashing through stalls to keep up with the other children. Constantly getting left behind had taught him to navigate well. Love dens and fighting arenas lay to the right; he remembered that much. The road straight ahead eventually became surrounded by housing, and beyond that towered the vibrant pillars and golden dome roofs of the noble families. He turned left.

Sweat trickled down his chest as he trudged on, activating the stench of a body long overdue for a bath. He'd moved, sweated, and panted more this trip than, well, ever probably, if his blister-laden feet were any testament. He could've made better time had he sailed with the horse he rode from Agaas to the Tangeesh docks, but she'd given him one too many scares. Besides, saddle sores were hardly preferrable to aching feet.

A merchant jumped out from behind her stall and rubbed a strip of silk against Zavik's cheek. "You like?" She yanked him toward her wares. "For your lady, sir? Or your man?"

"No, thank you. No one for me." Zavik slunk away, this time grateful for a crowd to disappear into.

Oh, Orillon. The nation of a thousand pleasures. He didn't suppose he would've survived here, nor did he care to imagine what life would look like had he stayed.

Afraid of getting stopped again, Zavik raced through the streets as fast as his stiff legs could carry him, searching stall after stall for his old... friend. But while many spice merchants lined his path, none had the graying, waist-length beard he remembered on Lanston. The few he'd dared to question shooed him away once they learned he wasn't buying anything. One was kind enough to accuse him of plotting theft. No one was acquainted with a Lanston. For all Zavik knew, it was one of the merchant's many names. Or he'd closed up shop long ago. Or died.

Zavik collapsed against a wall crusted in dirt (and feces, most likely, if he was being honest) and rubbed his temples. The last of his tepid waterskin beckoned him, so he raised it to his lips and tried to avoid counting the days since his departure. He craved the crisp air and shaded woods of Agaas, but he'd disappoint Elaysia if he returned emptyhanded. Sure, she'd punch him in the arm. Flash a smile. Maybe even pull him in for a quick hug to let him know it was alright. But deep down, she'd wish she sent Davier. If she could stand to be away from the starry-eyed ex-soldier that long.

No should've been his response to Elaysia's dubious request: a journey south in search of famed scrolls penned well over two thousand years ago by an ancient order known as the Prophets. It was said the scrolls, seven in number, contained Quinaria's true history, secrets of the gods, and divine magic. The shaktar were rumored to hoard some, assuming one could locate the haunted caverns of the ancient Vysilliam race. Assuming the damn things even existed. There was a reason scroll hunters always came up emptyhanded. The same reason prayers went unanswered and life proceeded with little to no order.

Divinity was a myth.

Still, Elaysia was nothing if not persistent, and Zavik caved. He knew better, especially after years of entanglement in her schemes. But there she'd been, wide-eyed and hopeful.

And here he was, in the heart of Orillon's capital, the place he swore to never return. Empty things, his promises.

"Flicker? Is that you?"

The voice startled Zavik from his stupor. He tripped over his pack as he rose, but instead of tumbling onto the path, he landed in a pair of thick arms wrapped in silk.

"It is you," his rescuer said, laughter rumbling from his belly. "They told me some foreigner was asking for me."

Zavik fumbled with his seers. Though wrinkles marred the man's leathered brown face and his hair had gone white, there was no mistaking those amber eyes. No one else referred to him as *Flicker* either, a jab at both his hair and meekness. At least not aloud.

"Lanston." Zavik fought an urge to hug the old merchant. "Am I glad to see you."

"Wish I'd be saying the same about you." Lanston's brow furrowed. "I think the last time I eyed you, you was scurrying off with one of my best imports."

Zavik swallowed. Sure, he'd taken things from Lanston's stall, but no more than the other children. He hadn't thought the old fart noticed.

Lanston's face softened. "Har, har, come on, boy. I just wanted to see if ya still turned the color of beets when prodded. Let's have a look." He straightened Zavik's shoulders and spun him around as if inspecting a piece of meat. "Grew as much as nature willed, I suppose. Much to catch up on. Mayhaps a drink, or five." He loosed another howl and slapped Zavik's back. "Come on back to the stall. We'll see if Lanston can't help an old ferret."

Despite Zavik's exhaustion, a smile tugged at his lips. "Sorry excuse for a ferret I was. Don't think I successfully stole more than a few trinkets for you."

"Naw, Flicker, you always made a mess of it, but you distracted people so I could do my shopping. I grew fond of ya." Lanston stopped at an unattended stall and snatched a bottle of wine and some hard cheeses. He tossed the latter to Zavik and continued on his way as if he'd done nothing out of the ordinary.

As Zavik trailed Lanston through the streets, he searched for the words to explain his impromptu visit. He'd been so consumed with arriving, with questioning his decision at every turn, that he'd neglected to prepare a speech.

Brilliant, Zav. Just brilliant.

"Been years since yer poor love-giver of a mother ran off with ya," Lanston said as he ensconced them in two over-sized, cushioned chairs in a tent five times the size of his old stall. He grinned, revealing a row of mostly golden teeth, and set the stolen wine between them. "What brings ya to my humble abode? Missing yer old life?"

Zavik crammed some cheese into his mouth to bide time. "In the area," he said finally. "Thought I'd check up on an old friend. Has business been good?"

"Whaddya think, boy?" Lanston gestured to the rich tapestries and filigreed screens ornamenting the space. "Business is better than ever now that more of ya northerners come down to taste our sweet life. By me mum's left tit, even the tight-ass sprigs in Az Zar sneak over to Munskahan in droves. Mayhaps you came seeking such things." He winked and took a long swig from the bottle.

"I'm happy for you." Zavik meant it. Lanston wasn't a trustworthy individual, but he'd always treated him well and provided opportunities to earn coin when times were tough—and they always had been. "But that's not why I'm here. I'm on a mission of sorts. Looking to help a friend, but I'm coming up dry. I hoped you might share knowledge with an old ferret."

"Course." He took another drink. "Go on."

Zavik forced himself to meet Lanston's gaze. He deepened his voice as much as possible, which wasn't very deep at all. "I know you trade with a variety of"—*unsavory characters* probably wasn't the wasn't thing to say—"rather, that your business takes you all over Orillon." Lanston's wild eyebrows bunched at the center. "I thought you might be able to, um, verify a location for me? Maybe? I mean, it's alright if not." *Wonderful, Zav. You're oozing confidence.*

"Well?" Lanston chugged the last of the wine and hurled the bottle through the tent flap. The sound of shattering glass followed. "Spit it out, boy. I've business with the ladies at Oasis."

No shortage of Lanston's favorite kind of *lady* there, provided one had a purse heavy with aspar. The lyvium currency established by Az Zar had long since bled into Orillon, and it was near impossible to do business outside Neharem without it.

Zavik squirmed in his seat. "I'm not certain it exists. It's an ancient place."

"I see, I see." Lanston regarded Zavik with weary eyes as he used a knife to pick his teeth. "And what would you be seeking in the Shaktar Caverns, assuming they exist?"

"Uh..." Zavik pulled a loose string from his tunic and rolled it into a ball. "Adventure?"

The wrinkles around Lanston's eyes deepened. "Wanting to spur a little excitement outside of your hand and the bedroom, eh?" He erupted in laughter.

Zavik ignored the flush in his cheeks. "Sure, something like that."

"Adventure, my ass. I don't buy it, Flicker. Not you." Lanston's laughter died as he wiped tears from his eyes. "I think you're going treasure huntin'. And I think it's to please a woman. Bet my right nut on it."

Zavik opened his mouth to deny it, but no words came out.

"I get it, boy. The only time a man does something unnatural to him is when a woman's involved."

Zavik shrugged. "The why doesn't matter." He thought he sounded firm. Hopefully. "So, can you help me?"

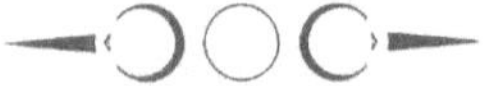

The next morning found Zavik clinging to a zaka-zaka as it bounded west toward Teth across the endless dunes of the Vashi Desert. While the animal's front pouch was useful for storing supplies, he couldn't get used to the erect way he had to sit in the saddle. Riding a creature that moved on two legs was… unnatural. Fast hopping. Slow hopping. Those were his only options. If he smashed his face against the back of its head one more time—

—well, he probably wouldn't do anything. Maybe one day.

Lanston had surrendered his knowledge with minimal prodding. Then again, the merchant's directions were rumors from a colleague down the street, who'd heard from a love-giver, who'd heard from a backhander, the tales of nomadic clans who left sacrifices at an abandoned temple to appease blood-thirsty gods. Zavik shoved the last bit of information into the far reaches of his mind. No need to focus on what might be. For all he knew, the shaktar were long extinct, and some starving desert beasts fed off the offerings every moon cycle.

Yes, extinct.

Like the stormbirds.

Bile crept up Zavik's throat, bitter and burning. He buried his face in the zaka-zaka's dust-laden fur. Why couldn't he say no? Stand his ground? Just once? He hadn't planned to wring information out of Lanston, much less get pointed toward a life-threatening discovery.

The zaka-zaka halted, throwing him headfirst into the sand.

"Thanks for the warning," Zavik mumbled.

He pushed himself up and dusted off the jacket he'd acquired from Lanston. It tapered around his waist and reached past his knees. Not exactly Neharem's style, but he liked how it looked, and, more importantly, it protected him from the blazing desert sun *and* the icy temperatures that settled in at night.

Map in hand, Zavik stepped into the shadow of his mount to avoid the sun's glare. The altar site Lanston crudely scrawled appeared to be several days' ride beyond Teth—not accounting for however long it took him to locate the cavern entrance or cross paths with a shaktar. Assuming either existed.

Zavik leaped onto the zaka–zaka, his stomach straddled over its back like a cat caught in a tree. As he maneuvered into position, he caught sight of riders in the distance racing toward him at an alarming pace. Doubtful they sought to ensure his wellbeing. He clenched the reins. They'd be on him in moments. He wasn't a good enough rider to outrun them, nor capable of fighting the bunch, let alone one.

Talking it was.

He shut his eyes. When the coughing growls of incoming zaka–zakas signaled time was up, he eased his grip on the reins, smoothed his jacket, and forced himself to look up. Four riders menaced him, all built for battle and armed for assault. One clenched a chain attached to a panther. Its golden eyes narrowed, claws flexing into the sand. Zavik instinctively raised his hands in the air.

"My good fellows," he said, voice cracking. "How can I assist you?"

The panther handler spoke first. "Hand over your aspar, and we'll consider letting you live." The gaping holes in his ears looked large enough for the tusks he wore as a necklace to fit through. A red cloth covered his face from the nose down. He pointed a scythe–tipped spear at Zavik's throat. "And we'll have your mount, too."

Zavik gasped. "I'll never make it back to Munskahan alive." He meant to process the thought in his head, but out it tumbled, destroying his shreds of resolve. Sweat dripped from every pore on his body, yet he was cold. "Please, don't. I mean no harm."

"We do." Panther bandit gave the cat some lead, and the beast leaped forward. Zavik's mount reared. "And I've changed my mind." He snapped his fingers. The other men dismounted and prowled toward him, weapons at the ready.

Zavik slid his knife from his boot. He tried to still his trembling hands by breathing the way Anahi had shown him. In. Out. In. Out.

Now or never.

He tumbled off his mount, knife slashing wildly.

He got someone. He must've, because his blade caught, and someone cried out in anguish.

Zavik's pulse quickened. He scrambled away blindly from the cry. "Stay back," he shouted. "I'll strike again."

He dared a glance. Two bandits lay in the sand, motionless and surrounded by blood. How'd he manage to hit two?

Before he could reason it away, another bandit was on him. Zavik rolled out of the way as the bandit brought down a club that could end his life with a single blow. The weapon caught in the sand and sent the bandit tumbling.

"Stick 'em now, lad," someone shouted.

Zavik didn't recognize the voice, but he didn't question the advice either. He lunged at the bandit scrambling for his club, and drove the full weight of his body into the man's legs. The bandit dropped. Zavik plunged the knife into his stomach. The blade sank into the skin like pudding until all that remained was the antler hilt.

"Cut his throat," the voice commanded.

Zavik couldn't take his eyes off the crimson blade as he lifted it to the bandit's neck. He hesitated. Those eyes. So full of hatred.

Zavik's head snapped back with a *crack*. He was on his back, gasping for air. His vision blurred; his seers had come off. The bandit was on top of him, fist reeling back for another punch. Toes clenched inside his boots, Zavik slashed the blade across his throat. The bandit collapsed atop him. Blood seeped from his wound and onto Zavik's chest.

Seers in hand, Zavik wiggled out from under the corpse. He started for his zaka-zaka, then froze. In between him and freedom stood two men: panther bandit and a newcomer, fighting in a blanket of dust. The panther's body lay beside them, a good two feet from its severed head.

Panther bandit swung hard but slow, the newcomer so swift in comparison that Zavik didn't notice he'd completed a killing stroke until the bandit crumpled to the ground. His head tore away from the slice in his neck and landed beside the panther's corpse. The newcomer huffed above the body, then cranked his head toward Zavik like a hawk.

"Shit." Zavik scrambled for a zaka-zaka, but before he got to it, the newcomer flung a knife. It landed between Zavik's feet.

"If I wanted you dead, I would've let them finish you," the newcomer said in broken Zarith. He was a burly, bronze man with a half-shaved head and unkempt braids running down the other side. A dagger and a curved sword were his weapons of choice; a simple tunic accented with leather armor, his protection. He took a step forward. Zavik thought he glimpsed a glimmer of amusement in his eyes, but he couldn't be sure.

"Why did you help me?" he squeaked.

"Had a promise to keep. Benefited you by accident."

"Oh." Zavik plunged his hands deep into his pockets and rocked from side to side. "Guess I owe you thanks."

The man didn't reply.

"You speak Zarith well, but I can speak Westmun if that's easier for you. It's my native language."

Still nothing. Zavik cast a longing glance at the zaka-zaka.

"What are you doing out here, slaver?"

"I'm not from Az—" Zavik stopped himself. It wasn't worth the argument. "It's personal. Travel."

The man folded his arms. "Your travels might end sooner than you'd like. There's plenty more of their kind 'round these parts."

"Thanks for the warning." Zavik fought the sick feeling in his stomach and hurried to his mount. He hesitated by the beast, one hand on its neck and the other digging fingernails into his palms.

The man sauntered around the other side of the zaka–zaka. "I could arrange safe passage for you."

"And why would you do that?"

"I'm a generous fellow." The man winked. "Especially when aspar is involved."

Great. A backhander. Still...

Zavik's eyes wandered back to the bodies strewn in the sand. There'd probably be more, and he wouldn't get out of the next attack so easily. But there was one problem. "I don't have enough coin with me."

The backhander shrugged and made to leave.

A wave of panic rippled through Zavik. "Wait." He grabbed the backhander's arm. The man shoved Zavik off and knelt to loot a body. "I can pay you later. Something far better than aspar when you safely return me to Neharem."

The backhander held one of the bandit's jeweled collars to the sun. "Nevethium."

Zavik answered before his conscience could catch up with his mouth. "I'm certain we can arrange that." He stuck out his hand. "Deal?"

"You have my word." The backhander swatted Zavik's hand away.

"My name is Zavik." He knelt to loot a body himself. Rifling through a dead man's things was better than letting the back-hander think him weak. "And you?"

"T'Vak, and that's your only question for the day. Where are we going, Zavik of Neharem?"

"Chasing ghosts." *And love,* he thought, but T'Vak didn't need to be privy to that information. No one did. "To us." Zavik raised his wineskin in comradery.

"Don't do that." T'Vak knocked the wineskin on the ground and piled his recent acquisitions into Zavik's arms. "Load these up and hand over your map. We've riding to do."

Oh, this would be a pleasant trip.

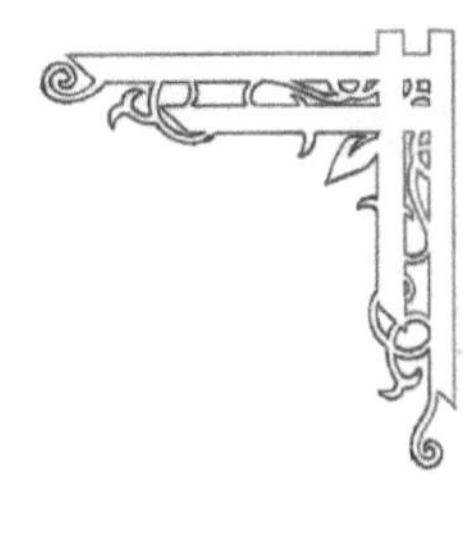

DAVIER

D avier cursed Xaren under his breath as he mashed berries into a pulp. If the idiot hadn't opened his damn mouth, they would've docked in Cadar ages ago instead of sailing south all the way to Za'alna, then traipsing through the desert on a paranoid whim. Not that he was entirely to blame. The pirate attack, intentional or not, made Lumira, and thereby the others, suspicious of Cadar's reception to them, and *then* Xaren riled them up further with tales of soldiers from his unit disappearing at the Caman Altars. Naturally, everyone agreed rerouting last-minute was a brilliant plan.

Davier reached into his pocket for the char he'd snatched from the firepit. As he ground it into the berries, a movement caught his eye. He slipped a sword free and scanned the brush doused in the pale light of dawn. Something sizzled to his left. He spun. There, camouflaged in the dirt, was a viper, coiled and ready to strike.

He struck first.

Snake beheaded and slung over his shoulder, he finished mixing his ink and unrolled a strip of parchment. If he could convince Elaysia to stop at a nearby village for supplies, a local might be willing to deliver the message for him.

Davier pressed quill to parchment, willing the words to flow.

Your Holiness,

> *We were thwarted by pirates*
> *and rerouted to the Caman*
> *Altars. We will arrive within*
> *a day. Four stormbirds travel*
> *with us, and four remain in*
> *Neharem. They have bonded*
> *with their riders, but are still*
> *young enough*

Ink pooled where he'd paused, seeping into the parchment until the word drowned in a sea of ashen red. He dipped the quill and tried again.

> *enough to accept new mas-*
> *ters. Still twenty strong.*
> *They will fight to the death*
> *for the high chieftain and the*
> *birds. I think it best to*

To what? Take the birds but spare their lives so Neharem could avenge the wrongdoing? Warn them to turn back and hope they never use the birds against the empire? Peace wasn't sustainable between Az Zar and Neharem. The die had been cast long before Elaysia's parents were murdered in cold blood. But she held the power now, and uncovering the secrets surrounding their deaths was what drove her, even more than the vanishing nevethium. The latter was a perplexing conundrum Davier refrained from giving much thought to. From what he'd seen, everyone in Neharem genuinely believed they'd been robbed—a far cry from the story the All-Sovereign told him before departing Cadar. One could only speculate what His Holiness plotted in that crimson tower. Like two wolves prowling around the last known food source, destiny intended the All-Sovereign and Elaysia to collide. Davier needed to get out of the way before it happened.

The parchment glared up at him, imploring him to finish. He tore it up. It wasn't worth risking suspicion. Besides, when they'd first reached Za'alna, he'd pressed one of his patches and a scrap of his tunic, inscribed with *headed to altars*, into the hands of a dock worker. With luck, it had already reached Cadar. If not, the All-Sovereign could use a lesson in patience.

Davier opted for the roundabout way to camp so he could stroll alongside the stream. Though a shadow of the roaring river it'd once been, it still provided enough water to nurture patches of teal and orange flowers. They speckled the desert, thickening and arching around the base of the Mavetahn Mountains as if they worshiped them. They were worship-worthy, with their red-dusted crevices begging to be trodden to the summits. Someday he would. Mountains even larger and more beautiful. Mountains he'd discover in his travels. Finish the mission, get the promotion, save a shit ton of aspar, and one day he'd have enough coin and courage to say goodbye to Quinaria forever.

Laughter echoed further upstream. Davier instinctively crept toward the sound, brushing against the patches of dry grass that grew along the path until he came to a place where the stream widened. Two figures stood waist-high in the water. Their backs were turned, but the white marking curved around the left shoulder blade of the otherwise russet-brown woman made her identity indisputable. If he'd any doubt, the beridian beside her confirmed it.

Davier ducked behind a spiny bush to admire Elaysia from afar. A rush of shame tainted his pleasure. Nyrian-human coupling was the greatest sin, an indecency to Mavet and the natural order of the world, but watching Elaysia now, as the sun caressed her skin and cast a soft glow to frame her hips, he questioned it. In fact, she made him question everything. Every conversation, every look, blurred the lines between right and wrong, the absolutist worldview he'd been born into.

A fly buzzed by his ear. He swatted it and took the opportunity to remind himself that fantasies belonged in bedside tales. As he stepped back to make his escape, his boot loosened a rock from the dirt and sent it tumbling into the stream. It wouldn't have been a problem, save for the stormbirds perched on the bank a stone's throw away. The female's plumage rose.

Please don't.

It shrieked, long and piercing.

Shit.

Elaysia dropped to her shoulders in the water while Lumira glided like a seaserpent, ears twitching. "Show yourself, and I'll think twice about killing you," the beridian growled.

Davier flattened himself into the brush as he edged away. It poked through his clothes, but he resisted the urge to scratch it and focused all his energy on calming his breath. He could've talked his way out of the intrusion. Chances were, Elaysia would've received it well. But he'd been playing the game too long, flirting a touch more than necessary, letting the conversations verge beyond polite inquiry.

He couldn't afford more vulnerability. Not this close.

He sprinted toward camp, shrieks filling the sky behind him.

A smokey, gamey odor greeted Davier at the campsite. Most of the warriors huddled around the fire watching Grokhion turn scraggly hares over a makeshift spit. A stormbird nestled against the beridian's shoulder. It opened one eye briefly to regard Davier before shutting it again.

Grokhion considered the snake strung over Davier's shoulder. "Does my cooking fail to satisfy your refined cravings?" The gruffness of his voice contrasted the gleam in his eyes.

Davier tossed the snake at a disgruntled Xaren who went about roasting it with no shortage of grumbles. "I do typically find your peasant fares an abomination. This morning, however, it almost smells appealing. Almost."

"Someone thinks you smell appealing, too." Grokhion gestured to Davier's leg.

Davier looked down. An iridescent beetle with a bulbous shell the size of his fist crawled up his calf. He flung it to the ground and raised his foot to crunch it when Jörd, a Daruk warrior who was overly fond of warpaint, shoved him back.

"That's good meat," she snarled.

Davier rolled his eyes and backed away. "Be my guest."

Jörd grabbed the beetle by its shell, speared it, and held it over the fire, all while maintaining a steady scowl.

Grokhion slid a hare off the spit and offered it to Davier. "Did you see Lumira and Elaysia out there?"

Davier tore off a piece of meat and tossed it to the stormbird before trying some himself. Chewy, but not terrible. "No," he said between mouthfuls. "I wondered where they went."

As if sensing his lie, Lumira tore into the camp, water droplets still clinging to her fur. Davier braced himself for an accusation, but she didn't spare a glance his way. "Are you all blind? Look up!" She thrust a finger into the sky.

Davier tipped his head back. Swirls of something akin to smoke, though thicker and darker, stained the sky. It was too large to be a rain cloud, but it hovered due east like swollen billows before a storm. How long had it been like that? They'd made camp after dark the previous night, so there was no way of knowing.

Elaysia raced up to Davier, hair and face damp. "The altars lie in that direction, do they not?"

He nodded.

"How much farther?"

Grokhion retrieved the map from where it was nestled between his belt and tunic. Unrolled, it looked like a napkin in his massive paws. "According to Konar's notes, a day's ride ahead."

Davier resisted the urge to scoff—as if Konar had sanctified the mission. The crusty nyrian was likely still stewing over Elaysia's audacity to nab the map from his chambers.

Elaysia slung her bow and quiver over her shoulder. "Lumira, Grokhion, and Jörd, with me." She walked past Davier as if she didn't see him, then called over her shoulder, "And you, slaver. Time to prove your expertise." She stopped beside Xaren. "The stormbirds will stay with you for safety. Ride to the closest village for supplies, but I only want you to enter."

Xaren's dark eyes drooped. "I'm honored to serve the high chieftain however she sees fit."

Davier knew the response, a product of years of military grooming. The boy would honor her wishes even if he felt ill-used by the task assigned to him.

Ten minutes' time found the party of five headed east on hesitant mounts, the squalls of the abandoned birds haunting them as the camp faded from view. The sky grew darker with each passing mile. Coincidence, Davier told himself. Weather was always more tumultuous down south; that's why few communities resided there. That and the utter lack of fertile land. The Caman Altars was just an old religious site frequented by the Lord Priestess and her lackeys to promote the idea that the All-Sovereign was a god. Rumor was Mavet either blessed His Holiness or he was the Creator reincarnate, and that he saw and heard everything—even people's hearts. Based on Davier's brief interaction with him, it was all an elaborate façade to better control citizens. He reminded himself of this as the shadows encroached on their small band.

If he refused to believe, he couldn't be manipulated.

Davier wasn't certain if dusk had set in or if they were fully enveloped in the shroud of darkness surrounding the altars, but there was no moonlight. The air had grown thick and sticky where it'd previously been arid. Bloodshot mountains loomed in the distance.

The sound of clopping hooves marred the eerie stillness as the remnants of an ancient stone path appeared. Ahead towered two massive, menacing nyrian statues guarding the temple, their spears raised to ward off intruders. Wrapped in the linen skirts of ancient Az Zar and adorned with head cloths, they'd long since started crumbling into disarray. One had lost half of its face, and the other looked on with cold eyes and a stern jaw. Further up on a plateau stood a gated archway accessible by a wide set of stairs. The archway rivaled the enormity of the palace doors in Cadar, but where the All-Sovereign's home boasted power and riches, the tone of the altars exuded death. As they drew closer to the stairs, smaller statues leered from pillars like demonic, winged gods guarding their sanctum. Barbed backs hunched with scorpion tails. Horned heads. Gnarled fangs poking through sneers.

Davier kept his eyes on the path.

A low growl rumbled in Grokhion's throat. "Khiev-Tatamic have mercy. Who could've carved all these? Such detail. It almost feels like…" He hesitated, head cocked as though he didn't want to speak his thoughts into existence.

"They're alive?" Jörd concluded. She tightened her grip on her axe. "We should ride back for the others. The gods don't bless our passage here."

Davier was inclined to agree. Nothing good could result from this venture.

Elaysia pursed her lips. "That means this is exactly where we need to be. Besides, the horses need to rest." She dismounted and led her gelding to a statue. The horse whinnied and reared as she tied the reins around the statue's wings.

A chill rippled down Davier's spine. *Spook-easy mount.*

When they reached the foot of the stairs, Lumira jabbed him in the ribs. "You first. You know best what traps might await."

Davier sized them up. They were wide enough for the entire party to climb side by side and roughly three hundred steps to the top. "Your vision's allegedly better than any human's or nyrian's, but whatever appeases you, night-stalker."

Lumira scowled at the insult, but she didn't defend her honor or assault his. Her subdued manner did little to soothe his own nerves.

Bits of the stairs crumbled as they climbed, reverberating like clashing cymbals in the silence. The feeling of being watched loomed over Davier with every step. He unsheathed his swords and studied their sleek edges, sharper than ever and ready for a fight.

At the top was a second archway adorned with curve-horned skulls, and through that, a courtyard filled with stone pews arranged in semicircles around a simple stone altar. Behind the altar lurked six statues. Davier couldn't make out their races, weathered as they were, each frozen in a grotesque position wrought with eternal agony, eyes locked on a vacant spot before them. The air reeked of sulfur and decay. He got the sense that something beyond time and life lingered beside him, separated by a thin veil.

He didn't want to find out what.

Elaysia made to sidle past him.

Davier blocked her path. "We should go. There's nothing here besides the remnants of a failing religion."

Jörd spat and muttered a curse in a Daruk dialect. "And you say we're barbaric."

Elaysia jutted her chin in defiance. "Xaren believes there's something to find here, and so did my parents. They just never made it this far."

"Fine. Wake me when you're done." Davier crumpled into a pew and reached for his wineskin. It was empty. *Fuck.*

Grokhion drifted through the pews, ears flicking this way and that. He stopped between the statues and knelt.

Lumira imitated him. "I hear it, too."

Despite himself, Davier joined them. He listened for a solid minute. Nothing. Before he could open his mouth to unleash a torrent of sarcasm on the cats, Lumira grabbed the back of his head and shoved his ear toward the ground. Davier started to fight her, then froze. Chanting, though not audible enough for him to make out the words.

"Mavet Almighty," he murmured.

Grokhion was already up, shoving at the altar. It gave with a groan. Below, a hatch cover without a handle. Davier handed the beridian one of his blades, and together they pried it open, revealing a dark hole. Cool air wafted through the cobwebs clustered at the entry, carrying the muffled chorus of chants. Davier volunteered to go first. He descended the rickety wooden ladder until the light emanating above was no more than a small sphere.

"What's down there?" Elaysia called out.

"I can't see shit. I'll forge ahead. Everyone can come down, but tell them to keep quiet and alert."

The tunnel wasn't tall enough for Davier to stand, so he crawled, hands extended in front of him. He found comfort in the anonymity darkness offered and wasn't entirely inferior to a beridian in his ability to maneuver in it. The chanting grew louder the further he delved, and it wasn't long before the crawl space widened into a beam-supported entrance flooded with nevethium light. He crept toward the edge of what appeared to be foundations for a balcony. The chamber below was about the same size as the All-Sovereign's throne room and lined with shimmering black gemstones and nevethium sconces. Hooded figures were the source of the chants. Although they wore the ornate, crimson trimmed robes of Mavist priests, their bone masks hardly conveyed holiness. Some sprouted serrated beaks. Others had fangs curled into wicked grins. One had no mouth at all, only a skeletal nose and hollowed eyes.

Twelve priests in total lined the elongated hall leading up to an altar where a more elaborately robed but unmasked nyrian flailed his arms above a body. A human body. Straggles of hair drooped down on either side of the priest's face. Blood trailed from his chin to his stomach. It pooled around the body and dripped off the altar onto the floor, where it slowly filled a serpentine eye enclosed in a diamond. Mavet's symbol. The nevethium sconces flickered. Chanting gave way to shouting as the priest bit a chunk of flesh off the corpse. It cried out in agony.

Alive.

Davier covered his mouth with a fist. What kind of convoluted ritual was this? Mavism taught one must consume the living flesh of the pure to atone for great sins, but he'd only seen fish or calves used. This went beyond faith. It was...

"They're trying to summon something," Elaysia whispered. She grabbed his arm, fingers cool on his flesh. "We have to intervene."

Davier surprised himself by laying his hand atop hers. The others hovered behind them, faces twisted with shock and horror.

For a moment, he envisioned slicing the priest's head off. It wouldn't be hard to take them, especially with the element of surprise. Elaysia would feel vindicated. The warriors would have no reason to doubt him again. But what was the point? They'd know his true motives soon enough. And if the All–Sovereign found out he'd attacked priests, it could mean the end of his promotion. Or worse.

No unnecessary risks. Az Zar needed him. His family needed him.

Davier considered the soft soil on the ledge and placed his foot in a weak spot. He drew Elaysia toward him. "On my lead."

He allowed his full weight to sink into the ledge. It crumbled beneath him. He tightened his grip on Elaysia's arm as he fell, landing on his back with a slam that knocked the wind out of him. Elaysia landed on top of him, cushioned by his body. The priests faced them in unison, their masked eyes a great deal more unsettling up close. He jumped to his feet and pulled out his swords—not entirely in show; he didn't trust the priests—and Elaysia her bow.

"Stay back," she shouted, aiming her arrow at the altar priest. "I'll kill him."

"Elaysia, wait." Davier's plea drowned in a sea of dozens of footsteps as Az Zarian soldiers poured into the room. He craned his head and found the source of their entrance: a passage near the back, concealed behind a shadowy veil.

The All–Sovereign had received his message. Davier should've felt relief, but dread weighed heavily in his stomach as a soldier shoved him to his knees and pressed a crossbow to his back. Elaysia knelt beside him, teeth bared. Someone bound their hands.

A snarl echoed above. On the remnants of the ledge, Grokhion fought to hold Lumira back and dragged her into the tunnel. Jörd had slipped down amid the commotion. She cut through two priests and started on a third. Nevethium arrowheads loosed from Az Zarian crossbows glowed vibrantly as they whizzed past. One sunk into Jörd's back. The other, her leg. She yelled, axe cutting the air as she squirmed toward another priest, then collapsed—far earlier than she should've with all that adrenalin. A faint yellow showed through her skin in the routes of her veins. Davier grimaced. Exposure to the crystals promoted health and healing, but inserted directly into the body, especially via a weapon, it resulted in inevitable death. Not unlike poison. He'd heard it was like burning from the inside out. Jörd writhed for what felt like minutes before a soldier with a shred of mercy loosed an arrow in her eye socket.

Elaysia sobbed. The maskless priest glided toward her and raised her chin with dirty, long-nailed fingers. "Barbarian empress," he said in a hollow voice. "The Lord Priestess will be most pleased."

Davier's skin crawled, but he took advantage of Elaysia's distraction and nudged the nearest soldier. "Look, I'm not sure how
much His Holiness has explained of my mission, but—"

The soldier drove the butt of his crossbow into Davier's skull.
His world went dark.

KONAR

Konar awoke on the floor tangled in his blanket, body slick with sweat. Dread sunk its talons into his spine and melded deep into the marrow of his bones. He swiped at the darkness until he found the pointed edges of his chest and cracked it open to expose the light of the nevethium pendant inside. His heartbeat slowed as it bathed the room in green splendor. The voices faded.

He paced, taking long draws from his pipe. Hastily made his cot as though someone intended to pay him a surprise visit. Massaged his temples. Wrote a letter to Elaysia and tore it up. When his eyelids burned with exhaustion, he retreated to his cot and snuffed the light of the crystal beneath his head roll.

The nightmares returned as soon as he shut his eyes. Vivid detail. Always the same.

He hadn't slept well in years. Why should tonight be any different? It was one thing to reason away a monster, and quite another to face the one you'd become.

Konar threw a cloak over his rumpled day clothes and trudged into the night, sap pulling at his bare feet with each step. The moons beamed unabashedly. Frigid air stirred around him, alive with the screeches and chatters of nocturnal creatures. A watcher nodded as he passed. It was well past the time for reasonable people to be asleep, but there wasn't a trace of concern on her face. High Elders could come and go from the buildings of Agaas as they pleased. Besides, this was scarcely abnormal behavior for Konar.

The floor groaned beneath him as he crept into his sanctuary, the place he felt most at home, barren as it was: the library. Driftwood walls hollowed into crude shelves lined the room. More were vacant than not, and the ones in use contained ten artifacts for every dust-laden scroll or leather-bound book. While Neharem valued the histories, they relied on oral tradition, not written record. Parchment could be destroyed. The stories passed down through generations withstood time.

A nice sentiment, but ancient tales had a way of exaggerating the truth until little of it remained.

Konar slid the table back and flipped the rug, then ran his hand across the floor until it caught on a small notch in the wood. He pried the hatch open. Below, a winding staircase led to a secret room no larger than his loft located in the heart of the tree. A few crates of nevethium sat in the corner, alongside a table piled high with books and scrolls. His personal library outnumbered the one upstairs. But for all the knowledge he'd gleaned, the false identities he'd assumed, the years of research, of painstaking expeditions, he was no closer to securing the Prophets' Scrolls. The ones he'd located were out of reach, guarded by a throng of beasts who deemed him unworthy.

He'd resolved to let the knowledge die with him. If he couldn't obtain the five remaining scrolls, chances were no one else would.

Then Elaysia ran off, no doubt seeking them, determined to unravel the fate of the nation he'd worked so long to protect. Perhaps she would've heeded his warning had he shared his knowledge.

Not that it'd stopped Elishon. It only made him hungrier. And she was too much like her father.

Konar clutched the worn doll he kept hidden in the folds of his robes. It was a risky game, confiding in no one, but better than handing over leverage. A slip of the lips was easy. It only took a moment of trust, of vulnerability. But once shared, things couldn't be unshared, unless one removed the potential threat: the confidant.

He tried to avoid that at all costs.

Still, unless he planned to live forever, he'd have to choose a successor soon. Zavik had long been a forerunner of interest. The only risk the lad proposed was blind allegiance to Elaysia. Konar strived to keep them apart, to destroy any traces of friendship or attraction, but Zavik always burrowed deeper. And now he'd set off on a foolhardy mission where he'd un-doubtedly lose his life—or worse, find what he so desperately sought. Zavik hadn't said as much to Konar the night he caught the lad scouring for scraps in the kitchen to prepare for his journey, but his intent was clear. Few things would send Zavik back to the land he'd escaped, and even fewer would interest Elaysia.

Footsteps echoed above, shattering Konar's musings.

His stomach twisted into a knot. The hatch was open. No time to conceal it. How could he have been so careless? Teeth clenched, he retrieved the dagger from his robes.

"Konar?"

The voice was calm, a whisper on the wind. Relief poured over him like a waterfall as feet pitter-pattered down the staircase. "Maseeya, what are you doing up so late?"

"You mean early?" she teased. She wore an Az Zarian evening gown adorned in golden fillagree, and her dark hair fell past her breasts. Teacups jostled in her hands. "I haven't slept well since..." She offered tea to Konar, round lips thinned with worry. "I hate that she left without our counsel."

Konar pulled a chair out for her. "She left because she didn't receive our counsel. Facing us would've forced her to logically approach the decision." He sipped the tea. It was scalding, the way he liked, and infused with dried berries and tungata root. "And I doubt that slaver encouraged our blessing."

Maseeya looked away.

Konar winced. "Forgive my crass disregard. I meant no offense." He rested his hand on her arm. "You've been with us so long; sometimes I forget you had another life before this."

Her arm tensed beneath his grip. "I've never forgotten. That's why I can't bear her being there." Tears welled up in Maseeya's eyes. "I know what he's capable of."

No, Konar wanted to say. *You can't begin to fathom what he's capable of.*

He drained the rest of his cup. "She's a smart girl. A survivor."

"And her parents weren't?" Maseeya dabbed the tears running down her flushed cheeks with her sleeve. "Annalee was the strongest woman I knew. She loved her children and would've fought through The Abyss to come home to them."

Konar slammed his cup on the table. "Annalee is the reason Elishon threw caution to the wind. They acted on impulse and wound up in a trap. It will be Elaysia's fate unless she comes to her senses."

Maseeya's face turned a violent shade of red. "How can you be so callous? She's like a daughter to me. I thought you felt the same, but maybe you're incapable of love."

Konar bowed his head. He couldn't bear her gaze.

"All those years spent caretaking, nurturing, guiding—it all sloughs off you like a snake shedding its skin. Always adapting, never feeling. Sometimes I think you're already dead." She stomped up the stairs, liquid sloshing out of her cup. The hatch slammed behind her.

Konar started after her. He made it halfway up the stairs, then trudged back down and lit his pipe. Nothing spoken would heal the wounds he'd inflicted. Not tonight.

He retrieved the doll from his robes and traced his thumb across its beaded eyes. Oh, to be incapable of love. If there was a draught to remedy it, he'd down it without question. Love was the gods' way of keeping mortals obedient, a curse disguised as a gift.

For no matter how long it lasted or how sweet its taste, love ultimately left one shattered beyond repair.

Konar peeled his cheek off the table and gingerly rotated his neck to alleviate the stiffness. He must've fallen asleep while reading. He rubbed his eyes. Teal light rippled on the walls like water, casting a shadow of a hulking beast, thick-necked and broad-shouldered, where his frail, mortal form should've been. Hot breath wafted against his back. Then a voice, richer than soil and older than time, spoke in the sighs of waves.

"Konar Gidmon Lightfoot. Long has it been since you sought my counsel."

Fifteen years. The nightmares pried at the threads of his consciousness. His stomach roiled. "Forgive me, Chai'Tik, Guardian of Life."

The teal light intensified. "Look upon me. Or have you spent all your courage on treason?"

Konar considered fleeing, but who could hide from a god? A chill wriggled down his spine as he rose from the chair. Even after multiple encounters, her magnificence never ceased to take his breath away.

The creature standing before him most closely resembled a bear, but to reduce her to such would've been an oversimplification of the greatest offense. Her black fur glistened silken splendor to rival the night sky, imprinted with teal symbols in the language of stars. Paws large enough to crush skulls. Claws thick as spears. She seemed to fill the entirety of the room, yet he could absorb her with a glance. A brilliant teal light shone through holes where eyes should've been. Beautiful and terrible as a storm.

Konar bowed. "Forgive my negligence. I thought you had no further need of me."

"I have never needed you." When she opened her mouth, teal light poured out, as though her spirit were tangible, the very breath of life. "But running from your past does not erase it. It merely lessens your aptitude to confront new problems. One might have thought you already learned that."

Nausea swept through him. He harnessed his anger to stifle it. "You know well I confront it every night, or do you not send those visions yourself?"

Her nostrils flared, emitting a huff of teal smoke.

"I did what was necessary. It prolonged the peace *you* appointed me to keep."

"Peace?" She drew out the word, savoring it like the rarest of wines. "Is that what you call this blind control and deceit, sinking your talons into decision-makers and disposing of them when they become burdensome?"

"You leave me no choice when you constantly move behind my back. You never told me about the stormbirds. Why?"

"Am I a beast to be commanded?" Chai'Tik snapped gleaming white teeth. "You have proven yourself untrustworthy. Or do you think me unaware of your dependency on my brother's magic?"

Konar's throat tightened. "Everything I've done is for this land, these people. If the scrolls fall into the wrong hands, if Az Zar succeeds in its conquest, Quinaria as we know it will cease to exist. I must change our fate. Please, tell me it's not too late."

"Anything is possible, but most things will never be."

"I will sacrifice everything."

She cocked her head. "But not yourself."

"I'm the last hope. Everyone else is... is..." Konar couldn't bring himself to say it.

He didn't have to.

"Expendable."

Chai'Tik slapped the ground with a massive paw. Elishon and Annalee appeared in the room. Not reflections he'd conjured out of memory, but vibrant and real as day, as if he could reach out and touch the beaded fringe of their tunics. He tried. They shirked away, the mistrust in their eyes so apparent it racked his stomach. He heaved his meager evening meal onto the floor. Everything went numb. The room ebbed in the distance like a dream. A nightmare.

"I should've never confessed to you," he screamed. The tears burst like a dam, rushing down his cheeks and spoiling his lips with salt. "You were supposed to understand and bring me comfort."

"There is no excuse for your malevolent deeds."

Konar lurched toward Chai'Tik. She swatted him against the wall. He couldn't breathe, couldn't move, couldn't fight the rage–tinted sadness engulfing him. He expelled soundless, tearless sobs. Chai'Tik ambled toward him, ears flattened.

"I warned them countless times about the danger," he rasped. "They wouldn't listen. The remaining scrolls shouldn't be recovered. They're safer hidden."

"You told them everything but the truth, and when they acted of their own accord, you had them slaughtered to maintain control." She snorted, the scent of pine rolling off her breath. "But they weren't the only ones who suffered for your arrogance."

Chai'Tik pressed her nose to his forehead. His vision tunneled into darkness. A chill set in.

He screamed.

His voice drowned in oblivion. He stumbled in the darkness until his hands found a wall, then a door. He rubbed his fingers down the graining until they brushed against the smooth protrusion of the handle. He knew that handle.

"Please," he whimpered, "I can't bear it anymore."

Chai'Tik didn't grace him with a reply.

Face taut, he creaked open the door and unleashed a flood of light.

Inside, it's as he remembers, and some things he's forgotten.

His scout, his apprentice, his son, cradles Annonitus's bloody body, face swollen with pride. Elaysia, only six, screams in the corner, small arms trembling as she levels a practice arrow like a spear.

"Kayrune," he says, just as he did fifteen years ago. He isn't sure if Chai'Tik forces the words out of him in her cruel justice or if he simply knows no other response. "What have you done?" Legs quaking, he takes a step away from his son, placing himself between the murderer and Elaysia.

Kayrune grins. A white rage flickers in his eyes. "The Moon-riders are a blight upon the land. They make Agaas eager for progress and greedy for power—no different from Az Zar. I'm ending the line to ensure peace."

"You had no right. Only the paren—" Konar catches himself, for Elaysia still shivers in the corner. Old enough to process. Old enough to remember. "He was an innocent child."

"So was Elishon." Kayrune dumps the boy like a bag of grain and starts for Elaysia.

Konar reacts on instinct. He retrieves the lyvium dagger from his sleeve and flings it across the room. It finds its home in Kayrune's neck. His son grasps at the hilt and pulls the blade out. Blood. So much blood. In his final moments, Kayrune glances up at him, his face equal parts shock and horror. And, right before his eyes shut forever, hurt.

Konar clutches his chest, emitting a hollow, dried-up moan. Elaysia taps his shoulder, her face muddied with tears and snot, but alive. He scoops her up. She won't speak for many moon cycles.

The dark tunnel envelopes him again. Chai'Tik's roar fills his ears.

"Kayrune made his choice." Her voice is lightning. "Yet you fostered his lust for power. You knew he wanted to rule, that he hated Elishon from the day he drew his first breath."

Konar finds no words to reply. He hangs his head, chest heaving.

"Your control is an illusion and your undoing. Free it and find the peace you so desire. Or grasp at it like fistfuls of sand and watch the few people you still care for slip through your fingers. The choice is yours."

Emptiness swallows Konar. His world and spirit are an endless void of darkness.

He weeps.

Konar peeled his cheek off the table, his memories sharp as a fresh wound.

He leaped from the chair. The room was empty. A book lay on the table, open to a few pages in. No odd lights or voices.

Just a dream, he told himself, even as a knot formed in his stomach.

He hurried upstairs and latched the door behind him, disguising it once again with the rug.

A knock sounded at the library door.

Konar drew a calming breath as he smoothed the wrinkles in his cloak. "Enter."

A boy no more than seven with enormous eyes and missing front teeth cracked the door, hesitating at the threshold. Sunlight streamed in.

"High Elder Lightfoot?"

Konar suppressed a smile at the boy's awkward formality.

"Chief Rajar's arrived at base camp with his warriors. They wish for a gathering with the high chieftain."

Konar's face hardened. "See that they are fed and rested, and let High Elders Strong-spear and Sower know of their arrival. The gathering will have to be on the morrow, I'm afraid, but assure them it will take place at dawn."

The boy nodded and skipped away, leaving the door ajar.

"Protect her," he whispered. Whether praying to Chai'Tik or simply wishing for luck, he knew not.

He wasn't past redemption. He had to believe that. It wasn't too late to make it up to Elaysia, to restore the life he'd stolen from her.

And he'd begin with Rajar.

JAKKI

Skulmor territory wasn't living up to its name.

They'd begun their search around the Daruk border of the Lesser Quentarri Mountains, where the days were short and the nights endless, the land frozen and rocky with rushing rivers that zig-zagged down mountainsides. Everything was amplified, from the size of plants to the viciousness of wildlife. Jakki witnessed the latter first-hand while scouting with Yerakai one evening. They'd settled on an alternative route (thanks to her insight) when a guttural snarl sounded from the bushes. A helgin emerged, pawing at the ground. Jakki had only heard stories about the monstrous boars of the north and stalled upon seeing its five-hundred-pound frame and quad tusks. Yerakai shoved her onto a bed of pine needles just before it gutted her. He took it down by lodging an arrow in its eye. She finished it with a dagger to the throat. The warriors celebrated their victory, and they had meat for days, but that was the last of their good fortune.

Nomadic or not, two fortnights of scouring skulmor land should've resulted in an encounter—at least a straggler or some sign of carnage. The few tracks Yerakai found faded within a day or dead-ended at some long-abandoned den. And though the landscape lent itself to more forgiving temperatures the further south they surveyed, the lack of discovery made for poor motivation. Hope ran thin and parallel to their sanguinity. The others wouldn't follow her through trailless forests and fields of boulders much longer. Not without proof.

Siren stirred behind her. The stormbird's eyes were slits, and her budding feathers cushioned her cheek against the edge of the pack. Jakki kissed her white down. It was midday and less windy since they'd crossed from a tundra plain into a wooded area where the trees grew as tall as—though not as girthy—the ones in Agaas. According to Davier's makeshift map, they weren't far from Gohla, the skulmor's sacred place.

"We're in agreement this is our final destination, regardless of what we find, yes?" Yerakai said, treading softly beside her. His stormbird gave her an equally suspicious look.

Jakki glared and removed the outermost layer of her furs. Yerakai wasn't one to challenge, but she grew tired of the way he subtly questioned her decision-making.

"Do you have previous engagements rivaling the importance of this mission?" she asked in a tone .

Yerakai drew an arrow from his quiver and ran his fingers over the fletching. "Only concern for the assumptions likely circulating about our high chieftain due to her absence and our own. Our return would put the council's minds at ease."

Jakki set her jaw and ignored him. The thought had occurred to her, but she didn't dare admit it.

Anahi, overhearing the conversation, matched Jakki's strides. "I agree. We already have proof the skulmor are at least partly to blame for the raids." She yanked a needle-covered twig off a low-hanging branch and tossed it back for her stormbird to chomp on. "Not sure what this is accomplishing."

Jakki scowled. If the Orillon filth mustered the balls to protest, the others would soon follow suit. "Oh, I don't know, maybe a chance to learn the why behind it? Uncover some of our stolen crystals? Maybe you'd care if you were one of us."

Yerakai quickly inserted himself between them. "We aren't undermining you. We're only offering insight so we can make the wisest decision as a group."

"Elaysia's orders were clear," Anahi said, her eyes challenging.

"Don't you think I know what she wanted more than anyone else?" Jakki shoved past them and continued through the brush, hacking at branches before they dared to strike her face.

Thanks to the dense blanket of fog settled over the woods, no one made out the skulmor settlement until they were face-to-face with an enclosure fashioned from sharpened logs of varying lengths. Jakki summoned Yerakai and Mardus to her flanks and, staff readied, heaved her shoulder against the gate. It swung open with a groan. Inside, crude dens sprouted from the dirt like winter-stripped bushes, all circling a building akin to a Daruk longhouse. It was more elaborate than she'd expected, with skin flags hanging from each structure and a watchtower looming in the background.

But Gohla was vacant, like everything else.

Jakki groaned and lowered her pack to let Siren out. "Enjoy the freedom while you can." The stormbird cocked her head, then hopped out of sight. Jakki let her. She wouldn't go far.

"Orders, Captain?" Anahi said, none too kindly.

Jakki didn't give her the courtesy of a glance as she barked commands. "Search every crevice of the village and the surrounding woods. They must've left something behind. Hints to where they've gone, how long they've been gone. Find it."

Grumbles ensued, but the warriors spread out as Jakki made her way to the longhouse. It was an odd shade of rusted-white, composed of smooth pieces with unnaturally round angles. Unlike any wood she'd—

She froze outside the entrance. Rubbed her eyes.

Bones. They'd constructed the entire building from bones. The wooden stairs creaked under her weight as she climbed to the deck. Massive tusks barred the entryway with tanned hides draped behind them like a screen. She pushed them aside.

Skulmor weren't the leisurely type. The room contained piles of furs for sleeping, a crude firepit, and a chair resembling a throne. Markings covered the floor at its feet. Skulmor runes? Did they have a written language? A metallic scent stained the air, so Jakki scraped off a bit of a rune and pressed it to her tongue. Blood, but sickly sweet, as if it'd been laced with something.

She approached the throne. Also bone-made; it'd been draped in furs for comfort. She lowered herself onto it and curled her hands over the skull armrests. Not human or nyrian skulls. Skulmor. What people slaughtered their own?

Mardus entered the longhouse and, upon seeing her in the chair, narrowed his eyes.

"Come off it," she snapped. "What did you find?"

"More of the same. Completely abandoned with no signs of struggle." He rubbed his jaw with a massive hand. "Maybe they're rallying against Az Zar."

"Then why invade Neharem? We never provoked them or stole their land." Jakki slumped in the chair. "We're missing something."

"Maybe we're looking in the wrong place."

She leaned forward, eyes twitching with irritation. "Elaborate."

"What if the skulmor are a distraction? A tool in the hands of something, someone, more sinister?" Mardus sat cross-legged on a pile of furs and placed his hands on his knees. "Chief Orandus"—Jakki rolled her eyes at his formality; who referred to their parents by their official titles, chiefs or not?—"said an Az Zarian trader from Quovana told him he was fleeing to Orillon. The All-Sovereign takes over half what the people make, earn, and grow. When they can't pay, they become slaves of the country."

Jakki didn't understand taxes, but that hardly seemed ethical. "People would revolt. The firstborn draft is one thing, but to enslave your own people? Seems extreme, even for the All-Sovereign."

"That's not all." Mardus looked very much to Jakki like an impatient child who presumed he held all the answers. "He also said they speak of the dawn of a new era in Az Zar. They summon the power of the one who always consumes and is never satisfied."

"How's that new?" Jakki drew her hair to the front and worked through the tangles. "Az Zarians have always worshiped Mavet."

"Not like this." He lowered his voice as if others lurked outside the room. "Their priests are rumored to summon angels to bestow gifts."

"Gifts?" She suddenly became acutely aware of the parchment tucked into her waistband. "Like what?"

Mardus shook his head. "The chief said it's best for the Moákun not to entertain rumors."

Jakki groaned. The Moákun were the primary source of trade for Neharem's Az Zarian imports, and Mardus's father wouldn't want that relationship tainted. Ignorance was bliss.

Yerakai moved from the doorframe like a ghost, face hardened. How long had he been standing there? "Caman don't bestow gifts. They exchange evil for evil deeds."

Jakki's arms prickled beneath her furs as she recalled the fireside stories from childhood. Caman were lyda. Demons. Mavet's bastard children.

"The Caman were destroyed thousands of years ago alongside Mavet," Mardus blurted. Sensing Jakki's eyes on him, he rose, clearly flustered. "If you believe that sort of thing."

"Perhaps," Yerakai said. "But if not, I suppose one might perceive them as angels. It's said they each had a gift to sway mortals: jealousy, betrayal, greed, prejudice, power, and fear."

Jakki cleared her throat loudly. "We've all heard those parables told by the elders to keep us mannered. Believe your ghost stories, Brother, but I'm more concerned with the very real skulmor that should occupy these lands."

"Might be they're intertwined," Yerakai said.

She glared back. "We can only track the living."

They locked eyes. Yerakai's gaze softened, which only further unnerved her. He tucked a silken strand behind his ear and shrugged.

"South, then," Mardus said, voice on edge. "To Az Zar?"

Jakki gave Yerakai a look that said *we'll agree to disagree*, and nodded to Mardus. "Tell the others to make camp. We'll set out in the morning." She didn't care to hear Yerakai's opinion.

He looked like he was about to give it anyway when a shout arose from outside.

They raced into the gray light. The voice came from the watchtower. One of their own. Jakki ran up to its base.

The Apáasutai on watch, an older man with beaded hair and a stern brow, climbed down to meet her. "Something advances due north. There's movement in the trees."

Jakki's eyes widened. If something was rustling the trees, it was no small creature. Tulek bears didn't thrive this far south, did they? "How far?"

"It will reach us soon. I couldn't see through the fog until now."

Before Jakki could issue a command, Mardus motioned two Moákun to him. "Tawiri, Oanya, with me. We'll post up on the northern ramparts."

They didn't so much as give Jakki a passing glance as they heeded Mardus's command, let alone ask her for the plan. Heat flared in her chest. She started after them, but Yerakai grabbed her arm.

"Don't take it to heart, Sister. They're his people. They owe him loyalty."

"They owe me loyalty." She shoved past Yerakai and climbed onto the ramparts. A few choice words danced on her tongue, but as she made to unleash them, a scream pierced the air.

Jakki whirled. Twenty feet below, a warrior lay pinned beneath a beast she'd heard of countless times yet never laid eyes on. As if sensing her, the skulmor looked up. Blood seeped from its victim's throat like a crimson waterfall. Its eyes were so intelligent. So cold. Not the eyes of a beast, but of a murderer. It held her gaze for a moment, then leaped toward another warrior. More spilled into the encampment. They must've had a tunnel system feeding from the woods into one of the dens.

She crept down from the ramparts, her pace slowed by the ferocity of the wolven race. They were roughly the height of a beridian, but it was hard to be certain since they prowled on all fours to take down prey. She swallowed hard, gripping her staff. Even a skilled nyrian struggled when pitted against a skulmor warrior, and their forty-year lifespans and harsh living conditions made them all the more reckless. They had nothing to lose.

"Circle up," Yerakai shouted below as they closed in. "Find someone to watch your back." The grounded warriors flocked to him like prey while the hunters closed in. There were at least two dozen skulmor. Almost an even match.

Except it would take more than a few of her warriors just to take down one.

A bird's shriek shattered her concentration. Her breath caught in her throat. Siren. Jakki ignored the fear twisting her stomach and flipped down, landing softly on the ground. The stormbird was backed against the longhouse, downy wings and plumage flared to appear bigger. A skulmor crept toward her slowly, as though curious. Siren showed no fear.

Jakki sprinted across the clearing, jabbing her staff into a skulmor's skull as it tried to thwart her. She reached Siren first and scooped the stormbird into her pack. The skulmor who'd cornered her snarled, flashing rows of uneven, rotting fangs. Ragged fur covered most of its body, thinning out near its brawny chest. It wore a simple loincloth and armor bits comprised of the bones and skins of what were likely its past enemies. She raised her staff. Told herself it wouldn't be any different from her years of combat training or the handful of tussles she had with bandits. With a shout, she sprang toward it and drove her staff into its neck. It dodged her with ease. Sunk its teeth into her leg.

The pain nearly blinded her. She screamed until her throat was raw. Instinct forced her to retrieve the dagger from her side and drive it into the beast's neck.

It unlatched with a yelp, but not before tearing its teeth further down her thigh.

Jakki clutched her wound. Blood seeped between her fingers and pooled on the deck. Her vision throbbed with her pulse, drawing her attention from the external to the internal. But the skulmor had already recovered. Its red eyes seethed with hatred. It prowled toward her, jaws salivating.

Get up, get up.

Ignoring the searing pain in her leg, she crouched, fingers locked into the woodgrain.

The skulmor lunged.

Jakki leaped at the last moment and clung to the rafters. It hesitated, stunned, for the briefest moment. That was all she needed.

She dropped, driving her weight into her staff as she fell. Her weapon met its skull with a satisfying crunch. The beast crumpled on the deck, twitching. Jakki struck it again and again until its face became concave.

Her heartbeat echoed in her head like a war drum. She blinked, sucked in air, and blinked once more.

"Jakki, watch out!" Yerakai shouted.

The warning sent a chill down her spine, but not in time for her to act.

A skulmor tackled her head-on like a boulder to the ribs. The stench of blood, dirt, and rotted carcass filled her nostrils. She shoved at the skulmor's chest, holding its snapping jaws inches from her face. It pressed a massive paw to her throat. She couldn't breathe. The sting of a claw scraped her neck. Her vision faded. Heart slowed.

This was it.

Amid all the things she'd not accomplished, the role of chief she hadn't claimed, and the lovers she'd yet to lie with, there was Elaysia's face, paling everything in comparison. And she'd never know what they could've been because she'd never taken the chance. She'd never confessed her love. Mother Itaso, why hadn't she told her?

Jakki's eyes shot open. Gnashing teeth dripped saliva onto her face. *Die,* the beast's eyes seemed to say.

"Like Haeshol I will." She heaved the last of her strength into the skulmor's chest. It flew off her, hurtling through the air until it smacked against a hut with a finite crunch.

What?

Jakki sat up. A pair of lyvium-plated boots stood before her, boots three times the size of what should've suited a larger nyrian. She scrambled back, clutching her wounded leg. Her rescuer carried the look of her kin with his pointed ears and white hair woven into intricate braids swooping down his back, but he was easily twice the size of Grokhion. His skin was ice blue with pink undertones, and he wore a tunic also armored with lyvium that exposed arms and legs corded in muscle. Starlight-colored eyes regarded her with care.

A nazrath. One of the giants of old.

The nazrath extended a hand the size of a shield to help her up. She recoiled. The nazrath frowned. He leaped over her and snatched another skulmor up by its tail, then finished it the way he had the last.

Jakki forced her quivering legs to stand. Carcasses covered the ground, both her warriors and skulmor, the latter mostly crumpled against fences and buildings thanks to the nazrath—there were at least two others—tromping about. Mardus knelt above a skulmor a few feet away. He was smeared with blood. Jakki prayed it wasn't his own. She started toward him but collapsed in agony as her leg trembled and throbbed. Blood still spilled from the wound. She held back tears and tried to crawl forward.

Anahi appeared, her face sheened in sweat. "Give me your arm."

Jakki had no energy for pride, and as much as she hated to admit it, the foreigner had managed to survive the assault without so much as a scratch, proving herself a formidable warrior if nothing else. She slung her arm around Anahi's neck and hobbled to the survivors, who'd regrouped around Yerakai. He tended to a Tangeesh who couldn't have been more than sixteen. Jakki almost retched; the girl's arm was ripped to shreds. She'd lose just the arm if she was lucky. Yerakai bandaged it as best he could with the minimal supplies they had while the others looked after the remaining wounded in silence.

"Are you alright?" Jakki asked Yerakai as the girl slipped into an alcohol-induced sleep. She wrapped her leg twice over with a cloth torn from her skirts and winced at the deadening pain setting in. She'd have to clean it soon, otherwise she'd risk infection.

"I fear I did better than most," he whispered. He rested his hand lightly on his stormbird's head. "The gods were watching out for us. Wind Chaser is well, and it looks like the other stormbirds fared the same?"

Jakki shrugged. The birds had survived, thankfully, but the gods hardly favored them. She counted ten Neharem warriors dead. Just under half the group they'd departed Agaas with.

The nazrath who'd saved Jakki stomped up and motioned for them to follow. His companions lingered at the gate with unreadable expressions. They hadn't even broken a sweat.

Yerakai placed his right fist over his heart. "Thank you, my friend. Can you speak the ancient tongue?"

The nazrath's stoic expression didn't change. He gestured for them to follow again.

"Yes, we'll come with you. But we must find a way to transport our wounded." Yerakai motioned to the Tangeesh girl, and the nazrath nodded.

Jakki used her staff to brace her weight and hobbled over to block Yerakai's path. "What are you doing? We don't know where they're going or what their intentions are. They showed up just in time to save us from a complete massacre. It's bit convenient, don't you think?"

Yerakai pulled a wounded Daruk to his feet. "They came to our aid. That's enough to earn my trust for now. We have few supplies and cannot shelter in the den of our enemies. Have you a better resolution?"

She didn't. Their ravaged group was more vulnerable than ever, and there was no telling how many more skulmor lurked in the woods, alerted to the murders of their kin.

Yerakai, taking Jakki's silence for compliance, rounded up the surviving warriors. A female nazrath ripped fabric off her tunic, scooped up the wounded Tangeesh girl, and swaddled her in the cloth like a newborn babe.

Jakki lingered while everyone shuffled out through the gates. Dusk had fallen, and the creatures of the forest released growls and howls echoing through the trees like the whispers of malevolent spirits. The thick canopy of branches overhead cast a green-tinted gloom upon the ground, where a carpet of moss and dead needles muffled the footfalls of those brave enough to venture within.

Siren chirped in her ear.

"Fine. We'll go. Stay low." She folded the top over her pack, hiding Siren's snowy feathers from view, then limped out of the encampment, trailing the muddied footprints of her companions.

She looked from side to side with each step.

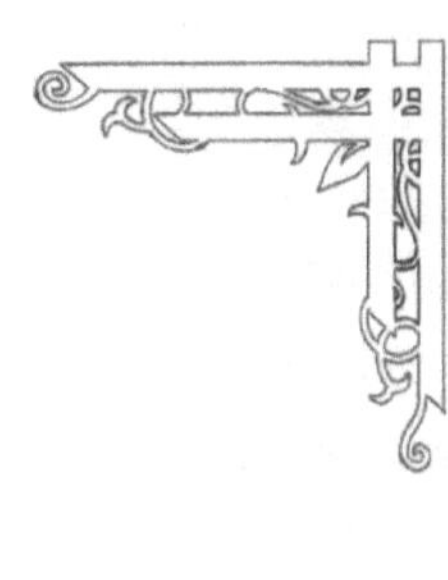

ELAYSIA

The darkest hour, even barren of moonlight, couldn't mute the rusted tones of the Tsabian Desert. It spilled across the landscape like old blood, speckled with hooded trees and enchanted by the distant lullabies of coyotes.

Under different circumstances, Elaysia might've enjoyed the thrill of new scenery. The bite of the wind against the warmth of a fire. The freedom of being somewhere that wasn't Agaas. Throw in Davier and a good drink, and what wasn't there to love?

But she had no drink. In fact, thanks to the generous daily ration of a half-filled canteen and gristle from the soldiers' meal, cracks marred her lips, and she swam in her once fitted tunic. And while she trembled against Davier's body, a primal need to stay warm overshadowed any hint of arousal, for the desert at night felt as cold as the northern lands, and they'd been offered no blankets. Rope chaffed against her wrists, and nightmares of Jörd's dying face evaporated her hope like dewdrops in the sun. Every day made her less certain she'd live to see the ocean again.

Davier stirred beside her, shaking his tangled locks to reveal a bruised face crusted with sweat and dirt. The grime adorned him in a way not altogether unflattering, as though he was made to withstand the elements and let his hair grow unkempt. Oddly enough, she preferred him now as to when he'd first arrived at her tent threshold, groomed and gleaming like a rich man's stallion. Not that her judgment was trustworthy at present. Anyone besides her captors would seem appealing now.

She must've stared too long, for he looked down at his body and asked, "That bad, eh?"

"Worse. You might be the most hideous creature I've ever laid eyes on." She forced a smile and, genuine or not, it felt good.

"They must think I'm handsome"—he inched toward her with all the grace his bound limbs would allow—"otherwise they would've slit my throat at the temple."

"You do have a way with words."

Not that it had helped. Davier's attempt to reason with the soldiers the night of their capture resulted in a beating that left him unconscious until the next morning. She'd lost track of how many days they'd been gagged and hooded for travel since. No word as to where they headed or why. No sign of her warriors or the stormbirds. And in case pending doom and starvation weren't enough, she'd acquired a cough that rattled her chest day and night.

All in all, she made a splendid leader on a flawless expedition. If Konar saw her now, his smugness would likely outweigh his pity.

Elaysia shivered as Davier pressed against her, chest to back, crotch to bum, legs intertwined. He radiated heat. They fit perfectly, the way a nut nestled in its shell. She wanted to enjoy it. Savor his touch. But there was nothing romantic about sharing body heat to survive the night. Might as well have been Paukton, the outspoken and overfed son of a chief who'd eyed her during cast-sessions as a child.

The wind shrieked, tearing through the holes in her clothes. She glared at the Az Zarian pigs huddled around the campfire twenty feet away. They slapped each other's backs and guffawed at lewd jokes about women and races they deemed lesser, all while draining their wineskins.

Elaysia shut her eyes. "It's taking a long time to get to Cadar."

"Assuming that's our heading." A pause. "I hope it's not. Cadar's impregnable, her prisons more so."

"I don't even care anymore. I just want answers." She did care. The mention of Cadar knotted her stomach. Dying in the same city as her parents was poetic, sure, but she'd carry questions to her grave. Not just why they died, but why they left in the first place. And why the raids? The attempt on her life? And Jörd's death...

She rolled over to face Davier. "Do you commonly use nevethium in your arrowheads?"

His face was stone. "Sometimes."

"What did she feel?"

"I don't know."

"Don't lie to me."

Davier's nostrils flared. "The crystals are broken down and melded with lyvium. It was our main weapon during The Skulmor Rebellion, though they were invented long before either of us was born." He rolled onto his back. "It flows through the bloodstream and targets the victim's heart. I hear it's a painful death."

Tears stung Elaysia's eyes. She blinked them back. "You must use a lot of nevethium. It's not sustainable." Her fists clenched and unclenched behind her back. "Is that what the raids are about?"

"I've already told you what I know. Try to get some sleep." Davier shut his eyes.

Elaysia scooted away from him. Wine splattered onto her cheek as the soldier assigned to watch duty succumbed to sleep, wineskin in hand.

They'd scared her at first, outnumbering them twenty to two, the majority battle-seasoned nyrians. But her fear receded with her waistline. Only the dull ache of spite remained, burdened by inadequate strength to employ it. Every night, she lay like a hare caught in a trap, cursing her own inaction, her inability to fight back.

Konar was right. She'd been stupid to come and hasty in her decision-making.

Maybe she hadn't sought answers or justice so the council might finally deem her capable and pledge steadfast loyalty. Perhaps she simply wanted to prove she could commandeer her destiny. That she was capable of anything.

But she wasn't.

Elaysia woke to Davier's lips brushing against her ear. A wave of pleasure rippled through her.

Then reality set in.

"What?" she croaked. Her voice cracked from dehydration.

"Shh. Look."

Elaysia blinked to adjust her vision. She sat upright, immediately forgetting the chill biting through her clothes. At least ten pairs of amber eyes glinted in the faint light of the coals. The hulking forms encircled the camp. Crept closer.

One leaped onto a sleeping soldier and tore out his throat.

Elaysia's breath hitched. More terrifying than the kill was the calculated grace with which it was executed. Silent as a dancer.

No one stirred as the soldier bled out onto the dirt, hands clutched around his throat until they collapsed at his sides. His killer was a beast half the size of a horse with a bobtail too dainty for its stocky frame. Fangs hung past its jaw, slick with blood.

Another leaped into the circle. This time, a soldier woke, groggy and unbalanced. He'd just claimed his swords when the beast took him down with a slash.

Carnage ensued. Screams filled the air as swords clashed with fangs, and a swirl of red dust slowly clouded the campfire. The soldier guarding Elaysia and Davier lurched to his feet. He took one look at his comrades and fled on the nearest mount.

Davier found his footing. "Sandcats. They'll be on us any minute. Wait here." He hopped toward a fallen soldier on the outskirts. A dagger lay a foot from the corpse.

As soon as he left, Elaysia felt eyes on her back. Hot, foul breath wafted against her neck. She froze. Everything in her screamed *run*. Her limbs refused to comply.

The sandcat nosed around her jaw, cheek, lips, until she found herself gazing into its unblinking eyes. Her heart skipped a beat.

Of all the ways to die.

But it didn't attack. It chuffed, then lunged for a soldier who'd crept into her peripherals, claws tearing into his innards.

"Elaysia!"

She flung herself toward Davier. He braced her with a strong hand and freed her bonds.

"What the fuck just happened? Are you alright?"

She couldn't muster a reply. The air was rife with blood and screams. Most of the soldiers lay sprawled on the ground, either pinned by sandcats or already stilled with death.

Davier pressed the dagger into her palm. "Horses and rations. I'll find our weapons." He sprinted back into the fray.

Elaysia willed her shaky legs forward. In the soldiers' drunken neglect, they'd left horses saddled with food and canteens. She approached a spry mare and reached for the reins.

A hand shot out, seizing her wrist.

"Going somewhere, half-breed?" The cleft in her captor's chin was so prominent it created the illusion of two small chins. He roved over her with his good eye. "If you don't fight me, I may see fit to give you a reward when we arrive." A wolfish smile crawled up his face.

Elaysia didn't realize what she'd done until his expression contorted in horror. The blade vanished into his stomach, leaving the hilt exposed. She yanked it out and vaulted onto the mare's back. The soldier stumbled to block her. She plowed over him.

A buzz coursed through her body. She secured a mount for Davier and searched for him amid the massacre. The sandcats, immersed in their recent kills, spared her few glances before returning to the feast of bodies that would undoubtedly last their pack a long while. Davier raced to meet her, swords strapped to his back. He thrust her bow and quiver into her hands.

His eyes lingered on the bloodied dagger. "Are you hurt?"

She shook her head. If she was hurt, she wouldn't know until the rush of the attack left her.

Davier mounted. "I don't think we'll be followed, but just in case, want to show me some of that riding you're always boasting about?"

Elaysia urged her mare forward. "Try to keep up."

They rode hard for miles with nothing but the stars to guide them. Elaysia didn't mind. It gave her an illusion of freedom, of control. For a short time, all was right with the world.

When it was clear no one pursued them, she eased her mount to a trot so Davier could catch up. "Nice of you to join."

"I won't take it easy on you next time." Davier peered over his shoulder and let out a whistle. "I still can't believe our luck."

"Maybe the sandcats wanted to help." Elaysia regretted the words as soon as they tumbled from her mouth. Davier raised an eyebrow. She bit her lip, cheeks flushing with heat. "They didn't harm us," she added quickly.

He wasn't convinced. "Like I said, luck. That pack was half-starved, and sandcats have been getting bolder. We've had reports of attacks on hunting parties, small villages—even our own squads. Aggressive creatures."

"Maybe they wouldn't be so aggressive if they hadn't been stripped of their land and prey." This time, the words left her mouth with unbridled intent.

Davier cracked his knuckles. "I'm just thankful we got away."

"That we can agree on."

A gust of wind slammed into them, relentless and cold. Elaysia tugged her sleeves down to salvage a little more warmth and caught sight of dried blood on her hand. She rubbed it with fervor, but the blood stayed put. Bile crept up her throat. Davier's expression suggested he sensed her discomfort but didn't want to discuss it. What else had she expected from a trained killer?

"Where are we?" she asked, no longer willing to bear the memories roused by silence.

Davier arched his neck skyward. "Given the slight change in weather and terrain, I'd say northeast of the altars. Opposite direction of Cadar. But if we continue north, we can cut through Or Zahal and follow the Ashaat to the capital."

Elaysia brushed her fingertips down the mare's neck. Cadar sounded tempting, but the repercussions of her recent bout of rash decision-making still stung. "The others must be looking for us. We need to find them."

She urged her mount in the direction she assumed was west, but Davier blocked her.

"I'm not in the mood." She maneuvered around him.

He repeated the action, eyes paling the stars' splendor. "I am."

Their horses danced around the desert, kicking up clouds of red dust until Elaysia's frustration gave way to amusement and, eventually, joy.

"Davier." She tried her best to take an assertive tone. "They'll want to know we're alright, and Onitus needs me."

He pulled his mount alongside hers. "You're a smallish person, and it's a rather large country."

She rolled her eyes and nudged her mount forward, but he grabbed the reins. The humor vanished from his face.

"I've lived here my whole life," he said, "and even with the aid of a battalion, I'd struggle to find them. The soil in this region is too dry to track, and we don't know if they followed us, went to Cadar, headed home—"

"They wouldn't abandon me. I don't know what kind of scum you're used to befriending, but we're loyal people."

He raised both hands in the air. "Sorry."

"Stop that."

"Apologizing?"

"Being so damn sarcastic."

"Fine."

"Fine."

Davier jumped off his horse and strode away.

"Where are you going?" Elaysia shouted after him.

"Taking a piss, if that's alright with you, High Chieftain. Look on, if it pleases you."

Bastard.

Elaysia faced her mare in the opposite direction. The desert unraveled in endless monotony, spattered with a few shrubs and ragged trees hinting at its former glory. The histories claimed Az Zar was once the richest of lands, the origin of life, gardened by the gods themselves, eternally sustainable. But for some, cohabitation wasn't enough. The land was an unruly beast to be tamed. A virgin with untainted goods. An enemy to conquer.

And that mentality spread like a wildfire.

"I won't make a decision until we've eaten and rested," she said when Davier rejoined her.

He regarded her with playful eyes and pointed to the nearby rocky hills. "There's an inn ahead. Race you. Winner gets first drink?"

But she'd already taken off at the word *race* and was well ahead of him. Riding was natural, invigorating, and one thing she excelled at. No one back home had bested her, not in a long while. As she fell into a rhythm with the mare, she dreamed of riding Onitus. Would it be similar? Stormbirds would likely have more power, more sway in what they did. The idea of soaring among the clouds made her head tingle.

A pang of guilt struck her. She'd never ride if she didn't get herself and the stormbirds home safely.

She clenched her jaw and urged the mare on.

A small crater, no more than a spear's throw in diameter, lay at the mouth of a cave in the foothills. Likely a dried-up lake. If they dug deep enough, it had the propensity to supply adequate water for them and the horses. After boiling, of course. Inside, a fire pit filled with charred wood warned of other travelers, but the rest of the cave was empty. No tracks or signs of recent occupation. Still, one could never be too sure. She'd completed a loop around the perimeter when Davier trotted up.

"My horse is older than yours," he said, dismounting.

"Right." She rolled her eyes and gestured to the campfire. "What do you make of this?"

"Probably smugglers. They use this route to make untaxed trades with Orillon."

Davier reached to help her down. She allowed it. This time. His hands fit halfway around her waist. Her cheeks flushed at the contact, and she became painstakingly aware they were alone.

She moved a safe distance away. "Can we risk a fire?"

"Don't see why not. They would've set up camp by now if they were planning on it. Dawn's only a few hours away. Besides, we need the warmth."

While Davier patted down the mounts and dug for water, she built a fire even Konar would praise and laid out the rations. It took all her resolve to wait for Davier. When he returned, she rehydrated the compact vegetable cakes with some water and fat from the salted pork, then spooned the concoction over the dried bread and meat. She wolfed down her portion, any care for how Davier perceived her overshadowed by the need for satiation. When she'd had her fill, she reached for the wine. An ever-reliable friend, it always comforted her, especially after one of Konar's guilt-ridden lectures or a failed council gathering. Sometimes she even drank before, just enough to awaken courage for speeches or to tolerate debates masked as feasts.

She was halfway through the wineskin when she caught Davier staring. "What?"

"You look happy."

"I don't normally?" She took another sip and tossed it to him.

"Not often." He lay on his side, propped up with an elbow. "You scrunch your face a lot. Maybe you don't frown so much, but you smile even less, and when you do, your eyes betray your worry."

Elaysia stiffened and yanked the wineskin back for another drink. "Wasn't aware you knew me so well."

"I'd probably do the same in your shoes." The firelight bathed Davier's skin in a golden glow and cast shadows on the grooves of his muscled forearms. "Carrying the burden of a nation is enough to make anyone go mad. Look at the All-Sovereign."

"I'm not mad," she snapped, more to silence her longing than unleash rage. "And it's my responsibility."

"People should be responsible for themselves."

"That's hardly an Az Zarian outlook."

"Just because I fought for my country doesn't mean I agree with it."

"Doesn't it?"

Davier pried the wineskin from her fingers. She watched, wide-eyed, as he drained it and reached for another. "Guess I'm a hypocrite. People should be free to do as they like."

"Like the skulmor?"

"Anarchy? Hardly." He blew air through his teeth. "But you have to admit, they fend for themselves well enough."

"Like you." The fire licked her skin. She scooted away from it and, not coincidentally, closer to him.

"I try. I wish I didn't have to."

"I wish I did."

"What do you call this?" He gestured around the cave. "I'd rather have your life, if we're being honest."

"We are. But you wouldn't. Trust me." Elaysia tucked her knees beneath her chin. Everyone loved the idea of power, but few knew the sleepless nights that accompanied it.

Davier's gaze bore into her. She felt it without looking to confirm it. Warmth spread through her body and lightened her stomach. "I'd give anything for peaceful living and freedom."

"Agaas"—she jabbed her finger into his chest and let it linger—"is a prison."

"Lock me away."

"You don't understand."

"Does anyone? Life always looks better when it's not your own." He pressed her hand to his chest and rubbed it with his thumb. "We can pursue happiness, even catch her sometimes and steal a lingering kiss, but she always runs off again. And then we crave her incessantly and die grasping for what we'll never own. It's life's greatest illusion. Sharing our miseries with others is all that keeps us sane." He locked eyes with her and leaned closer. His nose brushed hers. "Perhaps we can share in misery for a time."

"I'd like that." Warmth flooded her cheeks. "I mean—"

"I know what you mean."

Davier pressed his lips to hers, awakening every part of her body. She kissed him back, drawing his head in as he wrapped his arms around her waist. There was no gap between them. Her fingers combed through his hair; his ran down her collarbone, her breasts, her thighs. He kissed the hollow of her neck. She shuddered. Reached for his belt.

Davier stiffened. He wrenched himself away and shook his head as if coming out of a trance.

Elaysia backed to the other end of the cave and drew a blanket over her shoulders with trembling hands. Why the fuck had he done that? Had she done something wrong? Misread his intentions?

She dared another look at him. He gazed at her, his eyes filled with longing yet tainted with apprehension.

She understood. *She* was wrong. For him. He was wrong for her as well. And this, the wine, the kiss, the vulnerability, was a terrible mistake. She wouldn't make it again.

Davier rubbed his face with both hands and let out an exasperated moan. "I shouldn't have done that. I'm sorry. I just... you're beautiful, but"— he bit his lips and stared into the flames—"it's complicated."

"I doubt that." She wanted to scream, but letting him see her weakness would only hurt worse.

"We're both lonely right now. I don't want it to be misinterpreted as—"

"No problem." She flopped onto her bedroll and faced the wall. Pincers of anxiety tightened her throat. "Don't worry, I won't touch you again."

"Elaysia—"

"For Khiev-Tatamic's sake, shut it and get some rest, alright? We've a long way to go in the morning."

He complied. It was for the best. She needed to stay in her head, not her heart.

And hating him made that easier.

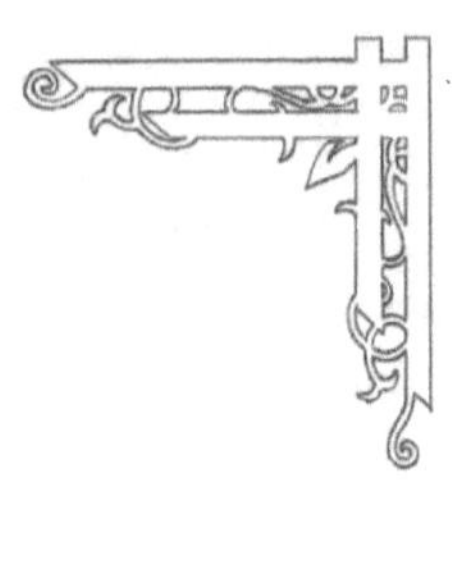

LUMIRA

"**L**ovely home you have here, slaver."

Az Zar's landscape had improved little since departing the Caman Altars. Zjensa, the village they now approached, looked much like the previous two: huts made of the reed-like poles growing alongside the Ashaat River; frail, stick fences teetering in the wind, the livestock within too malnourished to trample their prisons; people slogging under water pails and sacks of grain. No one smiled. Lumira responded in kind.

Xaren looked up at her and scowled. "It's not my home. My village is—"

"I meant this." Lumira swept her arm in an arc. "This whole moon-cursed nation of racist, greedy..." She didn't finish. Partially because Xaren looked affronted, but mostly because Grokhion cleared his throat loudly behind her. "I suppose you're an exception."

Xaren mopped his face with his mask, still frowning. His raven-black hair cut against his cheekbones like the night sky against the moons. "I've been a victim of nyrian prejudice, too."

"Haven't we all."

"Humans used to be no better than your kind in their eyes."

"I doubt that."

"It's written in our histories." Xaren took a long pull from his canteen. "The initial migrations thousands of years ago to modern day Neharem and Orillon were spawned by nyrian oppression here. Some nyrians who opposed the politics of that time also journeyed to Neharem for a chance to start anew. The humans who remained in Nyzar—now Az Zar—were driven east and north to the less habitable lands. I'm descended from the eastern clans of what was once Xyrania."

"And your fair-haired friends?"

"The north. Davier's ancestors once occupied what is now skulmor territory."

"The land you just stole back."

Xaren's brow furrowed. "Technically, it was stolen from them then, too."

Lumira snorted. She inclined her chin toward the sky, hands braced on her mount's rump for a stretch. "Seems you're on good terms with the nyrians now."

"They needed human soldiers during the Nyzarian Civil War. We surrendered our territories and joined their war in exchange for citizenship."

"But not in Cadar."

Xaren muttered something unintelligible. A gaunt girl no more than six scurried past his horse with a basket of sticks slung over her back.

Grokhion shook his mane. It caught the sunlight in a show of fiery splendor. "So young. And skinny. I find it hard to believe the capital lacks the resources to care for its people."

"These aren't the capital's people," Xaren replied. "Human villages in Az Zar aren't much better than slave camps. You're free, but many spend their lives working as hard as slaves, if not harder. More move to Or Zahal every day, seeking work in the factories or mines."

"Are you from a village like this?"

Xaren's face darkened. "Worse." He urged his mount ahead of the beridians.

And we'll save that topic for a night of drinking.

Lumira rubbed the crevice in her ear where a chunk had been torn out. A cuff earring Elaysia gave her before departing Neharem adorned the spot below it—the first gift she'd received in decades. Touching it sent a wave of guilt over her.

Grokhion followed the movement of her hand and offered a sympathetic nod. He'd literally dragged her from the temple after Elaysia toppled into the enemy's clutches, and though his quick and dispassionate thinking helped them escape unscathed, she'd hated him for it. They could've fought back. They might've escaped unscathed *with* Elaysia. When they returned with Xaren and the others early the next morning, it was too late. No priests. No tracks. No bodies. They'd even scrubbed the blood off the floor.

Lumira and Grokhion spared the rest of the party the finer details of the incident, including a fabricated tale about Jörd being taken prisoner with Davier and Elaysia. They'd carried the secret since, only conversing in their native language of Hispen when the others rested. Few outsiders spoke the beridian tongue, and given Xaren's swelling bitterness toward his homeland, keeping the others in the dark proved a wise decision.

Xaren insisted a prisoner of value would be brought to the All-Sovereign, so they made for Cadar. The journey was long and grueling. Little game crossed their path, and the villagers wouldn't trade much—not solely because they lacked resources. Although impoverished, the commoners of Az Zar swelled with pride and often refused to service beridians, so they camped outside most nights, catching scraggly hares whenever possible and raiding the occasional garden when Grokhion slept.

And now, here they were, about to enter yet another shithole where her presence was less welcome than a horde of bandits.

Xaren halted a few yards away from the village gates and handed his reins to one of the warriors. "It's best if only a few of us go in."

Lumira nodded and pried Anadu's talons off her saddle. The stormbird squawked in protest. "You know we can't risk taking you in. No telling who watches."

Though attached to their respective Stormriders (that's what Elaysia called them, but Lumira didn't feel they'd earned the titles yet), the stormbirds tolerated the supervision of a gentle Apáasutai named Nikkóla. The nyrian was older and not fond of speaking, which was why all the birds—and Lumira—were taken with her. Save for Onitus. Elaysia's stormbird had hardly eaten since her capture, nor had he made a single sound. Only Lumira could approach him. It made her feel worse.

The warriors made camp by the river beneath a small grove of half-dead trees that shielded them from the prying eyes of the thoroughfare. Anadu hopped over to Onitus, who sat by the bank in his typical statuesque manner.

Lumira crouched beside them. "We'll be back soon."

Onitus narrowed his eyes.

Clever thing. Perhaps a little too clever. "We're trying. Cadar isn't much further. She'll be there." He turned his head away. To her dismay, Anadu mirrored him.

Lumira shook her head and hurried to join Grokhion and Xaren.

Swollen, angry clouds gathered as they approached the gates. Rain soon pooled in the muddied ruts, splattering on indifferent villagers who trudged through them. A boy darted past and approached a white-bearded man with a hunched back. He listened to the boy, expression transforming from placid exhaustion to tight-lipped apprehension, then hobbled inside a hut as fast as his stick-thin legs allowed. The boy scurried to the next villager, then another, whispering in their ears until the majority disappeared into their huts, slamming doors and securing ramshackle window coverings. Someone even left a freshly plucked duck unattended on a butcher's table.

"Beridian hate runs deep here," Lumira muttered, stifling a growl. She wasn't expecting a warm welcome, but to be shunned by the entire village? Grokhion hung his head, and her blood ran hotter. "I'd like to give them a reason to hate me."

Xaren fixed his eyes on one of the huts. "I don't think it's you. The other villages didn't react to you this way. Something else frightens them."

Lumira snatched the duck from the butcher's table and sank her teeth into it, tearing off a chunk of flesh. "What in Quinaria could be more frightening than us?"

Grokhion frowned at her theft, petty as it was. "How far are we from the capital?"

"Several day's ride, according to Xaren." The map had vanished along with Elaysia, so they relied on his local expertise. "Right, boy?" she asked, turning to him.

But he'd shot off, skipping through the square with such grace as to not disrupt the mud, and cornered a woman lugging a cart into the shadows. She tried to run, but Xaren grabbed her arm and spoke in Zarith. Upon seeing the semblance in her kin and hearing her tongue, she stopped struggling and jabbered away, voice high and arms flailing. When she finished, Xaren bowed and helped her push the cart inside.

"What did she say?" Lumira asked when Xaren sprinted back to them. The stillness of the village, now fully vacated, made her tail twitch.

"That they always seek shelter when the sun is highest on the thirteenth day."

"Right."

Xaren dug his fingertips into her arm. "I'm serious. She said the people hide because they don't want to be chosen for tribute."

"Tribute? What does that mean?"

"I don't know, I swear." He didn't. That much was plain in his eyes. "But they fear something. Something they can't fight."

Grokhion grunted and freed *Belzaith* from his back. "We should help them."

"We should leave." Lumira leaned toward Grokhion and whispered in Hispen, "They wouldn't help us."

"That's *why* we should help them," Grokhion said, refusing to reply in their native tongue.

"This isn't up for discussion."

Xaren paced, wringing his hands like a child subjected to bickering parents. "Lumi—"

The sound of hoofbeats throbbed in the distance, stifling his pleas.

Lumira leaped onto the awning hanging over the butcher's table and flipped onto the roof. Not twenty yards out, two dozen horses and their riders approached the village. She couldn't make out their allegiance, and she didn't want to wait until they were close enough to find out. The faces of the frightened villagers permeated her mind.

She landed silently beside Grokhion. "They'll be on us before we make it back to the others."

Grokhion stroked his beard with a sense of calm; at his age, she doubted much alarmed him. "Best assume they're hidden and take shelter ourselves." He headed toward some poorly crafted stalls that didn't scream stable or shelter.

"Over here," Xaren called out, waving them toward a shack that looked one storm away from collapsing. He ducked inside.

Lumira sprinted into the shack, hoofbeats drumming in her ears. She tripped over a rotted board and cursed. The room reeked of shit. "Lovely place you've found. Must've belonged to the last victim."

Xaren rolled his eyes. Grokhion, finished with masking the conspicuous beridian tracks leading to the shack, slipped inside and closed the door. Lumira crouched by the window, spear ready.

An Az Zarian squadron thundered into the square, smashing through gardens and knocking over workbenches, their mounts slathered in sweat and champing at the bit. Someone shouted, and they melted into formation. A soldier broke from the ranks. Although masked like the others, the figure was distinctly female.

"A woman soldier in Az Zar?" Lumira asked.

Xaren shrugged. "It's not unheard of, at least for high-born nyrians."

"How progressive of you people."

Xaren continued as if he hadn't heard her snide remark. "And that's a general besides. See, she wears the embroidered cowl and billowing pants. The three moons on her armband signify the rank."

Lumira wrinkled her nose. All Az Zarian soldiers looked the same to her: pawns of hatred.

The general barked a few commands and dispatched two soldiers to investigate the perimeter of the square. And their shack was up first. Of course, it was.

Lumira tensed as the soldiers approached. Their split toe canvas boots were made to mask sound, but any half-awake beridian could still make out the soft plop of mud as they neared. Barefoot was the only way to guarantee absolute silence, and it made her kind superior hunters.

A soldier, masked head to toe as Davier had been, paused at the threshold of the shack. He swung the door open. Cold light spilled in, stopping at the cusp of Lumira's feet. She looked to Xaren. He gripped his bow, nostrils flaring. She extended her claws. Nudged Grokhion. If they moved swiftly enough, they might escape.

The soldier shouted something in Zarith, followed by footsteps fading away from their shack. Grokhion murmured a prayer and lowered *Belzaith*.

Lumira poked Xaren with the blunt end of her spear. "Why'd he leave?"

Xaren peered through the shutters. "He said they already cleared out this shack on the thirty and fourth day of Onelar."

Lumira shoved him over to make room and pressed her nose against the dusty sill, ears flattened. The soldiers had stopped three shacks down. The bulkier of the two collapsed the door with one swift kick. His companion, bird-like in stature, entered. Someone screamed. The soldier emerged, dragging the boy who'd flitted through the village earlier, warning people. He writhed and shouted until the soldier silenced him with a blow to the face. The boy crumpled in the mud, unconscious.

Xaren gasped and started for the door, but Grokhion clamped onto his arm with a grip few could wriggle out of. The boy tried in vain to jerk his arm away. "Let me help my people."

"You can't help them if you're dead," Grokhion said in his impossibly reasonable voice. "Be strong, lad."

Lumira growled. "Quiet, both of you."

An older man stumbled out of the shack. He hoisted the boy up. His slight frame quivered beneath the dead weight. Lumira didn't need to speak Zarith to understand the emotion strangling his voice.

His son.

The thin soldier kicked him in the stomach. The father crawled to the boy again; earned himself another kick. The female general lurked in silence, like a ravager bird waiting for the predators to clear out. Relentless in his pursuit, the father fell at her feet and babbled through his tears.

"He begs them not to take his only son," Xaren translated, voice cracking. "He offers himself instead."

Lumira averted her gaze from Xaren's crumpled face. It kindled a rage within her.

The general lifted the father's chin with the toe of her boot. She spoke, voice deep and monotone. The father planted his face on the ground, palms upraised to the sky.

"What now, lad?" Grokhion asked.

"She says Az Zar is grateful for his sacrifice; he and his people serve the empire to the utmost of their abilities. He's still begging her to take his son's place."

The general waved a gloved hand in the air as though she shooed a fly, summoning the stocky soldier to restrain the father.

Xaren sniffed. "She says why take the aged goat when there's a fattened lamb?"

The father struggled and hurled curses, but the soldier held firm. Captivated by his passion, Lumira didn't notice the general had disappeared into the formation of soldiers and horses until she emerged with what looked like a weapon, but not any she'd seen before. It had a pommel like a sword, but instead of a blade, it featured a stout tube of shiny metal with a hollowed inside fastened to wood. The general lowered it to the father's head. Hissed in Zarith. Her fingers wrapped around a thin shaft resembling a crossbow's trigger. She pressed the weapon harder into the father's skull while the soldiers grabbed the boy and slung him over a horse.

Xaren no longer required prompting. "She prefers he serve the All-Sovereign willingly, but he'll oblige, regardless."

"What's that weapon?" Lumira whispered.

Before Xaren could reply, the father drove an elbow into the soldier's stomach and lurched for the boy.

The weapon jolted in the general's hands, loosing a blast of yellow-green smoke. The father snapped back as if struck by an arrow, but no visible projectile left the weapon. He collapsed. Blood pooled around his head. Far more blood than any arrow would've drawn.

The taste of metal danced on Lumira's tongue. Her heart thudded in her throat. She backed away from the window to secure a sense of anonymity in the darkness.

The general toed the body over to display the father's twisted expression. She raised the weapon and draped her gaze over the shacks as if saying, *this is what awaits those who dare to challenge the empire*. The villagers crowded their doorways. No one protested. She shouted a final threat, then whistled at the soldiers, who mounted in a flash, taking the unconscious boy with them.

They'd scarcely cleared out when Xaren burst from the shack and raced toward the collapsed father. Grokhion plowed after him.

Lumira forced herself to follow. She focused on the rain tickling her whiskers instead of the chill that seized her blood as she studied the gaping hole in the father's head. She couldn't tell what'd entered. Was it lodged inside?

Xaren knelt over the body and felt for a pulse.

"Anything?" Lumira asked, doubtful. The body was limp with death.

Xaren shook his head and slammed a fist into the mud.

She closed the father's eyes. "Have you seen that weapon before?" she asked again, trying to harness some gentility in her voice.

The villagers began trickling out of their homes and edging toward the body, brows knit in fear.

Xaren shook his head. A woman ran out of the same shack as the deceased man and stolen son. She threw herself over the body, wailing. Xaren reached for her arm timidly, but Lumira grabbed his sleeve.

"Give her space to mourn," Lumira whispered.

They retreated to the stables where Grokhion waited. She grasped the boy's arms. "We need you to focus. Tell us what you know about that weapon. Rumors, guesses, anything."

Grokhion elbowed Lumira in the ribs.

She glared at the elder beridian but released Xaren. "Please?" she added, somewhat grudgingly.

Xaren scowled and rubbed the mud off his clothes. "Military intelligence is on a need–to–know basis, and most of us didn't need to know. It prevents captured soldiers from being easily compromised. If there are answers to be found, they'd be in Or Zahal. That's where all the factories are located."

Refusing to believe he knew *nothing*, Lumira pressed further as they made their way out of the village. "Why did they come for the boy, then? Do you know what that's about?"

Xaren thought for a moment before replying. "When slave labor runs short, the All–Sovereign will force civilians behind on taxes to work as indentured servants in the factories."

"Seems like a lot of effort for one boy," Grokhion mused, ears twitching.

Xaren stopped walking. "Unless *she* needed him."

Lumira exchanged a glance with Grokhion. "Who?"

"The Lord Priestess." A vein threatened to burst from Xaren's forehead. "It wouldn't be the first time people have gone missing on her behalf."

Lumira recalled the greenish-yellow smoke erupting from the hollow tube. The booming sound it made. The father's vacant eyes. "That weapon, it's using nevethium, isn't it? Does the military conduct all nevethium experimentation in Or Zahal?"

Xaren nodded. "The majority of it."

"We're heading there."

"But the high chieftain—"

"She'd want us to investigate. It's what we came here for."

"I agree," Grokhion said. "I'll inform the others." He marched toward the riverbed where their warriors hopefully still waited.

Xaren looked back at the village. His shoulders drooped. "My patriotism blinded me to the injustice of my people. I should've deserted sooner, but maybe I should never have left home. I could be fighting for them."

Lumira set her jaw and regarded Xaren for the boy he was: soft features and innocent eyes masked in a warrior's garb. "No"—she gave his shoulder an awkward punch as she'd seen other humans do—"you were meant to come to Neharem when you did. The high chieftain values your sacrifice. You can make right your wrongdoings and help liberate your people." If he could, maybe, just maybe, she stood a chance at redemption, too.

Xaren narrowed his eyes. "Even if they believed me, now a traitor, they'd never challenge the All-Sovereign."

"He's just a man."

"Perhaps. But the Lord Priestess is not."

ZAVIK

If Zavik were a gambling man, he'd have lost a fortune on his bets placed against T'Vak's ability to stay upright in the saddle while intoxicated. The backhander teetered like a boat in a storm, but he'd always grab his mount's neck right before he fell. This was often followed by laughter and another pull from his wineskin. Assuming it was wine. Doubtful, given the stench on T'Vak's breath. He offered some to Zavik now and again, but it smelled like soured milk and rye. Besides, one of them needed to be aware, even though it should've been the person he'd paid for protection. The one time Zavik had dared to verbalize concern regarding T'Vak's sobriety, he'd earned himself a display of the backhander's weapons via an impromptu sharpening session.

He'd festered in silence since.

When T'Vak wasn't drinking—which was rare—he passed the time with stories of drunken brawls, populum-induced hallucinations, and his non-discriminatory sex life. The latter proved to be the backhander's favorite, and the detail with which he painted the retellings left Zavik flushing for reasons other than the unrelenting sun.

Vulgarities aside, Zavik was grateful for his company. The harsh monotony of the Vashi Desert hadn't lessened since they'd departed Teth days prior, and food was scarce and water scarcer. T'Vak ensured they never lacked sustenance and provided distraction from the discomfort of prolonged riding.

That alone made him a worthwhile investment—that and the two additional bandit attacks he'd thwarted, thus far. Zavik reminded himself of these things when T'Vak drank heavily, as he did now. He wouldn't have made it this far on his wits alone. And it wouldn't be much longer, T'Vak assured him. With luck, they'd find the sacrificial stone tonight.

A snicker assaulted Zavik's contemplation. T'Vak sat sideways in his saddle, facing him, a wide grin plastered on his face.

Zavik fought to mask his irritation. "Can I help you?"

"You ride funny," T'Vak slurred.

"Is there a non-funny way to ride a zaka-zaka? Besides, your technique hardly seems superior."

T'Vak guffawed, brown liquid sloshing out of his wineskin and onto his legs. "It takes talent to do this, my friend. I can teach you." He winked. "I'll be gentle."

Zavik turned away to hide his blush.

The sun began its descent, which meant he could finally remove his hood for the day. He thought of the cool evening winds in Agaas and wished the slightest breeze would kiss his neck. The silken sand rippled endlessly on like an ocean before him, and to his right, a rock formation with a sheer surface not unlike a wall cast a shadow, its height rivaling living trees in Agaas. Though he'd gawked when they'd first come upon it, it'd since grown as tedious as the desert. The Shaktar Caverns were said to lie beyond it. One only had to find the entrance.

And no one ever had.

Zavik caught T'Vak leering and bristled. "Look," he said, straightening his aching back, "I know you think little of me, but—"

"You're a little man, Zavik, Pretender-of-the-Neharem," T'Vak said, smile fading, "but if I thought little of you, you'd already be dead."

Zavik shivered at the thought. "Thanks, I guess." T'Vak apparently found that toast-worthy and took another drink. "I'm not a pretender, though. I've spent more of my life in Neharem than Orillon."

T'Vak raised an eyebrow. "Who said Orillon?"

"I was born here."

"And I was born in a love den. Does that make me a love-giver?"

There wasn't a good way to answer that question. Zavik feigned a cough and looked up at the sky. "We're all our own people, regardless of our backgrounds."

"Clever little lad with your words." T'Vak bit into day-old roasted snake and swallowed it whole. "Enough about me. You've only told me our destination and your name, neither of which fascinates me. Regale me with a story of your Orillon roots."

"There's little to tell." *But if it will shut you up for a while, I'll oblige.* "My mother sought a new life in Neharem when I was eight and found a place in Agaas as a cook. I've remained there since. There was nothing for me here."

"Old man's dead?"

Zavik threaded his hand through his sleeve to rub the scar on his forearm. He clenched his teeth. "Yes."

"Sorry." T'Vak offered a well-meaning nod.

"He was nothing to mourn."

T'Vak didn't pry further.

Zavik was nodding off in his saddle when T'Vak pulled his mount to an abrupt stop, startling both him and his zaka-zaka.

Darkness engulfed the canyon, but he could just make out a crudely carved slab of rock with a few bindings staked to it. The sacrificial stone? The wall behind it remained unbroken, no entrance in sight.

Zavik groaned. What had he expected? A long-sought, mythical location to appear for him because he wanted it *badly*? For all he knew, Lanston sent him on a wild hunt for a good story to tell the girls at Oasis. Zavik pulled out the map and rubbed his eyes, wincing as sand scratched them.

"Maybe we missed the magic door," T'Vak said, tone drenched in sarcasm.

Zavik ignored him and slid off the zaka-zaka (whom he'd be perfectly fine never seeing again). He'd ridden more the past moon cycle than his twenty-three years combined, and he missed his little loft more than ever. As if sensing his disdain, the beast twitched its long ears back and snorted through flared nostrils as he limped away, legs threatening to buckle beneath him.

The sacrificial stone was just as disappointing up close; a makeshift altar smeared in brown stains. Likely old blood. He cursed and kicked it with all the venom he could muster. Pain pulsated through his foot. He screamed and kicked it again, albeit lighter. Vitality depleted, he curled up on the stone and shut his eyes.

T'Vak shook him. "Eat something."

Zavik opened his eyes to T'Vak dangling a snake above his head. Sandflies swarmed it. He recoiled.

T'Vak took a bite with a sickening crunch and chewed, face radiating satisfaction.

"I'm not hungry," Zavik snapped. He was hungry, but for venison and berries. Not fly food.

"You need strength for the return trip. Can't have you dying before I get my reward."

"I'm not going back emptyhanded." Zavik snatched the snake and took a bite before reason could stop him. He held his breath to dull the taste. The dried out and gummy texture was bad enough.

"And I'm not staying here." T'Vak loomed over him, playful disposition gone. "We ride at dawn."

"Not if you want pay," Zavik muttered as he rolled onto his back.

T'Vak responded with the sound of metal sliding from a scabbard. Before Zavik could react, the backhander brought the blade down. Metal bashed against stone. Upon registering no pain, Zavik dared a glance. A severed scorpion oozed gel inches from his arm.

T'Vak wiped his blade on Zavik's tunic. "Hate for you to end up the sacrifice. Legend has it the shaktar prefer soft, naïve bodies like yours."

Zavik shivered. He'd grown up with tales of the shaktar like all Orillon children. If you didn't behave, they'd fly in through the window at night, sing you to sleep, and take you back to their caverns to eat you. The first people of Orillon were said to have sacrificed their own to appease the creatures' appetites. Some of the desert clans still did.

"Give me an hour," he said, remounting his disgruntled zaka-zaka. "There's got to be a break in the wall somewhere."

There wasn't.

Zavik returned hours later, shoulders slumped and mount in tow. T'Vak lounged across the sacrificial stone, wineskin in hand. He raised it to his lips, then dropped it, eyes wide and fixed above Zavik.

Don't move, T'Vak mouthed. He unsheathed his sword.

Silence stifled the desert. Not a shuffle in the dirt, nor a menacing growl. No gnashing teeth. But Zavik obeyed; he'd never seen the backhander shook. He held his breath, fearing one inhale would trigger his doom.

The zaka-zaka yanked the reins from his grasp and bolted. Zavik froze, planted like a wisp of a flower in the path of a wildfire as his mount barreled into T'Vak's. They both disappeared screaming into the night.

"Move your ass," T'Vak cried. "It's jumping off the fucking wall!"

Zavik never knew he could move so fast. Blood rushed in his ears, masking all other sounds. He didn't hear the *thud* behind him. But he felt it.

Though his body pleaded against it, Zavik faced his killer.

A warm rush trickled down his legs.

It had no eyes. Countless spikes sprouted from its armored, loft-sized skull. A bug-like exterior wrapped its torso and continued down its spiked club tail and four limbs—all ending in claws twice the size of T'Vak's sword. Its teeth were no less fearsome: row upon row of rotten, spear-sharp fangs. It threw its head back and released a roar that vibrated the ground.

Stiffly, Zavik retreated to the illusion of safety that was T'Vak. The backhander's face paled, sword dangling loosely at his side. "If you've any gods, best pray to them now."

"No." Zavik scrambled behind his protector. "I think we're alone here." His jaw quivered as the monster loosed another cry. It darted around them with surprising agility given its size, vibrating the ground and blocking their escape. Zavik dove under the sacrificial stone, breath catching in ragged rasps.

"What're you doing?" T'Vak shouted as he sprinted toward the wall. "Stay with me."

Zavik mustered enough courage to slink out after him. T'Vak banked right, but the monster leaped over and slid to cut them off, creating a wave of dust. They tried for the left. It matched them. No matter where they ran, it herded them back, narrowing the gap each time until it cornered them against the wall. Zavik dropped to his knees, fear overtaken by fatigue.

T'Vak slashed his blade on the ground, eyes crazed as a cat's before a storm. "What do you wait for? Kill us, you fucking shit." The curved blade flew from his hand like a dagger and bounced off the monster's scales with a clank. It bared its teeth but came no closer.

"I don't think it can." Zavik drew his knees to his chest. The longer he watched the creature, the more it reminded him of a domesticated dog than a ravenous monster. "Kill us, I mean. It would've already. It's as if someone controls it."

The creature stopped snarling and twitched, head angled toward the sky. It charged. Zavik winced, but it sailed over them, locked onto the wall, and climbed straight up like a lizard before vanishing over the side.

"That's our cue to—"

A torrent of shrieks drowned T'Vak's voice. Silhouettes of winged creatures, the forms of nightmares, littered the sky.

Shaktar.

Zavik stumbled back and grabbed T'Vak's thick arm.

The backhander shook him off and sprinted for his sword. "There aren't too many. We can take them."

Zavik remained rooted. He knew he should be terrified, but excitement bubbled in his chest as one of the winged Vysilliam landed before him, glaring. At least, it resembled a glare. Albeit an indifferent one. It stood no more than five feet tall with muddied skin stretched tightly over its unclothed body. No genitalia. No bellybutton. Stocky, veiny limbs. Nothing to contrast its skin besides its eyes: large, diamond-shaped, and black as night.

Its face haunted him the most. It might've been the way its pointed ears crumpled down near the tips, the flattened nose with upraised nostrils, or the sharp bottom fangs that jutted above its upper lip. Most likely, it was the wisps of hair dangling from the back of its head.

T'Vak rejoined Zavik and leveled his sword at the shaktar. "Don't try anything, demon." The shaktar hardly seemed impressed. "Zavik, take out your poor excuse for a knife."

At least a dozen shaktar encircled them. They shuffled on stumpy legs, winged arms dragging in the dirt, their wispy hair blowing behind them like strands of spider webs. Zavik lowered T'Vak's sword and cleared his throat.

"We seek your counsel, shaktar, first of the races and greatest of the Vysilliam," he said in Nyrinian.

They stared at him, unblinking.

"I thought they'd be able to speak Nyrinian," Zavik mumbled in Westmun.

T'Vak glowered at the shaktar. "You don't know their tongue?"

Zavik shook his head. Few alive could read—much less speak—Shaktari. Konar, maybe. Not that it helped him presently.

"*We speak all the languages of Quorath, including those unwritten and unspoken,*" a sea of voices replied. The sound echoed through the canyon, but none of the thin lips in front of him moved.

Zavik's mouth gaped. "Are you hearing this, T'Vak?"

This time, a single voice replied. *"We have no desire to speak with him. His eyes remain shut, his ears unopened."*

Zavik peered over his shoulder and gasped. T'Vak lay in the dirt, eyes closed. Zavik hurried to his side and checked for a pulse. Alive. But no matter how hard Zavik shook him, he wouldn't wake.

"He will be fine. Come."

"But—"

"We will not ask again."

They made for the wall. A song arose in a soft language, rich in vowels and elegance, the tone not unlike the eunuch choirs of Munskahan. Zavik stumbled after them, ghostly melody calming his racked stomach. When they reached the rockface, it split from bottom to top in an unwavering line and parted to create an entrance to the caverns. Zavik pulled up, gawking at the immense crevice. Impossible.

"The wall is not patient."

It was not. As soon as Zavik staggered in—which took a moment since the wall was roughly a quarter-mile thick—it slammed shut with a bone-jarring thud, leaving not so much as a crack to suggest an entrance. *Not going back that way, am I?*

He touched the outline of the knife in his boot. "Lead on."

Moonlight spilled from gaps in the cavern ceiling and onto the path. It reeked of treachery, marred by jagged rock formations and sudden holes that increased in severity the further they ventured. The shaktar hovered in indifference, leathery wings beating, while Zavik struggled through the maze. Whenever he caught glimpses of others perched on ledges, blackened eyes shrouded in perfect anonymity, a chill ran down his spine.

They came to a tunnel that required Zavik to crawl. The shaktar disappeared through a crevice above, and he reluctantly pressed his palms to the cold edges of the stone to begin his solitary journey. The deeper he went, the more the space condensed. He dropped onto his elbows and stomach to squirm through. Rocks jabbed his belly and snagged his clothes. When there was no room left between him and the tunnel walls, a stream of light caught his eye. Eager to stand, he moved faster, eyes on the light.

The ground gave way beneath him. A sick puff of air filled his stomach as he careened down. He fought the sense of helplessness, the tightening of his chest, the racing of his heart, as though he could stop the fall through sheer will.

He landed in a brittle pile with a clatter and scrambled down as fast as his cramped limbs would allow. Only then did he dare a glance at what cushioned his fall.

Bones. They lay there in a jumbled heap that towered halfway to the ceiling, spears of moonlight illuminating their cracked and worn surfaces. A pile of the past, a warning for the future. His blood ran cold.

Brilliant, Zav. Just brilliant. You've served them up a fresh sacrifice.

Zavik took in the room. The rock walls bore the same ruddy colors and sharp edges of the cavern. Unless he sprouted wings, there wasn't a way out.

"We know what you seek."

Zavik spun toward the source of the voices. Three shaktar lurked above the bone pile, seated cross-legged on perches. He couldn't tell if they were the ones who'd led him to his doom; they all looked identical. One fluttered down. It beckoned him with clawed fingers.

Nails digging into his palms, Zavik took a step toward it. Another. Two more. His body was stone, breath shallow. When he reached the shaktar, he squared his shoulders and released all his tension in a winded, anxiety-ridden outpour.

"I've come on behalf of Elaysia Moonrider, high chieftain of Neharem, who begs you to lend her the Prophets' Scrolls, should you still hold them. Nevethium has fallen prey to greed. War is on the horizon, and we are vastly outnumbered. We seek the means to protect ourselves and the heart of Quinaria."

"*The scrolls cannot be trusted to the races of land.*" The voices strained thin, as if they'd snap in an instant. "*The ones in your possession have proven that already, Zavik of Az Zar.*"

"I'm from Oril—"

"*You are from Orillon as much as you are from Neharem,*" another voice answered.

"*Where you are from matters not to us,*" another quipped, "*although, to you, it should matter a great deal.*"

Zavik's heart throbbed in his throat. He forced himself to meet the abysses that were their eyes. "I don't understand. We don't have any scrolls."

"*Years have we worked to keep you from tearing each other and Quinaria apart, yet you have still created imbalance.*" The shaktar in front of him flexed its wings as if it made to leave.

Panic seized Zavik's voice. "If you've read my thoughts, then you know our intentions are pure. There are others not so well-meaning. The high chieftain seeks to restore balance."

"*The scrolls are chaos, not balance,*" a single voice replied.

"*They do not protect,*" said another, "*but enlighten. They are of the gods. Of Quorath. It is too risky. Your kind is unworthy.*"

Zavik's gaze wandered to the bone pile. He wouldn't fail her. Not again.

He thrust his knife onto the ground.

"Take me as a sacrifice. Bring the scrolls to Elaysia. You'll see she's worthy."

The shaktar ambled toward him. Zavik winced as it snatched his hand and pricked his palm with its claw. It tasted his blood.

Its eyes rolled back in its head revealing a murky white, then it chuffed and fluttered back to its post.

"Um, I—"

"*He is worthy,*" it said. "*The blood tells true,*" echoed another. "*But only confusion can be exchanged for knowledge. Only darkness for light.*"

The shaktar who'd pricked him swooped down with not one, but three scrolls clutched in its feet. Zavik reached for them, then hesitated. The cool grip of fear tightened around his throat.

"What do you ask for in return?"

"*It remains to be seen,*" the voices said in unison. "*It could be asked of you tonight. It could be the end of time. But you must pay it when demanded of you, no matter the cost.*"

"How will I know?"

"*Balance will tell,*" said one.

"*Time will tell,*" said another. "*You will know.*"

Zavik thought of Elaysia. Not of her duties. Not of his potential debt. Just the look on her face the moment he presented the scrolls.

"*The night grows old to be supplanted by a young day,*" they said. "*What is your decision?*"

Zavik stepped forward and held out his hand.

DAVIER

Davier halted his mount at the crest of the hill. Sunlight clawed through the clouds, scattering the residual morning fog that smothered the valley below. It seemed impossible that only days prior they'd abandoned the red desert and traded rock mounds and spiny grass for flourishing fields and slim-leafed trees with tender stalks. Their trail unfurled around the mountainside and disappeared beneath the full-breasted greenery of the forest. It would reemerge on a cliffside with an unmatched view of Az Zar.

Then home. At least, the one he wanted to remember. He'd grown up in the fertile lands once drafted, and visits to his family's house seldom occurred. The sooner he got them out of there, the better.

Elaysia stopped her horse beside his and leaned back, palms on its rump. "It's less hideous than I expected."

Davier shrugged. "So were you."

Elaysia's eyes widened. Her mouth curled into a scowl. Still, he detected a sense of good humor about her. She hadn't spoken to him for days after his blunder in the cave, but lately, her mood changed with the scenery.

"Not all Az Zar is a wasteland, nor all her people evil," he added softly.

"I wouldn't dare judge an entire nation based on the actions of its leader, Captain Zadel." With a tilt of her chin, she rode out in front of him. "Not that the people I've met here have proven otherwise."

Davier rolled his eyes at the flippant use of his title, but his gaze lingered on the arc of her hips, the way her legs hugged the curve of her mount's flanks, fingers intertwined in the mane. For all the finesse of a lady she lacked, she rode better than most of his soldiers. If she discovered his intention before they reached Cadar, she'd vanish in an instant, and he'd never catch her.

He clenched his teeth and forced his gaze down.

A breeze swirled around him, carrying the nutty aroma of kuba plants, and it prompted a vision of his mother making porridge from the nutrient-dense grains. They'd struggled to survive in Or Zahal, as most did, but his parents always worked hard and maintained steadfast pride. It'd been over a year since he'd seen them. The longest gap yet. How much had the girls grown? Did Eumma still pray daily for his safety? Was Eudna in good health? They'd beam when he returned decorated in a colonel's uniform.

"You're quiet today," Elaysia said.

She tugged on the torn sleeve of her tunic as if its fibers would magically reknit to cover her down to the wrist. The other arm was fully exposed, thanks to a run-in with some thick brush the night before. Davier squinted at the cream patch on her upper arm. A tattoo he hadn't noticed before adorned it: three feathers above a filled circle, with arrows pointed inward on both sides.

"What?" She followed his gaze and snorted. "Oh. Are tattoos so rare here?"

"Forbidden," he said, relieved she'd forgotten her initial question. "What does it mean?"

She pointed to the feathers. "A mark of three signifies the role of high chieftain; a chief would have one symbol. I chose feathers because of the relationship my family, the Moonriders, had with the stormbirds. Never thought I'd follow in their footsteps." She chewed her lip, eyes darkened by some unknown memory. "And this"—she gestured to the arrows and circle—"wards off evil spirits."

"How's that worked out for you?"

"You're here, so not very well."

Davier bit back a smile as she slipped off her horse.

"Honestly, I seem to attract trouble wherever I go. Konar says I was born under a blood moon."

"And that means?"

"I'll bring war." She pressed her leg against a tree to stretch.

Davier dismounted and pretended to busy himself with his horse's hooves while he watched her.

"It all sounds ridiculous to you, doesn't it?"

"No more than stormbirds taking to the skies again."

"They're a way's off from that still." Worry flicked across her face. "We need to find them. They're more vulnerable here than I thought."

"You told Xaren to return to Neharem if we didn't come back," Davier offered. "He's a good soldier. I'm sure he followed orders."

"And Lumira and Grokhion?"

Davier feigned checking his mount's saddle. "Could be they await us in Cadar." *Could be they ran off as their kind often does. Could be they're already dead.*

"Could be."

Davier's foot slipped out of the stirrup. "What?"

Elaysia's eyes shone like gems in the sunlight, betraying her nyrian roots. "I agreed with you? As in, yes, that's a possibility?"

Damn it. Get out of your head, Zadel. "Right, sorry."

He mounted and ran his fingers through his hair, gaze lost in the sea of green ahead. The same green as her right eye.

Eyes that were hot on his back. Did she know? She didn't act suspicious. Shouldn't that make him feel worse? He bit down on his lip hard. She was royal, at least to the extent they had royalty in Neharem. The All-Sovereign would use her as leverage for the birds and allegiance, and that would be the end of it. She'd live out her life, and he'd live out his. Besides, if he didn't do it, someone else would, and they'd get his reward. Better him. He might even persuade the All-Sovereign to let her companions live. If he received the stormbirds and fealty, what would it matter?

She'd hate you the rest of her life. Does that matter?

"What's that?" Elaysia pointed to a trail branching off from the main road to the right. It was a switchback path that vanished into the mountainside.

"Looks like a warning to stay on the main road." Davier dug his fingernails into the reins and pressed on. She didn't follow. "Come on, we're making good time."

Elaysia tucked a loose strand of hair back into her braid. "There are fresh tracks and droppings. Can't be more than a day or two old. What if Lumira and the others went up there? It won't take more than an hour to make sure."

"That's a bit optimistic. More likely to run into thieves or something worse." Davier searched the trail for justification. "Besides, it gets too steep for the horses halfway up. We'd have to tether them and finish on foot."

"Good. I could use some time on my feet." Elaysia took off cantering toward the trail.

Fuck. If she got herself killed, he was as good as dead, too. He trotted after her, cursing all the while.

Sweaty and horseless, they summited as the sun reached its highest point in the sky, their reward an entrance to a cave no larger than Davier was tall. Light poured into its crevices, bending around the twisted formations. It was heavy with dampness, and the air smelled of algae and rich soil. Elaysia brushed past him and vanished into the darkness, her footsteps silent as a beridian.

Davier gave a longing look down the hillside. Unclenched his fists. Clenched them again. This mission had well exceeded what he signed up for.

He took a step inside.

"What exactly are you hoping to find?" The gruffness in his voice reverberated off the cave walls.

"Adventure," she called back, heavy with sarcasm.

"There's no such thing. It's just the feeling you get when coming across something foreign to you. You eventually learn it's all the same." Davier dodged a stalagmite the size of a child hanging above. Drops of water ran down its slick surface and pooled into puddles beneath. "I've had my fill of adventure."

"You're endlessly charming." The tip of Elaysia's braid flashed between a gap in the rocks. "Have you always been this cynical? Didn't you have aspirations as a child?"

"I wanted to be a soldier." He jumped atop a flat rock that sparkled in the remaining light. She poked her head around another and wrinkled her nose. "I mean, I had little choice."

"You never dreamed of something else?"

She was gone before he could reply. He dashed around the corner, nearly slamming into her.

"Sailing," he whispered. The heat of her body radiated in the darkness. She smelled of campfire smoke and wild berries. "I dreamed of sailing to the uncharted isles in the far north. Above skulmor territory." Her lips were inches from his. His heart raced.

"What's stopping you? You aren't contracted to me."

The breath caught in his throat. He considered an excuse and, for a moment, the truth:

Because I'm contracted to another, your freedom the price for mine.

And at what cost? For all his praise, the All–Sovereign regarded Davier as little higher than his underling dwarf, scurrying about Quinaria to carry out tasks too unclean for his holy hands. A decorated bitch. But what else was there? This was the only path to see his dreams through. The only one that saw his family flourish.

He said nothing.

Elaysia sighed and ventured further into the cave, leaving a cold shadow in her absence.

An emptiness ached in Davier's chest. He slammed his fist against the rock until his hand went numb.

They emerged at the foot of a stone bridge stretched thin over a ravine. Roughly thirty feet to the other side and—Davier peered over the cliff—three times that distance to the ground. A gust of wind crashed into them, followed by kisses of rain. Cracks scarred the bridge's surface, and moss sprouted from the scowling faces carved into its sides. The eyes seemed to track his movements.

"I don't know about this." Davier pressed his boot to the surface, expecting the stone to crumble. It didn't. He grumbled, stepping back. "There weren't any signs of travelers in the cave. We're wasting time."

"We've come this far. Aren't you curious what's on the other side?" Elaysia pressed her hand against his chest to guide him out of the way. She let it linger.

Davier wrapped his hand over hers. "A little."

He dared a step closer. She backed away.

"I'll go first. Lighter, you know. I can make sure it's safe."

The sting of her rejection surprised him. "Whatever you say, High Chieftain."

She rolled her eyes and started across, bridge holding strong under her slight frame. Davier lowered one foot, then the other. No trouble greeted him, so he followed, quickening his pace as he went.

He was two-thirds of the way across when he heard a *crack*.

Toes ground into his boots, he froze and clung to the waist-high railing. Elaysia looked back, mouth agape, and crouched. Another *crack*. Another. Chunks of rock fell away beneath them.

Davier quelled his desire to run. "Keep going. Same pace. Nice and easy."

He pried his hand from the railing and crept forward as more pieces of the bridge plunged into the ravine. The rain came down in sheets. Black skies. Violent wind. His rage swelled with the storm. Why had he let her come this way?

A voice cut through the downpour.

Davier craned his neck. A figure clad in black robes and a lyvium mask with slits for eyes stood at the foot of the bridge. A flail hung at his side. Temple guards? This far from Cadar?

"I said halt in the name of His Holiness," the temple guard shouted.

"He can't reach us in time," Elaysia urged. "Come on."

The temple guard whistled. Two more guards emerged with readied bows.

Davier held up his hands. "We're travelers. We mean no harm."

"Then come hither that Mavet may determine the intent of your passage." The archers stepped onto the bridge.

"Elaysia," Davier started, but she was gone, sprinting across the bridge. "Slow down!"

It was too late. The ground crumbled beneath her feet, sending her plummeting toward the ravine. She snagged the ledge with one hand.

Davier's scream scraped his throat as he raced toward her. Elaysia brought her other hand to the ledge, struggling to find purchase. An arrow zinged past him, barely missing its mark. He sidled up to the remaining railing. Grabbed the back of her tunic. Another arrow whizzed by. With a grunt, he lifted her up and tossed her ahead. She scrambled to safety and sent the last chunk of the bridge careening down from her weight. The gap was longer than he was tall. He skidded to a halt at the edge.

Someone screamed behind him. More crumbling stone. He dared a glance. One of the temple guards had vanished along with a section of the bridge. The other backed away slowly, stringing another arrow.

"You can make it." Elaysia drew her bow, teeth bared. She loosed an arrow. It struck the other archer in the neck. "Davier, now!"

No room left for a running start. Davier coiled and sprung over the gap, stretching his arms forward. He latched onto the rock and clawed until his fingers were bloody.

Elaysia reached over the ledge. "Take my hand."

He peeled a hand free to catch hers. Her eyes bulged as she struggled to heave him up, and though much of the feat fell to him, he couldn't have made it without her. When he finally reached the surface, he scrambled inside the mouth of the new cave for shelter. Elaysia collapsed beside him.

"Where's the last guard?" he rasped.

"He fled."

Davier peered across the ravine. No bridge. No temple guards.

Had the All-Sovereign sent them? No. Even if they were searching for him, they couldn't have known he'd end up here, which meant they were hiding something in the mountains.

And Davier wasn't sure he wanted to find out.

He clenched his fists and winced. The rock had ripped patches of skin off his palms. He poured wine to clean the wound and tore off a strip of his tunic to wrap it.

Elaysia cleared her throat. "Well, this is... exciting."

"That's a nice way of saying we're fucked. I told you we shouldn't have left the road. Now we have no mounts and no path. You're lucky we brought our packs."

The smile fell from Elaysia's face. "I didn't know your friends would join us."

"How dare I suggest you take any blame, High Chieftain. Forgive me."

"There's no one to blame. Unless you knew they were coming." She leaned toward him, hand clutching an arrow. "Is that why you tried to stop me?"

"You caught me. Care to end it now? Duel? I'll even lose a sword to make it a fair fight." Davier held her gaze. If those guards—guards he had *nothing* to do with—ruined his ploy now...

"I'm sorry." She backed away and pulled her knees to her chest. "Sorry you're hurt. I thought—hoped—we'd find the others."

Guilt pressed on Davier like the cave's shadows. "It's naught but a scratch." He offered her a hand up. She refused, rightly so. "Maybe we'll find them yet. After you, my lady."

The new cave was more treacherous than the first, overrun with steep drop-offs and jagged rocks. Their only salvation was a radiating sphere of green cast by the nevethium in Elaysia's hand. At least an hour passed without a word between them. Davier was about to suggest they stop for food and drink when Elaysia gasped.

"What in Haeshol?" She shoved the crystal into her pouch. A new blueish light, much fainter than nevethium, illuminated her face.

Davier rubbed his eyes. Blue and white luminescent tubes clung to the ceiling with stringy bits hanging down like falling stars. They swayed gently, but there was no wind to move them.

Though the creatures were at least twenty feet above, Elaysia reached her arms up as though she meant to touch them, her eyes catching their glow. Davier wished he could collect some of her wonder and save it for days when he no longer felt like living. Maybe part of him wished he could collect *her*.

He didn't realize how long he'd stared until she spun to meet his gaze. Heat flooded his cheeks.

"Had enough time with your new friends?" he asked as disinterested as possible.

"No. I prefer their company to yours."

She brushed against him as she passed. There was no need. The space was plenty big enough. His skin came alive with her touch.

"I can see where the path continues now. Let's go."

Davier tucked his hands into his armpits and followed, the dampness weighing on him like a cold, wet blanket.

"Hardy little things," Elaysia called over her shoulder. "They thrive here where there's nothing. No sunlight, water, nutrients."

"You speak as though they're alive."

"You assume they aren't? Everything from rocks to clouds brims with life. We all share this world. This journey. Even when something dies, it returns to Quorath to give something else life."

Davier didn't reply. A pretty thought, but death was finite. Everyone learned that. Eventually.

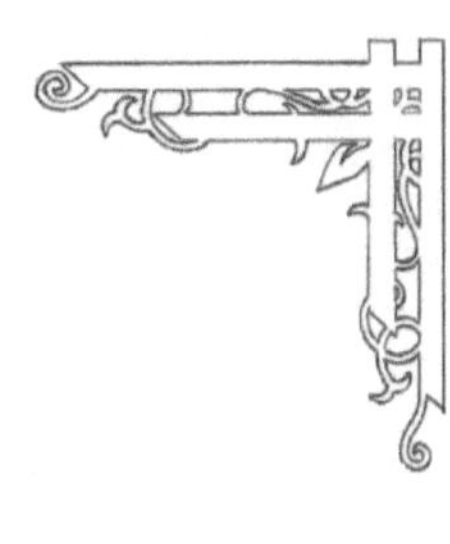

LUMIRA

Lumira hated Or Zahal the moment she laid eyes on it. Thanks to excessive mining of local nevethium, the landscape was scarcely superior to the shriveled villages of the outer regions. Large Mavist banners hung from a crumbling stone wall lined with beggars and other undesirables, and a handful of soldiers trudged across the ramparts and leaned out from the watchtowers. The road to the gate was so crusted in shit she could hardly decipher it from the dirt. It was also stifling hot, and her nose had gone dry.

And Xaren wanted to make it worse.

Lumira eyed the rough spun tunics in his hand and scowled. "I'm not wearing that. If my freedom makes the locals uncomfortable, all the better."

Grokhion stood beside her, arms crossed and teeth bared in un-Grokhion like fashion. They'd decided it'd be easier for the three of them to enter alone and left the rest of the warriors camped a safe distance away in the steppe with the stormbirds. On their way to the gates, however, Xaren led them past a small enclosure piled with loose mounds of dirt. It was a massive, unmarked graveyard for slaves and servants, and to her horror, Xaren had turned the soil up on multiple bodies until he located tunics fitting for her and Grokhion.

Xaren wiped the sweat from his furrowed brow. "Please, Lumira. Without this disguise, you'll be accosted before we even make it to the gates."

"Good. I'm itching for a fight."

"You can't take on the whole city."

"I'd paint it in slaver blood before they—"

"Lumira." Grokhion stilled her with a touch. "The government is poisoned, not her people."

Lumira spat. "Compliance is solidarity."

"Sometimes compliance is survival." Grokhion retrieved the tunics from Xaren. "I understand your reasoning, lad. We'll play along. Just know we don't assume this role lightly."

Lumira snatched a tunic and marched toward some densely packed brush to strip off her chest wrap, belt, and sashes. She touched each of the arrowheads on her necklace. They'd adorned her chest for half a century, and she wasn't removing them now. Tunic on and pride suppressed, she trudged back to her companions.

Grokhion looked up as she approached. His arms and neck tore the seams of his tunic, and his chest threatened to burst through the fabric should he move suddenly. "Convincing?" he asked.

"Undeniably." Lumira stifled a laugh, then glared at Xaren who'd transformed back into a soldier. "No one will take us for slaves."

"We don't have a choice." Xaren's voice was timid. His eyes darted beneath his mask. "And we'll need to bury your weapons here. Slaves shouldn't be armed."

"Neither should slavers," Lumira muttered.

"We'll follow your lead, lad," Grokhion said, eyeing Lumira. "The rest is in Khiev-Tatamic's hands."

Xaren's plan worked. The guards didn't so much as bat an eye at his uniform, much less at the *slaves* accompanying him.

Inside, Or Zahal looked like a small village that'd been built upon again and again until it could host the population of a city. There was little order to it all. A temple here, an academy there. Wooden houses were jammed in thick rows lining the streets, some stacked two or three stories high with frightfully thin balconies. Chatter arose from the locals as they milled about the main square, rushing to complete the day's work before merchants closed shop. They passed well-stocked market stalls displaying no shortage of imported goods: Orillon cheeses, Daruk furs, casks of Beridian Moonlight. A butcher's cart bustled by, rousing Lumira's stomach with the scent of blood. As the elderly merchant turned a corner, she snatched a raw steak off the edge of the cart. Grokhion's eyes narrowed.

Lumira tore off a chunk with her teeth and swallowed it whole. "Too good for stolen slaver meat? This isn't Neharem." She offered him some, but he shook his head and frowned. "Your loss. You'll regret it when you're eating your ragged, day-old hares for the hundredth time tonight."

Xaren motioned to them, eyes creased with worry. "Hurry, we need to get to the South District before sundown, otherwise we'll look suspicious." He marched down the street.

Lumira inhaled the rest of the meat and stole a wineskin for good measure before following.

As the moons rose and street urchins climbed poles to light lanterns (Or Zahal flaunted no public display of nevethium), the stone road gave way to dirt, and rickety shacks replaced the tiered houses. Dogs with protruding ribs raced through waste trenches in pursuit of an abandoned carcass, stirring up the stench of feces. Lumira peered into the fray of snapping jaws and bloodied flesh as they passed. The fur on her back raised. She blinked, wishing the scene away. The dogs weren't tearing into a beast, but a small human girl no more than eight. Death hollowed her eyes. Her stick-thin legs bent at unnatural angles.

Xaren touched Lumira's arm. "The city's overrun with poor villagers seeking work in the factories. Few have the means to take orphans in, and those who can do not."

Lumira flattened her ears and turned from the carnage. "Your nation has every means necessary to take care of its people. This is what becomes of unchecked greed."

"We could... bury her?" Xaren whispered.

"The dogs need to eat. Lead on. The sooner we rid ourselves of this place, the better."

Xaren trudged forward, shoulders slumped. Before they turned the corner, Lumira caught Grokhion closing the girl's eyes.

The South District—better known as the Slave District—began with a large dirt clearing enclosed in a barbed fence twice Lumira's height. Two sentries prowled the perimeter, streamlined swords at their sides with blades too pristine to have seen battle. Rows of longhouses layered the inside of the pen like a field of crops. No light in the windows, no movement within. Ragged clothes stained brown with sweat dangled from a line above the only water source: a large barrel slick with algae.

"It's quiet as a tomb," Grokhion said once the sentries passed. "Where are they?"

"They aren't allowed out after dark unless their work demands it," Xaren said.

Grokhion's claws extended, then retracted. The movement was fast, subtle, but Lumira noted the slight loss of control, the way his pupils constricted into slits. "Common beasts in Orillon are treated better than this."

Xaren's dark eyelashes brushed his cheeks. "Not everyone believes this is right, but what can anyone do? It's always been this way."

"You're doing something." She allowed him this one kindness. He wasn't like the others, and he deserved to know it.

"I, uh... thank you?" Xaren stammered.

"Not that it will matter if you don't get us to the moon-cursed factories safely." She crossed her arms and glared past him in the direction of the sentries, but not without catching Grokhion's devilish smirk out of the corner of her eye.

"This way."

Xaren darted around the pen and down another alley. It wound behind a guardhouse and dumped them outside a corral overstuffed with gaunt cattle. Xaren froze, cocking his head like a rodent alerted to prey, then scampered down a narrow path next to the grain shed. It dropped so steeply in some parts that the boy skidded on the dirt during his descent, and Lumira had to dig her claws in to avoid doing the same. At the bottom was a clearing roughly the size of a small village. It was a newer addition with pristine walls and leftover brush from the natural world, and in the center stood a round, wooden structure with a dome-shaped roof. Two smaller buildings hemmed it on either side, likely more guardhouses. A faint green ambiance showed through the central domed roof, and the clanking sound of metal on metal echoed within.

Lumira scanned for sentries and, upon locating them, frowned. "Only four on duty for a perimeter this size?"

Xaren pulled out hooded cowls for her and Grokhion. "The majority of the factories are in the Labor District. Most of the goods are there, so are most of the guards. This is a special location. Experimental."

"And you're sure it's here?"

"They wouldn't risk testing weapons in the public eye. Too many indentured servants and civilians work in the Labor District. Slaves don't talk, and if they do—"

"No one believes them, anyway."

Lumira forced her tail inside the tunic and tugged the mask over her face. It smashed her ears and weakened the sensitivity of her whiskers, but it was best to pose as human to minimize detection. On her signal, they snaked across the clearing, sticking to the shadows. The two sentries patrolling were her first targets. Once they fell out of each other's line of sight, she yanked one behind the smaller building and drew her claws across his throat. Two swords were her reward. His cohort met the same demise.

When she circled back around, Xaren and Grokhion had taken down—but not killed—the two posted at the entrance. One lay unconscious. The other clutched his wounded arm and spewed rapid phrases in Zarith. Before her companions could react, she lobbed off the sentries' heads in two swift strokes. Xaren gasped. Grokhion regarded her as a disappointed father might.

"Those were unnecessary kills," he growled.

Lumira rolled her eyes. "You've lived among the Ni'anko too long. This is how we survive."

Xaren approached her with a trembling sword. "That man surrendered. You murdered him."

"Better him than us. We have no rope; what would've pre-vented them from escaping and rallying the city guard?"

Xaren seethed beneath his mask, but he didn't object further.

"Help bring the bodies around back. Now." She dragged one sentry to a bin filled with scrap metals. His pockets jingled as she heaved him up. Perfect. Keys in hand, she marched back to the entrance and, after a few tries, unlocked it.

The clanking echoed loud enough through the chamber to mask her entry; with any luck, it had dulled the scuffle with the sentries, too. She slipped into the shadows to survey the room. It was much warmer inside, due to the lack of windows. Level upon level stretched above her, each exposed to the central floor with small railings offering the only protection from a fall. A tower of balconies, and the windowed dome above it all. Curious structure. Perhaps so one could monitor the building's activities regardless of location?

Dust covered an assortment of tools scattered atop rows of tables on the main level. She ran her paw through the film. It came back glinting silver and gold and gave her a tingling sensation. She brushed it off as Xaren and Grokhion crept in beside her, blades drawn. They climbed to the second level with-out incident, but upon reaching the third, a soldier paced in front of the landing.

"I'll take care of him, so you two don't have to dirty your hands," Lumira whispered.

Before the soldier turned his back and allowed her the killing stroke, Xaren burst from their hiding place and sprinted into the light. The soldier whirled, blades drawn. Lumira started after him, but Grokhion yanked her back.

"Give him a chance," he whispered.

Lumira wrenched herself from Grokhion's grip and braced for the worst as the soldier advanced on Xaren. The boy raised a hand in a show of camaraderie and said something friendly in Zarith. The soldier's eyes creased with laughter. He patted Xaren on the back. Xaren gestured to the level above, prompting the soldier to follow him to the balcony.

"He cleared a path for us," Grokhion said. "Let's go."

"We can't just leave him."

"He can maneuver better without us. They don't suspect him."

Grokhion led the way, striped tail flailing in front of her. His paws were nearly twice her size and his claws thick as knives.

Thank the moons her kin accompanied her on this foolish mission.

Lumira's zeal wilted with each flight they climbed. The situation was nearly identical on each floor: slaves hammered away at armor, sewed garments, and labored on other trade-driven tasks such as glass blowing and basket weaving. No giant contraptions. No new weapons.

When they reached the tenth and final floor, they ducked behind a row of supply barrels just as an overseer snatched a pot from an elderly slave and hurled it against the wall. The shards clattered around Lumira's feet. The overseer struck the slave's face, and she collapsed, cradling her head. Lumira gripped her hilt. The overseer would go down easily. There weren't too many on duty. If she snuck up on them all—

Grokhion lowered her blade. "I want to help, too," he whispered, "but now's not the time. We have a task at hand."

Lumira slumped against a barrel. "This is pointless. There's nothing out of the ordinary happening here. Not for Az Zar."

"Are you so certain?" Grokhion stroked his whiskers, emerald eyes sparkling with some secret he didn't want to divulge. "Look again. Displace your venom for a moment."

Just say it, old man. Lumira dug her claws into the barrel and returned her gaze to the room. This time, she forced herself to see beyond the people. Though it had appeared busy upon a first glance, there weren't more than a dozen slaves present, and few fabricated items filled the workbenches. The other floors had been similar; the slaves too sickly or old for skilled labor, and only one to two soldiers on guard.

She faced Grokhion. "No output. At least not enough to warrant a structure this size. And the slaves are too weak for the tasks assigned."

"Good, and what does that tell us?"

"It's a decoy."

Grokhion patted her on the back. "I knew your mind was as sharp as your claws."

Despite herself, Lumira prickled with pride at the older beridian's praise. They snuck out of the room and back down the stairs to the main floor, but not before she shredded the overseer's satchel and swallowed his rations.

Xaren waited for them outside, leaning against the building in the shadows. "What did you find?"

"This workshop is a decoy," Lumira said. "You two keep watch. I'm going to search the guardhouses for information. It shouldn't take long."

She stole across the clearing and tried the keys on the smaller guardhouse. None fit. The door was too solid to kick in. A window, perhaps? The sound of a door bar raising stopped her mid-search for a rock. The door swung open, and a man stumbled into the night, clad in an undertunic with a sword. She pounced, driving her blade into his chest before he could utter a cry. Someone inside gasped. Lumira wrenched her blade free and raced into the room. A human girl fresh to womanhood trembled atop a floor bed covered in nothing but a sheet. Zarith lettering was burned into her wrist. She cried out and buried her face in the sheet as Lumira approached.

"It's alright," Lumira said in her best gentle voice. "He's gone. Forever." The girl flinched at her touch. "You're free."

"Best to leave her."

Lumira sheathed her sword and turned to find Xaren in the doorway. Grokhion loomed beside him, eyes narrowing as he looked between the girl and the body.

"Leave her? Tell her to flee."

"It's better for her to stay. She's a house slave. There are far worse assignments, and she wouldn't make it far as a branded woman." Xaren whispered something to the girl. She nodded, blinking back tears, and skittered out the door, cloaked in the bedsheet.

"She won't..." Lumira's heart pounded as darkness swallowed the girl's figure. "Give us up, will she?"

"I don't think so," Xaren said. "How would it benefit her?"

Grokhion barred the door. "Let's have a look at this place."

Lumira assessed the room. It was no larger than a standard loft in Agaas. Slabs of stone were stacked in the corners. A lone table hosted a bowl of still steaming stew. Planks and benches of various makes towered by the fireplace. The bed in the center. Shelves covered the walls, most of them hanging on by a hinge or two, and the few still bolted in place supported jars so darkened with dust that their contents were a mystery. Random crates were strewn about, some half opened.

"It's a storage building," Xaren said after they'd searched for several minutes. "They wouldn't keep any documentation in here."

Lumira cursed. "Let's try the other. Grokhion, come on."

The great beridian lingered beside the floor bed, stroking his whiskers. "Odd place to sleep."

Lumira ventured closer. It was odd. Who slept in the center of a room? She shoved the mattress aside. "By the moons," she hissed through her teeth. A trapdoor lay beneath.

Grokhion chuffed and extended his arm with a bow. "After you."

Lumira lifted the trapdoor. A faint rumble echoed below. She leaped down and landed silently on her paws, then waited for her eyes to adjust to the darkness. A dirt tunnel unfurled ahead with some wooden-framed sections constructed for support.

"It's clear," she whispered. "Cover the trapdoor as best you can."

They walked no more than half a mile before the roar grew deafening and the ground beneath their feet turned to rock. Lumira halted as the tunnel mouth widened into a cavern rich in formations and heavy with moisture. Nevethium green saturated the walls and ceiling. A yellow haze darker than fog but lighter than smoke burned her lungs and drew tears from her eyes, its source a giant metal contraption the size of a ship. It screamed and groaned, trembled and spun. Lumira could hardly track all the moving parts amid the huffs of steam and the licks of flame spouting from the domed boiler. A drill plunged into the rock, somehow powered by the metal monster, and slaves with sweat-slicked torsos scooped loads of nevethium into the broiler while overseers shouted, whips cracking above their heads.

Grokhion nudged her. A patrol approached. Lumira searched until her eyes fell on a stack of supply crates on a ledge above. She climbed up and slipped behind them, Grokhion and Xaren on her heels. She peered over the crates, whiskers twitching. Stairs and ramps had been constructed to navigate the rocks, and below the metal monster, rows of slaves bent over tables of nevethium. They hammered at the crystals, smashing them into chunks before tossing them into pots on the ground. Others gathered the pots and took them to new stations where they further ground them down with pestles, mixed it with other powders, and loaded it carefully into weapons identical to the one wielded by the general at the village. Soldiers patrolled the length of the cavern. A cluster of them stood motionless beside a giant crate overflowing with nevethium. It was large as a house, and ladders were propped up on all its sides for easy access.

Lumira sucked air through her teeth. "I've never seen so much nevethium in my life, let alone all at once."

"They aren't likely to store it all here, either," Grokhion mused. Both beridians faced Xaren.

"I'm learning to trust you, slaver, but I can unlearn in a breath," Lumira said with a snarl.

He wrung his mask between his hands. "I didn't want it to be true."

"I like you, lad. Truly, I do. But if you're holding anything back..." Grokhion trailed off, leaving Xaren to imagine the rest.

The boy's head perked up, jaw set in defiance. "I didn't know about *this* factory. I swear it by your gods and mine. They're always poking and prodding to see what more nevethium can do, but there'd been little success with weaponry. I didn't know we'd made progress. They said it was too hard to control."

"What about that?" Lumira jabbed her finger at the metal monster.

"Arkthanax." They met Xaren with blank stares, so he added, "It means little gods. They can do the work of a hundred men, much faster, and with little to no breaks. Like little gods. They're made of lyvium and powered by nevethium. They weave our textiles faster and more efficiently than slaves. But we recently discovered it can be used to mine."

"How does it work?" Lumira asked.

Xaren chewed his lip, dark eyes distant with thought. "When nevethium is burned at high temperatures, it releases a yellow gas that fuels the machines. It uses a lot, but the return is great. We've uncovered more nevethium this past year than we have in decades."

Grokhion leaned against the crate beside Lumira. "Hardly seems sustainable. Is this how you've stripped the surrounding areas so fast?"

"And why your villages are wastelands?" Lumira added, none too kindly.

Xaren looked away.

Lumira studied the metal monster for weaknesses. There weren't too many soldiers, and the slaves likely wouldn't put up a fight. She might even be able to get some weapons back safely.

"I'm destroying it," she whispered. "Throwing that powder in its fire box ought to do it."

Grokhion frowned. "The slaves would die with the soldiers."

"And it's not the only arkthanax," Xaren added.

Lumira crossed her arms. "It would slow their weapons production. You said the others above ground are for textiles."

"Doesn't mean this is the only one." Xaren inched toward the exit. "Besides, the explosion would alert the city watch. We'd be dead before we reached the gates."

"What about this tunnel system? It can't have only one entrance."

"I told you I don't know it. We're just as likely to walk into a trap."

Grokhion shook his head. "Here's what we're going to do. Xaren will cause another distraction while we collect some weapons. Then we'll leave as silently as we came and make for Cadar."

Lumira growled. "But—"

"It's not a suggestion, Lumira. We aren't prepared for an attack, and we need to get this information back to Neharem."

Moons be cursed, he was right. "Fine," she huffed. "But next time, I'm leveling this place."

Grokhion flashed a fanged grin. "And I'll help you."

ELAYSIA

Water dripped from the stalactites and pooled into a puddle between Elaysia and Davier, shattering the cave's silence. The humidity curled the ends of Davier's hair around his ears and the nape of his neck. His lips curled the opposite direction, into a frown. Elaysia took a step toward the source of tension: eggs (shells, actually; the occupants had vacated) nestled in a rock nest gouged into the wall at waist-height. They'd caught her eye while searching for a way out of the cave. Thirteen in total, longer and thinner than stormbird eggs with bumpy shells thick enough to pierce flesh. Goo oozed from the cracks.

Davier edged toward the tunnel they'd entered from. "We need to keep moving. It'll be dark soon."

Elaysia ignored him and ran her finger through the goo. It came back thickly coated and reeked of rot and fish oil. She picked a piece of shell up, gently turning it over in her hands. On the inside, where it should've been smoothest, it was jagged. Her toes curled in her boots. What creatures could break through such a cage, let alone grow in a dank cave, void of light and a mother's warmth?

"I'm going now," Davier persisted behind her. His tone carried the bite of a threat, but he made no move to leave.

"Do you know what creatures these belong to?"

He shook his head, but a flicker of uncertainty betrayed his eyes. "No, and I don't want to find out."

"We might not have a choice." Elaysia slipped the shell into her satchel. Her thoughts rolled down a dangerous hill filled with the monsters of childhood. "Do they tell you stories of the Great Beasts of Old in Cadar?"

"The military has little use for myths."

"Shame, seeing as how your nation is founded on one."

Davier's smile didn't reach his eyes. "Enlighten me, if it pleases you."

Elaysia crossed her arms to make sure he knew it didn't please her, but she was going to damn well tell him, anyway. "Along with the Vysilliam, Khiev-Tatamic created six eggs, a male and female for each Great Beast. They were the first of the beasts, wise as the Vysilliam and blessed with long life and special abilities. The stormbirds were given the sky, the seaserpents the water, and the deathstalkers the land. The latter was said to have deadly stingers and plated exterior skeletons like insects, only much larger. The adults grew big as a wolf, maybe bigger."

"*Dzvadra,*" Davier muttered.

"What?"

"It's Zarith for deathstalker."

"*Dzvadra.*" The word tasted like poison on her tongue. "The stormbirds survived all these years. Could they also—" Elaysia swallowed, unsure if she wanted an answer to her question. "Have you seen one?"

Davier sorted through imaginary tangles in his beard. "Elaysia..."

"Tell me."

"They found fossilized eggs a while back. I know they'd been experimenting with nevethium. Praying. I don't think it's been successful."

"Unless there are other bug-monsters native to Az Zar, I'd argue otherwise." Elaysia pulled another shell off the pile and studied it with newfound horror. "Why didn't you tell me sooner?"

"I'm done discussing this." Davier started down the tunnel, fists clenched at his sides.

Elaysia summoned all the venom she could muster. "Dark caves frighten the legendary skulmor warrior?"

Davier whirled on her. "Getting caught frightens me. The longer we take, the more soldiers we're likely to run into. We've lost time, thanks to your spontaneous detour."

"Don't blame this on me. If your friends hadn't shown up, we wouldn't be trapped over here." Elaysia smashed the shell on the ground. It bounced off the rocky surface with a *smack* and plunked into the puddle. She shuddered. "Khiev-Tatamic protect us from whatever creature could break that shell."

Davier's eyes widened. He masked it by quickly rubbing his face in feigned exhaustion. "You probably didn't throw it hard enough. We're weary from travel."

Elaysia resisted the urge to chuck another shell at his back as he walked away.

They wound through the tunnels in silence. Hours later, they emerged beneath a moon and star-speckled sky, light shrouded in a sheen of clouds. Straight ahead was a steep ledge that wrapped around to the right. To the left, a clearing, and some trees beyond that. Wind hissed through the leaves and rattled the dewdrops clinging to the grass. Davier knelt to pull out his bedroll.

A faint trail was worn in the grass a few feet away from where Elaysia stood. Perhaps a way down? She marched past Davier, huffing.

"Where the fuck are you going?" He slammed the bedroll on the ground.

"We need to make up for lost time, remember? You want to get to Cadar as quickly as possible, so you can complete your atonement and move on with your life."

Davier retied the bedroll to his pack with no shortage of aggression. "So I do."

The admission stung more than she anticipated. "Is that honesty? How refreshing."

"Anything I've withheld is for the safety of you and the others."

Elaysia peered over her shoulder as if addressing someone behind her. "And we're safer than ever, aren't we, Lumira?" She turned back to Davier, glaring. "Oh, wait."

Davier loosed a clipped laugh. He caught up with her in two strides, eyes cool as frost. The rage didn't dampen his beauty, the cut of his jaw, the sweat beads on his chest where his tunic cut low. Curse her traitorous heart.

A fallen tree lay a few paces from the ledge. She shouldered past him and sat before he could unfurl another insult. Every time she thought she'd peeled back his final layer, there was another hidden beneath. Maybe that's all he was. A charming maze of lies.

Davier stood at the ledge, hands clasped behind his back. "I have been keeping something from you."

A thousand questions formed in Elaysia's mind, each more accusatory than the last. She retrieved her wineskin and clutched it to her chest.

Davier's throat bobbed. He took a tentative step toward her. "We've been using nevethium to fuel new machines that hasten the production of clothes and building materials."

"That's hardly a secret." Az Zar's production rates had quadrupled the past few years. The council assumed nevethium had something, or a lot, to do with it.

"With that mastered, they've moved on to mobility. And weapons."

She pulled the wineskin to her lips but didn't drink. "How?"

"The raw power of nevethium is unfathomable. They think it'll be enough to fuel ships without slaves and land vessels without beasts."

"And the weapons?"

"Made of fire and light. They shoot further and kill faster than arrows."

Elaysia took a swig from wineskin. Her hands went cold, clammy. She latched onto her anger to silence the fear coiled in her stomach. "Why are you really helping me?"

"You think so little of me?" The kindness melted from his voice. He tilted his chin toward the sky and ran his hands through his hair. "I could've killed you the night we met. Run off with your stormbirds."

"They would never follow you. They can smell an outsider."

"They seem to like Xaren well enough."

Elaysia bristled at the mention of his name. "Xaren's loyalty is not in question. Yours is."

"You think you would've gotten this far without me? I have everything to lose." He softened his face, though something about it felt disingenuous, and knelt before her. "You're a smart girl, Ellie. So, tell me, why would I be here except to help you?"

"Don't patronize me."

Davier stormed to the cliffside. He hurled a rock over the edge, then kicked another. "I'm trying to make things right, so if you give a damn about your life, listen. We should go to Or Zahal and investigate—"

"No, you listen." Elaysia swallowed to steady the tremble in her voice. "My father wouldn't have sent a rogue party after weapons advancements, even if it threatened Neharem and our nevethium caches. There's something beneath all this, and I need to go to Cadar to find out."

"I can't let you do that." Davier moved toward her with unnatural calm, emotion replaced with the detached motions of a soldier.

Elaysia ran.

Davier was on her before she could string her bow. She dove out of the way, but he stopped abruptly, mouth agape and arms limp at his sides. A clicking sound filled the silence. Elaysia followed his gaze and stifled a scream. Not twenty feet away, a cluster of insects the size of village cats gathered on the rockface. They were armed with serrated front pincers and six-inch stingers dripping venom. Large wings lay against their backs, glistening a blue-black in the moonlight. Deathstalkers.

Elaysia nocked an arrow. "Don't look directly at them. Back away slowly—"

Davier barreled into the fray with skilled slashes that severed two of the deathstalkers. The rest swarmed above the cave entrance, spindly claws digging into the crevices. Their hisses transformed into piercing cries.

There was no time to curse Davier; one flew at her, pincers snapping. She sprinted away, trying to gain enough ground for a clean shot, but the deathstalker matched her pace. The thrum of its wings deafened her ears. She was about to take aim when her foot caught on a root and sent her sprawling. She rolled onto her back. Grabbed her dagger. The deathstalker was on top of her, pincers snapping. She plunged the blade in. The lyvium sunk into its abdomen like a knife piercing ripe fruit. It dropped to the ground, stunned. She stabbed it over and over until its body was littered with holes that oozed a pus-like fluid.

She stumbled away from her kill. The world was muffled, her own hand foreign to her body. Up the hill, Davier engaged three deathstalkers. The others were dead or vanished. She pulled up abruptly. One creeped down the rock face like a spider, ready to descend on an unaware Davier.

Her arrow found its head with ease. She loosed two more to be safe, then hurried to Davier, who stood panting above his kills.

"Did they get you?" She grabbed both his arms to inspect for signs of stings.

"No." He brushed a thumb over her forehead, eyebrows knit with concern. "You're bleeding."

"I fell. It's nothing." Warmth flooded her cheeks. She turned from him to count the carcasses.

"Some retreated into the cave," Davier said regretfully.

"There may've been more nests, too. We need to leave. The mother must be nearby, and I don't want to be standing idle when she seeks revenge." Elaysia started down the path, but Davier grabbed her arm.

"Their stingers, what do they do?"

"I was told growing up that the young's stings cause life-threatening damage. An adult female dooms one to death with a single sting." Elaysia couldn't peel her eyes from the cave. She dragged Davier down the path as she continued. "Their venom turns your insides to liquid, and then they suck it up and spew it back out to feed their babies."

"And the males?" Davier dug his fingers into the straps of his pack, knuckles white.

"Impotent. The females usually eat them after mating. Once they reach sexual maturity, the females can lay eggs once a moon cycle, but each time they do, it takes a great toll. They die after a few egg lays, except for the hive empress, who never lays and grows to an unfathomable size." Davier stopped walking, so she added, "So the legends say."

Early that morning, as the sun pierced the darkness in ripples the colors of wildflowers, Elaysia plopped her bedroll down next to Davier's. The air was cold enough to fog her breath, but her body felt like it carried a fever. When Davier spoke, she wasn't entirely sure it *wasn't* a dream.

"Hmm?" she murmured.

"I'm sorry for being an asshole earlier. This is... new for me. I'm trying to figure a lot of things out right now." He cleared his throat and turned into her, so his chest pressed against her back. "I don't want anything to happen to you. I hope you know that."

She did, didn't she? He could've betrayed her so many times already. Refused to help her escape. Let her die. The screams of doubt that had plagued her earlier now faded to whispers as she leaned against his muscled chest. It didn't feel wrong.

"I do, and I'm sorry, too," she whispered. "I get caught up in my head and Konar's suspicions."

"No, you're right to question. I'd suspect me, too." Davier chuckled, beard tickling the back of her neck. "But there's another reason I want to go to Or Zahal."

Elaysia stiffened. She was going to Cadar. There was little he could say to convince her otherwise.

"My family's there," he continued. "When the military hears of my desertion, they'll punish them for my crime." His breathing hitched. "I need to warn them. Convince them to escape with me."

Her resolve melted. How could she dispute that? His breath was hot on her ear, his legs nestled into her own. She wanted to face him, pull his arms tight around her waist. But she hadn't enough wine to be so forward.

"We'll go. And they are welcome in Agaas."

Davier relaxed against her.

"But promise we'll ride to Cadar once they're safely on their way."

"Of course. You surprise me yet, Moonrider. I'll make good on my promise." He pressed his lips to her neck and let them linger.

At that moment, as she drifted off into a warm, protected sleep, nothing else in Quinaria mattered.

JAKKI

The nazrath paradise made no more sense than the giants' existence.

They'd borne them deep into the north, through the snow-crusted Quentarri Mountains, nearly all the way to the edge of the skulmor border where the great forests gave way to tundra, a brutal frost desert hedged in by the icy waters of the Tulek Sea. Wind ripped off hoods and chapped lips, as cruel and biting as the landscape. Without the nazrath's aid—their food and drink and arms to carry the wounded—they wouldn't have survived. The Tangeesh girl didn't. Jakki buried her in rocks and wept for the unfulfilled life and for the girl's resemblance to her first lover, another Tangeesh woman with the same ebony locks and warm brown skin. She, too, had been taken before her time.

The next day, they arrived at a small wood rich in berries and mushrooms. Though its existence alone was a marvel, the greatest blessing lay half a day's walk within: a lush clearing adorned with icy blue flowers and, at its center, a lake teeming with fish.

Her first sleep there was fitful, filled with nightmares of skulmor ripping limbs off her friends and painting the soil with blood and gore. Coated in sweat, she awoke to her nazrath rescuer looming above, his massive hand extended. Tucked in the middle of his sweaty palm were healing herbs pounded into a poultice. Jakki hesitated, pride swelling. But her leg was on fire, and the others slept soundly atop furs in the field. Quickly, before she could reason it away, she snatched the herbs and applied them to her wounds. She didn't thank him. He wouldn't have understood if she tried, anyway.

Even now, days later, lounging on the hillside with Siren while her warriors splashed in the lake below, Jakki struggled to embrace the gift. The gods would expect a great sacrifice in return.

So would the nazrath.

Yerakai emerged from the lake and wrapped a tunic around his lean frame as he made his way to Jakki. Wind Chaser hopped behind him, black eyes set on Siren. Perhaps they were already friends in their own way, not unlike her and Yerakai. When she'd first taken up in Agaas, it was he who'd made her feel welcome, who'd taken her on hunts where she'd ramble the whole trip, who'd surprised her with her favorite meal when she was homesick. The friend she'd never deserve but couldn't survive without.

Jakki patted the spot beside her on the log as he approached. "Enjoying yourself?"

Yerakai's face beamed. "It's as if Khiev-Tatamic carved a sanctuary." He retrieved a handful of herbs from his tunic and offered them to her. "You really should apply these. I can grind them for you. Mix in a little of the clay from that bank, and you'd be—"

"I'm fine." She'd refused the herbs beyond that first night. Her leg still ached, but it was more of a dull throb now. "I'd rather not take advantage of their generosity. The less they expect back, the better."

Yerakai shrugged and set the herbs beside her. "I don't think they expect anything back."

"We'll see."

Jakki searched the clearing for any sign of their giant blue brethren. The nazrath spent most of their time hunting, eating, sleeping, and fucking—the latter a nightly event executed with no regard for their guests sleeping ten feet away. Under other circumstances, she might've been aroused, but she loathed the nazrath and buried her ears beneath furs until it ended. She hated the way their stares penetrated. She hated them more for refusing to speak. She hated them most for making her feel both indebted and imprisoned.

"They're hunting," Yerakai said casually. "Won't be back until nightfall."

"Did they nod once for yes and twice for no?" Jakki scoffed.

Yerakai told her early on he recognized some of their hand signs; his people used similar variations when hunting. For the past few days, while everyone else recovered and rested, he followed the nazrath around like a puppy. He'd learned they lived with more of their kind in the uncharted north but sent hunting parties south when game ran scarce. The skulmor sometimes made off with their kills. Their timely arrival in Gohla had less to do with rescue and more to do with vengeance—at least that's how Jakki interpreted it.

Oh, and Yerakai swore they shared thoughts and feelings by perceiving each other's minds, not unlike the Great Beasts of Old. He wanted to learn. Jakki wanted proof.

"They've agreed to arrange a means of travel for us to head south toward Cadar," Yerakai continued, unscathed by her contempt. "We can leave tonight, if that's still what you want."

"Isn't that what you want?"

"Does it matter?"

Jakki clenched her fists. It was more of a genuine question than sarcasm, but it implied he didn't agree with her. Not fully.

"We've wasted too much time here. Thanks to the nazrath, we're even further from Az Zar than before."

"They saved our lives, Jak. More than once." Yerakai's frown deepened as he tightened his woven armor over his tunic. "Forgive me for wanting to repay them by learning their ways."

Jakki pressed up, keeping most of the weight off her injured leg. "Finding Elaysia is more important than appeasing some mute kin, who haven't had the decency to surface in thousands of years."

Yerakai stiffened. She waited for his wrath to unfurl. Instead, he exhaled and softened his face. "All Khiev-Tatamic's creation are our brothers and sisters, regardless if you can relate to them or not." He started for the lake and said over his shoulder, "I'll inform the others of your decision."

"*Our* decision," Jakki muttered when he was well out of range. Eager for solace, she hefted Siren onto her back and hobbled into the woods.

There was no clear path through the thicket. Jakki had a vague sense of where the camp lay and allowed herself the freedom to explore the wood's boundaries. It was sparser than the temperate rainforests of Agaas and much quieter. Brisk air stung her nose, and she found herself longing for the warm beaches of her homeland. A visit was long overdue.

As she walked, the environment stirred memories of her encounter with the creature in the woods outside the Daruk village. She'd done her best to forget, but now his words echoed in her mind: *Like most things in life, potential is often wasted.*

Her hands went to her pouch. She withdrew the ground leaves and lifted them to her nose. She prepped her pipe. Hesitated. The last time she'd smoked them, *he'd* appeared.

Fuck it. Anything to shake this feeling.

The relief hit her instantly. A warm cloud embraced her head, traced down her neck and spine, until it dulled the pain in her leg. Her mind quieted. Siren was weightless on her back. She pressed on, exhaling sweet fog.

When the pipe burned out, she found herself at a river's edge. The water ran quiet close to the lake. A lullaby of calm. Too calm.

Jakki pivoted on her good leg, unsure of what she sought until she located it ten feet up the river on the opposite side of the bank. Her skin prickled. Siren screeched behind her.

A fallen log bridged the sides. Staff raised, Jakki crossed it and approached the intruder. The creature looked the same as it had their first meeting: gaunt and nearly naked, with bits of twigs stuck in his wispy beard. Seated on a rock, he stared up the river, head angled away from her. A thin smile pulled at his lips.

Jakki tapped him with her staff. "Are you following me?"

"I was going to ask you the same."

"Seems a bit far from your home to be aimlessly strolling."

"I do not know *aimless*. My home is wherever I am."

"Spare me your riddles, old man." She reached into her waistband and retrieved the parchment she'd found that night in the woods. It had haunted her since, and he could either substantiate it or take it back. "You can, however, explain this." She thrust it in his face.

He regarded the parchment as though it were one of many trees in the woods. "What is it I am to explain?"

"Don't act like this isn't yours. It appeared in the pond after you left."

He nonchalantly rubbed his staff against one of his antlers. "Do you recognize the language?"

Jakki unrolled the parchment. It was a random assortment of symbols, few of which held any meaning for her. She'd tried to make sense of it, but without a fluent reader, her efforts were broad guesses. She glared at the old man. "Is it skulmor?"

"Clever girl." His voice suggested he thought the opposite.

"Take it back. I want nothing to do with it." The parchment was warm in her hand. She held it out to him, though a part of her didn't want to relinquish it.

He loosed a cruel chuckle. "It outgrew their usefulness long ago. It requires a bearer of strength and intelligence. The skulmor possess but one of those traits."

"What does it say? You must know something about it."

"I am entrusted to guard it and ensure it winds up in the hands of the worthy. It is a powerful weapon."

It was Jakki's turn to laugh. "Words are only weapons against the weak-minded." She plopped onto the ground, legs crossed, and plucked a ruffled Siren from her pouch. "I respect whatever lies you spun to thrive among the skulmor, but I'm not falling for it."

"What are lies but the truth reconstructed?" He hopped off the rock with the spryness of a young man and sat beside her. "The power is not within the words, but the wielder." His boldness took her aback; no one had ever stared so intently at her. "Perhaps it was wrong to choose you."

The parchment dented beneath Jakki's fingertips.

It might've been the look in his eyes. A desire to prove him wrong. The effects of the pipe weed coursing through her body.

But maybe she was simply curious.

Jakki nudged Siren off her lap. "I assume you know their language after spending time with them?"

The old man's lips curled. He nodded.

"Prove it," she whispered. "Tell me what to say so I can be free of you and this madness."

"As you wish."

A throaty, clipped phrase rolled off his tongue. His pupils dilated until both eyes were black as a bear's before the kill. The crystal on his staff flickered. He paused, waiting for her to repeat it.

A shiver raced down her spine. Something in her begged to refrain, but something greater called to her. She was meant to find this parchment.

The words lingered on her lips as if she could taste them. The more she spoke, the more certain she was she could. Her mouth watered, craving the next phrase. A warm sensation spread through her belly with the ease of wine, but the alertness of a crisp morning tingled at her fingertips. The world pulsated vibrant colors. She saw the heartbeats of trees. Heard the songs of rocks. Felt the embrace of the wind.

The old man was gone. Or was he? She felt his presence. Heard his cackle.

She found herself knee–deep in the river.

Would you like to unleash your potential? The voice wasn't hers, nor the old man's. It was a harbinger of death, a deep and guttural growl that echoed in her soul like a nightmare. Yet, there was a seductive edge to it, a dangerous glint like the flash of a blade, warning of the price to be paid for giving in to its allure.

Yes, she answered.

She stepped forward. The water slid over her chest. Her lips. Her head. The chill stiffened her muscles, but her mind had never been so free. She saw within herself and without. A flock of birds flapped miles above her. She followed their path as if she soared beside them, close enough to trace the details in their feathers. The ground sighed beneath her, groaning as it drew the trees' roots deeper. She would've been content to bask in her newfound awareness for ages were her lungs not burning for air. She tried to make for the surface, but she couldn't find where the world ended and she began. A scream caught in her throat as she fought for control over her body. *Stop,* she commanded the voice that had lured her in. *Let me go.*

It denied her. There was no moving her limbs, and no more air. She inhaled, braced for the pain of drowning.

The water never made it past the threshold of her mouth. Instead, rich air smelling of soil and pond musk filled her lungs. She pulled another tentative breath. Air. Filtered without gills. But how? Her limbs went slack. She was allowed to move again.

Jakki thrashed for the surface. Safety was a hand's breadth away when she stopped, unsure she wanted it to end. She wasn't frightened. Quite the opposite. Her pulse quickened, skin alive with the slightest of sensations, and she felt no pain, not even in her wounded leg. It was better than any alcohol, better than smoking kinawa—Haeshol, it rivaled the ecstasy of love-making. A few more moments wouldn't hurt. She closed her eyes and sank back to the riverbed, allowing the soil to conform to her shape.

A pebble plopped into the water and nestled beside her. It wasn't something she would've normally noticed, but in her current state, it sounded like a tree crashed into the river. Someone moved above her on the bank. Without opening her eyes, she sensed the presence was harmful, painted in red and throbbing like a wound. The voice returned, wispy as ash.

Attack, it said. *Or be attacked.*

The malevolent form drew closer, shouting. Everything in Jakki's body tensed.

Kill or be killed.

Streaking through the water like a seaserpent, she broke through the surface and dragged the would-be assailant into a watery grave. It struggled, but Jakki's grip was stone. She hardly flinched; the creature she damned weighed no more than a feather. Its thrashing ceased.

A braid of fear rippled through her chest and up her throat. She didn't dare open her eyes.

Siren shrieked, but it sounded distant. Jakki fell away from the darkness, from the warmth. Icy water bit through her skin. Her body was her own again. Every weak, trembling part of it. Something—someone—was slack in her hands, weighing her down. She screamed. Water slammed into her lungs as she clambered toward the surface, dragging the body, limbs as weak as though she'd been bedridden for days.

Sunlight. Air. Jakki sucked in both and heaved the body onto the bank. She checked for a heartbeat. Nothing. Siren nipped at her elbow. She shrugged the stormbird off and pushed on the chest, pressed her lips to the mouth, filling it with air. She listened again. Still nothing. The woods echoed the body's stillness. She stumbled back, eyes darting wildly. Her mouth went dry.

What have I done?

She stumbled into the trees, but scarcely made it a few feet before she halted, sobbing. She had to look. It pulled at her like an itching scab. The poor soul deserved that much.

Fingers contorted around each other, she trudged back to the body. Forced herself to study its face, its... *his* eyes...

No.

She clutched her stomach and heaved into the river.

The old man's laughter filled her ears.

ZAVIK

The port of Amiren knew not sleep or peace. Drunkards staggered to and from brightly colored inns, satchels swollen with aspar, seduced by the coos of rose-scented love-givers dangled over porch railings. Its streets pulsated with heat despite the evening breeze and filled Zavik's nostrils with the reek of ale and smoke. He edged closer to the buildings, seeking refuge from the crowds.

Someone stroked his shoulder.

"Aren't you a rare find," purred a love-giver. She wore fabric so sheer it revealed the bulge beneath her waistband.

Zavik lurched back into the fray, not caring *who* touched him so much as the fact someone touched him without his permission.

And to think people enjoy this.

T'Vak winked at the love-giver and wrapped a sweaty arm around Zavik's neck. "Someone's popular tonight."

Zavik's cheeks flushed. "Isn't there a less congested route?"

"We can always go in there, if you'd rather be touched by blades than fingers."

T'Vak used his wineskin to gesture down an alleyway. A cloaked man lurked in the shadows, hooded eyes lit by the embers in his pipe. He flashed a smile that made Zavik's insides crawl.

"Just hurry up," Zavik muttered. "I want to be back in Neharem by tomorrow evening."

"Then stop slowing me down." T'Vak stole across the street in large, clomping strides, draining the wineskin as he went.

Zavik clutched the scrolls to his chest and followed. It had been a fortnight since he'd departed the Shaktar Caverns with his prize. T'Vak had been curled up in the sand beside the zaka-zakas, well-rested with no recollection of the ancient Vysilliam or their monster, and demanded they ride for Amiren at once, stopping only for food and rest at night. Zavik, accustomed to sleep abstinence when researching, spent much of those precious evenings perusing the scrolls by firelight. The first two were written in Shaktari and Myremese, respectively, Vysilliam languages long forgotten by the races of land. Zavik was no exception, but he'd studied enough to recognize the ancient scripts. Thankfully, the author of the third wrote in Nyrinian. So far, it mentioned a great deal about the stormbirds. Elaysia would be proud.

Zavik picked up his pace and hurried after the backhander.

Moonlight glinted on the harbor when they reached it, creating parallel, silver lines like a path in the water. Any moment now, Zavik would see his little boat again. Only...

No boat. A gold-rimmed pleasure yacht in its place. Zavik nearly dropped the scrolls.

T'Vak let out a shrill whistle. "That's a ship and a half if I've seen one."

Zavik ran up and down the dock. He scoured every slip and squinted into the horizon.

Gone.

"I don't understand," he said, pulling up breathless. T'Vak sat cross-legged on a barrel of fish, clearly more fascinated by his wineskin than the predicament. "I left the dock lord enough to keep my boat here another fortnight past this." T'Vak raised a scarred eyebrow, mouth pulling up on one side. "What?"

"You gave them everything upfront and thought they'd hold it for you, a foreigner, outta the kindness of their money-grubbing heart?"

Zavik leaned against the barrel, fists balled, arms crossed. "I expected honesty. Good people don't—"

"Good people don't exist. Some are just less selfish than others." T'Vak took a drink and shrugged. "Have you anything left to barter?"

Zavik reached into his pocket and ran his fingers over a few aspar. "Barely enough for supplies and food."

"Shit."

"I could promise nevethium?"

"Word's no good here. I'm a rare breed on that account." T'Vak winked and stretched his arms overhead. The moonlight cast shadows along the curves of his muscles, as if they weren't intimidating enough to begin with. "In the interest of protecting my investments, I'm going to locate us a ship by whatever means necessary. In return, you're going to see to it that my pay is doubled, and"—he nodded to a horde of stumbling men dressed in the robes of city officials—"I'll take a bottle of Beridian Moonlight for the trip."

"But I—"

"Unless you're gonna pull a boat out of your ass, get moving."

Zavik decided against further antagonizing the backhander. *Double nevethium. Konar's going to kill me.*

Well, it would all be worth it to see the look on Elaysia's face when he presented not one, but three scrolls.

Zavik tucked the encased scrolls into his belt, securing another rope around them for good measure, then buttoned his jacket over them. "How will I find you?"

"Dock's not that big." With that, T'Vak strode away, hand on his hilt.

Zavik took a deep breath and wound his way up the rocky hillside. The city shone like a beacon, buildings stacked on the incline creating an illusion of a towering fortress—typical of a coastal town near tumultuous tides. He didn't walk far before the musk of other humans assaulted him. A sloshed drink here, a bump there. He maneuvered around a particularly boisterous group only to step in a pile of feces. Foul words piled on his tongue as he shook off his boots, but he didn't loose them. Not aloud.

A lively strum pattern drew him to a teardrop-shaped building with doorless archways and lattice-framed balconies: The Maiden's Voyage. His lips twitched at the name. He doubted many in Amiren fit that description besides him.

A gaggle of love-givers lounged on overstuffed divans in the courtyard. Eyes down, he shuffled past them. One caught his arm.

"Are you as fiery in bed as your hair is colored?" she purred through populum-stained lips. Dark circles framed her smudged eyes. An all-too-familiar warmth spread through Zavik's cheeks and ears. "Don't be shy." She pulled down her top, exposing her filigreed breasts.

Zavik ran inside and nearly collided with a serving girl. Liquid sloshed out of the overflowing cups and onto her pantaloons. Her eyes narrowed into slits, her teeth bared.

"I'm so sorry," he stammered over the music. "Here, let me—"

"Don't touch me." She shoved past him with an elbow to his chest.

Zavik ducked behind a drape to assess the room. Smoke from the communal water pipes hung thick, ripe with honey and sweat. It curled around the upper level's open balcony where patrons copulated atop silk-covered beds. Zavik was glad he couldn't hear anything over the music. The main level centered on a large bath—clothing optional—and clusters of horseshoe booths surrounding square tables. Not a seat to spare, and little standing room beside. With a grunt, he emerged from his hiding place and shuffled in the direction of what he hoped would be the counter.

Sticky bits on the rugs pulled at his boots as he sidled through the crowd. Try as he did to avoid others, love-givers grazed his torso, and his clothing caught on the occasional table. When he reached the counter, he wedged himself between a man garbed in the golden headwrap of a city official and an elderly dock worker, to whom bathing was a novelty. The proprietor eyed Zavik with a frown, then waited until there was no one left to serve before approaching him. When she finally returned with the Beridian Moonlight, she shooed Zavik away to make room for more deserving patrons who'd likely be spending half a week's wages by night's end.

Zavik practically sprinted for the exit. One moment, he had the door in sight, the next, he was free-falling, thwarted by a leg in his path. A meaty arm slung around his stomach at the last moment and hurled him into a booth.

His rescuer was a potbellied man with blackened teeth. A love-giver lolled naked in his lap, and another massaged his shoulders. "Lotta drink for not a lotta man," he sneered. Zavik eked out a nervous laugh. "Pour me a cup and I'll lend you one of my best girls."

The woman behind him winked. Zavik realized, belatedly, she was the one he'd snubbed outside.

"I really should be going." Zavik rose, but the love-giver straddled him back into the booth.

"What's the rush?" she teased.

Zavik shoved her off as gently as he could manage, taking care to avoid touching her exposed skin. "I, uh"—he scrambled for an excuse—"sorry, you're not my type."

"Don't imagine you have one." Her voice was ice. She adjusted her clothing to suggest modesty and stormed across the room to find someone more receptive to her writhing.

Face hot, Zavik sprung for the door, taking care to avoid any feet. He ran all the way back to the docks.

It wasn't until he slowed his pace that he felt it. A lightness. His stomach knotted. He ran a trembling hand across his jacket to count the scrolls. One... two...

Zavik's stomach dropped. Wood creaked under his feet as he tore down the boardwalk. "T'Vak, where are you? Quickly!"

The backhander caught Zavik by the collar as he raced by. "You trying to summon every kuza in the area?"

"I'm missing a scro—"

T'Vak covered his mouth. "Wanna try that again?"

Zavik lowered his voice. "I don't understand. I secured them, see?" He opened his jacket to show how he'd bound them. "Who could've known I even had them?"

"Calm down. When did you have them all last?"

"Here. With you. I took them to the inn."

T'Vak gave his head a knowing shake. "Lots of snatchers in these parts looking to make easy aspar. One likely set on you as prey. You look the type."

Zavik grit his teeth against the insult. "We have to go back and find it."

"The snatcher's long gone by now. Besides, you still have two." T'Vak shrugged.

"You don't understand. These are... sacred." And dangerous in the wrong hands, but now was hardly the time to fill T'Vak in on that secret. "I'll retrace my steps. Maybe it's lying on the ground." Even as Zavik spoke the words, he knew he'd wind up back at the inn.

"If you think I'm going to let my only means of payment get killed for sticking his tiny nose—hey!" Zavik had started up the hill, hoping desperately the backhander would accompany him. "Wait for me, you little urchin," T'Vak called out.

Good.

T'Vak stomped into The Maiden's Voyage, curved sword brandished. "Everyone, hands where I can see them."

The musicians stopped playing. A hush fell over the room. To Zavik's relief, no kuza were present, at least on duty. Then again, it wasn't the cleanest of establishments to draw a noble's eye, nor the most... erotic.

"My friend, don't ruin a good night, eh?" the proprietor shouted from behind the counter.

"That depends on your cooperation." T'Vak nudged Zavik forward. Eyes bore into him like hundreds of readied arrows. "Someone stole from my client. Empty your pockets and satchels."

No one moved.

"Now!"

"If I'm not emptying my pockets for love-givers, what makes you think I'll empty them for you?" The challenge came from a half-clothed man in a corner booth, who, judging by the pile of mugs at his table, was three drinks past reasoning. His braided hair ran down to his waist, and his stature was notably larger than T'Vak's, who wasn't a small man himself.

"We mean no trouble," Zavik said. He winced as the man rose and leveled blazing eyes at him. "Please, I'm looking for a scroll."

"I don't labor all week to lose my one night of pleasure to an Az Zarian ra—"

T'Vak hurled a knife across the room. Its blade wedged in the wall a finger's length from the man's head. Zavik braced himself for the wrath his companion unleashed, but—impressed or entertained—the man erupted with laughter and revealed the contents of his bag: aspar, lubricating oils, ground populum root. The rest of the patrons took far less convincing, but no one carried the scroll or claimed to have seen it. People soon returned to their smoking and fornication.

T'Vak shrugged and headed for the door. "Come on, lad. We tried. Your snatcher's long gone."

As Zavik followed, shoulders slumped, his hand brushed against the booth the greasy man had tossed him into. Both he and the love-giver were gone. His eyes widened. "Wait, one more thing."

The proprietor placed her hands on wide hips when Zavik appeared at the counter. "Haven't caused enough trouble tonight, slaver?"

"There was a large man at that booth earlier tonight. Do you know him?" The proprietor met him with a blank stare. Zavik tried again. "There was a love-giver, too. She, um"—*assaulted me with her breasts probably isn't the best descriptor*—"had short, curly hair. Raspy voice?" Still nothing. "Tattoos around her breasts?"

"Oh, Twyla?" The proprietor rolled her dark-lined eyes. "She's probably upstairs doing her job. Get in line."

Zavik didn't want to search the upper level for fear of catching her performing said job, but T'Vak had no such qualms and took the stairs three steps at a time. A few shouts and curses later, he returned empty-handed.

"No love-giver by that description, and no scroll. It's gone, Zav." T'Vak frowned and rumpled Zavik's hair.

"But it can't... there's no replacement." The room spun. Zavik clung to the counter.

"You don't look so good." T'Vak grabbed him by the arm and guided him back to the docks where the newly acquired boat—a noble's yacht—waited.

For hours, Zavik lay on the deck in silence. The waves rocked the boat with gentle creaks and groans, but he found no solace. He chewed his lips and tried to recall what he'd read in the nyrian scroll—because, of course, *that one* had been stolen—turning each bit over in his mind the way a baker kneaded bread. But the more he sought to draw it out, the further it burrowed in his memories. He cursed the shaktar for entrusting it to him. He cursed T'Vak's need for alcohol.

But his carelessness was to blame.

Brilliant, Zav. Just brilliant.

"It's not your fault, you know," T'Vak said, as though he could read Zavik's mind. The backhander rested on a supply barrel, back propped against the railing. His expression attempted sympathy. "I wouldn't lose sleep over it. In the gods' hands now, it is."

"Don't lose sleep?" Zavik sat up, body trembling. "It's one of the Prophets' seven scrolls."

T'Vak cracked his knuckles. "So?"

"*So?* The Prophets were a sacred sect coinciding with Az Zar's foundation. The scrolls contain years of research from some of the greatest minds to ever exist. They studied the natural world, kept records, explored alternate histories—some swore they learned the powers of gods. It's the greatest discovery of our time. And I've *lost* one." He smashed his fist on the side of the boat. Pain splintered up his arm.

"But you've read it. I saw you."

Zavik swallowed his rage. "I barely scratched the surface. Ancient Nyrinian varies from the modern language. Even if I had uninterrupted time with it, I couldn't have memorized the whole thing."

"Maybe it will turn up."

"And maybe I'll learn to fly."

T'Vak spat on the deck and smeared it around with his boot. "You best be getting some sleep. Not doing yourself any favors right now." He went about adjusting the sails, humming.

A coiling, white heat boiled in Zavik's belly. "Why couldn't you make do with wine, you drun—"

T'Vak closed the distance between them in a single stride. The words died on Zavik's lips. "Go on."

Zavik opened his mouth. Closed it. The wind ceased, and his courage deflated along with the sails. He retreated to the corner of the boat. T'Vak took a sip of Beridian Moonlight, and with a show of satisfaction, he returned to his barrel, shut his eyes, and started snoring. The last bit was forced, but Zavik got the message.

When T'Vak's fake snoring gave way to the heavy breathing of true sleep, Zavik grabbed a blanket from one of the supply barrels and wrapped it tightly around his body. The ocean sprawled before him like black blood, thick and cruel. No moons. No stars. Utter silence, save for the sloshing of the waves. Zavik's throat tightened. The weight of his failure pressed upon him, stole his air. He gripped the railing and retched.

He'd bring Elaysia more questions than answers.

KONAR

K onar waited until the last possible moment to act. When he could no longer bear the pain, when his bones grated with each step and his breath rattled his chest with long, wrenching rasps, he stole away from Agaas, shrouded in moonlight. He told himself he needed air. To stretch his legs. Escape from the questions, well-meaning or not, that plagued his every waking moment.

The communal sense of agitation was no longer confined to Agaas; people throughout Neharem grew weary of his excuses for the absent high chieftain, and Rajar tipped on the precipice of a coup. The Lautei chief had sent him a tuross message not an hour past. It demanded a summit of the tribes on the first day of sub-Vynar—less than a moon cycle away—where he'd invoke hoksanu to unseat Elaysia from the High Tree. It was Rajar's right as chief, and it would come to pass should Elaysia not return in time. Even if she returned, her chances of beating the seasoned nyrian in the ancient trials were...

He drew a sharp breath and hurried on.

The slaps of his footsteps on the weathered ramp gave way to the soft pattering of soil underfoot, signaling the end of his descent. Fog hung thick as the mossy coats adorning the trees. He shivered, feverish skin intensifying the bite in the breeze. A spear's length away sat a dual-stump that marked the entrance to a trail only he knew. It led to the coastline.

He hesitated. It had been too long without a worthy soul. He'd grown gaunt, with wrinkles set so deep into his face that he hardly recognized his reflection. Fish were no longer viable. Even the nytak fawn had only lasted a fortnight.

A human, then. Perhaps one of the older ones on watch.

He heaved himself over the thatched fence surrounding base camp. The mock village supervised entry to Agaas and maintained the little livestock they raised, along with several massive gardens and lofts for caretakers and watchers. One of the latter rested on a supply barrel, eyes weighted with sleep. A weathered man nameless to Konar.

He'd do.

Konar prowled through the shadows, relying on his instincts lest guilt drown his intent. Hopefully, this would be the last time. He stopped behind the man. Eased the dagger from his sleeve to his fingers. The blade peeked out from the folds of his robe and glinted in the moonlight. It was a necessary evil to protect Neharem. To protect Elaysia. Soon, she'd be strong in her rule, no longer in need of his guidance. Then he'd tell her everything. Or most things.

Or maybe you should disappear altogether, you old fool.

"High Elder Lightfoot?"

The blade nicked Konar's finger as he shoved it back into his sleeve. Grasping for composure, he turned to find a watcher scarcely older than Elaysia. The woman's head was freshly shaved and accented her elongated ears in the torchlight.

Konar cleared his throat. "Good evening."

The old man on the supply barrel rose, his face equal parts exhaustion and curiosity. "What brings you down so late, High Elder?"

"Couldn't sleep." Not entirely a lie. The woman appeared satisfied with his response, but the old man's brow furrowed. "I fear I've neglected base camp with the chaos up top. Is everything in order here? Crops and animals well?"

"Better than ever." The woman puffed with pride. "One of the mares bore twin foals this evening. A good omen."

"Khiev-Tatamic be praised," Konar said through clenched teeth.

"Gods bless your watch, Myra. My bones need rest." The old man gave Konar a curt nod. "High Elder." He trudged into the watcher commune and slammed the door behind him.

"I'm happy to accompany you back, High Elder. It's dark tonight, and the ramp is slick with mist." Myra's eyes brimmed with genuine concern. "A little Daruk mead should convince Ratcha to extend his watch." She winked and started for the commune, but Konar caught her arm.

"A gracious offer, but I prefer the solitude. Gives me time to think."

"Fair enough. That's why I wanted to be a watcher at base camp. Agaas is too crowded for me."

Konar bowed his head to hide his frustration. "Goodnight, Myra. The Daughter keep you."

"And you, High Elder."

Konar waited until she left, then trudged toward the corral, humus soft beneath his sandals. There was no guarantee he'd have the same strength tomorrow as tonight. Maybe one of the foals would do. The young blood might last long enough to—

A branch snapped behind him. Instinctively, he ducked behind a tree. A lone figure strode past the corral and disappeared into the woods. Myra. Likely checking traps.

Konar's gut wrenched, but he forced himself to follow. She was young and nyrian, away from firelight and prying eyes. A better opportunity couldn't have presented itself.

He followed her through overgrowth and streams. Down hills and around trees. When she knelt to check the first trap, he readied a stone, its weight cold and finite in his hand. He forced his mind to Elaysia. The stone struck the back of Myra's skull with a sickening crunch. She crumpled. The woods sighed. Konar cradled her body, pressed his ear to her chest. The beat of life still pulsed within her.

"Forgive me," he whispered.

With a grunt, he hoisted her onto his shoulders and returned to his hidden trail. He pushed the overhanging branches aside. Ferns strangled the path alongside rocks and fallen logs. He scrambled through the maze, ducking to avoid the twisted roots tunneled overhead. Though Myra weighed heavily on his neck, a giddiness overtook him as he neared the coastline. The air grew colder. A gentle thunder of crashing waves. It wouldn't be long now.

The ocean greeted him beneath a pallid sky. Stars winked through the fog, casting a faint light on the waves as they drowsily reached for turosses burrowed in the sand. Konar fixated on a cave cut from the rockface one hundred yards away. His cave. The tide was low enough for now, if he hurried.

Wet sand clung to his sandals with each step, weighing down his legs as though they were made of stone. The chilling coastal wind did little to prevent the sweat from drenching his clothes. He struggled to stay upright as Myra's weight bore down on his shoulders, sapping his strength with each passing moment.

Konar's legs buckled twenty paces away. He groped the sand, panting. How could such a small woman be so heavy? Maybe he could close his eyes and rest, just for a moment.

Myra stirred.

Konar groaned and used the last of his strength to get them both inside.

The stakes and ropes were as he'd left them. He bound her wrists and ankles, then tore off strips from his robes to blind and gag her. He needed her alive for the ritual, not aware. Knowing his identity would only add to her suffering.

Ancient speech dripped from his lips like poison, words that, even after all these years, felt foreign in his mouth. The air thickened with the scent of rot. Myra writhed and moaned as he cut open her tunic. She shouldn't have woken. It was always worse when they did.

Konar drew the blade across her throat, releasing a waterfall of blood. She gurgled, then stilled. He cracked her ribs and worked quickly to carve out her heart. Painted the wretched sigil with her blood. Muttering the final words, he placed her heart in the sigil's center and retreated to a rock at the mouth of the cave. He removed his robe and sat facing the ocean. Closed his eyes.

A burst of ice chilled him from behind. Hooves clacked over the rock, silencing when they trod the silken sand surrounding his perch. It smelled of loosened bowels and decay.

Konar didn't look. He never did. One glance into those soul-wrenching eyes years ago snuffed that curiosity.

He hated this part. Not the moment itself, but the emotional stupor to follow. He hated it because he craved it. And he shouldn't. Every act in the ritual tore at his spirit and left toxic, sleep-crippling guilt in its wake.

But this, this transcendence, this rush of life he'd yet to match—not in the heat of battle or the climax of love-making—was the best and worst part of his threadbare existence.

Icy breath washed over his back. The tip of the scythe pricked the skin over his spine. A snort. The pressure increased until metal met bone. It didn't hurt, or if it did, the euphoria careening through his body masked it. Everything tingled. His aches vanished along with the chill of the coastal air. No hunger. No thirst. In this moment, his strength was a young man's again. He was a god.

Konar rolled onto the damp sand. The cave faded around him. In a distant dream, he heard footsteps clacking away as the Caman returned to its master.

Sleep overtook him, the deepest slumber he'd had in moons.

Konar awoke to frigid waves sloshing against his face. His extremities were numb with cold, and sand irritated the crevices of his skin. Shivering, he shrugged into his robe. It, too, was soggy. But he was rejuvenated. He sprinted toward the beach with his newfound strength.

A lump in the sand tripped him.

Myra.

Water all but covered her body. It pulled her closer to the cave mouth with every sigh of the waves. Konar winced as he helped it along, guiding it with a piece of driftwood until it met open ocean. Her absence wouldn't draw much suspicion, if any. With her body gone, they'd assume a beast made off with her or, more likely, she deserted. It wouldn't be the first time a young watcher discovered their service to Agaas was less than rewarding. And the old man? Assuming he could even place Konar as the last person to be seen with the girl, who'd believe his claims over the High Elder's?

He waited until Myra's body blended into the horizon, then hurried up the trail much faster than before.

Murky golden rays cut through the fog as Konar returned to his loft. Though he'd ensured he hadn't been followed, he secured the door with a wooden plank designed by Zavik before he stoked the coals in his firepit. Upon removing his damp clothes, he found his robe stained with blood. He thrust it into the flames.

"I don't process your death lightly. I will honor your sacrifice," he whispered.

After inhaling a small loaf of bread and two grilled fish he'd neglected the night before, he threw on a simple nytak skin tunic and hurried down to the library. At the bottom of one of his many research piles was a book he'd not opened since he first adopted Agaas. He freed it from the stack. On the cover were three crescent moons interwoven behind an eye, and within the pupil, a sun: the Prophets' sigil. A journal penned by one of the members. Anonymous. He'd refused to touch it for so long. Simply glancing at it brought a wave of painful memories.

He shoved them away and leafed through the journal. Only a third of the pages were filled, and most of it was a cryptic code he'd yet to crack. But if Elaysia managed to secure even one scroll, it might be enough to unlock the message.

Foolish girl. If she only knew what danger they could bring. What danger they already brought. A danger he embraced with the utmost disdain for his own hypocrisy. He'd prolonged his life more than double its reach, and for what? A coveted position and a stack of bodies that would make a warrior blush? Crazed dream or not, Chai'Tik was right. His secrecy had starved the threat but not eradicated it. It waited in the shadows, growing hungry and vengeful. The resurgence of the stormbirds set things he could no longer manipulate into motion. At least two scrolls recovered and in the enemy's possession. It was only a matter of time before everything he'd fought for crumbled beneath him.

No turning back now.

Konar tucked the book under his sleeve and crept back to his loft.

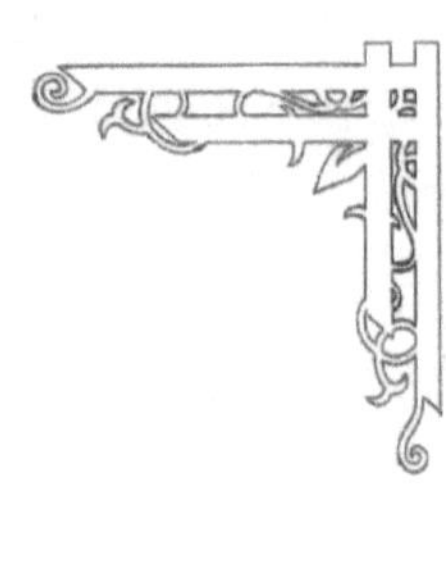

ELAYSIA

Despite all the dangers present in a foreign city, Elaysia's attention was wholly fixated on one. Her stomach fluttered, like a bird was caged within. Sweaty palms. Dry mouth. She tried to quiet her fears by studying her surroundings: curled roofs, intricate murals on the sides of buildings, clusters of greenery in the courtyards, pockets of sun-blood trees. Other than the sticky heat that lingered past sunset—and her impending introduction to Davier's family—Or Zahal wasn't entirely unpleasant.

Davier fought to convince her otherwise.

"Some districts aren't any better than the poverty-stricken villages we passed through on our way here," he said with a toss of his shoulders. "Constant droughts, heavy criminal activity, disease—compared to Cadar, Or Zahal's a slum."

Elaysia rolled her eyes. As soon as they'd set out for Or Zahal, Davier had seized every opportunity to belittle it in one fashion or another. Not that she cared for his home city, but hearing him sing Cadar's praises made her ill.

Davier halted at the head of a descending stairwell. "Down here. It's the fifteenth home on the right." He removed his mask and led her down the stairs and onto a narrow street lined with small, identically shaped homes on either side. Little light made its way through the crowded roofs, and no nevethium had been spared to light the way.

Elaysia tripped over a protruding stone slab and cursed.

Davier rushed to help her up, but she brushed away his hand. "I'll keep the little dignity afforded me, thanks."

"Told you this place is a shithole."

She scowled at the loose stone. Or Zahal's roads had long since succumbed to the weathering of hundreds of winters and ten times that many feet, leaving a gauntlet of jagged edges in its wake. Pointless. Dirt worked well enough and didn't needlessly waste materials and labor.

Shutters covered the windows of Davier's childhood home, but a light glowed within, and the scent of steamed grains and roasted vegetables rolled off the porch. Elaysia's mouth watered at the prospect of eating something not dried and cold. She rubbed her tunic to coax away remnants of dirt and ran her fingers over her braids to tame the frayed ends. Davier gathered his shoulder-length hair and tied it into a bun. It suited him better than the cropped heads and waxed faces of the soldiers she'd seen patrolling. A part of her hoped he wouldn't cut it again.

Davier raised his hand to knock, then hesitated. Studied her with his silver eyes. "Can you keep your hood on? The paint is holding up alright, and they usually keep it dim inside, but we have to be careful. And don't let your sleeves ride up past your gloves."

Elaysia gritted her teeth. He'd suggested she apply face paint before entering the city to even out her skin tone and minimize the curiosity of locals; nymans were considered an abomination and killed at birth under Az Zarian law. But she wasn't a citizen. The worst punishment she could suffer was being ostracized. She was starting to think it was more for his family's sake than her own.

"I'll just wait outside. Don't want to tarnish your image." She turned to leave, but he caught her elbow and pulled her close.

"I'm not ashamed of you. But they aren't going to take news of my desertion well, especially when I tell them why. It'd be a lot for one night and—"

Elaysia held a finger to his lips. "I understand. Just tonight."

"Thank you." He kissed her finger and smiled. Anger melted from her like the last frost of the Resting Moons. "And remember, say nothing about—"

"Davier, shut up. We've rehearsed this more than my induction speech."

Her head spun with the endless instruction he'd spewed over the past few days regarding how to interact with his family. Don't speak during the meal. Do smile and accept anything offered. Don't speak ill of Mavism. Do stick with the story he'd concocted about how she was a Neharem runaway he'd taken under his wing. And when in doubt, remain silent.

"You look better without the makeup." Davier added. An afterthought.

Elaysia rolled her eyes, but she tucked the compliment away. "Do you often tell women they look hideous before meeting your family?"

Davier opened his mouth to object, but the door swung open. A fair-haired, light-skinned girl no more than six stood there, her face scrunched in suspicion at Elaysia.

Davier stepped into the light. "Hello, Xi."

The girl's eyes widened. "Davier!" she squealed, diving into his arms. She clung to his neck until he peeled her off.

"That's Xianna," Davier said as she scampered off to tell the others.

Elaysia didn't know his voice—and face—could soften so much. He held the door open, and she stepped into a simple but clean family room, no larger than her loft. The table in the center had seen better days, but a fine fillagree adorned the top and matched the chair cushions. A fire crackled in the far corner, casting shadows on a uniform display complete with a cluster of medals. No weapons, though.

Two more girls, one around ten and the other new to womanhood, trailed into the room behind a bouncing Xi. The younger of the two embraced Davier and kissed his cheek.

"Kiska," he said, rumpling her hair. "And Dynah"— he nodded to the tallest girl—"playing at eldest while I'm away." Dynah smirked and regarded Elaysia with skeptical eyes.

"Eumma, come quick," Kiska shouted as she disappeared around a corner.

Xi sprung onto Davier once more, leaving Elaysia standing awkwardly across from Dynah, who stared her down with not so much as a smile. The girl's silks were clean, though sized too small and frayed at the edges. Elaysia's throat tightened. For all Az Zar's wealth, few beyond the capital had any taste of it.

She dared a step toward Dynah. "It's a lovely home."

Dynah scrunched her forehead in disbelief.

A woman about Maseeya's age entered the room and saved Elaysia from tossing out more conversational fodder. Her golden hair faded to gray, but she shared the same starry eyes as the rest of the family. A calm surrounded her, like the forest after it rained. Behind her strode a man of the same age and look, though with his rigid shoulders and deep-set frown, his demeanor was every bit her opposite. A barbaric practice, arranged marriages.

The woman kissed Davier's cheek and held his face at arm's length as though she basked in the beauty of a painting. "What's all this?" she asked, running her fingers through his beard.

"He's undercover for a mission, Eumma," the man said in an authoritative voice, rivaling Konar's. He shook Davier's hand firmly.

"Eudna." Davier straightened, sliding back into his soldier persona with unsettling ease. "I'm sorry I've come unannounced."

"We always have plenty of food, boy, especially for a servant of Az Zar." No smile, but he puffed his chest and bestowed a nod of approval. "Our neighbors ask of you often. I tell them you'll be a colonel soon and that you bring our family the highest of honors." He took in Elaysia, his expression unreadable. "You've brought company."

All eyes locked on her. She dug her fingernails into gloved palms. "I'm—"

"Vanya." Davier touched the small of her back and urged her closer. "I met her while undercover in Neharem. She's helped our cause. She's a refugee now."

Elaysia fought an instinctual grimace and replaced it with a veil of forced pleasantries normally reserved for council gatherings. "It's been an honor to serve with your son. I'm pleased to meet you all." She offered her hand to his father, but he simply nodded and gestured to the table.

"Please, sit." He waited until Elaysia and Davier sat, then chose a chair opposite them. "You speak our language well."

Elaysia lifted her chin a bit higher. "I was taught in Agaas." Not a lie. "It was an honor to learn the language of your people." Most certainly a lie. Learning all the dialects of Neharem was bad enough, and Zarith had a sharp, abrasive quality she loathed despite it being her mother's native tongue.

Davier's father folded his arms. "It's good you're working with Az Zar to help liberate Neharem. Few of your people are so wise."

Elaysia's jaw tightened. She concentrated on the tea Dynah poured in front of her.

"Kyreena"—he motioned to Davier's mother—"our guests are hungry from travel."

"I can help," Elaysia offered, eager for escape. It wasn't uncommon for guests in Neharem to join their host in meal preparation, but as soon as she spoke, Davier nudged her leg under the table.

"It's no trouble," Kyreena said, tone light. "We're always prepared for visitors. Davier never announces when he's coming home."

She chuckled and herded the girls out of the room. They returned with enough dishes to fill the table: vegetables soaked in vinegar, steamed kuba grain, smoked fish, sweet and tangy sauces, boiled eggs, and sauteed greens. It took all Elaysia's restraint to wait, enticed as she was by the new spices and flavors.

Davier's father asked for Mavet's blessing, a lengthy ordeal focused on damning those who strayed from—or altogether avoided—the holy path. When they finally ate, no one spoke. The whole meal. She swore they heard her swallow.

After bellies were filled and the dishes cleared, Davier's father dominated the discussion. It revolved around pride, both familial and national, and how excited they were to relocate to the capital after Davier's promotion. Which district would be best to live in? Would they have access to the coveted bathhouses? Shop on the sun-blood strip with the finest vendors? The girls would do well there. Kiska excelled in her religious studies. Dynah's homemaking skills were certain to win her a suitor. Xi—

He didn't get to finish, for Xi smashed her fists on the table and shouted, "I'm going to be a soldier like Davier." With her flushed little cheeks and piercing eyes, Elaysia didn't doubt her.

Davier's father shot down her zeal with a huff of disgust. "A woman's place is in the home or serving our Lord and Savior."

"But there are lady soldiers," Xi said, lip quivering. "I've seen them."

"Nyrians, highborn at that, and unbecoming still. It tarnishes one's image for a potential husband. Don't cloud your future with childish fantasies."

"I don't want a husband."

"Silence," he spat. Xi sniffled. "Help Eumma fetch dessert."

"Yes, sir." Xi trudged to the kitchen, an exaggerated slump in her shoulders.

Elaysia gripped her chair. Her father would've never spoken to her in such a demeaning manner.

The elder man returned his attention to Davier, and his irritation melted away. "Now, boy, how long are you staying?"

"Not long." Davier cracked his knuckles. "Perhaps we can speak in private later?"

His father stiffened; a subtle tensing of the shoulders. Before he could respond, Kyreena and Xi returned with a loaf of sweet bread alongside bowls of fresh berries and cream—a luxury, Davier whispered, saved for the most important guests and occasions. Elaysia thanked Kyreena, who accepted the compliment with a smile but politely declined her offer to help clear the dishes.

They remained at the table the rest of the evening, visiting over a fermented kuba grain drink. Rather, the men shared the drink; Mavet-fearing women knew their weaker constitutions would be compromised. At least, that's how Davier's father put it. Elaysia snuck sips from Davier's cup anyway, partly out of spite, partly because she needed it.

She happily accepted Kiska's cot for the night, exhausted as she was, but her thoughts wouldn't let her find immediate sleep.

Despite the dogmatic and cruel framework they'd been bred into, Davier's family wasn't so unlike those in Neharem. They loved, worked hard, reminisced about the past, breathed hope into the future. Her heart twisted a little. It was one thing to hate a people from afar and quite another to be welcomed into their home. Would she be like them—believe as they did—had she been born in Az Zar?

No, she thought bitterly. *If by some miracle I was born in this wretched place, I would've been killed soon after my first breath.*

A rage, hot and righteous, burned inside her. She channeled it toward the one she knew to be responsible: the All-Sovereign.

Elaysia woke to the sound of muffled shouting.

The house was dark, and the spicy scent of dinner lingered in the air. She lowered a cautious foot. The floor creaked beneath her weight. She winced as Dynah stirred, muttered something in her sleep, and rolled over.

For Khiev-Tatamic's sake.

She crept into the main room and parted the wooden slats covering the window. Davier and his father stood in the yard.

"Eudna, please listen," Davier was saying, his words slurred. "There's plenty of opportunity in Orillon. You and Eumma can get your own land. Settle down. Raise the girls right. Be free of all"—he gestured wildly to the surrounding homes—"this."

His father crossed his arms, face twisted into a snarl. "You'd throw away your rank, your family, your own life—all for this girl?"

"It's not just her." Davier leaned against the porch and took drink from a bottle. "I've given my life to this empire, and for what? Worthless accolades from the All-Sovereign? Even if I completed my mission and got promoted, I'd still be his bitch. I'm disposable to him. And so are you." Davier's father was stone. "His Holiness," Davier continued, laden with disdain, "is starting another war, and I won't be a pawn in it. Not this time." He took another drink and staggered toward his father. "We don't have to go to Orillon. Shit, we can go anywhere. Let's leave Quinaria and see what the world has to offer us."

"I won't listen to your treasonous talk, boy." Davier's father slapped the bottle from his hand. "Why should I leave my country after all it has done for me? The All-Sovereign blessed us, and you spit in his face." He jabbed a finger into Davier's chest, his face inches from his son's. "It was stupid enough to bring a heathen into our home, but to ask us to commit treason? To throw away the opportunities your eumma and I've worked tirelessly to give to you and your sisters? You dishonor me."

Davier flinched. "Why are you so stubborn, old man? This isn't about honor." He reached for his father's arm. "At least leave Or Zahal for a time. Take new names. You're not safe here."

"If we're not safe, it's because of you." He ripped his arm free and spat. "If we are punished, it's on your conscience."

"No." Davier blocked the porch. "I'm washing my hands of this. This is your decision and your family."

Davier's father shoved past him with an elbow to his stomach. He paused at the door, back to his son. "I'm not afraid like you. This conversation is over."

The door groaned open.

Elaysia was halfway across the room, tiptoeing back to sanctuary, but her foot caught on the uniform display. It crashed to the ground with her.

Davier's father stormed toward the commotion and snatched Elaysia's arm. "You creep about even now. Going through our things, were you?" Spittle flew out as he spoke.

Kyreena and the girls stumbled into the room. Someone gasped.

"Let her go." Davier's voice was calm, but Elaysia made out his hardened features in the moonlight streaming through the door. His father's grip loosened. Elaysia seized the moment and rushed to Davier's side. "We can talk more in the morning."

The older man shook his head violently. "There will be no more talk. You know where I stand. Where this family stands." He grabbed their packs from the corner and hurled them into the yard.

Kyreena broke off from the girls and grabbed his arm. "Davkahl, please," she croaked.

He shrugged her off. "I said no, woman. He's no longer our son. It's the choice he made." He angled his body toward Davier and Elaysia without looking at them. "Go, before I alert the sentries."

Davier froze, dead to the world. Elaysia grabbed his hand. It trembled.

Xi fell into his arms, crying. Dynah and Kiska didn't approach. Whether out of shock or fear, Elaysia knew not.

"I said go!" Davier's father yanked Xi back. Kyreena took Davier's arm and urged him and Elaysia outside.

"Eumma," Davier's voiced cracked. "Take the girls and leave. Promise me. It's not safe. Think of them." She didn't reply, but she wrapped her arms around him before retreating into the house.

When they reached the gate at the edge of the yard, Davier's father shouted a final threat. "I'll help the All-Sovereign himself hunt you down if I must, to serve the empire and protect my family. You're dead to me, boy."

They slunk through the streets in silence, nothing but stray dogs and the occasional sentry to break their stride. Elaysia almost spoke when they reached their horses tethered outside the city, but one look at Davier's sunken posture convinced her she had nothing to offer him. They rode through the night until wisps of sunlight stained the horizon. When they passed an abandoned campfire next to the river, Davier hopped off without warning and retrieved his bedroll.

"Davier," Elaysia said, summoning her courage. She rested her hand on his arm, but he quickly shrugged it off.

He threw his bedroll on the ground, not bothering to remove the rocks from underneath it, and lay down.

"What can I do? Please tell me."

No reply. Elaysia patted down the horses, then arranged her bedroll beside him. Pressed her back to his as they'd done countless nights prior. "Sleep well," she whispered.

"If only it were so easy." His words dripped bitterness as he stiffened his back against hers.

Elaysia rubbed the grooves of her necklace. Staring up at the dawn, thoughts caught somewhere between prayer and plea, she wished safety for Davier's family. Even his father.

It's too late, a small voice said as exhaustion pulled her eyelids closed.

Those who don't bend break.

JAKKI

J akki loosened her grip on the riverbank and wiped the vomit from her lips. The body loomed behind her. She splashed some water on her face and turned to face it.

Him.

It was Unleto, a young warrior with ice-white eyes distinct to the Moatiwe tribe. His head lay at an awkward angle, eyes glazed over with death. A foul stench revived Jakki's nausea: his bowels had loosened.

A deep burn seized her throat. She rubbed her eyes to prevent tears from falling. The old man. It was him. She couldn't have—wouldn't have—on her own.

"What did you do to me?" she screamed. "Show yourself."

The woods offered no reply.

Jakki refused to look at Unleto as she dragged him from the bank. His lean frame was much heavier than she'd anticipated, slick with water, skin lax and cold.

An hour later found her peering over a cliff, filmed in sweat. Whatever happened in the river had sapped her energy, but her leg was healed, marred by a fresh, reddened scar. A gift.

A curse.

Jakki searched the clearing to ensure she hadn't been followed, mumbled a prayer, and shoved the body off. She didn't watch it fall.

Siren shrieked and hopped away from the cliffside. Jakki started after her, but the pull to take a final look was too strong. She peered over the edge. Swallowed bile. Save for the gray–blue skin, any resemblance to Unleto was gone, dashed atop the rocks in bloody disarray. At least she couldn't see his face.

"Find peace, Brother," she whispered. It wasn't the burial he deserved, but the ravager birds would appreciate her offering. Life had its order.

Jakki was a few minutes from the camp when black tendrils obstructed her vision. Chills rippled through her body as she stumbled through the tall, spindly grasses. Her foot caught. She lurched, headfirst, and struck something hard.

Darkness overtook her.

Jakki awoke to a throbbing temple. Large hands cradled her head, stroked the back of her neck. She stiffened. Tried to rise. The hands held her fast.

"Easy, Jak. You're safe."

She blinked. A face came into focus above her. "Mardus?"

The Moákun grunted. He dabbed a damp cloth around her eye to remove the crusted blood. "You've been unconscious for hours, maybe longer. What happened?"

"I—fuck." Jakki drew in a sharp breath as he encroached on her wound. Siren squalled and nipped at Mardus's fingers.

"She's been worried," he said, jerking his hand away. "Wouldn't let us near you at first."

Jakki calmed the stormbird with a brush of her hand. "How bad is it?"

Mardus smirked as he slathered a poultice on her temple. "With this and your leg wound, you'll rival Chief Gibrund's scars."

Jakki pressed to her elbows. They were back in the nazrath valley, warmed by the rusty rays of the setting sun. She motioned for Mardus's waterskin, which he offered without question. Pouch pressed to her mouth, visions of Unleto flooded her mind. Maybe it was all a dream. She searched for him among the Neharem gathered in the clearing. No Unleto. Her chest tightened.

She passed the empty skin back to Mardus. "I went for a walk to strengthen my leg. I remember feeling faint, then darkness." Not entirely a lie. "I'm sorry to have caused worry."

Mardus patted her arm, albeit awkwardly, but before he could respond, Yerakai crouched beside them. She hadn't heard him or his ghostly stormbird approach. His skin looked a midnight purple in the fading light, his eyes alive with the colors of a sunset.

"Praise Khiev-Tatamic you're safe." Yerakai's tone was anything but sincere. "It was unwise to wander off in your condition, though I'd expect it of you." He maintained unbroken eye contact. She fought to match it. "You were gone a great while. Did your injuries also weaken your sense of time and direction?"

"We're all weakened right now, Brother," Mardus said. "Body and mind." Jakki could've kissed him.

"I sent Unleto after you long before the rest of us went looking," Yerakai continued, ignoring Mardus's attempt at peace.

Jakki kept her face calm. Studied the curves of his armor, the outlines of leaves and branches blending into the lyvium.

"Did you happen upon him?"

Jakki—perhaps too quickly—said, "I saw no one. I found a river and followed it for a while. Rested. Prayed." She swallowed. Forced herself to look at his face. "Has he not returned?"

"No." Yerakai's eyes simmered. "It's strange. He's our best tracker in my absence."

Silence hung between them, thick as a hide.

He doesn't want to think it's possible, she thought as she watched his face contort.

"If there are skulmor nearby, not one of us could survive an attack alone," Mardus offered.

Yerakai pursed his lips. "We'll split into two parties and scout until nightfall. If we can't find him by then, we'll bless his spirit and head south as planned." His normally musical voice sounded scratchy and thick. A wave of sickness washed over Jakki.

"You should rest," Mardus said when she made to follow. "We'll be back soon. With Unleto." The disbelief in his eyes betrayed his confident voice.

Jakki started to protest, then remembered her leg. Scarred, but healed. It wouldn't do to share that secret, though, not yet. She lay down to appease Mardus, but once alone, she paced, too anxious to rest, too nauseated to eat. Every time the wind rustled the leaves, she jerked, startling Siren. They'd never let her live if they found out. Or worse, they'd drag her back to Agaas to await Elaysia's punishment. Assuming Elaysia ever came home.

Jakki tamped down the thought.

Night fell. The moons hung high, unhindered by clouds. Jakki, layered in furs, decided the least she could do was start a fire.

The giants didn't have piles of wood stacked like sensible folk, so she took to the edge of the forest and cut some with an abandoned Daruk axe. She was sprinting back to the camp with a final load when someone cleared their throat. Loudly. The wood slipped from her arms.

Anahi emerged from the shadows, a wry smile on her face. "Feeling better?"

Jakki cursed her racing heart. She picked up the wood slowly, as though it pained her. "A little. I didn't want to be useless and thought everyone would appreciate a fire when they returned."

"Clarity of mind would've been more appreciated."

"Sorry my head injury's an inconvenience for you."

"Inconvenient for Unleto."

"You didn't find him?"

"My party didn't." Anahi's hand flicked to her hilt. "Something tells me no one else did either."

Jakki's jaw clenched. Siren fluttered toward Anahi's half-sized male and screeched. The Stormriders assumed the stances of their birds, toe to toe, a breath's distance apart. Jakki's eyes roved over the foreigner. Even wounded, she could take the Orillon bitch.

But that day would have to wait.

The others trickled into the camp, weighted with sorrow and silence. No need to cause a commotion. Jakki spat at Anahi's feet and sought Yerakai. Best to face him head-on.

He didn't look up as she approached. "Nothing?" she asked.

Yerakai shook his head. "Not even a body. I fear skulmor ate"—he covered his mouth—"he's gone. It's likely he came upon a hunting party and misjudged his ability to handle them." He grasped Jakki's hands and pressed his cheek to hers. "I was wrong to infer your involvement. I hope you can forgive me."

Tension dripped from Jakki's muscles. She fought to keep her tone and face somber. "I harbor nothing against you, Brother."

Yerakai pulled away just as Anahi stalked by. The Orillon woman's gaze could kill.

They prepared Unleto's sending within the hour. The Moatiwe funeral process required offerings of hair, blood, and bone, so the dead could be remade anew in the next life.

Jakki was honored with lighting the pyre—a kind gesture suggested by Yerakai that only worsened her guilt—where Unleto's body should've lain. She hurried to rejoin the circle with the others. Eeshta, a Moatiwe black as the night sky, moaned in deep-toned agony. She stood near the pyre, white locks goldened with firelight. In lieu of a drum, Mardus knocked wooden paddles together in a heartbeat's rhythm.

"We ask Moartea, harbinger of passing, to deliver our brother, Unleto, to Everworld," Eeshta said. She spoke first in the dialect of her people, then repeated each phrase in Nyrinian. "May he thrive forever, unshackled and unsleeping, running with our ancestors and drinking from Khiev-Tatamic's river of eternal life." Mardus stopped pounding. The wails halted with it, leaving only Eeshta's voice. "We rejoice for Unleto and others who've passed, for there is no death, only a change of worlds. Khiev-Tatamic be praised."

One by one, the warriors placed their offerings and departed.

Jakki stayed. She watched the fire turn to embers. The Yustano believed in new life as well, though by means of rebirth. Wherever Unleto's spirit settled, Jakki hoped he'd understand. Forgive her.

A hand rested on her shoulder. She wiped the tears from her eyes and spun to find Yerakai.

"Sister, it's time to depart this place. The nazrath are waiting." He touched her cheek with tenderness, a gesture of genuine concern and friendship. "Something haunts you. Won't you tell me?"

Someone. Mother Itaso, she wanted to tell him. Yerakai could pry honesty from a pirate and carry a secret through ten lifetimes.

Instead, she said, "I'm tired is all," and hurried to the sleeping circle they shared with the giants.

The rest of the Neharem warriors huddled around a dying fire. Above them towered the male nazrath, arms folded over his exposed chest. He regarded Jakki with a grunt and held out an unidentifiable slab of meat on a stick. She refused but forced a smile. The two females were nowhere to be seen, and their belongings—giant bedrolls, extra furs, and drinking horns belonging to larger creatures than any she'd laid eyes on—had vanished.

Yerakai came to stand beside her. "His companions are headed home with their kills. They came south to hunt and delayed their return to aid us." He brought a hand to his lips and extended it in front of him. "Thank you again, Brother," he told the giant.

Brother? Jakki rolled her eyes and struggled to fit Siren into her pack. The stormbird would have to hop along on her own soon or, better yet, fly.

Yerakai continued his nonsensical motions and grunts, which the nazrath apparently understood well enough to return. After a few gestures, the giant rushed into the woods as swiftly as any nyrian.

"He's arranged a means of travel to Denjuu for us," Yerakai said, motioning the others to follow. "Be quiet and respectful as you approach."

A few choice responses flitted through Jakki's mind, but considering recent events, she kept them to herself and trailed her warriors to the tree line.

The wind carried an icy bite and rattled the frost in the trees like crystals in the moonlight. A few yards away, with a face stoic enough to make Mardus look lively, stood the nazrath. He stepped aside and revealed two pale eyes hidden in the shadows. Jakki pushed past the others to get a closer look. The owner of the eyes snorted. A horn as long as she was tall emerged from the shadows, sending her stumbling back into the grass. She raised her staff in defense, but the nazrath ripped it from her grasp. Nostrils flared, he pressed his forehead against the creature's horn and grunted. It huffed back, and several more creatures appeared.

Jakki snatched her staff back and moved a safe distance away to evaluate the beasts. Their bodies were half the height of the giants, but elongated and stocky. Instead of hooves, toes covered each of their four legs. A thick, coarse hair protected their bodies, save for their faces, which resembled hides. A smaller horn rested above their primary defense.

Anahi dared to offer a creature her hand. To Jakki's dismay, it pressed a massive snout into her palm. "I bet one of them could carry four of us," the Orillon woman said, eyes wide with wonder.

"We aren't riding these things." Jakki turned to Yerakai. "You can't be serious. They're wild."

Yerakai lifted a shoulder. "No more than our horses."

"But the nazrath hunt them. You've seen their drinking horns."

"And we hunt the nytak, but they respect us. We return to them and nourish their soil." He slung his bow over his shoulder and tied his hair in a low knot. "These creatures have a similar relationship with the nazrath, only more dependent. They will take us to the Az Zarian border."

A grin cracked across Mardus's face as he ran his hand through a beast's matted coat. "It's a harsh aroma, but they are kind, Jakki. Don't worry."

"I'm *not* worried." Jakki marched toward one and thrust her hand onto its horn. It shook its head and pawed at the ground.

"Don't approach them so aggressively." Yerakai rested his hand on the beast. It settled instantly.

Jakki's cheeks burned. She glared at Yerakai and gritted her teeth. "How in Haeshol do we get on the damn things?"

"Observe." He tilted his head toward the nazrath, who hoisted a wide-eyed Eeshta onto one.

Jakki cursed inwardly when the nazrath wrapped his hand around her waist and set her atop a beast's shivering back as though she was a child's figurine. To make things even better, he placed Anahi behind her. Jakki smoldered, struggling to stay balanced on the thick spine, while Yerakai flapped and flailed at the nazrath. When the goodbyes ceased, the giant gave a final bow and vanished into the woods.

"How do we make them go?" Mardus shouted.

In reply, the beast he shared with Eeshta snorted and barreled down the path leading out of the valley.

Anahi chuckled behind her. "Like that, I suppose."

Jakki dug her fingers into the beast's hair as it lurched forward. Anahi held onto Jakki's waist with a tenderness not offered to her hours prior and, thank The Daughter, she had the decency to avoid further interrogation.

Alone with her thoughts, Jakki tried to cling to the anticipation of seeing Elaysia again. But Unleto's empty eyes haunted her. As they raced through the night, growing accustomed to the beast's heavy-footed gait, she swore she heard a cackle. Somewhere in the dark, the old man sneered at her from his rock perch. She had a feeling she'd see him again.

When she did, she'd kill him.

DAVIER

Sunlight beat down on Davier's face like an overseer full of self-righteous anger. He chewed his lips to remove the rough edges and studied the red dirt stretching miles ahead with no relief from the violent rays. Normally, he traveled north of the Ashaat, the standard route from Or Zahal to Cadar, a journey filled with greenery and chirping birds instead of nevethium-stripped drought land plagued with screaming vultures. But it was too risky. His father had likely notified the local authorities. Besides, this was the journey he deserved.

"Davier, wait," Elaysia shouted. Her tone implied it wasn't the first time she'd called out. "There's a path branching off toward the river."

Davier didn't turn or slow his mount.

"I know you want to avoid the main roads, but our horses need water. So do we. Besides, we're on the opposite side." The demanding bite in her words sounded eerily like his old general barking orders. He gave a curt nod and turned a sharp right toward the path. "Wonderful speaking with you, as always," she shouted behind him.

The silence between them was more suffocating than the heat, but still better than pretending everything was fine. She'd tried to console him the first few days. Little jokes, more wine, extra space—complete avoidance of the issue at hand. In return, he ignored her during the days and lay awake at night, trying to identify the exact moment she'd fucked his life over forever. Was it the quirk of her lips? The spontaneity of her actions? The warmth of her skin?

Not that she was fully to blame. It was his mistake for letting lust impede duty. For letting his heart destroy the future he deserved. If he'd just stayed detached a little longer, hadn't allowed her to wander off into dangerous situations where he realized he cared about her safety, he'd already be headed home with his promotion and reward. To make it all worse, he wasn't even sure it was love.

Elaysia gasped, returning Davier's attention to the trail. Or the river, rather. This part of the Ashaat ran large and still enough to imitate a lake. Fields of water lilies stretched as far as the eye could see, swathed in a vibrant red, the color of freshly spilled blood. A warm breeze pressed against him, rich with algae and mud.

Elaysia took a hesitant step toward the bank. "What is it?"

"The Red Beach. A special vegetation grows around this part of the river between Or Zahal and Ba'albehk. Supposedly fertilizes the soil and cleanses the water." He dismounted and ran his hand across the tops of some lilies. Slick and fuzzy as a wet puppy. "See? Just plants. They grow so close together that it often gets mistaken for soil or a swamp."

"It's beautiful."

"I guess."

Elaysia lifted her mare's leg to check her hoof. The horses they'd acquired from a settlement east of Or Zahal were sickly, prone to missteps, and just a few missed meals away from protruding ribs.

"I know you're grieving for your family, but you've hardly said anything to me since we left days ago." She faced him, her form stark against the sea of red. "Days. What happened between you and your father?"

"Don't pretend you weren't listening." He shoved past Elaysia to lead his gelding to the water, but she grabbed the reins.

"Why'd he react so harshly?"

"I told him I'm done serving the empire, and he's not one to take dishonor lightly." Davier ripped the reins from her grasp. "I should've known better. Should've lied to him. Now their lives are at stake."

"You did everything you could. He would've found out, eventually. Does it matter that it was now versus later?"

"Later would've meant they'd be out of harm's way when they disowned me." Davier marched to the bank. Elaysia's eyes burned into his back as he knelt to drink. "It's safe," he muttered. "I told you it cleanses the water. Hurry and drink. Neharem is a long way still."

"We're going to Cadar." Elaysia's controlled tone slipped into high-pitched panic. "I can't return emptyhanded."

"Better emptyhanded than dead."

Elaysia's eyes widened, then narrowed. "You're still hiding something from me. Why?"

"This again?" Davier laughed, an aggravated cackle leaving a bitter taste on his tongue.

"Maybe Konar was right about you." Elaysia made for her horse, but Davier clasped her wrist mid-mount and yanked her back. The mare bared her teeth and snapped, missing Davier's arm by inches.

"I have nothing left to hide from you!" he shouted.

"I wish I believed that." Elaysia dropped her gaze, dark lashes brushing against her cheeks. "Why are you even still here? If it's only pity, then go. I've had enough of that to last a lifetime. And if it's guilt, I'm not some tool to clear your conscious."

Davier's grip on her softened. Why couldn't he turn her in? Or better yet, leave? *Because you lov—*

No. He refused to think it. To feel it.

"It's too risky, Ellie." He smoothed back his hair and stared beyond her in the direction of Cadar. "They'll know of my desertion by now, and the All-Sovereign will heighten patrols."

Elaysia sought her necklace and rubbed it between her fingers. If she noted his avoidance of her question, she didn't divulge it. "We've discussed the risks at length and were in agreement. Besides, the others might be waiting there, and we can't leave without them."

"If they're there—and that's a big if—we'd be lucky to find them. Cadar's no small village."

"It will work out. It has to."

Davier's palms began to sweat. "We've seen enough to convince the council. We could return with more warriors."

Elaysia climbed atop her mount. "I'm going, with or without you."

The sun kissed the horizon, alighting her frame in a fiery glow. Her eyes danced; her nostrils flared like a wild mare about to bolt. She was a lamb willing for the slaughter. A more perfect situation couldn't be devised. But...

"I can't let you do that." His voice cracked.

"That's the second time you've said that. That exact phrase." She nudged her mount forward, eyes on his hands. "Go back to your family. I'm done—"

A woman's scream drowned out her voice. Shrill. In pain.

Without warning, Elaysia took off, racing toward a cloud of red dust in the distance.

Everything in Davier's body screamed *stay*. His muscles stiffened. Heart raced. But he forced himself to ride after her. Bodies deprived of proper sleep and rations did strange things.

Elaysia had dismounted a few yards from the scene: two low-ranking soldiers set upon a woman. They tore at her clothes like ravenous animals while she struggled to keep her breasts covered with the slivers of fabric left from her gown. Davier leaned forward in the saddle at a gallop. When he drew close enough, he dove off the gelding and rose amid the skirmish, both swords drawn. He prowled within an arm's reach of the woman. One soldier scrambled to put a blade to her throat. The other lowered his swords at Davier.

"Stay back, or she dies," the latter said.

Elaysia entered Davier's peripherals, bow drawn. He took a step closer, lowering his swords to meet the soldier's. "Your funeral."

The man's eyes narrowed beneath his mask. He looked from Davier to Elaysia. "We mean you no trouble. This one ran away from our camp, and we're collecting her to finish her duty. What do you care about a whore? Unless"—his eyes roved Elaysia's figure—"you want to trade yours? Never fucked a half-breed before."

Davier flinched. Without thinking, he brought a blade down on the soldier's arm, slicing it clean off. The soldier gaped at the waterfall of blood. Davier slit his throat and started for the other, but Elaysia's arrow had already found its home in his chest. He lay on the ground, fingers grasping at the arrow. Davier severed his head from his body to be sure.

Elaysia rushed to the woman's side. "Are you hurt?"

The woman was a few years older than Davier. Narrow eyes, pale skin, dark hair—features of a southern Az Zarian human. Two grotesque creatures with flaming eyes and horned heads tattooed the innermost parts of her breasts. Something about the tattoos was familiar, as if from a dream. She caught his eye and smiled with blood-red lips. The film of dirt and tears did little to mask her beauty. He averted his gaze.

"All is well now that I've found you, High Chieftain," the woman sang. "They came upon me, and I tried to run, but—"

"Wait." Davier tensed, fists taut at his sides. Had the All-Sovereign sent a spy? But the soldiers... "What did you say?"

"That the gods guided me to the high chieftain." The woman, who hadn't stopped smiling since her rescue, took Elaysia's face in her hands. "I've been seeking you, Daughter of Quinaria."

Davier searched the darkening horizon. No mounts in sight, nor any tracks besides their own. "Where's your mount? Or your attackers' mounts, for that matter?"

"Who sent you?" Elaysia stuttered. She appeared paralyzed in the woman's hands, unaware Davier inched toward her, blades still drawn.

"The Guardian of Life herself," the woman cooed. "Chai'Tik heard your prayers and shepherded your journey. And now she has need of you."

"The Daughter." Elaysia's voice was barely a whisper. She grasped her necklace. "I've always hoped, but...." Her eyes closed for a moment. "I'm hers to command."

Davier ripped Elaysia from the woman's grasp and shoved her behind him. "An ordained messenger, eh?" He raised his blades to hover above the woman's throat. "Let's put it to the test. I cut you now, and we'll see if you bleed and die like us mortals."

"Davier, stop." Elaysia lowered his swords. "She's alone and unarmed."

"That's what concerns me."

"Captain Zadel," the woman purred. "Let me show you I mean no harm." She slithered up to him, flaunting her lithe body.

Threats formulated in Davier's mind, but when he tried to speak, the words wouldn't come. His entire body stilled, save for the rise and fall of his chest. He couldn't blink, swallow, twitch. The woman ran her fingertips down his arms and pried his swords away with ease. With her hands no longer holding the fragmented gown in place, it fell open and exposed her breasts. Davier tore his gaze away and sought Elaysia's. The woman blocked his view. She pressed her lips to his ear.

"She'll be your downfall," she whispered, "and you'll do nothing to stop it." A shiver prickled across his skin as her lips drifted to his neck and down his chest. "Best enjoy the present, Davier San Zadel." She tilted her chin to him and blinked. For a fleeting moment, her eyes were an abyss. Beastly and otherworldly. Another blink returned them to deep brown. "It's all that exists." She tugged at his belt and sauntered back to Elaysia, who stood dazed, eyes on the woman. Davier pressed at the invisible bonds holding him.

"What does Chai'Tik require of me?" Elaysia asked. If she feared for herself or Davier, she didn't show it. She drank the woman in, lips parted in wonder.

"She requires nothing, yet offers an opportunity to succeed where your parents failed." The woman lifted Elaysia's chin and traced snow-white fingers over her face. "You're destined, my dear," she murmured. "Unique as a filly among sows. You will succeed where others have not." She kissed Elaysia softly on the lips—a common enough gesture in Orillon where Davier doubted she hailed from—and whispered something in her ear. Elaysia's eyes went wide.

Davier's throat tightened. He wanted to cut the woman down. He glared at the back of her head with all the spite he could muster. *Cowardly bitch. Come, fight me.*

As though she'd heard his thoughts spoken aloud, she vanished, then appeared directly in front of him. He tried in vain to shut his eyes. *Awskada.* Witch.

"Sleep now, sweet warrior. Your time is soon." The woman grabbed a handful of dirt and blew it over him like a gentle sandstorm.

Davier grunted and strained, but the world around him faded into a red glow until all he saw was the witch. She blinked again. This time, more than the color of her eyes changed. Gone were the long lashes, smooth skin, full lips. In its place, a beast's face. Curved horns. A monster, like the ones on her breasts.

"Elaysia," he croaked. But his eyes grew heavy. His body quivered. He fell to the ground, swallowed by a red haze.

Davier awoke to claws of thirst scraping his throat. He drained his canteen and rose, stumbling around in a drunken stupor he was no stranger to. But this time, he'd consumed no drink, *and* he recalled the preceding events. Mostly.

Night had fallen. Dust tendrils danced in the wind, teasing the naked branches of bushes, making ghosts in the air. No Elaysia. No bodies. No witch.

A snort cut through the night. Their horses waited a few yards away. They pawed at the dirt, ears flicking.

Davier ignored the prickles on his skin and dared to call out, "Elaysia."

A shadow moved in a nearby brush cluster. "Davier?"

He sprang toward the voice. Elaysia's body was elongated in the dirt, propped up on her elbow, eyes half-open. He slid an arm around her waist, pulling her to his chest.

"Are you alright?"

"Of course," she said, voice raspy with sleep. "I'm alive, and so are you."

"What happened to you? Did you see me struggling? She put a spell on me. Froze my body."

"I know." No trace of concern in Elaysia's voice. Her hair blew free from the remnants of her braids. She ran a finger along his jaw. "She was enchanting. I didn't dare move or speak until she asked it of me." A smile passed over Elaysia's lips. She parted them, inching closer to Davier.

Davier held up his hand. "I'm not saying she captivated me. I couldn't *move*. Couldn't speak. She said—did—unnatural things." He rubbed his eyes. "Didn't you see me fall?"

Elaysia's expression remained oblivious. "I thought you fell asleep. It was all so... strange."

Davier ran his fingers through his hair. "What happened after I"—he swallowed—"fell asleep?"

Elaysia lit up, eyes sparkling in the moonlight. "She said to continue to Cadar. There's something I must find, and if I wait too long, the opportunity won't arise again."

"Is that all?"

Her brow furrowed. "When she kissed me, she said, 'To have success, you must first know failure. To have love, you must first learn loss. To have true power, you must experience utter helplessness.'"

Davier's stomach tightened. He looked away.

"This is the sign I've waited for. Don't you see?"

"No." Davier untangled his fingers from hers. "We don't know where she came from, and your enemies are many here. She's lying. Maybe one of the All-Sovereign's spies."

"She's a goddess." Elaysia leaned away from him, frowning. "How else would she appear and disappear without a trace? No Az Zarian spy would claim to be a messenger of The Daughter."

Davier laughed, though it lacked any sincerity. "Then you're more naïve than I thought."

Elaysia drew her knees to her chest. "Not everyone's a snake like you."

He closed his eyes to mask the hurt. "That's a bit harsh."

"Deity or not, something awaits me in Cadar, and I won't ignore that calling." She grasped his hand with a fierceness to rival his own. "Go. Return to your family. Sail to those distant lands you crave. I won't think ill of you, Captain." She bit her lip. Hesitated. But then she kissed him, a lingering press of her mouth against his.

His throat tightened, his mind at war with his body. And heart. He leaned into her. Ran his hand along the curve of her backside.

She groped the back of his head, then pulled away. "Sorry, I"—she wrapped her arms around her stomach—"I wanted to feel you one last time." She made to leave.

He didn't let her.

"It doesn't have to be the last time." The desert held its breath as he drew her near. Not so much as a rustle in the brush. Here, now, the light of the moon softening her skin and the musk of exertion emanating from her chest, she was the most beautiful woman he'd ever seen. His lips hovered above hers, tasting, not drinking. "If you ask it of me, I'll never leave your side."

"I need no allegiance." She kissed him again, hands drifting down his stomach to unfasten his belt. The breeze cooled his bare skin. He pulled at her gauntlets. Her tunic. Ran his hands down her exposed back. "Just tonight."

He kissed her back fiercely and pulled her to the ground on top of him.

ZAVIK

Zavik tugged his collar back and blew down his chest. It wasn't hot out. Quite pleasant, actually, with a breeze carrying the familiar tingle of salt. And though he remained in the shade, avoiding spears of sunlight that penetrated breaks in the branches and spilled onto the High Tree platform, sweat pooled in the most inopportune places. Elaysia would tell him to shake it off; he couldn't control most of what was about to happen. But she wasn't here, and her absence further inflamed his nerves.

"Are we doing this?" T'Vak asked mid-yawn.

Zavik wiped his palms on his pants and cleared his throat. "I will translate these with or without your help. I risked my life for this knowledge, and it might be the only way... what I mean is, it's necessary to, to"—T'Vak raised an eyebrow—"Konar, the very survival of Neharem depends on..." Zavik shook his head. "Is any of this convincing? Do I need more force? Less?"

"You're overthinking it." T'Vak drained the last of his wineskin. "The more you babble, the worse it sounds. What's so scary about this, anyway? You held your own against bandits."

A monster, and the shaktar, too. Of course, his only witness conveniently forgot those little details. "It's different. Konar's, well, he's..."

"Now you've gone and used all your words up for the day." T'Vak cracked his knuckles and shot Zavik a wink. That stupid wink.

"You're a funny man, T'Vak. I'll hate to see you go."

"Eh, might stick 'round if the pay's right."

"I don't exactly make those decisions."

"I do," a familiar voice cut in.

Konar. Zavik brought his right fist to his heart in greeting, but Konar surprised him with an embrace.

"Khiev-Tatamic be praised. You've returned to us safely."

"Of course," Zavik stammered, trying to match Konar's cavern-deep register. "Why wouldn't I have?" T'Vak snickered, and Konar frowned, studying the backhander. "This is T'Vak"—Zavik nudged him, lowering his voice—"your family name was?"

T'Vak gave a sloppy grin with an air of defiance. "Don't think I told you. Don't think it matters. Don't know for certain, love-giving mother and all."

Zavik's cheeks flushed. "I, we, owe him a bit of something well deserved. He offered me protection on my journey and saved my life more than once."

T'Vak snorted. "I count thrice."

"I see." Konar's eyes darkened. A cluster of women, fingers stained with dye, gawked as they passed, eyes on the high elder. Konar apparently kept to himself as of late. Not a good sign. "Chala." Konar summoned a nyrian watcher on patrol. "Ensure this guest"—he gestured to T'Vak with disgust—"is fed and rested."

The watcher nodded. T'Vak shrugged at Zavik and followed an unenthused Chala to the guest quarters.

So much for support.

"I must speak with you, High Elder." Zavik hoped his voice sounded more certain aloud than it did in his head.

Konar flashed a row of gleaming teeth. "I expected so. Saw you ride in last night." Did he have fewer wrinkles since Zavik saw him last? Was that even possible? "But first, I've had a meal prepared to break your fast. I'm sure your journey's left you exhausted and in need of proper food. Care to join me?"

Zavik's stomach rumbled. Perhaps food would quell his nerves. "I'd be honored."

Inside the summit lodge, bean soup, grain salads, baked squash with dried fruit, and smoked fish covered the table—enough to feed a standard council gathering. Maseeya alone awaited them. She wore a simple fringe tunic with her hair tangled around her shoulders, far from the usual care she put into her presentation. Her tired eyes lit up when Zavik entered. She wrapped him in a hug and ushered him to the table where she doubled-stacked cushions and slid the platters up close. They ate in silence while Konar looked on, pipe in hand. Zavik chewed slowly, biding his time.

"Well?" Konar asked after Zavik finally pushed away the last dish. "Were your endeavors successful?"

Maseeya leaned forward and rested a hand on Konar's arm.

Zavik reached into his cloak and ran his fingers across the scroll tips. He'd grown accustomed to their weight pressed against his chest. He started to pull one out, then reached for the wine instead. He took a swig and choked. It spilled down his tunic, missing the scrolls by mere inches. Konar tossed Maseeya an irritated look while Zavik blotted his chest with his cloak.

For the love of Quinaria, can something go according to plan?

"Zavik," Konar urged.

"You should know I'll honor Elaysia's wishes over any objections, be it the council's or yours," Zavik said, meeker than intended. He cleared his throat. "I won't be dissuaded."

"If I wanted to dissuade you, do you think I would've let you run off after ransacking my loft for maps?" Konar's lips twitched in amusement. "On the contrary, I regret not lending aid sooner. I'm eager to hear what you've learned." He laid his pipe on the table and regarded Zavik with unhindered attention.

"Oh. I thought..." Zavik's planned speech slipped from his thoughts like water through fingers. Of all the reactions he'd planned for, approval wasn't among them. "I sought relics to aid us," he stammered, adjusting his seers.

"Relics?"

"Scrolls."

Konar's brow furrowed. "Go on."

"I found them. Well, two."

Maseeya gasped. She begged Zavik to recall his journey, and he did, neglecting unfavorable parts like the stolen scroll. No need to upset Konar's recently changed heart. By the time he'd concluded his tales, they'd finished the wine (sans Konar) and been interrupted by a cook inquiring about the evening meal.

Konar waved the cook off. He pressed his fingertips into the table, gaze steady. "Something unsettles me. Why would the shaktar give you not one, but two scrolls, and keep the third? You confirmed it's written in Nyrinian, so they must've at least shown it to you?"

"Briefly." Zavik shrugged and rose from the cushions to stretch. Why did he even mention that scroll? *Brilliant, Zav. Just brilliant.* "They didn't say why I couldn't take it. Odd creatures. Void of emotion. I didn't press them for fear of losing their hospitality. They might've refused to let me take any of the scrolls, or worse."

Maseeya squeezed Zavik's shoulders. "Elaysia will be so proud of you. Now, if you'll excuse me, I've sewing to attend to."

Zavik blinked. Considering her reaction when the nevethium heart went missing, she handled the whole sudden-appearance-of-long-lost-scrolls-that-could-change-destiny situation well.

"I'd like to have a look at them," Konar said once she left. "Inside the library."

Zavik tried to suppress the excitement bubbling inside him. By *library*, Konar meant the secret study below it, a place Zavik had only visited once, years ago, when Konar first took a liking to his inquisitive mind. He'd been invited down one afternoon to study nevethium and stayed well into the night discussing theories—until he pried into Konar's past. The high elder hadn't liked that. He'd ended the session abruptly, never extending the offer again.

But now Zavik had another chance, and he'd sew his lips shut before spoiling it.

The room was as Zavik remembered: scattered, stuffy, and imbued with the scent of old parchments and dust. Empty mugs and journals covered the table, and Konar had pushed chairs together and draped a blanket over them like a makeshift cot. Unsure of where to sit, Zavik slid a scroll from its leather case and offered it to the high elder.

Konar marveled, hand hovered above the parchment. "Smaller than I'd expected, but more beautiful. And these details"—he traced the scroll from tip to tip and let out a little moan—"particular to the myrem culture, no?"

"Oh, undeniably." Zavik wiped his seers clean and studied the scroll, determined to find what made it *undeniably* so. The handles? They were dyed a deep blue, the wood carved into intricate shells and speckled with nevethium. The edges of the parchment were cut to mimic the shapes of waves.

Konar unrolled the scroll and held it up to a nevethium sconce. "See how they used waterproof ink from mizol crustaceans?"

Zavik nodded. He was as familiar with mizol ink as anyone in Neharem. Many tribes infused it with their tattoo ink to add a fluorescent glow.

Konar dashed to the table and sprinkled some liquid from a mug onto the scroll. The parchment resisted. "Ha, look! They cured it so it's impervious to water damage. Remarkable. If only we knew how." His voice rose as he spoke, rushed and giddy as a child. "Perhaps with some tests, hmm? Let's have a look at the other."

Zavik retrieved the carved bone scroll embellished with berry-sized nevethium crystals at the ends of each of the four handles. "I think this one's Shaktari."

Konar unrolled it, unveiling rows of ambiguous shapes and symbols.

"Can you read it?"

"It's not something I use every day," Konar said gruffly, eyes scanning the parchment. He set the Shaktari scroll aside suddenly, as though he'd read something upsetting. "But yes, with time and research, I should be able to translate them."

"Could you teach me? I have an eye for languages."

Konar rubbed his beard, considering

Zavik added, "It'd be faster with both of us translating."

"Not if we account for the time lost educating you." Konar dipped a quill in some ink and scribbled in his journal.

"I'll leave you to it, then." Zavik trudged up the stairs, dragging one foot after the other. If finding the scrolls didn't render him worthy, nothing would.

"Gather some food and drink and return promptly," Konar called after him. "With The Daughter's blessing, we'll be down here a while."

Zavik froze. "We—right away, High Elder." He sprinted up the remaining stairs, skipping two at a time, a smile stretched across his face.

Konar wasn't a patient teacher. Zavik told himself the knowledge was invaluable—worth tolerating snide comments and redirecting misplaced frustrations—but time dragged on in the windowless lair. They studied until one or both fell asleep at the table, ancient text in one hand, quill in the other, half-eaten platters strewn between them. Maseeya visited twice a day. She always grumbled in Zarith but ensured they never lacked sustenance. Trips to the waste shoot and occasional baths in Norcoos Lake were the only other times Zavik took conscious breaks. As time spent studying the scrolls passed a full moon cycle, he looked forward to those trivial escapes with fervor.

He'd been tasked with learning Myremese first because of its similarities to Nyrinian. It came much faster to him than the symbol-based Shaktari. Despite Konar's guidance, he struggled to find patterns and formulate cohesive phrases with the countless symbols, most of which were obscure and varied in style from Konar's Shaktari references. Still, he'd managed some rudimentary translations. The passage he'd just finished sent prickles down his arms.

"High Elder, does this..." Zavik hesitated as Konar peeled his baggy eyes away from the myrem scroll. Any illusion of youth had long since left him.

Konar chuckled and scooted closer. "You don't look your best either. Where are you stuck now? It better not be a simple color variation like the previous passage."

"Here." Zavik hovered a finger over a flat line with two half circles emerging beneath it. "It says this is the incantation for what?"

Konar's smile faded. He snatched the parchment out from under Zavik's finger, eyes flicking over the page. "Invocation, not incantation. And that symbol means *ownership of another's soul*." He rolled the scroll up and tucked it in his robes. "Why don't you take a stroll. It's been a while since we've had a break."

Days of pent-up frustration threatened to ignite Zavik's words. He fought to steady his voice. "I'd like to finish translating the previous passage."

"I said that's enough for today."

"Why are you scared?" Zavik immediately regretted his forthrightness. He squirmed but remained rooted as Konar advanced.

"Why aren't you?"

"It's not meant to be taken literally. Shaktar are ancient beings with no end to their lifespan," Zavik stammered. Konar's chest was level with his face. "Perhaps they were once more inclined to capricious storytelling."

"There's truth in myth and myth in truth." Konar retrieved his pipe, but the wild look in his eyes didn't recede. "The Prophets protected these with their lives, which suggests they believed in the power of the scrolls."

"Knowledge is power."

"That, my boy, it is. But don't be so quick to assume you've fully grasped it."

A retort danced on the tip of Zavik's tongue, but he busied himself with a cup of wine. "Can I just have the scroll back?"

Konar held it out of reach. "Have you asked yourself why they let you take them?"

It was arguably not the best time to reveal what'd been promised, so Zavik shook his head.

"It's rare for such a gift to be given freely." He narrowed his eyes at Zavik.

"Maybe there's something they wanted me—us—to see." Zavik took a swig, then another, to plot his next remark. "And you're right. The scrolls exist, and I must openly question what they represent and what power they might hold." He looked down to hide the heat in his cheeks. "They alone might be the key to separating history from fireside stories."

The sound of a chair sliding across wood gave Zavik the courage to look up again. Konar reclined, interlaced his fingers, and reached them behind his head. "You should complete the passages in order. You could miss something."

"Yes, High Elder."

"What was in the previous passage?"

"It regards the Caman." Zavik's voice cracked a little. He didn't care. As far as he knew, it was the first ancient text to support the peoples' legends of Mavet's immortal servants. Well-deserving of excitement.

Konar unrolled the scroll, stopping on a passage beneath the art of a dark figure rising from a corpse. "Go on."

"It said they're his most loyal followers, indebted to an eternity of servitude for their worldly gains. They aren't bound to the laws of the natural world. They can assume the forms of other races. Maybe even beasts. Only the shaktar can see through their guise."

"Pity they hide away in their caverns." Konar's white eyebrows knit together in an expression Zavik couldn't quite put his finger on. Something of apprehension speckled with re-morse.

"Anyway, it's scarcely enough to go on, and I have my doubts, but considering the Caman's existence *is* a bit terrifying, isn't it?" Zavik took another sip of wine. "To think anyone we know could be something else entirely."

"People do it every day, Zav. Pretend to be something they're not. Perhaps you'll learn that when you're older."

"Perhaps." Zavik reached a timid hand toward the scroll. "Guess I should be finishing that translation now."

Konar slipped the scroll back into his tunic. "We'll take the rest of the day to reflect. I think we could both use sleep in our cots." He wandered to a dust-covered shelf and stared into it as though he'd misplaced something.

Zavik balled his fists at his sides. "What about yours?"

"I'm sorry?"

"The myrem scroll? I give you daily reports on what I've translated, but you horde your discoveries."

"There's not much to tell."

A laugh escaped Zavik's lips, shrill and wavering. "I'm try-ing so hard, and you won't give me anything. Do you know I respect you more than anyone?" *And the wine's talking for me. Great.* His eyes burned, and his stomach felt like it was eating him from the inside. "I thought coming down here again would be different. Maybe you finally trusted me. But no, you're still treating me like a child."

Konar's face was a mask.

"Fine. Don't say anything. But I want the scrolls back. They were entrusted to me. Me." Zavik jabbed himself in the chest with his finger. "I earned them, and I want them now." He extended his arm. "Please."

Footsteps pounded into the room above them. Zavik nearly dropped his wine, sobering in an instant. The trap door creaked open.

"Konar, come quickly." Maseeya's voice. It dripped with worry. "Rajar is back. He demands an audience with the high chieftain."

Konar cursed, threw on his outer robe, and marched up the stairs.

Zavik stood dumbfounded for a moment, all traces of anger gone. Rajar took precedent over any dispute he had with Konar. He hurried up the stairs. Up top, Maseeya paced about the library, muttering in Zarith while Konar adorned the rest of his high elder ornamentation. The door had been barred. Maseeya followed Zavik's gaze to the entrance and wrapped her arms around herself.

"I couldn't get him to stay in the summit lodge," she whispered. "He's waiting outside."

"Why is he here?" Zavik asked.

Maseeya and Konar looked away. Their silence confirmed his suspicions.

"He means to invoke hoksanu, doesn't he?" Zavik caught Konar's sleeve. "You can't let him. Elaysia isn't here to accept his challenge. She'll be forfeit."

Konar ran his fingers down the leather-wrapped center of his staff. "You know our laws."

"Then I'll do something about it."

Zavik ignored Maseeya's protests and unbarred the door. A blur of sunlight blinded him. As he stumbled out, hand covering his face, someone remarked on the high elder's poor choice in ambassadors. He rubbed his eyes. Rajar leered before him, golden armor reflecting the sun overtop swaths of multi-colored fabric. He wore his ceremonial headdress. Club brandished. Six warriors flanked his sides.

Zavik glared at them and opened his mouth, but his voice caught in his throat.

"Chief Rajar," Konar bellowed behind him.

Zavik relaxed a little.

"We didn't expect you so soon. Your last tuross message reported you were waiting to depart until after the Sun Festival. Won't your god, Rayanti, be displeased?"

Rajar sauntered up to Konar and lowered his club between them. "Rayanti himself told me to come. He's touched me with visions regarding our high chieftain." He motioned to his warriors who formed a semi-circle around them. "I presume she's yet to return?"

"As I've told you, she's investigating the raids and will return as soon as she's finished." Konar stepped back, though from what Zavik could tell, not out of fear.

Rajar smoothed a flyaway strand into his skin-tight horsetail. "I've heard otherwise. Rumor has it she's been captured. Some across the sea claim she's betrayed our people to the likes of the eastern slavers."

"That's not true," Zavik squeaked.

Rajar flared his nostrils and regarded Zavik with disdain. "We find ourselves in agreement. I doubt it's anything so grand or deceitful. Most likely she's shirked her responsibilities. Runs in the family."

Zavik lunged at Rajar. The chief sidestepped and drove him to the ground. He landed face-first and cracked his seers. The taste of blood filled his mouth.

Rajar sneered above him. "Stay down, pup."

Konar spouted warnings, but Zavik pushed himself back up. He swung wildly at Rajar. His first punch struck armor and sent a throbbing pain up his arm. Rajar caught his second. Before Zavik wriggled out, a knee connected with his stomach. He doubled over. Shut his eyes to hide the tears. Maseeya tried to help him up, but he shooed her away. He couldn't let Elaysia down. She'd want him to fight.

"Please," Konar pleaded. "Give her another moon cycle. You can't enact hoksanu if she's not here to defend herself in the trials."

"My dearest high elder, I'm not enacting anything." Rajar hoisted Zavik up by his collar and shoved him toward Konar. "She's been gone many moon cycles. As far as anyone's concerned, Neharem is leaderless." He brushed some dust off his armor from the scuffle. "I'm here to fill the role she abandoned. The Banaxa, Morotôk, Moatiwe, and Atsukut support my claim. Even now, I have war parties positioned below the city. If you behave, I might kindly allow you to remain high elder for a time. You"—he eyed Zavik—"would make a fine wine bearer. I hear the All-Sovereign has one."

Despite the pain, Zavik mustered a scowl. "You cowardly—"

"Inside. Now." Konar shoved Zavik into the library and slipped him the scrolls. "Not another word," he whispered. "Go to the study and remain there until I come for you." Zavik started to protest, but Konar slammed the door.

Zavik lingered by the door until the footsteps and voices faded, leaving him alone in the library with nothing but his thoughts and fears. He trudged downstairs and settled for an overfull wine cup to ease the pain. Rajar was an opportunist, he reminded himself. There was no reason to believe his claims held any truth.

And no reason to believe they didn't.

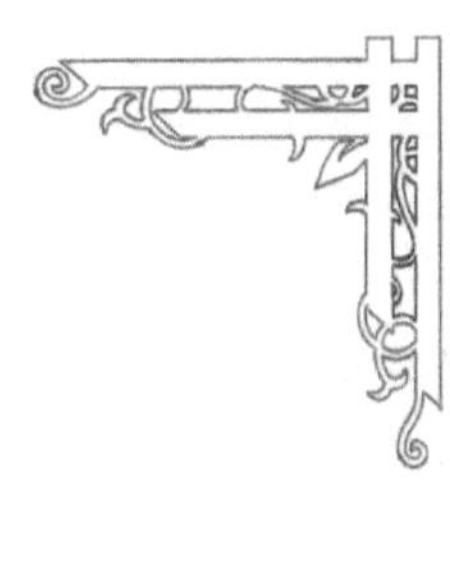

ELAYSIA

"That's definitely her," Elaysia said, urging her mount forward.

A hundred paces away, Jakki sat poised on a stallion, outline aglow with the sunset's radiance. Behind her waited roughly a dozen riders. Elaysia stifled a shout. Somehow, they'd found each other. Perhaps Chai'Tik's messenger guided them.

Davier cast a weary glance across the field. "I don't know."

"How many nyrians wander half-naked through Cadar's territory?"

"Could be another witch."

Elaysia ignored the jab and raced through the tall, pink-tinged grasses, grateful to be free of the desert. As she drew closer, Jakki's eyes widened in recognition. She dismounted and wrapped her arms around Elaysia, pulling her into a deep embrace. Her warm skin smelled of the coniferous trees of the north.

"Dearest Sister, I've longed for your company," Jakki said.

"And I've prayed for you every night." Elaysia pressed her forehead to Jakki's, then pulled back to subtly smooth her clothes and hair. Despite her relief, seeing Jakki stirred nagging feelings of inferiority. She shook them off and grasped Jakki's hands. "How'd you know we'd be here? Did Xaren send word to—" Her thoughts evaporated as she caught sight of a newly healed gash on Jakki's long, bronze leg. "What happened?"

"Long story." Jakki brushed it off with a wink, but tension lines creased her forehead. A fresher wound, though not nearly as large, cut into her hairline. "I'm better off than many."

A downy head peeked out from the bag on Jakki's mount. "Siren?" Elaysia asked, stepping closer. The stormbird nibbled at her hand. "She's nearly doubled in size since I saw her last."

"Hasn't Onitus?"

Elaysia wrapped her arms around herself. The guilt of leaving Onitus still ate at her daily. She peered over Jakki's shoulder to get a better view of the warriors as they dismounted. "How are Mardus and Yerakai? Anahi?"

"Alive and well." Jakki's eyes narrowed as Davier joined them. "Mother Itaso's blessing on you, slaver. I see she's kept you alive."

"Hate to disappoint." Davier's expression was void of amusement.

They stared each other down until Elaysia pushed between them on her way to greet the others.

Anahi noticed Elaysia first and hurried to embrace her, followed by Yerakai. Mardus waited until the commotion ceased before greeting her with a traditional fist over his heart. They wore a blend of northern furs and the garments of their respective tribes, save for Anahi, who, in her plated armor and calf-high sandals, looked like she'd just finished a round at the fighting pits. All the birds had grown and began shedding down for sleek feathers, though Siren's stature nearly doubled the rest.

A chill rippled down Elaysia's spine as she surveyed the remaining warriors; they'd lost over half the original scouting party departed from Agaas. On a second glance, everyone was ragged, stretched thin. Her throat worked, but no sounds came out.

Yerakai quieted her with a touch that could calm even the wildest beast. "We might celebrate the reunion for now and talk about our time later."

"Of course." Elaysia clung to the shame roiling inside her. She didn't want to forget what it felt like to expend lives on a whim. "How did you find us?"

Yerakai glanced at Jakki. "We were drawn into skulmor territory. Circumstances evolved and led us to the Az Zarian border." Hesitation crossed his eyes. He knelt to feed Wind Chaser some dried meat. "We've debated entering Cadar for some time, so finding you here is an unexpected blessing."

Mardus joined them, square jaw jutting in suspicion. "Where are the others?"

Elaysia lowered her eyes. She ran a hand through her hair and began securing it in new braids. "Hopefully back in Neharem. We got split up at the Caman Altars shortly after we arrived."

"Split up?" Mardus grunted and shot a glare toward Davier, muscles tensing under his exposed bronze torso.

"Nothing's gone as we planned," Elaysia replied quickly. Darkness sank around them, casting shadows on the hills. "We should find a place to make camp. Davier said the nearest village is half a day's ride away."

Davier tossed his bedroll on the ground. "Here's as good as any."

Jakki gestured at the surrounding landscape with her staff. "We're completely exposed. My scout said there's a grove near a farmstead a few miles ahead."

"The closer we get to Cadar, the more careful we'll have to be. I'll take my chances with the local wildlife over the All-Sovereign's spies."

"Who put you in charge?"

Davier laughed under his breath and turned from Jakki. He touched the small of Elaysia's back. "There's good fishing this part of the Ashaat. I'll see what I can scrounge up."

"I'll help you," Yerakai said, taking off after him.

While the others started a fire and set up camp, Jakki spread out a fur in the grass and motioned Elaysia over. "Want some stories?"

Elaysia plopped down beside her and offered a wineskin. "Want a drink?"

"You have no idea."

While they shared the last of the kuba grain wine, Jakki recounted their northern expedition, leaving out some details, Elaysia guessed, regarding the severity of the skulmor attack and the state of the Daruk villages. When she finished, Elaysia rested her head on Jakki's shoulder.

"I couldn't have done it, Jak. Thrown myself in front of a monster like that."

"I should've done more." Jakki ripped out a blade of grass half as long as she was tall and twisted it in her fingers. "I failed them."

"They knew what they volunteered for."

"It's not that."

"Then what is it?"

Jakki's golden-brown eyes widened. Her lips parted, and she leaned closer. "I..." She abruptly pulled back, shaking her head. "Nothing. I need to relieve myself." She wandered off in a daze and disappeared into the grass.

"She's been different as of late." Yerakai's voice startled Elaysia. He stood behind her with a fish-laden spear slung across his shoulders. "Many things have been."

Elaysia dug her fingernails into the wineskin. "She told me about the brutal murders. The decapitations. Sacrifices. Seems barbaric, even for skulmor."

Yerakai lowered his spear and studied the fish, running his fingers over the scales of the largest one. "Something sinister unravels beneath the guise of skirmishes. More than the raging of a dictator or the sudden viciousness besieging the skulmor."

Bumps prickled down Elaysia's arms. Smoke drifted through the air, stinging her eyes with the scent of cooking fish. The others huddled around a small fire in the dirt a few yards away. Davier waved her over.

"We should eat." She started for the fire, but Wind Chaser fluttered in front of her, blocking her path. His eyes gleamed in the moonlight.

Yerakai knelt, and the stormbird hopped onto his forearm. "Don't take my suspicions to heart. It's just a feeling."

Elaysia feigned indifference. "Of course."

"Our chief is the oldest in Neharem. I'll seek his counsel and refrain from further speculation until my vision is clearer." He bit his lip and nodded toward the fire. "Be wary, Sister. Of everyone."

"I always am." Elaysia hurried away before he said anything else.

Most of the warriors huddled silently around the fire, picking at fish, dried fruit, and nuts. A few dozed, wine in hand. Elaysia sat beside Davier. He offered her a still steaming fish before tossing more kindling on the flames.

"What's with them?" she whispered, tilting her chin toward Jakki and Anahi. They were engaged in a heated debate. Their food lay untouched by their feet.

"Jakki still wants to enter Cadar," Mardus answered, none too quietly. He set his jaw and gave a look suggesting utter madness.

"We came here to find you, and now we have. We'd be foolish to risk—"

"No," Jakki snapped. Siren, perched on her shoulder, flared her partially feathered wings in warning. "We'd be foolish to go back now, especially with no answers. Our people would've died for nothing."

"They died all the same." Mardus spat at her feet. Keera screeched beside him.

Elaysia grabbed Mardus's arm. "I understand your concerns, Brother." She forced the words out like a speech, and they sounded convincing enough. Konar would be proud. "Others feel similar."

Davier dodged her gaze but said nothing.

"I don't know if we'll find the answers we seek, but Jakki's right. We must try. We'll honor their sacrifices. Besides"—Elaysia steeled herself with a sharp breath—"Chai'Tik gave me her blessing."

Murmurs erupted among the warriors.

Mardus's expression transformed from tight-lipped anger to gaping awe. "She came to you? In a vision?"

"More or less." Elaysia tugged at her sleeves. "She said something awaits me in Cadar."

"Given your incident at the Caman Altars, I'm not certain we're welcome," Yerakai mused from where he reclined on the outskirts of the fire. "Still, there's Lumira, Grokhion, Xaren, and whomever remains of their party to consider. It wouldn't be right to leave them if they're still alive."

Everyone fell silent. Wind shivered through the grass, arousing the flames.

Elaysia unbound her bedroll. "It's decided. Rest well, friends. Tomorrow, we ride for Cadar. With Khiev-Tatamic's blessing, we'll arrive before rations run out."

"It's only two days' ride away," Davier mumbled.

Long after the fire turned to coals, Elaysia gazed up at the stars, lulled by the snores of those at rest. Was she leading them to their doom? Just because Chai'Tik wanted her to go to Cadar didn't mean she guaranteed safe passage. But Yerakai was right—if Lumira and the others still lingered in Az Zar, they weren't safe.

Fear, like physical pain, is a warning, her father used to say. *It's the spirit's way of protecting you. But you have to decipher threat from insecurity.*

Elaysia clutched her necklace and hoped she knew the difference.

The morning before they entered Cadar, Elaysia woke at dawn to a blanket of mist settled so thickly she couldn't see more than a foot away. The cool air smelled of soil and reminded her of the woods back home, only less fragrant and mossy.

They ate and packed up within the hour. No one cared to converse. Some rode eagerly ahead, while others furrowed their brows and looked west toward Neharem. The stormbirds were restless, Jakki distracted, Davier distant, Anahi solemn, and Mardus was never one for chatter. Yerakai would've gladly kept her company, but she rode as far away from him as possible to avoid rumination of unfounded theories.

Supple grasslands and fertile hills unfolded before them, chock-full of wildflowers and fat-bellied cattle. Elaysia could scarcely believe she'd been in a desert wasteland not a week prior. They rode through the day, stopping shy of the city gates on a hilltop at dusk. Citrus fruit made for a light, albeit sweet, evening meal while crickets and the rustle of wind through the leaves serenaded them. The river gurgled along the base of the hill and fed into the bay, glistening like liquid silver. Trees with red, feathered blossoms puffed overhead with a scent sweet as perfume.

To Elaysia's dismay, she admired Cadar, at least from afar. Unlike Or Zahal—a conglomeration of tightly knit quarters crammed inside crumbling walls—the sprawling city was intricately designed to be both practical and appealing. A dozen tiny islands, each endowed with ornate temples and two-story pavilions, fanned out before the peninsula. Nevethium-lit bridges connected them to the city proper, weaving around the bay like green snakes on the hunt. Boats drifted lazily about the docks while their masters requested access through one of the guarded entrances to the stone wall encasing the peninsula. In the city proper, resting atop the tallest hill, was the All-Sovereign's palace. It was unmistakably his, radiating such obscene light that one could make out the domesticated gardens in its courtyard and the golden edges of its curved rooftops. Not far from the palace, a grotesque, steepled building lurked atop a waterfall, its sharp forms darkened and otherwise camouflaged by the night.

Elaysia nudged Davier. "What's that?"

Davier laughed darkly. "The Lord Priestess's lair. They call it a place of worship, but few are welcome there." He rubbed his face—now clean shaven to make for easier entry. "Are you sure you want to do this? It's not too late to turn back."

"You know I have to."

He frowned but gave her the briefest peck on the lips. Her heart raced, and she almost leaned in for another before thinking better of it. There was an unspoken agreement between them to keep their newly found affection private.

"Only two can accompany us," Davier said, gesturing to the warriors. "We'd have a hard time getting this many outsiders past the sentries at once, even with people flocking to the capital because of Dzro Jiazin."

The Cleansing.

The mention of the Az Zarian holiday made Elaysia shudder.

"Keep your face covered as you did in Or Zahal. And hurry. No one's allowed in past a certain hour." He retrieved his uniform and armor from a bag. She'd forgotten he had it. The impracticality of their relationship struck her like an ocean spray.

But he's changed.

She donned a cloak that encompassed most of her body and left Mardus and Anahi in charge of the stormbirds and warriors. With Davier leading the way, and Jakki and Yerakai on either side, she crept down the hill and past a lyvium bridge spanning the width of the river. Clouds obscured the moons; a gift from The Daughter shrouding them in darkness. They sheltered behind a sun-blood tree a few feet from the main road to assess the sentries. Eight stood guard at the gates, and at least a dozen others paced atop the wall. Elaysia pressed closer to the ground. In the lush grasses surrounding the city, she felt almost invisible.

"Is there a less"—she swallowed, not wanting to sound weak in front of the others—"obvious way for us to gain entry? Smuggler passage? One of the island bridges?"

Davier shook his head. "The island bridges are equally guarded. If we get caught sneaking in, it will be far more difficult to talk our way out of it than if we attempted entering as visitors.

The All-Sovereign's akin to a god. It's not odd for people to journey here to pay homage."

Jakki lifted her newly acquired silk skirt (she'd raided a homestead on the outskirts to find clothing better suited to the locale for herself and Yerakai) and revealed a dagger strapped to her thigh. "If they're hostile, I've got a few tricks up my sleeve—er, leg." She punched Elaysia's arm affectionately and strode ahead.

"Oh, Jakki," Yerakai muttered, trailing after her.

"Ready?" Davier asked Elaysia.

She forced a nod and abandoned the grass's shelter with all the confidence she could muster.

"Damn these clothes," Jakki complained as they neared the gates. She huffed and tugged at the wide, structured belt cinching her waist. "It's impossible to breathe, much less fuck." She shot Davier a coy look, and Elaysia, grateful for a distraction, couldn't help but smile.

Davier glared back. "Do you want to blend in or not? And secure your hair in a bun. It's improper for women to wear it down."

"Too tempting?" Jakki walked backward, facing Davier while she piled her hair atop her head.

"You can't just stroll through the main gates looking like..." Davier's voice trailed off.

Elaysia imagined him biting his lip beneath the mask. She braced herself for Jakki's wrath.

"A savage?" Jakki handled the implied insult with a toss of her shoulders. "A proper savage would've been allowed to carry her staff in."

"Cadar has strict policies on civilians carrying weapons." Davier's voice was on the verge of snapping. "And we're already trying to smuggle you in without papers, in case you forgot."

Elaysia positioned herself between them. "We'll never get in if you two don't shut it."

By Chai'Tik's blessing, they remained silent for the rest of the walk.

Elaysia stopped in her tracks when they reached the foot of the marble staircase. Deathstalker statues with nevethium eyes hovered twenty steps above, and though they'd been reimagined with more elegance and coated in gold, her stomach still lurched. Behind them, sentries fanned out around a lyvium gate five times her height. At least ten more archers lurked atop the wall.

Her palms grew sweaty. A city this guarded during peacetime would be formidable, should it come to war. She pulled her hood down further and followed the others up the stairs.

"Halt in the name of His Holiness," a sentry bellowed. His garb was similar to Davier's, although more ornamental and embellished with a cape.

Davier cleared his throat and moved into the nevethium sconces' perimeter.

The sentry's eyes widened, and he bowed. "My apologies, Captain. I couldn't make out your uniform in the darkness."

Davier waved him off. "Your diligence is commendable. Open the gates at once; I'm in a great hurry."

The sentry rushed to notify the gatekeeper, but another sentry blocked his path. "We'll need to see papers on the civilians," the second sentry growled.

"They're my guests." Davier ushered them all in front of him, his demeanor calm and unsuspecting.

Sentry number two crossed his arms. "Visiting vouchers, then."

"I didn't exactly have time to secure them." Davier unmasked and leaned up against a statue as if he and the sentry were old friends reconnecting over a drink. "This is the first rest night I've had in a moon cycle. I'm sure you can relate."

"Whether I understand your position is irrelevant. No vouchers, no entry. No exceptions. Especially during Dzro Jiazin."

Jakki and Yerakai moved in closer, protecting Elaysia on both sides. She fingered her grandfather's dagger beneath her billowing sleeve. The prick of its tip comforted her.

Davier retrieved a small pouch from his belt. "Perhaps this could pay penance for my negligence?" He tossed it from one hand to the other, eyeing the sentries while the clinking of aspar filled the air. "Take this. Buy yourselves a drink and some company. It's a time for celebration, after all."

The sentries murmured among themselves until the aggressive one silenced them with a hand. "Don't expect a second pardon," he said, snatching the bag from Davier. He motioned to the gatekeeper. "Let the captain and his companions through. They've provided papers."

Elaysia kept her eyes on the ground as they passed the sentries, not daring to so much as breathe until the gate thudded closed behind them.

Inside, a ring of amber-leafed trees with smooth, twisted trunks encircled the courtyard. The wind loosened a few fan-shaped leaves, and they swirled around her before drifting into a crystalline pond brimming with fish of every color. Ten paces ahead, two statues garbed in ancient Az Zarian armor—clunkier versions of the current uniforms, complete with oversized chest plates and leather and iron face armor molded into terrifying masks—clashed giant blades overhead. Below their pedestals, etched into stone in Zarith, were the phrases *Victory in Solidarity* and *Strength in Order*. Elaysia shivered as she ducked beneath their swords and hurried down the stone path leading out of the courtyard. It fed into a wide street hemmed in by banners and flags, soon giving way to buildings. The first few, no larger than shacks (though they were anything but shack-like), appeared to be homes, but it wasn't long before the buildings doubled, even tripled, in size.

"Indoor market," Davier said when she lingered by particularly large one. Its three-tiered roof was rimmed in gold and supported by thick pillars carved with floral patterns. "So the high-born aren't exposed to unfavorable weather. Merchants sell garments, furniture, perfumes, rugs, pottery—all the artisan products."

Elaysia nodded like she knew, but the concept of paying for meals and clothing—things people made for themselves and shared with others as gifts—baffled her. "What's artisan?"

Davier arched an eyebrow. "Artistic, hand-crafted goods."

"Isn't everything hand-crafted?"

"Common people buy the bulk-produced items. They're faster to make and a fraction of the cost."

Realization struck Elaysia like a snake bite. "The ones made in your factories through slave labor." Fury burned in her stomach. Any admiration she felt toward the city vanished.

Davier exhaled through pursed lips and nodded to another soldier who passed by. "Free people work there, too. It provides a means to support their families."

"Perhaps they wouldn't need to labor in factories if they were allowed the time and means to care for themselves."

"And do what? Farm? Hunt? You saw the villages we rode through. They live on dead land."

"If you hadn't overmined their nevethium—"

"I had *nothing* to do with that."

"You didn't try to stop it."

Davier opened his mouth, but no words came out. He marched past her, cursing under his breath.

The streets of Cadar were deathly quiet. Guards frequented their path as they wound deeper into the city, but the only
civilians they encountered were a young boy scampering into
a house with a wooden sword and an older man hauling fire-
wood.

"Why is it so quiet?" Yerakai asked, breaking the silence. "I
thought a city this size would be noisy."

"The warning gong must've already sounded," Davier replied,
voice still on edge.

Despite her soured mood, Elaysia couldn't rein in her intrigue.
"Gong?"

Davier pressed on, eyes on the road. "It's an instrument. It
sounds the hour citizens are to remain indoors."

"Has it always been this way?"

"Since I was a boy. Maybe longer. It's the All–Sovereign's way
of keeping a hold on the peace."

Jakki appeared on Elaysia's other side. "Imprisonment will
have that effect. Nice home you have here, slaver."

Davier picked up the pace. "We need to move faster. Patrols
will increase soon."

"What? Can't use your captain magic to talk our way out
again?" Jakki sneered.

Davier whirled. He looked ready to strike Jakki down. "If we
get caught, you'll be the first to—"

"Davier," Elaysia croaked. They'd drawn the attention of
passing guards who now approached, weapons drawn.

"Shit." Davier pulled his mask on. "Follow my lead."

Elaysia swallowed and searched her surroundings. An alleyway branched out to the left. She edged closer to it.

"Mavet's blessings on you," Davier said as the guards drew
near. "These civilians claim one of their household is deathly ill.
They require medicine."

"Captain." The guard in front lowered his swords, eyes narrowing. "Seems a large party to fetch medicine."

If Davier's confidence wavered, it didn't show. "The sick member accompanies them, as they don't know the ailment. One is the husband, the other the sister."

Jakki elbowed Elaysia. *Guess that's my cue to be the sick one.* She lowered her head and leaned against Jakki for support.

The guard didn't waver. "I'll need their papers."

"I've reviewed their papers. Everything's in order." Davier's hand twitched.

"What did you say your name was? I don't remember any captains scheduled for patrol."

Davier retrieved his last aspar satchel. "Listen, friend, how about you let us pass, and I'll reward you with—"

"That's enough." The guards formed a semi-circle around them, blades encroaching. "You, mask off and weapons on the ground. Civilians, hands where I can see them."

"So much for a pleasant night," Davier muttered. He nodded to Elaysia, then drew his blades in a smooth stroke before tumbling forward and slicing the legs off the closest guard.

Elaysia's mouth gaped, horrified, yet she was compelled to linger by some invisible string of loyalty.

"Go," Jakki said, shoving Elaysia into the alley.

Neck pulsating, Elaysia sprinted into the darkness, banking left and right each time she encountered a dead end. When her breathing rasped and her sides ached, she ducked behind a crate and lowered her hood cautiously. Another alley, this one scarcely a body's length wide and backed against an oblong building. The smell of refuse permeated her nose alongside the sweet char of grilled meats. A drunkard slumped against the wall, snoring and oblivious to the fact he broke multiple laws simultaneously.

She squatted until her legs cramped, frozen by fear and indecision. What if they'd died? But even if she wanted to go back, she couldn't retrace her steps. *You shouldn't have fled. Coward.* She fingered the aspar Davier had given her. It'd be enough for a room.

A gloved hand closed over her mouth, cutting off the beginnings of her scream.

Elaysia writhed, but her captor's grip was strong.

No. Not alone in a dark alley. Not in the city that robbed her of her parents.

Not like this.

"Quiet, or you'll give away our position." A woman's voice, so deep it purred.

Elaysia stilled. She knew that rich, beridian accent. "Lumira?" She pulled free of the now loosened grip. Her captor's tall, slender form was well disguised and hooded, but the sapphire eyes shimmering inside gave her away. "You're alive." She threw her arms around the beridian's neck, gladly sacrificing what remained of her dignity for comfort.

"No thanks to the locals." Lumira returned the hug, albeit stiffly. "I thought you were dead. Back at the altars, I... I'm sorry I didn't stop them. Grokhion, he—"

"I'm glad you didn't. I don't think they would've let you live." Elaysia offered a sympathetic smile.

Lumira froze. She scented the air, whiskers twitching. "Someone's coming. Get behind me."

Elaysia obeyed. She clung to her dagger and prayed she wouldn't have to use it. The sound of footsteps reverberated through the alley. Three figures turned the corner. She squinted into the darkness. "Jak?"

"The one and only." Jakki's brow raised, a mixture of relief and contempt as she eyed Lumira. "Harder to kill than I thought, cat."

Lumira lowered her spear with no shortage of disgust. "I like to keep people guessing."

Davier paced, his gaze darting about the alley. "Where are you staying?" he asked Lumira. "We just slaughtered four guards back there, and it won't be long before a patrol discovers their bodies in the alley."

Jakki nudged the drunkard with the toe of her sandal. He toppled over. "I think you overestimate your people's ability to—"

Everyone stilled. Footsteps once again echoed off the alley walls, only this time, no allies awaited.

Lumira sidled between the buildings. "This way."

Elaysia and the others followed, darting down narrow passages that forced them to maneuver single file. Lumira halted in front of a door and knelt to pick the lock.

"Breaking into a random house is your big plan?" Jakki hissed.

Lumira muttered in Hispen, then addressed Elaysia. "Xaren and Grokhion wait inside. We've food and drink, and much"—she wriggled the lock some more until the door opened with a *pop*—"to discuss."

Elaysia took one last look down the alley and ducked through the doorway.

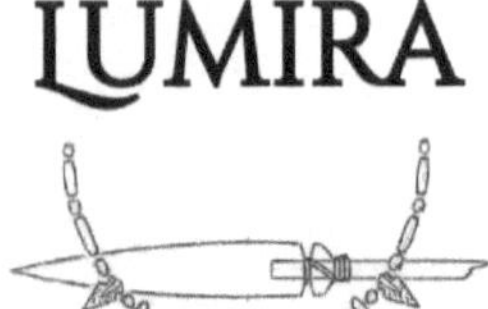

LUMIRA

I t had to be tomorrow.

Waning moons meant decreased visibility. An influx of pilgrims occupied patrols. The stormbirds grew anxious outside the city gates.

And if Lumira spent one more day suffocating in a servant's tunic, she'd tear out a slaver's throat.

Besides, each wave of pilgrims meant greater difficulty in securing lodging; at least lodging that allowed her kind. Tonight's inn consisted of middle-class humans drinking away the day's labors while a puffy harpist plucked some dismal rendition of Cadar's anthem. A boy dressed in a servant's tunic waited in the corner, tiptoeing out between patrons to wipe tables. Mavist tapestries hung from every wall, judging the sins unfolding beneath their ever-watching eyes. Reserved conversations made the environment more akin to ceremony than celebration.

Across the table, Elaysia fiddled with her untouched drink.

"It's not poison. Take a swig already." Lumira took a sip to verify her claim.

Elaysia obliged. She winced, eyes watering, and spit some back into the cup. "Very good."

"I'll order something else." Lumira reached for the cup, but Elaysia clung to it, tipping her head back for another drink. This time, she kept it down and smiled triumphantly.

"I said it's good. Strong."

"Beridian Moonlight isn't made for your kind." Lumira knocked her cup against Elaysia's and tossed back the rest. She stole a glance at the adjacent table where Xaren and Grokhion played at the roles of master and servant. Hardly convincing.

"High Chieftain, we've exhausted our time here. But we need to press our advantage before leaving."

Elaysia pushed her drink aside, a sloppy grin plastered on her face. "Elaysia," she said, lowering her voice as though she shared a secret.

"What?"

"It's Elaysia. I must've told you to call me that a thousand times. Or Ellie. Or sigh in annoyance. That's what Konar prefers."

Lumira's eyes widened as Elaysia took a sizable gulp. "Sorry. I'll work on it. But listen, if we attack—"

"Nope. Already told you that, too. I trust you've done your research, but we're here for answers. Not vengeance."

"The weapons we recovered from the factory in Or Zahal aren't answer enough?" Lumira caught wind of her tone—voice raised, words sharp—and softened it. "We've learned little since arriving in Cadar. War is coming, and you need to prepare your people. Best we strike now and tip the odds in our favor."

Elaysia fingered the worn edges of her tunic. "What do you propose?"

"Target their temple."

Elaysia blew air through her lips and shook her head. "Religion is the least of my concerns right now."

Lumira grabbed Elaysia's gloved hand. "They conduct more than services there. When I first arrived, I saw the temple guards drag a slave inside. I sneaked close enough to hear the victim's cries. And the chanting that followed. The voices sounded like they came from no mortal. It's happened at least three times since. Always at night. Sometimes it's an orphan. An elderly human. Also"—she guzzled the rest of Elaysia's drink—"the sky changes above the temple."

"Like the Caman Altars." Elaysia's voice was distant. Her two-toned eyes appeared unusually large and child-like in the ambient light of the inn.

Lumira nodded. "You said something's missing. This is it. We need to know what they're doing and why."

"You're probably right. I feel I haven't justified my expedition yet, even with the weapon discovery." Elaysia fidgeted with the necklace she kept hidden beneath her cloak. "My father always said a leader's actions matter more than their words. If I can't act on behalf of my people, what reason do they have to follow me—right?"

Lumira ignored the guilt bubbling in her stomach. She had personal reasons for attacking, but it would help Neharem, too. *Right?*

"Right. And imagine the looks on their faces when you return with information *and* a prize."

Elaysia tore off a chunk of bean pastry that the locals were fond of. "What prize am I to bring?"

"The Lord Priestess."

Elaysia stopped mid-chew. "First, you're crazy. Second, if I was crazy enough to go along with this, why not the All-Sovereign?"

"He might carry the title, but she holds as much power, if not more. Us women often do." That drew a smile from the girl. "Besides, she's the one overseeing the sacrifices—"

"We don't know what's happening for certain."

Lumira shrugged. "Fine. She's in charge of whatever *takes place* in the temple. I guarantee she's behind the nevethium raids, too. We take her, we cut the head off the snake."

Elaysia sat quietly for a moment, mushing pastry into the plate. "Seems risky. Konar wouldn't approve." Lumira started to grumble, but Elaysia held up her hand. "But it's a worthwhile risk. Capturing a leader is better than losing countless lives to war." She leaned forward, face glowing in the candlelight. "How? And when?"

"Tomorrow night. We've overstayed our welcome, and the slavers are distracted with their religious festivities."

Elaysia nodded. "Dzro Jiazin."

"What?"

"A fortnight from now commemorates Dzro Jiazin, or Az Zar's foundation day. It honors Ashaat the Victor, the All-Sovereign's ancestor and first ruler of Az Zar. Davier said the festival lasts fifty-one days—the length of the famed Siege of Cadar—culminating on the thirty-fifth of Vynar with a ceremonial sacrifice to Mavet. That's why we've been able to move around undetected. Everyone visits Cadar this time of year to worship and bring tithes."

"Giving all your earnings to a dead guy. Makes sense."

Elaysia's eyes darkened. "It's a terrible holiday. How people can blindly celebrate massacre astounds me."

"War isn't pretty."

"I'm not talking about the war. Do you know nothing of ancient Quinaria?"

"United people turned enemies over clashing ideologies. Civil war. Nyzar becomes Az Zar. The losing side flees to Neharem." Lumira studied her claws. "Similar things happened on my isles. Smaller scale, though. We've got countless clans today."

"Az Zar was founded on betrayal."

So was everywhere else. "Go on."

Elaysia stared off, pinching her bottom lip between her fingers. "With devastating losses on both sides and no end in sight to the civil war, Igtheos, the leader of the rebellion, agreed to sign an accord. Ashaat himself drew it up. To celebrate peace, everyone laid down their weapons for a night of feasting. But Ashaat conspired with the skulmor and bribed some myrem, who were eager to end the land war. While Igtheos and his warriors slept, and their stormbirds hunted over the sea, Ashaat attacked with the bulk of the skulmor forces and a fleet of deathstalkers. Meanwhile, the myrem unleashed their seaserpent upon the unsuspecting stormbirds. It was slaughter. Ashaat proceeded to wipe out anyone loyal to Igtheos, even the elderly and children. The survivors flew west on the last stormbirds, seeking refuge in Neharem. The Apáasutai embraced them. Together, they founded Agaas and united the tribes of Neharem over the next two centuries."

"Thanks for the history lesson."

Elaysia bit back whatever obscenity danced on her tongue.

Lumira folded her arms. "My people aren't strangers to betrayal. Hundreds of beridians were uprooted from our islands and sold into slavery after making the mistake of connecting with the landlocked nations, years ago."

"I'm sorry. I forget myself." Elaysia dropped her head and interlaced her fingers. "I just want to do right by Neharem."

Yerakai passed their table, tapping Elaysia on the shoulder as he walked outside. Time to go. It would be a quick debrief, then they'd pair off and find separate inns to sleep in as they'd done the past few nights.

Elaysia grabbed Lumira's arm with a newfound determination; a fire in the girl's eyes she'd not seen before. "My parents died here for a reason. Maybe they'd learned of the new weapons, but maybe it was more. I must see this through. They deserve justice."

"We'll make Az Zar pay. We have the advantage: surprise and distraction." Lumira nodded to her inn partners for the night, Anahi and Mardus, and gave Elaysia a subtle bow. "Tomorrow's the first step. Keep to your heart, Elaysia."

Tonight, Cadar's leadership would pay for their crimes.

Lumira clung to the rooftop, tail flicking back and forth freely. She hadn't bothered with a cloak. Distended clouds shrouded Cadar in darkness, and pilgrims overflowed from congested inns, occupying the soldiers. Besides, if they got caught after the last gong with no papers, her tail would be the least of her worries.

A rich, floral breeze rippled through her whiskers. Despite herself, she loved its scent. The air was one of Cadar's only redeeming qualities, far superior to its ability to assume the façade of a thriving nation while the rest of Az Zar deteriorated. Cadar's lords didn't care how they came by their abundance, happy to exchange blind allegiance for comfort while the slaves and impoverished extracted what little nevethium remained around their ramshackle villages.

She tightened her grip on her spear and looked to the slivers of moons for comfort. The Goddesses were with her.

As soon as the patrol below rounded the corner, she leaped to the adjacent rooftop, claws sinking into the crevices in the wood. A *thud* sounded beside her. Good. Grokhion kept pace. She craned her neck to find Davier, Xaren, Yerakai, and Elaysia racing through the alley. They stopped at an intersecting path to await a signal. Jakki motioned several streets down with Mardus and Anahi by her side, giving Davier the go-ahead.

Lumira's breath caught. Ahead, two soldiers marched down the path parallel to Davier's party. She raised her spear, but Grokhion grabbed her arm before she could position it for the throw. Lips pursed, he emitted a sound identical to a seahawk's shriek, drawing Davier's gaze to him. Davier's party hid in the shadows until the patrol passed.

She thanked Grokhion with her eyes. His posture boasted courage—much needed since her confidence ebbed and flowed like a tide. Yesterday's plan seemed intimidating in the absence of the inn's illusion of safety, but there was no going back now. She leaped down from the rooftop and wended her way up the temple path. A *plop* landed on her shoulder. She tensed and spun around, spear ready. No one. Another *plop* on her face. Rain. Lightning cracked from the south. She shivered and motioned the others forward.

"Move faster," she hissed, stomach bloated with tension. She couldn't remember the last time she'd been so nervous, if ever.

The rain transformed into a downpour, soaking her fur through by the time they reached the temple. Dark and towering, it loomed over the city atop a waterfall, accented by haggard stone creatures with gemstone eyes that guarded its courtyard. Unlike the rest of Cadar, its physique boasted sharp steeples instead of flat roofs with curved edges. In the center, above stone doors three times her height, was a single stained-glass window in the shape of Mavet's eye. Nevethium glow emanated within. Lumira hated that cursed symbol most of all. It watched her no matter where she moved. Leering. Consuming. She turned away from it to scan the horizon. No one followed, save for her companions, who hurried over, panting and wide eyed. Xaren and Davier had smuggled all their weapons in earlier that day, so each person was armed in their preferred way.

"Yerakai, enter there." Lumira pointed to the hedges growing up the side of the building like snakes. "Davier, Mardus, Elaysia, with me. Anahi, Jakki, Grokhion, Xaren, spread out and stand guard. We should be out soon after the chanting starts, but if something goes wrong, flee this wretched city and send word to Neharem." Her hands trembled as she spoke. She hid them behind her back.

"For Neharem." Grokhion dropped to his knees and closed his eyes in a silent prayer to either their gods or Neharem's. Maybe both.

"For the glory of Khiev-Tatamic," Yerakai added.

Jakki crossed her arms. "We're fucked if this goes wrong. We should've smuggled the rest of our warriors in for backup."

"And risk getting caught at the gates?" Anahi challenged.

"If we'd waited—"

"Mavet Almighty," Davier snapped. "Everyone shut up and get into position." He tugged his cowl on and marched toward the entrance.

Elaysia shot Lumira a concerned look as she followed him.

Lumira shoved an unblinking Mardus up the stairs. She offered a final plea to the moon mothers, then cracked open the temple door.

A green glow cut through the darkness. Lumira slunk in, gaze fixated on a nevethium crystal at the end of the great hall. Its size rivaled those of the living trees in Agaas. It had been smoothed and shaped to the likeness of an altar. A carved swirl fanned the ground beneath it like flower petals. The room was as long as it was tall, burdened with pews, lavish in marble, supported by pillars, and hemmed with domed ceilings. Mosaic art decorated the surfaces, images of Az Zar's heroes, gods, and conquests. The scent of ashes and incense saturated the air like a thick, sticky cloth. A tapestry of Mavet's symbol ran the length of the furthest wall behind the altar. Two nyrian statues, hand-carved with a delicacy mastered only by the Vysilliam bloodlines, guarded either side, arms crossed in warning, their nevethium eyes twinkling alongside the smoldering fires burning in their open mouths.

Mardus gasped and sprinted to the altar. "Crystals this size are rarely found outside Neharem."

"Stay on mission," Davier said, his gaze darting about the room.

Mardus shot Davier an accusatory glance. "How did you come by this?"

"Don't know, don't care."

"By the moons, would you both—" Lumira froze, ears craned. She could just make out the pads of footsteps and a monotone hum in an adjacent passage. Her companions continued to mutter among themselves, their ears not attuned to the incoming threat. "Quiet. They're coming."

They split off—Davier and Elaysia on one side, Lumira and Mardus on the other—and sheltered beneath pews. The hum grew louder. A dozen cloaked figures emerged from a passage at the head of the hall. They wore the same masks as the priests at the Caman Altars and split into two eerily straight rows, revealing an unconscious human woman carried between them. A thin line of blood trailed down her chin and dripped onto her ragged tunic. The humming transformed into chanting as two of the priests broke off to place the woman's body atop the altar. They bowed their heads. The chanting grew louder. Angrier.

Lumira advanced, careful to stay in the shadows and hide behind pillars. Twelve would be easy enough for the four of them, especially unarmed. She extended her claws.

But where was the priestess?

As if responding to Lumira's summons, a haunting wail dwarfed the priests' chanting. A woman swathed in satin—a startling, pure white that had never seen a smidgen of dirt, much less blood—emerged from a passage opposite the proselytizers. An embroidered cloak ran the length of her arms with sleeves dangling down to her feet. Its train trailed far behind her. The woman's face remained hidden beneath a bone-carved mask fitted with curled, wooden horns and jagged teeth, but corded locks of nyrian-white hair hung beneath the hood. She glided to the altar and raised a dagger above the victim's breasts.

Not tonight, witch. Lumira pressed herself to the floor. The stone was cool beneath her. She looked back to ensure the others followed. Davier held his hand up in a halting motion. She beckoned him forward. He shook his head, eyes stern.

Moons be cursed. Why would he hesitate now?

The victim stirred on the altar. She'd be damned if another innocent died on her watch.

Lumira launched her spear at the priest nearest her. It sunk into his abdomen. He collapsed.

The priests rustled like a flock of pigeons, squawking and tripping over their robes as they sought shelter. One fell victim to her claws, then another. Both dropped to their knees, clutching their throats as blood poured from their wounds and lined the swirl on the ground with red. On her tail, Mardus finished one with a club to the skull. Davier slashed another. A whizzing sound rushed past her ears as a priest collapsed beside her, an arrow lodged in his chest where Elaysia made her mark. Lumira leaped over the bodies, eyes locked on the priestess. Amid shouts and the clanging of weapons, she secured her prize, but not before the priestess plunged her dagger into the woman's chest.

Lumira grabbed her by the throat and slammed her against the wall. Despite her predicament, the priestess chuckled. A chill ran down Lumira's spine.

"The murder of your lackeys amuses you?" Lumira hissed, drawing blood above the woman's ebony collarbone.

"How freely you admit to your sins, night-stalker. It's unlike your kind," the priestess said, smoky voice taunting.

Lumira kicked her in the knees. The priestess collapsed, still laughing. Lumira drew back for another strike.

Davier caught Lumira's arm. He knelt to bind the priestess. "We need to leave. You can interrogate her later when we're safe aboard the ship."

The priestess cocked her head. "So eager to abandon your home and betray your people? For shame. It appears your latest mission's gone to your head."

Davier's eyes hardened. "Open your mouth again, and I'll rethink my mercy."

"But, Davier," her shrill voice sang. "I thought we had something special."

Davier brought his hilt down on the priestess's mask. It broke. She grabbed at her face, laughing and spitting up blood as he ripped the remnants of her mask off. Davier recoiled. He slit her throat and shoved the body aside like a sack of grain.

Lumira gasped. She tackled Davier, pinning him to the ground with ease. Her chest tightened as she ripped off his cowl. His face had gone white. "You piece of shit slaver. She's what we came here for. Now we have nothing."

Davier shoved Lumira off and gestured to the body. "That's not her. I've never seen the Lord Priestess unmasked, but I know *that* woman. They're about the same build and skin tone—rare in Az Zar—but she, Vanya, used to be one of my superiors. I thought she got promoted or reassigned."

Mardus finished a still twitching priest with his club. "I'm assuming your military relationship wasn't the *something special.*"

Davier's cheeks flushed. Elaysia retrieved the priestess's dagger and twirled it in her hand, eyes on the body. Neither spoke. The air felt thicker. Smoky. It burned Lumira's lungs. She stormed across the hall and yanked her spear out of a carcass. Davier cursed and made for the door.

"We need to clear out now. Abandon the plan," he called over his shoulder.

Elaysia marched the opposite direction toward the altar. "I'm not leaving empty-handed."

"Wait," Mardus shouted. He knelt over the sacrificed woman's body. "What about this woman? We can't leave her here."

Davier made a disgruntled groan. "With any luck, she's already dead."

"Then she deserves a burial." Mardus scooped the woman up.

Lumira stalked toward the Moákun. "Davier's right. Leave her."

The doors burst open, accompanied by a gust of wind and two figures. Jakki and Grokhion. The former rushed ahead, wiping the water streaming down her face.

"What's taking so long?" Jakki asked. "Why didn't you stop the ceremony?"

Lumira didn't want to admit the fiery nyrian sounded frightened for the first time since she'd known her. She took a subconscious step toward Elaysia. They'd all gathered by the doors, but the high chieftain lingered across the room, transfixed on the tapestry.

"I sent Xaren and Anahi out of the city to gather the others and prepare the boat," Grokhion said. He noted the bodies with the faintest flick of his tail. "Is everyone alright?"

Mardus kicked over a pew on his way out. "We did stop it. And we're fine. No priestess."

Jakki's lips stretched thin. "Then why is the sky changing above the temple?"

"They were expecting us." Lumira dropped her eyes. She could already hear Jakki's taunting remarks. "High Chieftain, with your permission—"

She stiffened, choking on her words as she turned toward Elaysia. Fur raised along her spine. Something lurked behind the girl at the far end of the hall. One of *them*. It had to be. It was sneering, hating, seething death from its pores. Reaching for—

"Elaysia," she forced the words out, gnarled and ragged as they scraped against her throat in the form of a scream. "Run!"

# DAVIER

D avier's blood ran cold as Lumira's roar rippled through the hall.

Somehow, even before he laid eyes on the monster, he knew. He knew better than to stray from Elaysia's side. Accompany her to the temple. Lead her to Cadar.

Fall for her in the first place.

The Caman parted its muzzle, goo stretching between its overlapping fangs. Davier shuddered. He'd heard stories of Mavet's messengers, but witnessing one wield a scythe as it advanced toward Elaysia, a curved smile to match its horns, made his skin crawl.

Like the woman in the desert.

The Caman shrieked. Its high-pitched cry forced Davier to cover his ears. Elaysia cowered, arms trembling as she leveled the dagger. It closed in, movements intentional and elegant despite its size: roughly twice his height and as burly as Grokhion. Davier was still closer to Elaysia. He could intervene. He screamed back and willed himself forward. It was fifty paces away. Forty. Thirty. He focused on Elaysia. Increased his speed. A surge of hope pricked his chest. He was going to beat it.

An arm shot out, catching Davier's stomach. It hit him like a wave, stealing his breath as he crashed to the ground.

Breathe. Just breathe.

His head throbbed. He touched it; felt blood.

Focus. Breathe.

The assailant, a priest who must've survived their ambush, lunged for him again. Davier dodged his grasp. Just like training. Just like any other mission. He unsheathed his swords and sprinted.

The Caman turned its hollow eyes on Davier as he dove, swinging at its legs. His blade sliced through. He felt the tension, the familiar pull of the flesh and crack of bone. But no blood. Ankles remained attached to cloven hoofs. The Caman peered down at him, a sneer plastered to its face. He slashed again. It caught his blade. The lyvium disintegrated in its hand, piling into ash on the ground. He scrambled for Elaysia.

Boom!

Davier's ears rang. A searing pain hit below his ribs. His side burned like he'd lain upon hot coals. He peeled his gaze away from Elaysia. Temple guards swarmed the hall wielding weapons he'd only heard rumors of.

Shieum. Thunder-makers.

Smoke billowed from the hollowed end of the weapon. Its wielder tipped it lengthwise and poured something from his robes inside. Davier started for Elaysia, but the Caman reached her first, pressing its scythe to her chest. Fire coursed through his veins as he dragged himself to his nearest ally: Grokhion. He stopped short of the great cat's paws and lay there, cheek pressed against the cool stone. Lumira raced by.

Boom. Boom, boom.

Grokhion knelt to pick him up. "Are you alright?"

"Fine," Davier lied, fighting the urge to cry out as the movement jarred him. "Get cover. These new weapons are"—he winced, clutching his side. Blood poured from his wound.

"I've seen the terror they unleash." Grokhion set him behind a pillar with the gentility of a mother. "Stay hidden."

"Elaysia."

"We'll save her." Emerald eyes constricted, the beridian crouched on all fours in a beastly stance and prowled into the shadows.

Glad you're on our side. Davier clutched his remaining sword and peered around the pillar. Jakki and Mardus huddled nearby. Another *boom* sounded, then another, leaving a mark on the pillar they sheltered behind.

Across the hall, Lumira slunk in the shadows. She popped out behind two unaware temple guards and slashed their throats. Grokhion emerged opposite her with a less discreet approach. Three guards reloading their weapons fell prey to his claws. He jerked the axe off his back and sliced through another, severing torso from hips in one swift stroke. A guard trained his shieum on Grokhion's back. Davier cried a warning, but an arrow pierced the guard's chest, vanquishing the threat. Another arrow sailed by, and Davier traced its origin to Yerakai. The Apáasutai perched on the balcony above, stringing arrows with honed skill as the remaining guards fumbled with their weapons. Good. Shieum were still new to them. Jakki and Mardus abandoned their shelter and joined the fray with battle cries, and Davier dared to summon hope.

It vanished when he glanced back at Elaysia. The Caman was gone, but in its place stood the Lord Priestess. She held a shieum to Elaysia's head. She faced Davier, cold eyes seething contempt beneath her mask. The dagger slipped from Elaysia's hand. His heart leaped into his throat.

"Call your filth off, or she dies," the Lord Priestess hissed.

The fighting dwindled, but screams still tangled with roars as the beridians unleashed their wrath.

"Do as she says," Davier cried, voice grating against his throat. Clutching his wound, he limped out from the pillar's shelter and hurled his remaining sword. It landed a few paces from the Lord Priestess with a clatter.

A temple guard sprinted to his mistress's side and yanked Elaysia up by the hair. Her scream reverberated off the walls. Davier ground his teeth as the guard bound and hooded her.

Mardus raged forward. "Let her go. You're outnumbered, *lyda.*"

The Lord Priestess aimed her shieum at Mardus. He relented. Together, she and the guard retreated toward the shelter of the pillars opposite them, weapons trained on Elaysia.

Davier weighed the odds. Lumira and Grokhion regrouped beside him, claws stained with blood. The larger beridian bled from his shoulder. Jakki cursed from somewhere behind him. The bodies of temple guards lay strewn about the hall. Even if they timed the attacks right, they'd never reach Elaysia in time.

Out of the corner of his eye, Davier caught Lumira advancing, spear in hand.

"Come any closer, and we'll kill her," the guard snarled.

Davier limped after her. "Lumira, stop."

Her ears flattened, but she halted.

"That's more like it, beast. Listen to your masters and—"

An arrow to the neck silenced the guard. Yerakai. The nyrian still lurked on the level above.

In the moments it took Davier to register the fallen guard and react, the Lord Priestess hit Elaysia over the head with the shieum and dragged her unconscious into the shadows. Yerakai loosed another arrow, but it missed its mark. Lumira sprung after them, Grokhion on her tail. Anguished roars filled the room.

Davier's vision blurred. He rubbed his eyes and crawled toward his sword. "Do you see anything?"

"They're gone," Lumira shouted. "There must be a trigger to a secret passage somewhere, but we can't find it."

"We're out of time." Grokhion's form stood dark against a tapestry that ran the height of the wall. Fire tears leaked from the serpent's eye embroidered in the center. "Our position's been compromised. More soldiers will follow."

Mardus made for the door, three shieum in hand. "I agree. Let's leave."

"No." Davier used his sword like a staff and hobbled forward. "We can't leave her. You don't know what they'll do."

"We'll come back for her," Yerakai called as he slid down the tapestry with his knives, slitting the fabric in two. He landed silently and sprinted to the door. The beridians followed.

Jakki approached Davier and offered her hand. "Come on, slaver. We can't help her tonight."

"It's death for her if we leave." Davier pressed past Jakki and limped toward the guard with the arrow lodged in his neck. He ripped off his mask. "Tell me what you know."

A faint smile danced across the guard's lips. "You know more than I. This bloodshed is on your hands. And now you'll never taste the rank of colonel."

Davier gripped his hilt. "I had nothing to do with this."

"Is that what you tell yourself?" He choked out a laugh. Blood dripped down his lips and pooled into the cracks on the floor. "Despite your wavering loyalties, you still brought the All-Sovereign his prize. Perhaps he'll take that into account when punish—"

Davier severed his head. Only Xaren and Elaysia spoke Zarith as far as he knew, but it wasn't worth the risk.

Mardus approached him with a leveled club. "I heard every word." His voice was winter. Unforgiving and cold. "He said Davier betrayed us," he shouted to the others.

Davier stiffened. A wave of guilt crashed into him, weight like iron. He tried to move, but his body refused to obey. His heart slammed against his ribs. The others didn't speak, but he could feel their eyes boring into him like readied bows.

"No, I—"

Lumira snatched his sword and hissed.

"I didn't want this, I swear." Davier looked to Jakki, then Yerakai. His throat tightened. "Please, believe me."

Grokhion pushed through and grabbed Davier's shoulders. "Say it isn't so, lad, and I'll believe you."

"I," Davier stammered.

Grokhion's face softened. Hoping. Waiting.

Davier crumpled. "I tried to warn you."

Jakki lunged for him. "You piece of shit."

Grokhion blocked her advance. He shook his head slowly, his face contorted in a mixture of disbelief and revulsion. "You betrayed us? Betrayed her?"

"The All-Sovereign ordered me to. I was just doing my job." Grokhion's claws moved to Davier's neck. "But I changed my mind. I've tried to keep you safe." *Just not soon enough.*

Mardus dug his knife into Davier's stomach. The blade encroached on his already throbbing wound. "What made you change your mind, traitor?" The Moákun's eyes looked dark as his hair, hardened and narrowed with a set jaw to match. "When you realized you'd lost, too?"

Davier offered no explanation. No matter what he said, they'd never believe him.

"You led us straight to ruin." Mardus pressed the blade deeper, puncturing his skin. Tears stung Davier's eyes. He blinked them back.

"I begged everyone to return to Neharem," Davier grunted, struggling against Grokhion's grip, which tightened securely around his throat. "No one listened."

"You didn't give us just cause," Jakki shouted. She stood beside Yerakai with her staff raised.

"Would you have wanted to leave Az Zar had I been honest? Keeping you in the dark was the best way to protect you all. If Lumira hadn't suggested—"

"Leave her out of this." Grokhion raised him by his throat.

Davier felt his vision slipping. "Escape in secrecy," he rasped. "That was the original plan, and it was our only chance."

"You mean your only chance." Grokhion hurled Davier into the wall. He fell to the ground with a *thud* and grasped for consciousness, his body pulsating. The others backed away without so much as a hint of compassion in their faces.

Grokhion raised his axe, stance like an executioner. The warm, merciful eyes he knew the beridian for were now icy slits of hatred. "I take no pleasure in this."

"Do what you must." Davier closed his eyes.

Instead of the whir of a blade cutting the air, the creak of a door filled his ears. Then the sound of shuffling feet.

"Run," Lumira shouted.

Davier's eyes shot open as several dozen arrows rained down on them. One struck Grokhion's leg. The beridian snapped it off, his face masking the pain, and gave Davier a final glare before trailing the others. They vanished through the main door, leaving him cheek-down on the stone. Several dozen soldiers poured into the room. They circled Davier and leveled their weapons. Cowards in masks. He struggled to his knees and forced some gusto into his voice.

"I know I'm an exalted warrior, but this is a bit much." He shoved the nearest sword out of his face, nearly losing his balance. He clutched his side.

A clap echoed off the walls.

The soldiers changed posture to stand at attention, then parted. Dread wafted over Davier as a figure glided into the hall from a darkened corridor. The All-Sovereign. He'd exchanged his favored silks for lyvium-plated armor and contained his hair in a military-style bun. His gray skin mirrored the stone floor and contrasted his gleaming teeth.

Davier forced himself to his feet. His limbs shook beneath him, and a spicy tingle coursed through his blood.

"You bastard," he snarled.

"Captain Zadel, how informal of you. And to think you had such potential." The All-Sovereign's crisp voice fell flat. He strode to Davier, stopping within arm's reach. "I suppose I should thank you. I thought my plan was sufficient, but your stupidity and lust proved far more effective." He clapped twice and turned a serpentine smile on Davier. "Bring out my prize. I imagine Zadel wants to say goodbye."

Somewhere in the hall, another door creaked open. Two temple guards hauled a drowsy Elaysia over. Her forehead was red and swollen where the Lord Priestess had struck her. Davier's lips pulled thin. Elaysia lifted her head, her gaze seeking his. Her eyes signaled for help.

He looked away.

The All-Sovereign raised Elaysia's chin, stroking her hair with the opposite hand. "I can understand why you deserted," he told Davier, "assuming you find interbreeding mutations attractive and have no desire for offspring."

Davier swung. He delivered a blow to the All-Sovereign's face, resulting in a satisfying *crunch*. Soldiers fell on him. One kicked his stomach. Another drove the hilt of a sword into his back. He collapsed. More kicks slammed into his arms, his back, his legs. The wound at his side throbbed, dulling the pain of the beating. He distantly registered the crack of a rib.

"Enough," the All-Sovereign commanded.

Davier's world blurred, but he could still make out the blood dripping from the nyrian's nose. The pink tinge to his cheeks. The balled hands at his sides.

"I want him conscious to tell her himself."

"Tell me what?" Elaysia pulled against her captors, soft features contorted by a furrowed brow and pinched lips.

The All-Sovereign's jaw ticked. "Shall I have my soldiers continue beating it out of you, Zadel?"

Bile crept up Davier's throat. He'd live through a thousand more beatings if it meant keeping her in the dark. But she already knew, didn't she? Some part of her had to.

"Do it now, or you'll watch my men slice the Az Zarian patches off her skin." The All-Sovereign spat blood onto the ground as he stomped toward Davier. "Confess the lies you breathed to lead her to ruin."

"Elaysia, I..."

Davier forced himself to look at her, savoring the trust in her eyes before he shattered it forever. There was no way to soften the blow, to appear the hero or convince her of all the reasons that led to his actions. The inner turmoil he'd faced every step of the journey. How much it cost to choose her over everything he'd built his life around. And now, as he lay bleeding into the temple floor, he knew he loved her. But he'd never deserve her.

And she'd never forgive him.

Davier extended a shaky hand. "What happened between us was real. I want you to know I chose you, in the end."

Elaysia winced. Shut her eyes. A tear snaked down her cheek.

"Beautiful delivery," the All-Sovereign crowed. "I'll make certain the street performers hear of it."

Davier glowered, fighting for scraps of resolve. "Fuck you, you pointy-eared prick. Just do it."

Mock ignorance flickered across the All-Sovereign's face. "Do what?"

"Kill me."

The All-Sovereign beamed. "No need. You've already paid for your crimes against the empire."

A chill gripped Davier's bones. "What are you talking about?"

"We couldn't find you, Zadel." He knelt before Davier and dropped his voice to a whisper. "So, I settled for blood substitutes."

Davier's chest heaved. He writhed and tried to get up, but the world fell further and further away. Darkness licked at the edges of his vision. He imagined his family tortured in dark cells. Or... *no. Don't think it.*

"I'm afraid you'll have to make peace with their ashes," the All-Sovereign continued. "We couldn't honor them with a tomb burial, after all. Treason doesn't beget resurrection in Mavet's new world."

"All of them?" Davier clenched his teeth and let the tears run freely. "My sisters. They're children."

"Bad seed." The All-Sovereign frowned and stroked Davier's head, voice frosted in feigned sorrow. "Was it worth it? You had it all. More opportunity than I've ever offered a human. I won't make that mistake again. Still, a reward was promised, and I always keep my word." He rose and dropped a bag of aspar next to Davier's head. "You're henceforth stripped of your rank and exiled from Cadar, effective sunrise." To the soldiers, he added, "If Davier San Zadel is found within city walls after tonight, kill him on sight. Hang posters with his face around the city.

Heighten patrols and spread word of the Neharem filth in our midst. I want them all dead."

Davier sank to the ground, wishing it would open and swallow him. The All-Sovereign motioned two soldiers over. They seized Davier's sword and stripped him down to his loincloth, aggravating his wound. He pressed his hand to his side. Blood seeped through his fingers. He locked onto Elaysia as the All-Sovereign guided her away, hoping she'd turn around one last time with some hint of understanding in her eyes.

Elaysia disappeared into the sea of soldiers and down a corridor. She never looked back.

Davier dreamed of death. His own. His family's. Elaysia's. His body ached with every pulse of his heartbeat, and his throat was a desert. The throbbing in his side became a slow ember of pain coming newly aflame with the slightest movement. Sometimes water trickled down his throat, but he could never tell if it was real or not.

When Davier finally awakened, his eyes were crusted over and burning. He cracked them open, and painful streams of light burst in. He rubbed them and tried again. The room wasn't that bright after all, illuminated only by a single candlestick. It rested beside a mug on a shoddy table. A tall figure in a dark, hooded cloak lurked behind it.

Davier's efforts to rise fell short as pain screamed through his body. He settled for propping himself up on elbows and squinted at the visitor, searching for signs of familiarity. The cloaked figure stepped into the light and removed the hood. Davier gasped. It sent a stabbing pain through his lungs and triggered a coughing fit. His visitor offered him the mug.

"Yerakai?" he croaked. His lips cracked as he spoke. He guzzled the water. "You... I thought..." Yerakai retrieved the empty mug from Davier's trembling hands. "Why are you here?"

Yerakai's ashen-violet brow furrowed. "It was a terrible thing you did. The gods don't view betrayal favorably."

The words stung anew; Davier looked down to hide his shame.

"I do, however, believe you've changed. I don't think you were an accomplice to what happened in the temple a few days ago."

"Days ago?" Davier swung one leg over the side of the bed, flinching as it activated the throbbing in his side. He was shirtless with a bandage wrapped around his torso. Blood stained the fabric.

Yerakai gestured to the table where a small, fabricated stone flecked in green lay. "I retrieved that from your abdomen. Never seen its like. Lyvium, I think. Mixed with compromised nevethium. Your new weapons somehow launch it from those tubes. It flies faster than an arrow. More distance. More damage." He tucked the stone into his pocket. "I'm taking it back to Zavik, so he can study it along with the weapons we recovered."

Davier cracked his knuckles.

"The wound alone was enough to endanger your life," Yerakai continued, "but having nevethium inserted into your body like that would've killed you if left unattended. Lucky for you, I gathered some ancient savage medicine"—he eyed Davier, letting the sarcasm sink in—"and it stopped the poison from spreading. I worried you wouldn't wake, but now it looks like you'll recover."

He offered Davier a hand, eyes unblinking but heavy as he helped him tug on a tunic. "You'll carry that scar for life, though."

Davier nodded, unsure if Yerakai meant a literal scar or the emotional one caused by his choices. "The others?"

"They're as well as can be expected. I wouldn't go searching for them. They're more apt to kill you than your ex-soldiers."

"I don't blame them." Davier's chest tightened. He looked at the floor, studying the trails of the woodgrain and stains from what he assumed were his bodily fluids. "Elaysia?" He hoped her name was enough to convey his intent.

Yerakai raised his hood. "She lives. They hold her in an island prison outside the city. I'm sure you're familiar with it."

"I know it well. No one's ever escaped."

"Tread carefully when you leave. The All-Sovereign has drawings of your face around the city, and there's a bounty on all our heads." He turned to leave.

"Yerakai."

The Apáasutai hesitated in the doorframe. Anyone else would've killed him in his sleep, not given him sanctuary and tended to his wounds. Davier searched for words to relay his gratitude, but as he sat humbled and wounded in an inn keep's room with nothing to his name, he realized he'd no flowery speech left to offer.

"Thank you," he mumbled.

"Goodbye, Davier. I pray you find peace in this life and the next. I truly do." Yerakai closed the door with a finite *thud*.

Davier sat on the bed, oblivious to time. He focused on his physical pain and the finer details of the cobwebs in the corners before succumbing to the blanket of loneliness. He'd no purpose now. Not enough money for a ship. No ranks to surpass. No one alive left to care for. No one to blame but himself.

A uniform—not his—lay folded at the foot of the bed, the blade of a sword glinting atop it in the candlelight. Yerakai must've gone to great lengths to obtain it. It'd provide the cover he needed to flee Cadar.

Davier ran his finger along the sword's edge, drawing blood. It wouldn't be a terrible way to go. Far better than he deserved.

But Elaysia still lived, and she needed him.

A heroic act wouldn't make up for what he'd done, no more than his meager thanks to Yerakai repaid his life-debt. But it would save her life. Give her a fresh start. That was enough.

Davier struggled into the uniform and fell to the bed again once fully clothed. After a brief respite and an attempt to pay off his room—an unnecessary venture as Yerakai already cleared the balance and left him a few day's rations—he stumbled into the street. It was raining. Angry clouds masked the sun, giving the appearance of a moonlit night even though it was still morning. He trudged through the streets he'd once marched down proudly, stopping often to ensure no one stared at him oddly or whispered as he passed by. Not that it'd be easy to pick him out of the hordes of soldiers clustering the streets, but one could never be too careful when it came to the All-Sovereign. He passed through the gates without so much as a raised eyebrow.

Climbing the hill overlooking the palace proved to be the most trying task of the day, but he conquered it, albeit breathless and on the verge of losing consciousness. From there, he had an unobstructed view of the prison. Overshadowed by the grandeur of Cadar proper, the small island harbored a simple stone building mostly masked by over-hanging willows and vines with walls twice the height of the city's. Guards lurked within, patrolling level upon level of cells burrowing deep into the island's core. Davier imagined Elaysia shivering alone in the dark, inhaling filth-stained soil, and clenched his fists.

"You'll get your freedom, Elaysia. Your justice. Your revenge. I'll do whatever it takes." He violently wiped away the tears building in his eyes. "And I'm sorry for all of this, though you'll never get to hear it from my lips. We were never meant to be. You are the ocean, and I was naught but a storm."

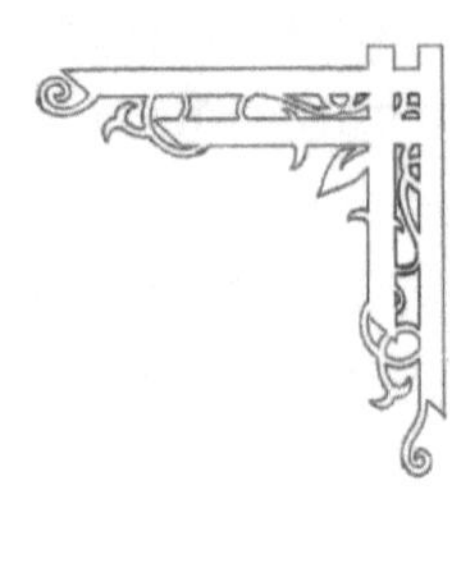

ELAYSIA

The crypt walls rippled like seaweed against the ocean floor, alive with streams of water trickling over mosses and molds before puddling into uneven crevasses on the ground. Spiders with glistening fangs and beetles the size of Elaysia's palm scurried around her cell. It was always cold, her clothes always damp, and the silence deadening. A path imprinted with pebble-sized nevethium fragments lined the stairs and cells, providing the prison's only source of light.

Elaysia shut her eyes and pretended she basked in the glow of a living tree crystal. Something had to comfort her. Remind her of home. Provide escape from the sneering voices of guards and beratement from self-imposed harmful thoughts. She didn't know the day for certain, but judging by the guards' rotations, her imprisonment treaded on a fortnight. Or maybe it just felt that long. She shuddered, scratching at the bumps inflicting her body. They itched fiercely and brought fever with them. Her lips were cracked and as rough as tree bark, despite her guzzling the daily half-skin of water and forcing down the tasteless gruel they shoved through the bars. She'd refused the latter at first—it was slimy, gummy, and often crawling with maggots—but nausea engulfed her when she didn't eat.

So, she sat, waiting for nothing, neither awake nor asleep, cross-legged in a feces-infested cell, blinking to avoid the burning sensation and shivering even though her hand reasoned her face was hot to the touch. The roughspun tunic they'd thrown her into the first night hung off her shoulders like a coarse blanket and dragged on the ground when she rose to relieve herself in the hole in the corner. She doubted they'd removed the last prisoner's refuse before tossing her in, given the pungent odor. A whiff of it hit her. She cupped her mouth and begged the contents of her stomach to stay put. She couldn't afford to grow weaker.

A harsh laugh escaped her throat as she reflected on the times she'd told Konar imprisonment would be preferable to council gatherings. He'd tell her not to speak lightly of such things. Life was bound to give her what she asked for.

And so, it did.

Elaysia drew her knees to her chest, burying her face between them. "You were right, Konar. All good things come at a cost. Freedom demands captivity. Adventure demands duty. And love..." She blinked back tears. "Love is as fleeting as a good meal. I wish I'd never tasted it."

The echo of approaching footsteps reverberated through the prison, forming ripples in the thin layer of water covering the stone path. The guard outside her cell stirred from his nap. She retreated to the corner.

"My turn to watch the whore," the new guard said, puffing his chest to increase the size of his already bulbous torso. He spoke in Zarith, as they all did, assuming Elaysia ignorant of their language. She gave them no reason to think otherwise. Not that it'd revealed anything of value. Their conversations revolved around crass remarks about women or fabricated war stories to establish dominance.

"Not much of her left to watch," said her current guard, a weasel-eyed human. Boils covered his face, and Elaysia imagined they riddled the rest of his slight frame. "She was weak to begin with and dying now, most like. Heaves up half of what she eats and coughs all night."

Puffy Chest pushed Weasel Eyes out of the way and studied Elaysia, wine-stained lips creeping into a smile. "She'll make it. Almost time for the witch's ceremony. Stupid order, though, if you ask me." He rolled his eyes, implying he should rule Az Zar, then banged on the cell bars with his sword hilt to get Elaysia's attention. "You hear me, Empress of Savages? If it was up to me, I'd have you now and after you die, then parade your naked body through the streets of your homeland while your villages burned."

Elaysia remained expressionless as she wrestled the tension seizing her chest.

Puffy's mouth pinched. "Dumb bitch," he told Weasel. "Hasn't got a clue."

The threats would've provoked Elaysia once, back when she thought hardship consisted of lectures and socializing, but now they had little more impact than disapproving grunts from the elders. Besides, guards on other shifts often spouted similar insults. She leaned against the grimy wall, fighting the looming question of when *it* would happen. Her Stormriders would've attempted a rescue by now if they intended to—not that she blamed them; they lacked the forces and risked imprisonment themselves—and she'd declined physically and mentally if the All-Sovereign sought proof of her extinguished spirit.

"All right, she's all yours." Weasel regarded her with eyes verging on empathetic, then trudged up the stairs, clinging to the rope with all the strength his little arms could muster so he wouldn't slip on the slick stone.

Puffy gripped the bars, baring haggard teeth flecked with rot. "I wish you understood me. I heard Zadel's staying at the finest inns with the best ale, entertaining new whores nightly with the money he earned from you. Some men have all the luck." He snorted, staring past her.

Probably wondering why the All-Sovereign didn't select his loveliness over Davier. Her lips started to curl upward, but the thought of Davier tainted any seedlings of joy.

"But he fucked himself. Large bounty on his head. Stupid way to get discharged. Stupid man." Puffy slumped against the bars. "Lucky bastard," he muttered.

Elaysia closed her eyes, grateful for silence. But soon enough, the memory of Davier's betrayal seized her. It haunted her dreams, unfurling in vivid detail and wrought with embellishments. Sometimes he mocked her and struck her. In the worst ones, he dragged her to the Lord Priestess himself.

Davier had never loved her. She was a means to his end. She couldn't even direct all her anger toward him; her naivety was partly to blame. If she hadn't been so bent on Cadar and had heeded Konar's warning, nothing would've happened. Now, even if she escaped by some divine intervention, the chiefs would never support the girl who followed in her parents' footsteps. Konar had fought for so many years to hold the position for her. To ensure people saw her as her own person. A fresh start. A new hope.

Another failure.

Maybe he'd lead in her stead, uniting the tribes to fend off Az Zar. Onitus could bond with someone else. And things would be as they were meant to.

The Moonriders no more.

Elaysia covered her mouth as nausea roiled her stomach. It wasn't the first time. Her breasts also ached and swelled despite her minimal sustenance. And her moon cycle was...

Coming. It was coming. Maseeya said stress could delay it. It'd happened once before when she'd worked herself up a great deal over leading her first council gathering.

She crumpled into the dirt, waiting for the nightmares to take her.

The sound of screeching metal yanked Elaysia from her slumber. The door never opened, not even for her meals, which they shoved through the bars or, if the guard was feeling amicable, slid beneath the door so the food remained on the plate. She scurried to the furthest corner of her cell to evaluate the intruder from a distance. The cloaked figure lurking in the doorframe didn't wear military garb. Was it time? It couldn't be. Not like this. She wasn't ready to die. Her heartbeat quickened as the intruder removed their hood, exposing one of the most exquisite nyrian faces she'd ever seen.

But she had seen him before. Eyes like hot coals. The cruel cut of his jawline. Their brief interaction in the temple seared his face into her mind for eternity.

The All-Sovereign.

Elaysia's gaze darted to the open door. Puffy was gone, and no other guards stood post. How far would she make it if she sprinted now? Her body was weak, but if she moved lightly and kept to the shadows, she stood a chance.

The All-Sovereign followed her gaze. He backed away from the door with a slight bow. "Be my guest." His voice tempted. A serpent coiling for the strike.

Elaysia rubbed her temples, feigning disinterest. "What do you want? Surely, you've enough slaves and soldiers to commit your atrocities for you."

"Proper execution often requires taking matters into one's own hands." He advanced, dancing around darkened patches of soil with disgust.

"You don't strike me as the type to dirty your hands."

"My heart's desire demands no shortage of self-sacrifice." He squatted before her and traced a scar running from the corner of his eye down past his jawline. "But I suppose you understand that better than most."

She glared at him. She wouldn't play his game, no matter how he baited her. Resolve was all she had left.

He inspected his fingernails. "It disappointed me how easy it was to lure you here, though I did handpick Captain—oh, forgive me, no need for formalities—*Davier* for a reason. Do you know why?"

Elaysia clenched her teeth. She focused on the texture of his cloak, how intricately woven the threads were for such a simple garment, to ease her anger.

"Physical aptitude is expected of all our soldiers," he continued, "but Davier's prowess in battle was remarkable. He also had the motivation: a strong desire to move up in rank—all humans do. But one thing secured my decision." He smiled a perfect smile, one she would've considered alluring if not for the beast lurking beneath. "The primal desires of youth." A chill crawled up Elaysia's spine. "His comrades spoke highly of him, and not in strictly platonic terms. A few whispers from my maidservants and a glimpse with my own eyes, and I knew he'd have little trouble wooing you."

Elaysia sunk her hands into the dirt and found a small buried rock. She tightened her fingers around it. It wouldn't hurt him much, but enough for her to escape.

"I worried he'd fall for you as well." The All-Sovereign pinched his lips. "I knew her, you know. Your mother. Beautiful Az Zarian stock, even for a human. She dishonored her family when she married your father. Dishonored me. I warned her." He glanced at Elaysia's hands.

"And the nevethium?" she asked, blurting the first thing that came to mind. "That was all a pretense to get us here?"

He rolled his eyes. "*Us?* If you think I care the slightest bit about your petty crew, you're even more foolish than I thought. We've great need of nevethium. Our stores run low, and unseating an enemy nation's newly ordained leader is not an ill-timed move that coincided with it."

The rock slipped from Elaysia's fingers. She recalled the barren wastelands yawning wider and wider, the impoverished villages, the hungry animals, the dry riverbeds, the depleted nevethium mines. Az Zar was nearly reaped beyond repair. The land could no longer sustain their greed and illusions of grandeur, at least not while maintaining the luxurious lifestyles of their nobles and the prowess of their military. They'd exhausted their resources.

And Neharem was next.

Elaysia scrabbled at the dirt, fighting for composure. "The gods support us, and we have stormbirds. They'll be unstoppable when they're grown. They'll—"

"Protect you? Please, don't be dense. You're savage but highborn still." He stood and straightened his cloak, making a sour face as he rubbed a spot of dirt off it. "I'll see to it those birds are mine or dead before the end of this moon cycle."

"Why keep me alive?" Elaysia licked her lips and inched toward the door. Now or never. She rose to meet him, tensing as nausea riled her stomach. "You've asked me nothing since throwing me in this cell."

"You've nothing of value left to share. We learned everything we needed from Davier's reports. I'd be satisfied with killing you now or seeing if your people would exchange a bird for you, not that it's a fair trade." He spoke low and watched her reaction closely. She didn't give him one. "Alas, the Lord Priestess has need of you. You'll fulfill the remainder of your purpose with her."

Elaysia recalled her confrontation with the masked woman and shivered. She wondered what she truly looked like. What powers the priestess held. Why the All-Sovereign didn't implement one of his ideas instead.

"She commands you," Elaysia said aloud, without thinking.

The All-Sovereign struck her. She collapsed. Fire burned in her cheek. Dirt and blood in her mouth. Her legs buckled when she tried to rise, sending her back onto her hands and knees where she retched the meager contents of her stomach into the dirt.

"I almost felt sorry you were spending your last days in this cell, so thank you for reinforcing my decision." His words unleashed in a torrential force, but he trembled. She'd struck something in him.

She leaned against the wall for support, studying him. Small imperfections like the enormity of his pointed ears and the slight wrinkles on his brow stood out. The faint bruising from Davier's punch. It gave her a taste of victory, seeing something so flawless flawed.

"Mavet thanks you for your sacrifice. I'm sure your people will thank you, too, when they become new citizens of the empire." The All-Sovereign turned to leave, but something inside her snapped.

"Does your god hide behind your Lord Priestess, too? Or is it the other way around?" she shouted.

The All-Sovereign halted. He clenched his fists and faced her.

"I don't know what you're plotting, but you won't get away with it." Her head swam, but she advanced, feeding on his shock. "You can't destroy us. Not you. Not your priestess. Not your god. If you should kill me, my people will remain united. Even now, I have someone searching for the Prophets' Scrolls."

The All-Sovereign chuckled. "Fool's errand. They're not so easily found. Do you think I just stumbled upon the ones in my possession?"

Elaysia's lips parted as the pieces fell into place. "Your immortality." A cramp twisted in her lower stomach, too painful to ignore. The All-Sovereign raised an eyebrow as she clutched herself. "I thought it was a rumor spread by your priests to convince people you're a god, but there's truth to it, isn't there? The sacrifices, they... you use them." She clenched her fists. "You're a monster."

The All-Sovereign pinched the bridge of his nose and shook his head. "Yes, a monstrous thing it is. Unfortunately, monsters abound in our world, and your only choice is to become one or be killed by one. You'll find out, eventually. We all do. Anything—an idea, person, lover, god—you hold in high regard will disappoint you. Mark my word." He leaned against the doorframe and gazed upon his body with bewildering fondness. "I don't doubt those you hold in confidence keep secrets from you. In fact, I know someone does." He bit the tip of his tongue.

"You're lying."

"Am I? It's a shame you can't ask High Elder Lightfoot about the shadows in his life before you die. Some might consider his secrets"—he cocked his head to one side, face alive with a sickening pleasure—"monstrous. Worthy of punishment, I'd wager. Even death."

"He's served my family for years. Not everyone is like you and destroys lives for personal gain. He'd never harm us. He raised me."

"*Anyone* will harm *anyone* for the right price, and the right price isn't always immortality or power. For Konar, it likely had to do with control. Did you ever ask yourself why he raised you? Why your entire family disappeared so conveniently at the height of your moldability?"

Elaysia chewed her lips. She fought to stifle the memories, the questions, the nagging *what ifs*, but the more she tried, the louder they screamed.

"I've done many things you'd consider"—the All-Sovereign twirled his finger in the air as if the word he searched for escaped him—"immoral? Which is amusing because morality *is* relative, isn't it? Regardless, I pride myself on the fact that I rarely lie. I find no need for it. If people fear you, then you've nothing to hide from them."

Elaysia breathed in ragged, shallow rasps that tore at her throat. *Say it. Just say it.*

"Boring you? Terribly sorry, but now that I think about it, perhaps it's not my place to tell."

"Tell what?" Elaysia slammed her fist against the wall. Throbbing pain coursed through her arm. She bit her lip to keep from crying out.

"Goodness. If you insist." The All-Sovereign, an amused look on his face, shook his head. "I saw your parents right before they died. They'd begged my audience; I gave it. One leader to another, after all. It was the least I could do. I ignored their pleas and their vain attempts at an alliance, but I provided them food and offered their small party sanctuary in the guest chambers."

"And you slaughtered them while they slept. I know the tale."

"I didn't kill them. Not like that. It's not my style, I assure you. It was one of your kind. My men saw it."

"Your men saw it? And what good are they?"

"Believe what you want. One of their party from Neharem killed everyone as they slept. You might ask yourself who sent him and why. I believe he delivered the terrible message to your people, and then surprisingly—or not so surprisingly—murdered your brother soon after. You would've been rather young, but surely you'd remember his face. It looked strikingly like someone else you know."

"I don't remember. I"—she cupped her mouth until the wave of nausea passed. Lies. The All-Sovereign breathed lies. But the warrior in her room. The one who killed Annonitus. He was Konar's son. "Konar had nothing to do with it. He couldn't have. He..." She froze, her mind locking onto the memory she'd smothered long ago.

The Moonriders are a blight upon the land, Kayrune had told Konar. *Eager for progress and greedy for power—no different from Az Zar. I'm ending the line to ensure peace.*

Elaysia clutched her stomach and gasped. Darkness clawed at her vision. She blinked it back violently.

"It hurts, doesn't it?" The All-Sovereign purred. "When a person you hold in such high regard betrays you? Does it hurt more than Davier, or the same?"

Elaysia grabbed her head as if it would stop the thoughts from spreading.

"No response? Fascinating. I'll leave you to mull over that." He slammed the gate shut. "Wyntz," he shouted.

Puffy rounded the corner and bowed.

"The High Chieftain has an important role to play in our upcoming ceremony. She appears ill, so see to it she keeps enough food and water down to keep her strength about her."

"Don't bother." Elaysia hurled her dish at the bars. "I won't eat to give you the satisfaction of killing me."

The All-Sovereign peered over his shoulder at her, closing and opening his eyes in an exaggerated motion. He turned back Wyntz. "Force it down her, if you must."

Elaysia lay down and shut her eyes. She tried to find sleep using the rhythm of the drips outside her cell, but it evaded her, leaving her alone with thoughts more terrifying than anything the All-Sovereign had planned. It wasn't true. Konar never could've...

He did. You know he did. You've always known.

Tears filled her eyes, trickling down her cheeks and stinging her cracked lips. She looked at her belly; she'd been rubbing it subconsciously. She withdrew her hand as if she'd touched smoldering coals.

No. It wasn't possible. Nymans were infertile. She was infertile. It'd never happened before, and Davier wasn't the exception.

Rest. She just needed rest.

She curled into a ball, muttering *no* over and over and over until a bitter sleep enveloped her, locking her into a nightmare of threats both past and present.

LUMIRA

Moons be cursed.

Why any mainlander chose a frigid, coastal climate over a tropical oasis like The Isles baffled Lumira. Damp air smelling of rotted crustaceans clung to her fur as she squeezed between the wooden shacks clogging the docks of Talza, their frayed splinters snagging her cloak and the satchel she'd concealed Anadu in. More like ruins than housing. She popped onto the main road where seahawks swarmed a deceased dog, their multicolored scales glittering in the bits of sunlight streaming through the clouds. They fanned their tails to hover, snatching morsels of flesh whenever the clusters of dock-dwellers grew sparse enough, then dove into the waves with their hoard.

Lumira sidestepped the bloodied corpse and approached a human boy carrying a basket of dried fish. She offered him the little aspar she had left after securing passage across Skyfall Sea, and gained four herring in return. They were tough and over-salted. As the boy scampered toward his next customer, she wondered if he lived off them. Little else provided sustenance in Talza, home to sailors, fisherfolk, and boat-builders. No harvestable land for miles. Anadu poked her downy head out of the satchel, black eyes fixated on the fish.

"Do you want to get us killed?" Lumira tucked her back in. At the rate she grew, Lumira wouldn't be able to hide her much longer. Or carry her. "Here." Lumira dropped a herring into the satchel and secured the covering.

Heaving Anadu back onto her shoulders, Lumira set off, cursing as she struggled to keep her tail beneath the cloak. It'd taken the bulk of the day to find a sailor willing to do business with a night-stalker, and the Orillon trader who'd finally agreed charged her double. Az Zar was plagued by bigotry. Even the poor boy selling fish would fall prey to Cadar's dogma soon enough. She shoved another herring into her mouth and choked, coughing it onto the ground. Before she could react, a seahawk swooped down and claimed it. She swung at the creature with her spear, but it soared out of reach, cackling.

"Enjoy it," she muttered. "You'll be someone else's meal soon enough."

The stench of shit stung her nose. She dared a glance down. Someone had dropped a massive pile not two feet away. Softened by the rain, it spread from its original parameters like the slow, creeping liquid fire that erupted from the mountains back home. She backed away just before a human man (she'd come to find most of Talza's citizens were human) trudged straight through the pile as though it were only a rain puddle. She gagged.

Lovely people.

Lumira hurried to the dock she'd paid at earlier, wooden planking weathered and smooth beneath her feet. Her hired sailor hadn't returned, so she sat, dangling her legs in the blue-green water, surprised by its mild temperature compared to the bone-chilling fog. The sea was always welcoming. She belonged to it, and it to her.

Across the bay, boats glided through the waves, sails billowing in the wind and dancing in and out of the fog. One drew closer, carrying the unmistakable frame of a beridian. The fur on

Lumira's back rose. She allowed herself the frailest of hopes that it was her papa, as if he'd survived that damning storm nearly a century ago.

Her fantasy dissipated as a scrawny adolescent with yellow and black patched fur took shape. She crossed her arms and lay back, facing the sky, no longer caring if raindrops splattered her face and stung her eyes.

Papa's gone forever. Like Elaysia.

A seahawk landed on her chest and shrieked, its beak splitting to reveal rows of teeth too small to cause her harm. It looked at her like it knew, as though it'd been there the night she ran, watching. Lumira's mouth went dry.

"What? I tried, alright? We didn't stand a chance."

The seahawk cocked its head and blinked as the memory washed over Lumira. After Elaysia's capture, they'd sheltered in a stable on the outskirts of Cadar. She'd awakened sore and distraught the following morning to find the others debating how to break into the best-guarded prison in Quinaria. Provoked by Jakki's snide comments regarding her reckless plan while battling the clutches of self-inflicted guilt, she'd crept out that night with only the light of the moons for company. And Anadu. The damned bird was nothing if not loyal. Lumira tried to sneak into the prison first and swam the perimeter of the barricaded island, but a quick assessment confirmed the improbability of entering unnoticed. With a solitary entrance and lyvium skewers fortifying the walls, a rescue attempt without the others would've been suicide. Even with their remaining warriors, it'd be suicide. So, she fled on a stolen mount, stomach twisting and aching as if hands wrapped around her insides and squeezed.

She'd never belonged in Elaysia's company. She didn't belong anywhere. Beridians only belonged on their isles, and even there,

Lumira felt like an outcast. Not that she'd been exiled. She remembered climbing the tallest tree on her island as her papa set sail, watching him wave a muscular arm. Even then, as a child, she'd known. A voice as fleeting as wind told her it'd be the last goodbye he'd ever give, but she'd ignored it, watching until his sails disappeared into the horizon. After word of her papa's death, she'd run away. Away from their home. From the places he'd taught her to sail and fish. From his ghost. She'd never stopped running. Not until Elaysia, the first person who'd dared to push past her shell in years. And now, Lumira ran from her, too.

"It's Davier's fault," Lumira told the seahawk. It had nestled into her chest, content to risk its life with a stranger for some warmth. "I trusted him too quickly." The seahawk opened one eye and stared at her, unblinking. "What? Everyone else did, and most far sooner than me."

Still, she'd noticed things, hadn't she? The way he'd sneak off in the quiet hours of late night and early morning. How the group always argued and found trouble around him. She sat up, knocking the seahawk into her lap. It hissed, spreading its wings to appear bigger, but it stayed with her.

"Bit desperate, eh? Hungry?" She fingered the last herring, then offered it to the seahawk, who looked between her and the fish with uncertainty. "Now or never, little friend."

It snatched the fish from her palm and disappeared into the waves. Anadu poked her head out of the satchel, chirping in protest. Lumira stroked the stormbird. The horizon called to her, sky blending seamlessly with the water in a dismal tapestry of gray that faded into the distance like a never-ending cave. She'd disgraced the moons beyond repair this time. So much for redemption. She ran her hands over her ears and crumpled into herself. A backhander. That's all she'd ever be.

"Ahoy there," a hearty voice called out in Westmun.

"'Bout time," she muttered, rising to meet the sailor.

The Orillon trader eyed her from several paces away, bottle in hand. His hair was cropped short, accentuating the overly round shape of his head. She couldn't tell if he had one massive chin or several small layers rolled underneath, and she thought of the starving boy who'd sold her the fish. She glared at him.

The trader took a swig and smashed the bottle on the dock. "Better stop muttering in that foreign tongue, or they're like to butcher you for rations and sell your fur to a high-born in Cadar." He snorted, slapping a meaty hand against his leg.

Lumira fought for composure. "Do you have food for the journey? I don't have enough to last to Amiren." The few bites she'd eaten wouldn't satiate most land races half a day, let alone a beridian with twice the average appetite.

"Do I look like an innkeeper, cat?" He shoved past her, humor gone from his voice "Get your own damn food."

She caught his sleeve. "Thought you might do me the courtesy since you're charging me double."

The trader fixed his beady eyes on her, face twitching. "You're lucky I'm taking you at all. Unless you want me to start a commotion about how you intended to rob me, I suggest you keep quiet and get on the boat. Otherwise, I'll charge you triple."

Lumira's claws extended. She considered taking the boat by force, but there were too many bystanders for a clean escape.

"Do you have a hook and line, at least? Or a net?" She asked in her best let's-not-start-a-brawl-on-the-dock voice.

He nodded. "But don't go pushing for anything else."

Lumira growled and followed him onto the boat. They pushed off, and she settled against the railing, eyes closed. She'd take him on the open sea.

"Lumira!"

Her eyes shot open. *Grokhion?* She crouched, inspecting the docks. Sure enough, her kin pushed his way through the crowds. If his bulk and towering frame weren't drawing attention, his shouting certainly was. Lumira begged the moons for anonymity.

Grokhion turned from the docks, heading inland. Lumira relaxed. A bit further, and they'd be unreachable. She leaned back against the railing, reaching for Anadu.

The satchel was empty.

Lumira's pulse quickened. She searched the boat. Anadu perched on the railing, facing the docks. She shrieked, long and piercing. Lumira lunged for the stormbird, but not before Grokhion spun toward the dock, locking eyes with her. Roth screeched back.

Shit.

Grokhion dodged the dock-dwellers with remarkable agility for his monstrous frame and plunged into the water.

"Faster," she hissed. The trader cursed and waddled to adjust the sails.

Grokhion emerged next to the boat, sinking his claws into its sides. Roth climbed out of his satchel and up his back, flapping and squawking to express his displeasure with getting wet. He jumped into the boat and puffed his feathers at Anadu.

"Why did you ignore me? I know you saw me," Grokhion asked in unbridled beridian fashion.

"If I'd wanted you to come, I would've told you back in Cadar." Lumira glanced at the shore. If she could outswim him...

"Wouldn't try it. Even if you outswam me, I doubt you've the aspar for another fare." Grokhion climbed into the boat, tipping it under his weight, and Lumira clung to the opposite side for balance. The trader started to protest until Grokhion stared him down. He backed into the corner, grumbling.

Lumira pressed against the railing, sides closing in on her. "I'm not going back."

"You would abandon her?" Grokhion's eyes widened enough to suggest genuine surprise. Had he thought her fleeing was part of a plot to rescue Elaysia?

Lumira faced the water. "She's already lost. Even if by some miracle she escaped, she'd never want me back in her service. I advised her to make terrible choices and failed to protect her. Everyone's better off without me, and I'm better off alone. It's just how it is. I warned her."

Lumira clutched the railing, her body tightening from the inside out. Even her breathing constricted. Grokhion draped a drenched arm over her shoulders, pulling her in for a hug. She resisted at first, but her body craved the comfort, and she buried her face into his chest. A sob loosened in her throat.

"It's my fault," she whispered.

"It's not, yet you force yourself to carry that burden. Then you act carelessly because you're afraid to let anyone see how much you care. Perhaps even yourself." His breath was warm on the top of her head. "When the pressure proves too much, you run. It's easier to start anew than to fix a broken thing, isn't it?"

Broken thing? No. It wasn't broken. It was over. Gone forever. Like her papa. She ripped away from Grokhion's arms and leaped into the sea, but he grasped her tail, yanking her back onto the boat with a smack. It stole the air from her lungs, and she slashed at him, drawing blood from his arm.

"I can't help it, alright?" she snarled. "I'm not a leader or a protector. I'm hardly a good companion. I do life alone, and no one gets hurt."

Grokhion regarded her with soft eyes "You're selfish."

"What?"

"If you're quite done with your dispute, I've a schedule to keep," the trader interjected.

Lumira bared her fangs. "I swear to your soul-sucking god, shut it before I do it for you."

The trader crumpled back into his corner.

She resumed glaring at Grokhion. "Selfish? Everything I did was for Elaysia and her Stormriders. You think I'd have come here otherwise? To the slavers' homeland? Selfish? I could've run off with my egg long before I met you." She ran her claws down the side of the boat, enjoying the feeling of the wood grains tearing beneath them. "I leave now to protect the others. They won't attack without me, and no one else will get hurt."

"You leave to protect yourself."

"I'm not responsible for them." Lumira's body heated. Why was it so warm out? The sky was still gray. She needed to leave. He shouldn't be here. "It's my life. Mine. I can't..." *Can't lose anyone again.* "If you care so much, you do it. I proclaim you leader in my stead. Now leave."

"Your life?" Grokhion sat beside the stormbirds and stroked his beard. His calmness amid her storm made her want to rage all the more. "Life is a web, Lumira. We are but single threads within it. We control our choices, but we must also take responsibility for them. Even if it doesn't seem like it affects others, our actions, or lack of, vibrate throughout the web, impacting other threads in ways we can't imagine. All things are bound together. All things connected."

Lumira wrapped her arms around herself, wishing she could disappear. Grokhion was right, but what of all the hate she'd seen? Prejudice against her kind and others considered lesser-races; the rich and powerful preying on the poor and the weak; her papa never to return while the All-Sovereign lived on; crimes she'd gotten away with for years while Elaysia's first-ever risk landed her a cell with a death sentence.

She knelt before Grokhion, feeling like a child seeking an elder's wisdom. "How am I supposed to know what outcome my choices will breed? Can a single thread make that much of a difference?"

Grokhion patted the spot beside him. She joined him, leaning her head next to his. "It can, if it unites with other threads, forming an inseparable bond. It only takes one voice to inspire change. It's not easy, nor guaranteed, but nothing's impossible if the right people believe in an idea, hold it dear to their hearts, and fight for a just world."

"How do you maintain it?"

"What?"

"Your unabashed optimism."

A laugh rumbled from Grokhion's belly. Lumira drank it in, basking in a blanket of security she'd not experienced in years.

"Love of life keeps me going. If I'm not fighting for it, am I any better than those opposing it?"

"What if it's not enough to defeat Az Zar?"

Grokhion's brow furrowed. "I never said it was. Perhaps we should consider the possibility Az Zar is not the true enemy."

Lumira huffed. "That's not how it looks to me, but you're right about everything else." She rose, sucking in the evening air as it rolled off the waves. The sun kissed the sea, summoning flashes of orange and purple to the otherwise dreary skies. "Why'd you come for me? Everyone else must be furious. I'm sure some hope I never return." *Like Jakki.* She shook her head. "Why risk making them hate you, too?"

"Because I believe in you." He grinned, fangs glinting in the sunset. "That, and because I refuse to be abandoned to a throng of arrogant nyrians and ignorant humans."

"I knew you had some beridian left in you." She butted her head against his. "I don't know what you see in me, but I'll take it. Can't afford to reject a compliment when I get so few."

"You're tougher than a mollusk, but I know a good soul when I meet one. These ancient eyes have learned a thing or two." He pointed to them and winked.

Lumira wondered exactly what they'd seen. Beridians weren't fond of prying into other people's business, but if she didn't ask now...

"Why did you leave The Isles for Neharem?" There. It was done.

Grokhion shook his head. "That's a story for another time."

"Sorry." Lumira stared her feet, painfully aware of how her body twitched. He'd tell her one day. She'd make sure of it.

"Don't be sorry." He retrieved her spear, placing it in her hand. "Just embrace who you are. All of it. When your purpose is clear and you burn with the fire of unbreakable will, no deluge can dampen your mission. Love yourself. Love others. Love the land. The Ni'anko say a good life is built on these tenets."

Lumira snorted. "Sounds easy enough."

"Don't underestimate yourself."

"I'll try not to." She touched his arm and nodded to the fuming trader who readied a makeshift weapon in the corner. "Thinking what I'm thinking?"

Grokhion's pupils constricted. "I never said I abandoned all our ways."

"Now?"

"Now."

They pounced on the trader as he lunged at them with a fishhook bound to a pole. Grokhion scooped up the protesting man while Lumira retrieved her aspar, and then some, from his pockets.

"For putting up with you," she said with a wink. They tossed him overboard, watching him flail like a bird in the water, spittle and profanities flying from his mouth.

Grokhion held up a map from the trader's belongings and outlined their path with an extended claw. "We can take this right down the coast to Cadar. Are you ready for a life-threatening rescue attempt?"

"Am I beridian?" Lumira unfurled the sail, chest puffing as Grokhion nodded in approval.

"Good. Time isn't on our side."

"They still hold her?"

"Yes." A cloud passed over his face as he checked the boat for supplies. "But her time draws near."

Lumira gripped her spear. "Grokhion."

He stopped scavenging, giving her his full attention. "Go on."

"I..." *I'm sorry you had to chase after me. I'm sorry I've shut you out. I'm sorry I made them think less of us.* She looked up. The moons hovered over her, watching. Papa watched, too. "I swear by our ancestors and the goddesses above, I'll never abandon you all again. Never."

"No need to swear. Just show me."

JAKKI

Jakki ducked behind an abandoned cart as an Az Zarian patrol rounded the corner—the third she'd dodged that afternoon. The soldiers' shadows danced before her feet in a never-ending parade. The All-Sovereign grew desperate. A hint of pride swelled in her chest, knowing he considered the Stormriders a threat. Now, to live up to it.

A cat slunk under the cart and rubbed against her leg. She nudged it with her boot. It returned, purring. Another nudge. Back again, tail sticking up. It slammed into her shin.

"Scram, you little shit," she whispered. "I don't have any food."

The cat yowled. A soldier broke formation, cocking his head toward the cart.

Keep marching, dammit.

She gave the cat a final shove. It scampered off, but the soldier strode toward her.

Fuck.

Jakki gripped her pilfered Az Zarian dagger, its hilt sleek and foreign in her hands. It wasn't an opportune place for a skirmish, but if the gods willed it, she'd die fighting.

Someone further up the line barked an order in Zarith. The soldier halted within arm's reach of the cart, mumbled something, and retreated. Jakki offered a silent prayer of gratitude. When the last of the soldiers cleared out, she sprinted to the next alleyway. The streets narrowed ahead. They'd have to march single file. If she'd timed it right, the last soldier would pass by—

Now.

She dragged him into the alleyway and slit his throat. The man was enormous. Great. At least height was on her side. She donned her new uniform and hoisted the stripped carcass into a feces bin.

The burial he deserved.

Jakki found Xaren browsing pottery beneath an awning's shade. "Enjoying yourself?"

Xaren's eyes widened. "Where's your mask?"

"I'll put it on when I'm good and ready." She plucked a vase from his hands. "Nearly got killed back there. Don't know if you noticed."

"You said you had it handled—"

"Save it." She tugged on the mask. It smelled of rotting teeth and ale. Of course, it did. "This will never work. Look at me." She gestured to the uniform that sagged like an oversized gown with cinches.

"Would you rather march in wearing the garments of the Yustano?" Xaren crossed his arms, his tone sharp and assertive. "Marksmen would take you down before we reached the citadel. Trust me."

"Watch yourself. I've little trust for outsiders now, especially another deserter who pledged fealty on a whim." Jakki shoved past him, slamming her shoulder into his.

They wove through the streets in silence until the citadel archway towered above them, polished jade gleaming in the sun.

Behind it, a courtyard with stacks of curved roof buildings decorated in murals, each with additional barricades and fencing. A dozen soldiers guarded the entrance alone. More likely patrolled inside.

Jakki elbowed Xaren. "There's no other way in?"

Xaren shook his head. "If we got caught without papers in a service passage, we'd never talk our way out of it. The main gate is less suspicious."

"And crawling with slavers."

"Do you want to triple our chances of dying?"

"Servant entrance. Now."

"Your funeral."

Xaren banked left, leading her past the last of the wealthy homes and down a narrow staircase that opened into a courtyard enclosed by stables. Children dressed in canvass tunics and skirts scampered about, dodging bales of hay as they batted at a ball with sticks. The palace slave quarters, though modest in size, carried the perception of wealth with green-flecked stone and stained roofs. They'd even taken care to position every plant and statue in the courtyard to accentuate the beauty and order of the citadel. Minimal guards clustered around the palace entrance.

Jakki nudged Xaren and strode into the courtyard, trying her best to imitate the marching pattern of a soldier. It felt ridiculous, but the handful of slaves that looked up paid her no mind. Sweat collected in her mask as they neared the guards. They'd made it halfway up the stairs to the entrance when one called out. She halted, her hand tracing her hilt. Xaren replied in Zarith. The guard nodded, laughing, and waved them inside. Jakki almost thanked Xaren.

The palace reeked of incense, a sickly-sweet smell carrying floral notes and spice. Gaudy tapestries fringed in gems slithered down blood-red walls, diminished only by the ornate carvings of sun-blood branches and blossoms wrapping around the pillars. Throat and eyes burning, Jakki followed Xaren down the hall. Paintings twice her height and embellished with jeweled frames lined their passage, commemorating Az Zar's rulers, dignitaries, and warlords over the years. She passed a recently painted portrait, presumably of the All-Sovereign. A few paces later, she froze. Another painting of the same man. But the second must've been painted over a millennium prior, judging by the clothing and wear on the canvas. No nyrian lived that long.

Xaren tapped Jakki's shoulder. "We need to keep moving."

"Hold on. Who does this look like to you?"

"The All-Sovereign's relative, I guess."

"You guess." Jakki rolled her eyes. "Don't you find it odd this *relative* looks like the All-Sovereign?"

"It can happen."

"They're identical."

Xaren walked away. "We're going to miss the meeting if you don't hurry."

"Right behind you." Jakki let the frustration bleed through her tone and stormed after him.

Xaren never hesitated as he wound them down halls, up stairwells, and through side doors leading to more of the same: luxurious room upon luxurious room. *Who needs all this space? An entire village could live here,* Jakki mused, glaring into another empty room that stored beds with satin sheets, which probably never got slept in.

"You seem well acquainted with this place," she said when Xaren stopped in front of an armor display.

"I was assigned palace guard when I first completed the exams."

"Close with His Holiness, were you?"

Xaren ignored the jab, prodding the wall with his fingers. It gave and groaned open, revealing a dark passageway. Cobwebs hung low, and the stench of musk filled her nostrils. Xaren ducked inside. She hurried after him, closing the secret entrance behind her.

Jakki slipped her nevethium necklace out of her uniform, highlighting the various pathways available before joining Xaren at what looked like a dead end. He pressed a cutaway in the stone, and the passage opened to a balcony overlooking a thriving garden filled with sun-blood trees and sparkling brooks. Exotic, long-legged birds stalked about the lily pads, pecking at the ground and water. Two guards paced the terrace. A delicate table with a single chair sat empty. No All-Sovereign.

Jakki gripped the railing. She'd expected a secret meeting room or the All-Sovereign's private quarters. "Why are we here? You said we'd see *him*."

Xaren didn't offer so much as a glance in her direction.

"Fine. I'll explore on my own."

Xaren yanked his mask off, exposing a scowl. "I told you yesterday."

"Like Haeshol you did."

"He prefers to meet in the gardens and other outdoor venues away from the *thin walls of the palace,* as he so often puts it. Satisfied?" Xaren turned away, muttering in Zarith.

Jakki sat on crossed legs with her back to him, determined to avoid conversing until the ordeal was finished. She found herself wanting to reach out and stroke Siren for comfort, but the stormbird was kept safely outside the city with the others.

At least an hour passed. Jakki's stomach growled. Shadows crept down the ceiling. Other than a small girl tending the birds, no one entered.

She flung her mask at Xaren. "Fucking waste of time. We could've looted several more uniforms by now."

Xaren wrung her mask in his hands. "He usually meets with a general or priest once a fortnight around sunset, I swear."

"Your swears mean noth—"

Jakki froze as voices flittered into the vicinity. She crept toward the railing, her body pressed to the ground like a snake. Two figures emerged from a row of bushes manicured to look like rearing stallions. They marched up the nevethium-flecked staircase to the terrace. The All-Sovereign wore a gilded collar and silk skirt that blazed whiter than the sun, and some variation of a soldier's uniform garbed his companion, albeit more lavish with jewels and billowing pants.

"General Zhia," Xaren said, hatred choking his words. "We saw her at the village where they—"

Jakki held a finger to his lips. She placed her ear as close to the bars as possible.

"... prepared for tomorrow," Zhia was saying. They'd stopped strolling and faced the gardens with their backs to the balcony. "And I'm to inform the people attendance is mandatory this year?"

"Our Lord demands it." The All-Sovereign's tone carried the faintest hint of disdain. "They will witness his power and tremble to behold him. Their whispers must carry across the sea to Neharem, Orillon, and whomever else dares to question the might of Mavet's chosen people."

"It will be done, Your Holiness."

"Everything must go perfectly. She's still in good health?"

Zhia hesitated. "She wanes."

The All-Sovereign paced across the terrace, hand on his jaw as he stared off. "See to it she survives the night."

Zhia bowed and started down the stairs, pausing halfway.

The All-Sovereign wasn't facing her, but he must've sensed she lingered. "You're excused, General."

Zhia rocked from one foot to the other. "Forgive my forthrightness, but is it wise to antagonize Neharem now? Weapons development is behind schedule. Our military's not fully recovered from The Skulmor Rebellion. I worry it's inviting—"

"Silence." The All-Sovereign snapped out of whatever trance he'd fallen into and marched down the stairs, stopping two steps above Zhia, bare chest in her face. "Did I ask for your counsel on the matter?"

"No, Your Eminence." Zhia lowered her head. "But shouldn't we focus on distribution and preparing our troops for war instead of the Lord Priestess's..." She bit her lip, raising her eyes to meet his. "We must evolve beyond archaic rituals and remind the people the empire comes before faith. You've said so yourself."

"Blasphemy." The All-Sovereign struck her face with a resounding slap.

Zhia fell to the floor, face down, palms upturned. "Mercy, Your Holiness."

The All-Sovereign lifted her chin with his foot. "It concerns me someone I hold in confidence is so easily misled by abhorrent gossip."

Zhia quivered. "It won't happen again, I swear. I'll eradicate any who dare to speak ill of you and our Lord Priestess."

The All-Sovereign patted her head as if she were a village hound. "There, there. All is forgiven. Remember, it is not your place to question our Lord's ways. This girl is a small sacrifice for the greater good of our empire."

"You are ever wise, Your Holiness."

Zhia backed out of the room, head bowed. Once alone, the All-Sovereign glided to the table and snapped his fingers. A dwarf appeared, presented a bottle of wine, and left.

Xaren nudged Jakki. "We've learned enough to inform our decision. Let's go." He disappeared into the secret passage.

Jakki lingered, wrapping her fingers around the Az Zarian hilts. Swords weren't her expertise and required abandoning the safety of her perch, but it would have to do. Below, the All-Sovereign reclined in his chair, sipping wine, with only two soldiers to defend him. It was too easy. She'd be a fool not to. She rose, searching for a landing to soften her leap. The pillars sported lips of varying lengths, and one was within jumping distance.

"Jakki," Xaren popped out of the tunnel. "What are you doing?" His voice suggested he already knew.

"I'm avenging Elaysia. I won't get a better opportunity."

Xaren shook his head. "We'd never get out of here alive."

"I'm not asking you to stick around." Jakki pulled herself onto the railing.

"And if you succeed? You think they'll let Elaysia live? Proceed with tomorrow as planned? They're more likely to behead her immediately in revenge."

Jakki froze, a knot forming in her throat. *Mother Itaso. He's right.* Gritting her teeth, she leaped down from the railing.

Xaren reached for her shoulder. "Thank you. I know it—"

"This has *nothing* to do with you. You don't know what loyalty means, so I assume my struggle is foreign to you." She shoved past him and tore through the tunnel, not bothering to ensure he followed.

The sky was dark and thick with clouds when Jakki and Xaren reached that night's gathering place: a brothel disguised as a tavern on the outskirts of Cadar's slave district, aptly named Mavet's Delights. Inside the courtyard, indiscreet merchants and off-duty soldiers stumbled around shit piles and loitered on the rotting porch, munching sedare mushrooms and fawning over whores. Jakki cringed. *Excellent choice, Yerakai.* He'd suggested changing locations every night, which made sense as it rendered them harder to track and predict, but they'd nearly run out of options. Leaving Cadar wasn't viable either; not if they wanted back in. Without Davier's military prowess, reentering the city proved treacherous, and they'd only sent Xaren out once to update the rest of the warriors. Last he'd reported, they ran low on supplies. And optimism.

"I thought this shit was illegal here," Jakki told Xaren as she stepped over a man snoring on the pathway, a bottle in one of his hands and an empty satchel in the other. He'd regret that in the morning.

Xaren shrugged. "You can buy your way out of punishment if you're from a high-born family. And not everyone obeys the laws."

"The All-Sovereign must know these places exist."

"If it's not affecting someone of influence, they ignore it. They'd be imprisoning half the military if they enforced the law. Besides, the whores are usually slaves."

"And no one cares what happens to them." Jakki yanked her mask off and blotted her face. "Don't ask, don't tell, and the empire uses it as leverage when needed."

"Can we just find the others?" Xaren removed his mask as a handful of topless women sauntered by. He averted his gaze.

A smirk tugged at Jakki's lips. "Never seen a naked woman?"

"It's not that. I don't like seeing anyone treated as a commodity." Xaren hurried ahead.

"Noble thought for a slaver." Jakki called after him.

She lingered, studying one of the women, a human with skin pale as the moons. The woman felt Jakki's gaze and scowled upon realizing whose attention she'd attracted, then turned away with a hand on her hip. *Bitch.* Jakki took a step toward the tavern, eyes still tracing the woman's backside, and collided with Xaren.

"Mother Itaso"—she shoved him back—"why are you always skulking about?"

Xaren gestured to the woman. "Don't take it personally."

Jakki's cheeks burned. "Never do."

"It's outlawed here. Even if she were a willing partner, she wouldn't dare act on it." Xaren's brow furrowed. "I'm sorry. I don't agree with the laws. I think love is—"

"I don't care what *you* think." Jakki hurried up the stairs and through the open door.

It was darker inside than out. Screens carved with Mavist symbols divided the seating areas. She narrowed her eyes, searching for her companions amid the bevy of Az Zarians reclining at communal tables. Mardus, Anahi, and Yerakai clustered in the corner of the room, cloaks drawn about their faces despite the tavern's warmth. It wasn't unheard of for Neharem traders to visit Cadar, but with the All-Sovereign's bounty at large, it was best to keep their identities veiled. Jakki wedged herself between the tables, keeping her head down.

"Did you learn anything?" Yerakai asked as she slid into the booth beside him. His face lacked its usual vibrancy, and it struck something in her. She rested her head on his shoulder.

"We've confirmed she'll be part of tomorrow's ceremony at dusk," Xaren said, joining Mardus and Anahi on the opposite side of the table. "It's the chance we've been waiting for."

Mardus shoved his drink aside and leaned toward Xaren. "What's the importance of this ceremony?"

Xaren looked down at his hands. "Tomorrow's Az Zar's foundation day. After feasting, tithing, and worshiping throughout the moon cycle of Vynar, it culminates with a sacrifice to Mavet."

"And Elaysia's the sacrifice." Mardus slammed his fists on the table.

"Easy, Brother." Jakki reached for Mardus's abandoned drink and took a sip of something tart. "Hope isn't lost. They're opening the citadel gates and demanding all citizens attend. That's our opportunity. We'll funnel in with the crowds and plant ourselves around the courtyard."

"We'll need a bit more direction than that," Anahi said, idly spinning her cup on the table.

Jakki's nostrils flared. "If you'd let me finish."

Anahi raised her eyebrows. "My humblest apologies. Continue."

"Even if we secure enough uniforms to smuggle more warriors inside, we still don't have enough people," Mardus said, oblivious to the standoff. "The beridians could've—"

"They abandoned us." Jakki's raised voice drew attention from the adjacent table, and Yerakai rested a hand on her leg. She fought for composure. "All that matters is who's here now. We're loyal, we're fighting back, and we'll rescue Elaysia under my leadership."

Mardus frowned and reclaimed his drink. "Grokhion's coming back. He swore."

"You're a fool to believe him." Jakki reached into her pouch and fingered the parchment the old man gave her. "I have a plan. Trust me."

"I'm equally a fool for believing you. We should've stormed the prison days ago. Tomorrow will be suicide. Do you know how many soldiers they'll have patrolling?" Mardus shoved away from the table. Anahi followed, and Xaren cleared his throat before creeping to the counter.

Jakki buried her head in her hands. Yerakai's hand moved from her leg to her shoulder. She shrugged away from it.

"They don't doubt you," he said. "They underestimate themselves and fear the odds."

"And you?" She forced herself to look at him, truly look at him for the first time since Unleto. Complete, unwavering trust. Her stomach tightened.

"I choose to acknowledge my fears and prepare to meet them. If you treat them like feasible conquests, they lose their power. Besides, this life is but a journey to the next. I worry not."

"Must be nice to be so confident in those old stories."

"I'm confident in Khiev-Tatamic and his plan. The stories are meant to give us hope and help us remember."

"Remember what?"

"That we're made for more."

"A bit vague to be inspiring, but whatever keeps your spirits." Jakki squeezed Yerakai's hand. "Let's gather the others. We need to secure a few more uniforms tonight."

As Jakki rose, two tall, cloaked figures strode in, drawing attention from the patrons. A tail peeked out beneath the larger one's garment. Jakki's jaw clenched as Mardus intercepted them. They embraced.

Attention-seeking traitors. Whatever they hoped to gain, she was going to make sure they didn't get it.

As Mardus guided the beridians to the table, Jakki sauntered to the countertop, ignoring Yerakai's bewildered expression. Excited murmurs drifted through the air behind her, signifying the party's reunion. She stole a glance over her shoulder and caught Anahi's gaze. The Orillon woman rested her hands on her hips, frowning. Jakki offered an obscene gesture. She took her time ordering her drink and returned to the table even slower than she'd departed. There was plenty of sitting room, even with the addition of two larger members, but Jakki stood, drinking in the hesitant look in Lumira's eyes. It was time the cat learned her place.

"I'm sorry I ran," Lumira said. Her claws poked through the gloves she wore to mask them. "It seemed hopeless, and I..." Her voice caught in her throat, and she turned to Grokhion for what was undoubtedly some sort of kindred support. "I was selfish and scared. Scared of forming attachments. Scared of being a part of something greater than myself." She faced Jakki, shoulders slumped. "I've no right to lead you any longer." Mardus objected, but Lumira held up her hand. "But I owe Elaysia a debt, and I want to help rescue her, if you'll have me."

Jakki scoffed and propped her foot on the bench beside Anahi. "We already have a plan in place, thanks to those who stayed. We might be able to use you—"

"We need you," Anahi interrupted. She grasped Lumira's forearm. "Elaysia will be proud of your honesty. Most people wouldn't have come back."

"Most people wouldn't have left in the first place," Jakki muttered. She looked around the table for support, but found none.

"You should still lead us tomorrow," Anahi continued. "We'll fill you in on the plan and see what other perspectives you might offer."

The others echoed their agreement, all except Yerakai, who simply nodded and smiled.

Jakki's face flushed. "That's all it takes? A half-assed apology from an outsider, and you welcome her back with open arms? Pathetic." Jakki shoved the table with her foot, spilling everyone's drinks and drawing eyes around the room. "Fine, devise your plans and have someone fill me in tomorrow." She shoved through the crowd and back out into the night air. It smacked into her like a rush of cold water, and for a moment, tears threatened to get the better of her.

"Jakki." Lumira's voice. The beridian joined her on the porch, wringing her hands.

Jakki finished her drink in one gulp and hurled the mug into the courtyard. "What in Haeshol do you want, cat?"

"I know we've had our differences, but I'm willing to see past it if you can." Lumira stepped closer. Jakki stepped back. "You've no respect for me, and rightfully so. But I appreciate who you are and what you mean to Elaysia. I don't have to lead. We'll need you tomorrow."

"Of course, you do." Jakki patted Lumira's shoulder condescendingly. "You're hardly capable on your own."

Lumira's eyes widened, then narrowed. She bared the slightest bit of fang.

Jakki spat and prowled toward the whores. If she was going to die tomorrow, copulation was a worthwhile risk.

But later that night as she reveled in ecstasy, the moon-skinned woman she set upon in the courtyard panting and moaning beneath her, Jakki only had thoughts for Elaysia.

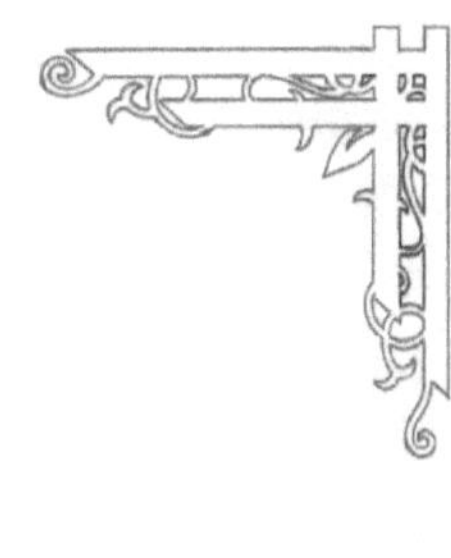

ELAYSIA

The cell door screeched like a ravager bird taunting its kill. Elaysia clutched her stomach, knowing she was the latter. No one had visited since the All-Sovereign, which only left one option.

It was time.

Her spirit withered like flower petals kissing the soil, ready to embrace the full circle of its journey. Death would seem welcoming if not for the life now intertwined with hers, this new entity she'd scarcely had time to process. Hopefully, it wouldn't feel pain. She traced her fingers over her stomach and tried to imagine the fragile cords of consciousness weaving together. A bit of her. A bit of *him.* Did it look like a baby already? Its anomalies worse than her own? A mob of scenarios flooded her mind. She harnessed the negative ones and buried them deep.

"Better you not see this world," she whispered.

Footsteps pattered in the dirt. Her eyelids fluttered open to find the webbed booting Az Zarian soldiers wore to muffle their movements. She gripped the wall to brace her ascent, darkness ebbing at her vision as the ground shifted beneath her.

"Stop wallowing," the soldier barked in Zarith.

"A moment, please." Every movement jarred her head and sent her heart racing.

The soldier unfastened a pouch from his belt and sloshed its contents on her face. The overpowering sweetness of kuba grain wine trickled into her mouth, triggering a bout of dry heaves. She collapsed, wheezing. The soldier cursed and yanked her up by the collar of her tunic. His eyes seethed hatred.

"Please—"

He brought a hand down on her face before she could finish her plea. She landed on her back, ears ringing. She clawed for air. The soldier shouted something, but it sounded muffled. Distant. She moaned, curling her knees into her stomach.

The soldier drew back for another strike. "I said, get your filthy—"

Another hand caught his at the last moment, preventing the blow. "I'll carry her," the newcomer said. "She's suffered enough."

Elaysia tucked her head between her knees and rocked. Thick, warm arms wrapped underneath her as the ground fell away. She fought the relief surging through her body. The newcomer merely sought to keep her alive for whatever end awaited her, but it was the only semblance of gentility she'd known in days.

Lulled by the cradling motion, she didn't rouse until the movement stopped. They'd entered a windowless room with the same crude stone walls as her cell. But unlike her cell, the glow from a small nevethium crystal revealed simple living quarters complete with a fireplace, a cushioned chair, and a bathing basin. A table in the corner held a pitcher of water and what looked like fermented cabbage and steamed kuba grain. Her mouth watered.

A humpbacked old woman with tiny feet hobbled over to meet them. "What does His Holiness ask of me?" she croaked.

"She's to be"—the soldier carrying Elaysia paused, as if unsure what words should follow—"prepared. For this evening. I leave her in your care." He set Elaysia down in the chair and left before she had a chance to thank him.

It doesn't matter, she reminded herself. *He still played a part in my death.*

The old woman squinted at Elaysia. "We'll get you something to eat before your bath." She gave Elaysia water, then used two smoothed, wooden utensil sticks to pinch the sticky grains and bring them to her mouth.

Elaysia glowered at first, but hunger overtook her desire to maintain resolve. Besides, based on the woman's ragged clothing and elderly state, she wasn't here by choice either. When it was time to bathe, Elaysia couldn't help but smirk at the challenge of her and the old woman, both in weakened states, struggling to get her out of the rags and into the basin. The water burned her skin, even though the woman insisted it grew cold, but eventually, her body relaxed. As she rested, eyes closed, trying not to imagine the bath was her last, she felt the woman's gaze on her.

"Do you find me so repulsive?" Elaysia snapped. The woman, however, fixated on her breasts. Elaysia covered them with her hands.

"You're with child." The woman spoke devoid of emotion, but it pierced Elaysia like an arrow.

"What do you know?" Elaysia submerged underwater and screamed. No one else had spoken it aloud. There was no denying it now.

The woman rested bony fingers on the edge of the basin. "Girl, I've been alive a long while now. I know the signs. It's too small to feel pain, if it's any comfort."

"It's not." Elaysia struggled out of the tub and sloshed to the table where a pile of silks waited. The woman offered a hand, but Elaysia shirked away. "Don't. I'll prepare myself to meet death."

The gown tied at the waist in traditional Cadar fashion, but it was far more revealing with a delicate cream silk bordering on transparent. The sleeves draped past her knees, and the train rippled on the ground like water.

The woman approached with a comb. "At least let me ready your hair?"

Elaysia nodded, too fatigued to defy her.

After the woman fashioned her hair in an Az Zarian-styled bun, sleek and piled high, Elaysia caught her arm. "I'm sorry. I know this isn't your doing."

The woman cracked a toothless smile. "Of course, dear. Take heart. It's better to go young than flounder in old age." She bowed and closed the door. The bolt locked into place with a *clank*.

Elaysia slumped in the chair. "Easy to say when you've lived long enough to compare the two."

She took the silver comb, eyeing her reflection in the splintered metal. A stranger peered back, frail with dulled skin. More white hair streaked the black. Had the cream patch beneath her nose spread? Dark bags saddled her eyes. Hollow cheeks. Cracked, flakey lips.

"You're not me," she told the reflection. "But it makes today easier. I'm already dead."

The lock jostled. A figure filled the doorframe, clad in a white, hooded robe with Mavet's symbol embroidered in blood-red on the chest. The comb slipped from Elaysia's hand, landing with a clatter. They didn't speak. They didn't have to. Elaysia forced herself to look the executioner in the eye as she padded across the floor. A probing, callous gaze was the last thing she saw before a hood snuffed out her vision. Rough hands slung her over a shoulder. Steady *thumps* signified a journey up the stairs. A door creaked. Warm, briny air tingled her skin. Soldiers barked orders. Eventually, she found herself seated in a small boat, gently rocked by the waves. She wished the sea would welcome her into its dark, numbing womb.

The boat struck the dock, and back she went into another's arms. More talking in low, surly rasps. More walking. Elaysia fought for consciousness until her carrier slammed her down, scraping her knees against stone. Someone tore off her hood as the last streams of daylight faded over the horizon to the west. Clear skies. All three moons full-bellied in golden splendor. The manicured foliage and tri-stacked buildings signified a return to Cadar. So be it. She'd meet the fate of her parents after all.

A gentle roar vibrated the city as they marched up the main road. It transformed into thunderous chants when they neared the citadel gates where costumed dancers crowded beneath the bodies of resplendent serpents with snarling wooden faces and streaming feathers of fabric. Citizens watched from rooftops, porches, in the roads, and around them, dangling nevethium lanterns and donning ostentatious masks with angry eyes and frowning mouths. "Long live the All-Sovereign," some shouted. "Mavet is Lord," and, "cleanse Quinaria," crowed others.

A simmering mob lurked at the citadel threshold, spitting and slurring curses. Elaysia's heart lurched as someone lunged at her. She sidestepped the attack, but something smashed into the back of her head, knocking her off balance. She crumpled. Beside her, a fist-sized rock. Another slammed into her spine. She covered her head. Blood pooled in her mouth from her recently bitten tongue. A gruff hand yanked her arm with a *pop*, and the soldiers hedged her in. She slogged forward, eyes on the ground, until her bare feet scuffed the foot of the stairs. After a few steps, her leg spasmed and buckled beneath her. A soldier growled and dragged her up by her hair until she found her footing. Somehow, engulfed in deadening pain, she found herself overlooking a courtyard overflowing with people. Had the whole of Cadar come to witness her death?

A priest shoved Elaysia toward an altar fashioned from nevethium. Its glow illuminated a woman wearing a sleeveless crimson dress, and though a hood shrouded her face, her nyrian white, roped locks tumbled down freely. A chain bearing a ravager bird's skull nestled in her cleavage.

The Lord Priestess. A chill seized Elaysia's flesh.

The All-Sovereign stood opposite her, his silvered skin contrasting her ebony hue, looking bathed and pampered in swaths of embroidered silk. But his face suggested inner turmoil distinctive to... fear? He refused to acknowledge Elaysia, focusing instead on smoothing his robes. The Lord Priestess tapped the altar, and the tip of a crossbow pricked Elaysia's spine, urging her forward. The crowd quieted. The altar was smooth and warm, almost welcoming. The Lord Priestess lay Elaysia back, tracing the outline of her stormbird necklace with fingers like ice. Like death. Above, clouds wrapped the moons in a gray film. Raindrops kissed the altar. Elaysia clutched her necklace. If the ancient stories were true, death meant reunion and a new life. She begged her trembling soul to believe it.

A gong sounded, and the crowd rippled, heads bowed and palms upraised.

"I implore mercy, Mavet, Savior and Lord, Almighty and Ineffable," the Lord Priestess began in a silver-tongued voice. "Your faithful servant intercedes on behalf of your people, beseeching you to deliver us from ourselves. Bless your ordained leader, the All-Sovereign, that he may champion your holy crusade and eradicate immoral peoples and false gods. Fill us with subservience and keep us strong in faith and service to the empire, that you may reign again on the day where sky, land, and sea become one. When the worlds above and below have no bounds.

When all life on Quorath trembles to behold your power. May all swear eternal servitude or else face eternal decay, unquenchable thirst, and insatiable hunger in The Abyss. Victory in solidarity. Strength in order. Hail Mavet."

"Hail Mavet," the people echoed.

Rain poured, blurring Elaysia's vision and soaking her thin gown. The Lord Priestess unsheathed a glowing red dagger with jagged edges. Terror gripped Elaysia's muscles. She focused on the rise and fall of her chest as she breathed.

In. Out. In. Out.

The Lord Priestess drew the dagger across Elaysia's palm, squeezing her blood into a chalice embossed with an ancient tongue. The sounds of clanking metal and pouring liquid reverberated through the courtyard.

"We drink the blood of our enemies that Mavet may transform their weaknesses into our strengths," the Lord Priestess said, raising her chalice. She tipped her head back to drink, revealing eyes violet as anderberries. A rare color, even for a nyrian. Elaysia had only seen it once before, adorning someone dear to her.

In. Out. In. Out.

The Lord Priestess lowered her empty chalice with a clank. A solemn, steady drumbeat seized Elaysia's heart, controlling its beat and filling her mouth with saliva while nausea festered in her stomach. *Thump. Thump. Thump, thump, thump, thump.* The Lord Priestess emitted guttural sounds more beastly than speech, resonating with the power of a voice beyond her own. Lightning flickered, thunder raging on its tail. A wind gust tore through the courtyard and whipped around Elaysia, threatening to knock her off the altar. Instead, it cradled her, lifting her until she came level with the Lord Priestess's chest. She raised the dagger above Elaysia.

"The Daughter forgive me," Elaysia whispered. She closed her eyes, seeking comfort in the weightlessness.

"Are you ready, child?"

The voice filled Elaysia's mind as if it originated within, but it wasn't her own. A feminine voice, but deeper in tone, as though it pulled from the depths of Quorath. It couldn't be the spirit walker. Not so far from nature. And the forest goddess spoke in airy tones, soothing and gentle. This voice was wild. Warm. Powerful.

I am, she told it. *I've accepted my fate.*

"But what of your destiny? Your story can end here, and no one will think less of you. Can you say the same for yourself? Is this your legacy?"

Elaysia opened her eyes, but all she saw was darkness. The Lord Priestess's blade should've dropped by now. She should be—

"I asked, are you ready?"

Elaysia bit her lip. She wasn't sure she wanted to trade death's finality for life's uncertainty after everything she'd experienced. Where there was opportunity for hope, catastrophe loomed nearby, eager to strike.

Can you promise it'll be worth it if I stay? Elaysia asked the voice. *That I'll even make it out of this courtyard alive?*

"The future is unwritten. I can, however, promise that every time you try, you'll become a stronger version of yourself. The rewards of this life are in the journey, not the result."

Elaysia thought of her parents, murdered in the same city she'd all but surrendered to, perhaps in the same way, for the same reasons, and shuddered.

I'm not ready, she told the voice. *How do I get out of this?*

"One step at a time."

The darkness melted away just as the Lord Priestess cried out and lowered her dagger. Elaysia clawed at her cloak, using the leverage to free herself from whatever magic held her in the air. The Lord Priestess hissed and slashed again, blade barely missing Elaysia's arm.

Elaysia rolled off the altar and willed her legs to the edge of the platform. It stood several body lengths above the stone courtyard with little to cushion her fall. Soldiers closed in on the platform behind her.

If it be death, it'll be my way.

The Lord Priestess bared her teeth and leaped forward, dagger extended. "Don't run from your fate, little kitten."

Elaysia clutched her stomach. "I determine my fate."

She closed her eyes and jumped.

JAKKI

"No!"

Jakki's scream cut through the courtyard like cracking ice as Elaysia careened from the platform and into the crowd. Even with the nevethium lanterns aglow, she couldn't locate Elaysia in the shadows. Tension seized her chest. She searched for Xaren amid the fray of soldiers surrounding the Lord Priestess. Why hadn't he taken the shot?

"To me," a voice rang out.

Jakki reverted her gaze to where Lumira hid among the sea of Az Zarians. The beridian ripped off the cloak she'd used to disguise herself as the Neharem warriors emerged from their hiding places and flocked to her, Mardus and Anahi included. Together, they barreled through the onlookers like a herd of helgins.

"Hold," Jakki shouted.

The beridian ignored her cries and launched a spear into the first line of soldiers blockading the stairs. A Neharem warrior followed, clubbing his way through a few soldiers before a blade found his throat. Civilians screamed and swarmed for the gates.

Cursing, Jakki leaped down from the battlement—a vantage point she regretted relinquishing—and landed beside Yerakai.

"What in Haeshol is she thinking?"

"No time to argue, Sister." Yerakai summoned Grokhion and the rest of their twenty-something warriors, save for the few waiting at the ship with the stormbirds. "We need to get to Elaysia before the soldiers do."

Jakki squinted at the line of uniforms snaking down the platform. She retrieved the parchment from her waistband. Now or never.

"I'll get Elaysia," she shouted, sprinting away. "Capture or kill the Lord Priestess and the All-Sovereign. Tonight, they feel Neharem's wrath."

Jakki kept her gaze low as she ran. The crowd split, and she glimpsed Elaysia lying unconscious on the stone. No blood. She prayed something had braced her fall.

Parchment trembling in her hands, Jakki evoked the ancient speech the old man taught her. It wasn't difficult to remember the phrases. The words fell from her lips as if she'd always known them. A rush rippled through her. Noise faded as if she'd gone underwater. Tension pulled up and out of her body, escaping through her breath. Smudges of color and distorted figures appeared in her peripherals as she plowed forward—later she'd recall running faster than ever before, far faster than should've been possible. But as she neared Elaysia's resting place, the Lord Priestess leaped down and scooped up Elaysia, then retreated behind a wall of soldiers like a spider hoarding its catch.

"If you want her." The Lord Priestess pressed a dagger to Elaysia's throat. Her eyes danced with intrigue.

Elaysia should've been dead already. The Lord Priestess played at something, and she didn't have a choice but to find out.

Jakki closed her eyes. Locked onto her targets as she had with Unleto. Lunged, wielding her staff with strength and mastery beyond her years. It was an extension of her arm driving into a soldier's eye, delivering a blow to another with a *crunch*. She parried an attack, catching the swords by the hilts with her staff. Grokhion and Yerakai arrived with more warriors, driving back the soldiers one by one. Jakki met the Lord Priestess's eyes.

"Clever." The Lord Priestess feigned boredom. "Self-taught, I assume?"

"We're not all lucky enough to—"

A loud clacking drowned out Jakki's voice. The hairs on the back of her neck rose as she squinted into the rain. Giant insects half her size charged on six legs, large, veiny wings folded against their backs and clawed front limbs lashing. An old fireside story popped into her mind: deathstalkers. But how? One set upon her, its silhouette stark against a moon. Jakki rolled out of the way as it slashed a sword-sized stinger dripping venom. It made a clicking sound and turned itself about for another attack. Jakki grunted and curled her toes in her sandals. The deathstalker hissed and charged. She waited, heart pounding, and ducked at the last moment to jam her staff into its underbelly. It clicked fast and loud, pincers chomping and dripping with ooze.

"Come and get me, you fucker." Jakki charged at the deathstalker and leveled her staff into its pincers.

It clenched the staff and knocked her down. Spiny legs cut into her sides. Gel dripped on her face, dredging up memories of the skulmor attack. When her arms threatened to collapse under its weight, an arrow lodged in its head. The pincers stopped flexing. Its body went slack. Jakki heaved it off with a shout, and it rolled onto its side, legs twitching. Another arrow struck its abdomen. Xaren nodded from the platform, notching another arrow. Blood covered his unmasked face.

Jakki rose, staff in hand. Several deathstalkers had fallen upon her warriors, and judging by the screams, not all of them fared as well. Jakki searched for the Lord Priestess and found more deathstalkers lined in front of her like a battalion.

Lumira leaped from the platform and landed beside Jakki. "The All-Sovereign got away." She pointed her spear at the wall of deathstalkers and snarled. "You with me?"

Jakki glared but nodded her consent.

Lumira's spear struck first, a clean penetration in one of the deathstalker's larger front eyes. Jakki brought one down with a blow to the head. She pounced, digging at its leathery wings with her dagger before slicing open its underbelly. Translucent, red goo oozed out smelling of rotted fish. She leaped back, ready to strike another when a *boom* jarred her ears. Her pulse raced. She'd only heard that sound once before.

The weapons from the temple.

"Watch out," she screamed at Lumira, ducking behind the deathstalker's body.

Boom.

A projectile struck the corpse, shaking it.

Boom, boom.

Jakki scrambled away. Something struck the back of her head with a crack. The world blurred as she stumbled, blood rushing in her ears. Another hit on her stomach. She raised her staff, blocking the third blow. A rock clattered to the stone. Her assailant, a boy of ten, dropped his other rock and disappeared into the flood of civilians fleeing the courtyard.

More booms rang through the night as she shoved back into the fight, eyes darting between sky and land. Lumira lay sprawled on the ground a spear's throw away, visibly wounded. Jakki started for her but caught sight of the Lord Priestess limping away. In her leg, what must've been one of Xaren's arrows. No Elaysia. More soldiers poured in through the gates. They'd be trapped soon.

"Retreat," she shouted, voice rasping. She rushed to Lumira's side and offered her hand. The beridian's eyes narrowed, but she accepted the help, teeth clenched as she rose. Blood matted her cream fur. "Can you run?"

"Can't afford not to." Lumira grunted and staggered toward the gate.

Jakki watched her flank, checking back often to ensure no one followed. Neharem warriors lay tangled amid the bodies of soldiers and deathstalkers like a bloodied carpet. Ahead, Grokhion charged the gate, one hand swinging his great axe while the other carried—

Jakki gasped. *Elaysia.*

Energy renewed, she picked up her pace, then froze. Over one hundred soldiers blocked their escape, and they'd barred the gates behind them. Her hope melted. Grokhion roared and ran back toward Jakki. She ducked as a sword came down on her and caught its wielder by the wrist. She gutted him navel to neck with her dagger. A deathstalker crashed beside her, two arrows in its head. One by one, the rest of her warriors fell or joined her in the center of the courtyard. The soldiers closed in, reloading weapons and bellowing threats. Jakki shrugged out of her cloak, now drenched with rain, and gripped her staff with aching fingers. Whatever the parchment bestowed had vanished, leaving her naked, weak, and trembling.

Elaysia's head dangled over Grokhion's arm. Jakki stroked her hair. The courtyard fell silent save for the *clicks* and *clangs* of weapons reloading, readying, the patter of rain distastefully gentle as it diluted the blood-stained stone. No civilians remained, leaving a ring of soldiers and deathstalkers around the surviving Neharem warriors. They encroached but withheld an attack, waiting for gods-knew-what. Someone had to face them. Jakki gritted her teeth and approached the stairs, staff raised high. She braced herself for the impact of a sword, an arrow, or whatever evil the new weapons spat.

A voice, strong and gritty, filled the courtyard. "Let them go." *Davier?*

Jakki searched for the speaker. On the platform, basking in the light of the nevethium altar, a masked figure held a dagger to the All-Sovereign's throat. Half the soldiers marched to the foot of the stairs, weapons ready.

"I'll do it," Davier said. "Nothing would bring me greater pleasure. Let them leave the city in peace, and I'll return *His Holiness*"—he punched the All-Sovereign in the stomach—"to you in one piece. Open the gates now."

General Zhia broke from the ranks and made it halfway up the stairs before the All-Sovereign shouted, "Stop, you impudent fool." His voice was shrill. "Do as he says."

"But, Your Holiness." General Zhia advanced another step.

"I think His Holiness already decided." Davier dug the tip of the blade into the All-Sovereign's throat until he cried out.

General Zhia retreated down the stairs, stopping in front of Jakki. She signaled to the soldiers to open the gate. "Run," she said, leaning close, voice slick as a serpent. "Return to your precious little village. Drink it in before we burn it to the ground."

Jakki's fingers tightened around her staff. The rain ceased. Grokhion led the Stormriders and few remaining warriors to the gate, their path unmarred by soldiers, while she lingered, eyes on the platform.

"Go," Davier shouted. "I know it's not enough to fix what I've done, but it gives her a chance. And"—his voice, rife with emotion, broke—"tell her I'm sorry. Please. Now go."

Jakki raised her staff to Davier and fled. Bumps prickled her skin as she raced by the soldiers and into the streets of Cadar. Xaren motioned her down an alley where the others waited, and together, they darted through the city until they reached the south wall. From there, he led them up what felt like endless stairs toward the waste chutes. The stench overtook Jakki while they were still a way's off, and up close, it was enough to turn her stomach.

"There's no other way?" she asked, inspecting the shit-crusted tubes. They were large enough for Grokhion to fit comfortably inside, provided he remained elongated, and plummeted into the Ashaat, where the waste dissolved into the sea—according to Xaren.

The ex-soldier peered over her shoulder, eyes on the stairs. "Not if you want to leave the city alive."

Shouts reverberated in the streets below. Soldiers. Davier was gone. Jakki tore off a strip of her cloak and tied it around her nose and mouth. "Fine, but I'm not going first."

Mardus gestured toward the tubes. "Lumira's already gone."

With that, the Moákun covered his face and slid down after her. Grokhion went next with Elaysia, followed by the rest, until only Jakki remained on the balcony. The clouds unveiled the stars, bathing her in soft light. She swept a final gaze over the city, searing the architecture into her memory.

"Next time I see you, you'll burn."

Jakki spat and plunged into the tube.

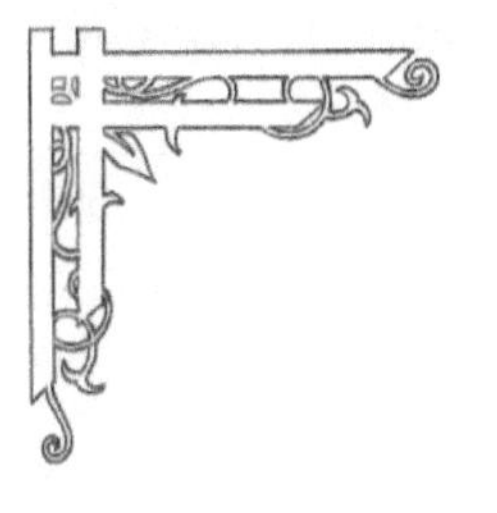

ZAVIK

Zavik tapped his fingers on the table, trying to think of everything and nothing all at once while Konar secured the library. The bar settled into place.

"Well?" Zavik blurted.

Konar gestured to the table covering the trap door. "The study, if you please."

Zavik shook his head. He straightened his back and puffed his chest like T'Vak did to intimidate people. "Here is fine. I've been waiting all night. What did Rajar say?"

Konar lifted the beaded pendants off his neck and laid them in a perfect circle atop the table. The council gathering had run late, but his eyes bore more than exhaustion. "A messenger from Az Zar came."

"You saw them arrive?"

"Zavik, please."

"Sorry." Zavik folded his arms and leaned against the table.

"I tried to intercept them, but one of the Lautei got there first. Rajar flayed the messenger before anyone else could speak to him. He read the parchment aloud tonight."

"And?"

"The vote to elect him high chieftain was unanimous."

Zavik's vision blurred. He removed his seers and wiped them down with trembling fingers. It didn't help. "How? Half the chiefs were adamant about waiting for Elaysia not two nights past. What did it say?"

Konar interlaced his fingers. He stared through Zavik, bearded jaw set with lips in a hard, unmoving line. "They captured her."

Zavik dug his nails into the wood grain. "No. Not possible. She's too smart for that."

Konar turned away, but not before Zavik caught sight of the moisture in his eyes. "They killed her, Zav," he croaked.

Blood drained from Zavik's face. "Rajar's lying. He wants war, and he'll say anything to gain other tribes' support." A weak laugh escaped his throat. "It's brilliant, honestly. I applaud him for it."

"The message bore the All-Sovereign's seal. I saw it with my own eyes."

"I'd like to see it."

"Can't you for once accept something for what it is? Not everything is some conspiracy to unravel, boy. I *know* that seal."

"And I know Elaysia." Zavik yanked the bar up and swung the door open. "She's coming home soon. I'll be waiting, even if I'm the last one in this cursed city to believe in her. Good night."

Zavik slammed the door. A warm breeze tousled his hair and teased a chime hanging from a loft. He ran across the platform and down the winding pathway, drawing the occasional eyeroll from a watcher, until his lungs screamed—which didn't take long. As he rounded the bend to the stables, unsure of where he was going, someone grabbed the back of his tunic. Zavik yelped. He tore away, knife ready, only to find T'Vak snorting.

"Easier to sneak up on than a drunkard," the backhander said, rubbing tears from his eyes.

Zavik glared and straightened his collar. "I'm not in the mood."

"Wanna talk about it?"

"No."

"Want some company?"

"I'm going for a walk to clear my head. Tag along, if you want. I suppose I'm technically still paying you."

"Every day, until I receive those glowing beauties you promised."

Zavik cringed. As if there wasn't enough going wrong. He shook his head at T'Vak and, with all the gusto he could rouse, tromped into the forest. In a fragmented display of empathy, T'Vak followed quietly, content to drink and burp his way down the trail.

Zavik was grateful for the silence at first. Since Rajar's arrival, Agaas had been anything but calm, and between assisting Konar's preparation for council sessions and doing his best to mediate the holy city's daily affairs in Elaysia's stead, his alone time was nonexistent. But as the trees grew thicker and a sheen of sweat developed on his face, he found himself missing the backhander's stories.

"T'Vak, you can—"

Snap.

The backhander grabbed his shoulder. They both froze, listening.

Snap, snap.

Zavik squinted. There. A flash of white in the branches.

"Did you see—"

T'Vak covered Zavik's mouth, sword drawn, as a hooded figure approached. A tail flicked underneath the cloak.

Zavik rubbed his eyes. "Lumira?"

The beridian lowered her hood and winked. Behind her hopped a stormbird as large as a dog. Deep blue feathers had replaced its fluffy white down, and its talons had grown large enough to crush a rabbit's skull. Zavik crept forward, stopping within arm's reach of Lumira. A hug seemed appropriate, but he hardly knew her and didn't want to appear more of, well, whatever she thought he was. Lumira confirmed his suspicions by crossing her arms. Ah, but there was a smile. He'd settle for that.

Zavik reached a timid hand toward the stormbird. "She's huge. Anadu, right?"

The stormbird cocked its head at Lumira as if asking permission. Lumira nodded. Anadu ignored Zavik's hand and nipped his pocket where he carried some salted venison he'd neglected from the evening meal. He offered some, earning a chirp from Anadu.

Lumira nudged Zavik. "Who's the meat slab?"

"Oh, right. Sorry." Zavik beckoned T'Vak closer. "Lumira, meet T'Vak. He's a... friend, of sorts."

Zavik made room so they could greet each other. Neither offered. He nudged T'Vak.

T'Vak grunted. "Been a while since I've seen your kind. Takes balls to survive Az Zar with the tail being so obvious and all that." He shrugged, perversely clear he cared little for formalities, and spat to the side. "Well done, then."

"Thanks." Lumira's tone matched her ears: flat.

Zavik cleared his throat. "I don't mean to be rude, but where's Elaysia?"

T'Vak smirked, and Zavik's cheeks heated.

"And the others, of course." There. That should sound less desperate.

Lumira averted her gaze. "She lives. She waits with the others."

Zavik thrust a triumphant hand in the air. "I knew she'd succeed. Tell me everything. Did you obtain samples of their recent advancements? Confirm their plots? I stumbled across a few trinkets in my travels, but I won't bore you with that now." His words tumbled out in one breath, like a harsh breeze.

Lumira traced her toe through the dirt and opened her mouth ever so slightly. She refused to meet his eyes.

Zavik fidgeted with the linings of his pockets. "There's something you're not telling me. What is it? Is she hurt?"

"She's not hurt, but she's not what you remember."

"Well, I'm sure she's been through a lot. It'll take time to digest."

The rustle of leaves and songs of crickets hung between them.

"I don't know if she'll *ever* be what you remember," Lumira said finally.

Zavik furrowed his brow at her cryptic message and balled his hands into fists. "I want to see her. Now."

Lumira glared. "She needs to rest. Does the city sleep?"

No, they move about all hours of the night like forest beasts. Zavik suppressed the remark. "Yes. A few may still linger, but we can enter discreetly if needed. However..." There was that minor problem.

"Spit it out."

"Rajar's taken over the high chieftain's quarters."

A thin hiss escaped Lumira's throat. "Moons be cursed. We'll wait for tomorrow."

Zavik opened his mouth to object, but Lumira stormed off.

"You can follow. Don't ask questions," she said.

Zavik stumbled after her, T'Vak on his heels, and most certainly asked all the questions. When they cleared the forest and crested a hill, the glow of a fire radiating below, Lumira relented and shared minimal details regarding their time in Az Zar. As Zavik listened, his movements stiffened as though he no longer controlled his body.

"I knew he was false," Zavik said, dodging a rabbit hole and tripping over a stone instead. "I should've insisted she listen to me or told Konar before she left. I could've prevented all this."

"It's dangerous to linger on what could've been," T'Vak chimed in. "I've seen many people get so lost in the past that they stop living for fear of the future."

Lumira shot T'Vak a look suggesting he spoke out of turn. "Davier was sorry in the end," she told Zavik over her shoulder. They drew close enough to the fire to smell smoke and make out the forms of those huddled around it. "I think he loved her."

"Hardly justifies his actions." Zavik brushed the hair off his forehead and hurried toward the Stormriders, grass slick beneath his feet.

Grokhion noticed—or sensed, given beridians' superior hearing—Zavik first and bounded over to smother him in a hug. He followed Grokhion to the fire and greeted each rider and stormbird with genuine affection. All but Elaysia and Onitus.

"Where is she?" Zavik asked after politely declining the communal wineskin.

A hush fell over the gathering.

"Down by the creek. Keeps to herself as of late." The answer came from Jakki, who'd neglected his greeting and now shrugged as if he'd asked something trivial. A scar the size of his forearm marred her thigh. He made a note to ask someone about it later.

"I'll head that way. She shouldn't be alone."

"Don't bother." Jakki reclined against her pack and propped her bare feet up on one of the rocks surrounding the fire. "She won't speak to anyone. Not even her oldest friend." She eyed Zavik and tore into a piece of jerky with a venom reserved for predators in the wild.

"Thanks for the warning." Zavik regarded her as the beast she'd presented to him and backed away. "Seeing you all safe brings me unspeakable joy," he told the others. "I'm sorry if it's not evident right now."

Zavik made to leave, but Lumira caught his arm. "I can't let you go. She doesn't want—"

T'Vak appeared beside Zavik in a flash, hand resting on his hilt. "Decision's not yours to make."

"I know you want to protect her"—Zavik pulled his arm free and sheltered behind T'Vak—"but I must see her. What kind of friend would I be if I didn't go?"

Lumira retreated, muttering in Hispen, and Zavik raced to the creek.

Zavik relished the endless, sun-kissed days of the Feasting Moons, and having Elaysia home should've rendered them perfect. But as he pointed out shapes in the clouds and laughed at the stormbirds fluttering around the meadow, he couldn't shake the feeling only bits of Elaysia remained. He'd hardly recognized her that night by the creek: gaunt with dull skin and unwashed hair sprawling across her back in oily, knotted strands. No sparkle in her eyes. No tension in her muscles. He sat beside her in the damp soil until his rear went numb before she acknowledged him with a thin smile and rested her head on his shoulder. That was all the affirmation he'd needed. They'd huddled in silence until sunlight streamed through the branches at dawn. After making her return to Agaas public, she'd stowed away in her reassigned chambers, surfacing only to empty her waste bucket and collect satchels of food and drink.

But today she'd break.

In a good way.

A stormbird's shriek yanked Zavik from his musings. Siren had pinned a squalling Keera with her talons and arched her neck as another piercing scream echoed through the valley. Two-thirds the size of her attacker, Mardus's albino female lay helpless while Siren nipped at her neck with a ferocity treading the boundaries of play and war.

"Growing fierce, aren't they?" Zavik said as Jakki and Mardus sprinted through the tall grasses to intervene. Even the males, though half the size of the females, boasted talons larger than his fist. Sleek wings flared off their backs, a myriad of blacks, blues, grays, and whites. Like a storm. The fluffy down only remained on the heads of a few; it wouldn't be long before their hopping and fluttering led to flight.

"Mhmm." Elaysia faced the stormbirds, but stared past them, eyes glazed over. Onitus was stoic beside her. Though the Stormriders lounged about the meadow, none sat close enough to eavesdrop on their conversation.

Not that it's much of a conversation.

"You won't believe what I discovered the other day." Zavik waited for her curiosity to pique. It didn't. "A fortress. On the coast."

Still nothing. He pinched a blade of grass between his fingers. *Come on, Ellie. You used to love exploring.*

"Alright, it's more of a hideaway than a fortress. Built into an old tree that grew on the cliffside. Rather large, though, and there's still some furniture and tools inside. Looks like people lived there."

Elaysia reclined and closed her eyes. "People did."

"Oh. Nice. Good to know for certain." Zavik tossed a chunk of rabbit to Onitus, who gulped it down. "At least taste it next time," he mumbled, wiping his hand on his pants.

Elaysia's eyelids fluttered open, a hint of a smile tugging at her lips. "I wasn't teasing you. Igtheos and his survivors lived there and in places like it before constructing Agaas. It's one of the earliest teachings I received from Konar."

"He's a good man."

"I'm not so sure."

Elaysia closed her eyes again, smile gone. She didn't speak the rest of the afternoon and disappeared during the chaos of rounding up the stormbirds.

That evening, Zavik ascended Agaas by way of the ladders, hoping he'd catch Elaysia on her usual path. He struggled through the climb in vain. Grokhion spied him near the top, clinging to the ladder and gasping for air, and hefted his log of an arm over the side to pull Zavik to the platform.

"Thanks," Zavik wheezed.

"Training to join the Stormriders, eh?" Grokhion laughed, warm and deep-bellied.

"Almost there." Zavik flexed his arm, triggering another uproar from Grokhion. "Did you see Elaysia on your way up?"

Grokhion shook his head.

"Oh. I thought she'd be here by now." Zavik dug at his cuticles as he searched the deserted platform.

"Sorry, lad. It'll take her time to sort through things, but I wouldn't worry. She'll turn up when she's ready." He patted Zavik on the back and resumed grooming his stormbird.

"It's more than that, beridian," Zavik muttered once Grokhion was out of earshot. A twinge of guilt pulled at his chest, so he added, "I wouldn't expect anyone else to see it, though." Everyone brushed off his concerns, insisting she was simply processing. Understandable, they'd add, given what she'd been through. And with Rajar's takeover? More than worthy of a few down days.

But there was something else: a void where a free spirit once champed at the bit. Detachment from everything and everyone. Konar, she avoided like a plague, and Jakki gave up shortly after their return. The rest of the Stormriders fared little better. Well, he wasn't going to give up, nor was he going to pretend any longer. Next time he saw her, he'd make sure she talked to him. Really talked. Whatever it took.

Zavik searched for her the rest of the evening. During the feast at Yerakai's loft, he forced himself to engage with the Stormriders while they carried on about their adventures, all the while glancing back every time the door creaked open. It was never her.

As he lay awake in his cot later that night, guilt gnawed at his consciousness until he finally threw back his blanket and sprinted to her new room in the guest quarters. He knocked quietly at first, then louder when no one answered.

Shoulders slumped, he shuffled back to his loft. As he rested his back against his pillow, however, something inside him snapped like a branch supporting too much weight. Something was wrong.

Do something about it.

"Alright," he said, the sound of his own voice startling him. "I will."

He ran back to her quarters, not caring how loudly his feet smacked the wooden path, and burst in. The room hadn't been touched since they'd first dumped her things in it. It wasn't a far cry from her typical standard of living, but even her chaos had some order.

"Where are you hiding?" he asked the darkness.

He nudged piles with his toe, making a path to a cot covered in maps and other finer belongings. The largest map, a parchment charting Neharem and all its territories, bubbled out. Underneath, a seashell. Part of a collection Elaysia began as a child with her mother. He'd helped them all those years ago, thrilled to take part in an expedition with the famed Moonriders. He cradled the shell, a spiraled marvel decorated in spiny bursts of sapphire and onyx. They'd found it in a hidden cove only accessible via a stout hike through the woods. It remained one of Elaysia's favorite hideaways. Forests and streams offered anyone solace, but the ocean was where one found answers. Or escaped from them.

Zavik's eyes widened.

He hurried outside and down the nearest ramp as fast as his body would go.

Zavik's voice grew hoarse from shouting as he darted through the woods with naught but the faint glow of the crystal around his neck to guide him. Branches slapped his face and snagged his clothes like grasping arms of undergrowth. When he broke through the clearing, Elaysia stood at the cliffside, one hand on her stomach, peering out across the waves. Onitus squalled and nipped at her skirt. Panic seized Zavik's throat. He lunged for her, tripping on an uneven patch of stone with a shout. Elaysia's toes curled around the edge. She swayed with the wind as it tugged her closer to death.

"Elaysia!" Zavik yanked her arm, sending them both sprawling.

She propped herself up on trembling elbows and faced him. Her brows knit together in an upturned arch while the rest of her face stretched thin. Her eyes were...

Vacant.

"Are you alright?" Zavik wrapped his arms around his knees. *Idiot. Does she look alright? She was about to, to...* He couldn't finish the thought, much less say it aloud. Onitus nestled beside him and ruffled his feathers.

Elaysia dragged a rock across the stone. "It's too much, Zav."

"What is?"

"Everything."

Elaysia hurled the rock into the ocean. Bumps covered Zavik's arms as it sunk beneath the waves, barely missing the jagged rocks protruding from the base of the cliff. He scooted back.

"All I wanted was freedom. To start fresh. Not be a Moonrider. But when I finally tasted independence, I wove myself a new prison. Guess I can't escape fate." Elaysia laughed darkly. "We're made to believe we control every decision, that each day is new, but the more we try to fight it, the stronger it binds us. I have nowhere left to go now. No way to dig out of this." A tear trailed down her cheek. "Choice is an illusion."

Before his instinct succumbed to reason, Zavik wrapped his arm around her shoulders. She was boney, yet warm, as if a fire glowed within. "You always have choices, if you summon the courage to see them."

Elaysia leaned into him, tucking her head in the crevice of his neck. "Do you believe in the gods?"

"I believe in what they represent." A chill from the stone seeped through Zavik's pants as a mist rippled off the ocean. He shivered.

"I'm not sure what I believe anymore. But if they don't exist, if there's no life after this—no grand plan for us all—then what's the point? None of this matters."

"You're wrong. It matters even more." Zavik clung to her. "What's more precious? The evergreen tree or the flower that blooms for a day? All things end. It's what gives life meaning. If we never die, then we never lived. Don't throw away what might be your only beautiful life."

"My greatest fear is dying alone, and my second greatest fear is being known." She chuckled. It was faint and swallowed by the wind, but a laugh still. "But not with you. It's what I like about us. You're the only one who doesn't shove opinions down my throat. You just... listen."

Zavik's heartbeat quickened. *Us. She said us.*

Elaysia pointed to her chest. "I wish I could lock you away in here forever."

"It'd be cramped." *Brilliant, Zav. Just brilliant.*

"Something happened, Zav."

"We don't have to talk about it."

"Everyone else will be soon enough." She drew her knees to her chest. "Davier's dead."

Rightfully so. Zavik squeezed her hand. "I'm sorry. I really am."

"I can't decide if I want to remember him or not."

"Time will help."

"Time's not on my side." She gripped Zavik's forearm. Exhaled sharply. "I'm with child."

"Funny." He studied her, waiting for the charade to fall. It didn't. "Oh. You... But I thought you couldn't, with the, I mean your parents... I..."

Elaysia looked away.

Zavik wrung his hands together. "Who's the, uh"—he cleared his throat—"father?"

"Who do you think?"

A gust of wind tore into them, arousing small bumps all over his body. But of course. He'd known the moment she spoke it.

He forced a sympathetic smile. "Have you told anyone else?"

"No, but I'm at least two moon cycles along. I won't be able to hide it much longer. Unless I"—Elaysia pushed herself up, tears streaming down her face. "I'm surprised it's survived this long."

"It's a fighter, like its mother." The thought spilled from Zavik's lips without warning.

Elaysia shook her head.

"There are ways to take care of it without harming yourself. Certain plants—"

"I don't want more blood on my hands."

"So, keep it."

"Keep it? Bearing the child of our enemy destroys any chance I have at reclaiming Agaas. As if Rajar needs more weapons to wield against me." She stopped pacing and faced the ocean. "I'll never live up to everyone's expectations."

"Piss on their expectations, and piss on your expectations."

Elaysia stiffened. Her tears ceased, leaving wet trails down her set jaw. "What?"

"You're setting yourself up for failure. The more you let outside voices define you and what your success looks like, the more you lose who you truly are. Life never goes according to plan, so don't kill yourself trying to find that perfect path."

Zavik led her to the cliffside and gestured to the thrashing waves. The roar commanded reverence, a sporadic yet expected collision of a magnificent force smashing against itself and into the rocks below. "I can't tell you what the right answer is, but I can help you sift out the wrong ones. *This* is the wrong one.

Just because you can't see your purpose right now doesn't mean it doesn't exist. As long as there's life, there's hope."

Elaysia sat and dangled her feet over the edge. Bumps flecked her bare legs peeking under her tunic. She patted the spot beside her. "When did you become so wise?"

"You left me alone for quite a long time. I had to do something." She rolled her eyes, but they glittered warmth. Zavik fought the urge to shy from her gaze. "Don't let them get to you. Az Zar. The All-Sovereign. Rajar. Even the lies you're telling yourself. Don't let them win. I've seen you fight back. How many times have you shunned the advice of Konar and the council?"

"About as many times as I've led to my own ruin." Her voice was light, and Zavik relaxed for the first time that night. Then, more somber, she added, "But you're right. You usually are." She brushed the hair out of his eyes, sending a spark through his body that left him feeling exposed. "I don't deserve you." She kissed his cheek.

Zavik's breath caught in his throat. Thirsty. He was so very thirsty.

"Are you with me?"

"Always."

More than you know.

As they wove back through woods and the sound of the waves faded, Elaysia halted and grabbed Zavik's arm. The breeze teased her hair, blowing it around her face like the limber, dangling branches of a pocoaon tree.

"There's something else I have to tell you." Her voice carried the weight of someone bearing ill tidings.

Zavik fidgeted with his pocket, unsure if he wanted to hear anymore. "Go on."

"It's about Konar." She steepled her fingers and brought them to her mouth. "I think he's done something terrible, and I need your advice."

KONAR

K onar leaned over Elaysia's cot and cleared his throat. Loudly. The guest loft she'd been reassigned to contrasted her old quarters in every way: small, stark, and stale. Onitus, perched at the foot of her bed, slid an eyelid back. Konar cracked the window, releasing a gust of dewy air that ruffled Elaysia's blanket. She shot up, knotted strands of hair tumbling around puffy, reddened eyes.

"Honestly, Konar, what the fuck?" Elaysia thrust her thumb at the open window. "It's freezing and dark out still. I don't feel well. Go away." She scowled, pulled the blanket over her head, and flopped onto her side.

"I thought you liked the moonlight." Konar tugged the blanket off, earning himself a painful bite from Onitus. Clad in her mother's silken sleep gown, Elaysia looked healthier after nearly a moon cycle back home. Maseeya's cooking did wonders for anyone, and he doubted few put such delicious Az Zarian twists on Agaasian staples. "Zavik told me you wanted to start training this morning."

"It wasn't specified we'd begin this early."

"That was intentional." Konar meant it in jest, the typical banter they'd always exchanged, but instead of a witty reply, she shook her head and looked away. His smile faded. She'd avoided him since her return, giving him little opportunity to repair the damage done during her departure.

"I'm not doing this right now." She glared and placed a hand over her stomach. She'd not confided in him yet, but Maseeya confirmed his suspicions. They needed to act fast for her to stand a chance against Rajar. "I'll find you after I've broken my fast."

"As you wish. I'll gather the Stormriders at the training grounds within the hour. And Elaysia"—the words caught in his throat as he tripped over a stack of paintings. Her father's. They didn't belong on the floor. He picked them up and cleared a spot on the table as he searched for a gentle way to voice his concern.

"What? Is it about this?" She pointed to her stomach with a trembling finger. Then, belatedly noticing Konar's tidying, she snapped, "Don't touch those. They're *my* father's, and I'll take care of them."

"I'm sorry." Konar dropped the paintings and took a hesitant step toward her cot. "And no, not about that. You seem... is everything alright? Between us? You've hardly said a word to me since your arrival. If it's about the—"

"Everything's fine. May I have some privacy, please?"

Per her tone, everything was not fine, but he nodded and softly closed the door, regretting his decision to wake her. He trudged toward Zavik's loft, caressing the doll in his pocket as worry sunk its fangs into his chest. She'd been in Az Zar a long time. Long enough to learn secrets. But who could've told her? It wouldn't be to anyone's gain. And surely, if she knew, he'd already be dead.

"Ready when you are, High Elder."

Heart racing, Konar raised his staff and spun as Zavik emerged from the shadows. "Gods, lad, don't sneak up on me like that. Did you even sleep?"

Zavik yawned and ran a hand through his hair. "No, but—"

"You're used to it." Konar beckoned him closer. "I was the same at your age, always up late, reading whatever I could get my hands on."

Zavik smiled; Konar was stingy with compliments. But then he shrugged it off, as if suddenly reminded he shouldn't show kindness. "Something like that."

Konar frowned. Since when was Zavik temperamental? He tucked his concern away to be dealt with another day. "Let the Stormriders know we're leaving now."

"Already done. The scrolls?"

"We need to focus on getting Elaysia physically ready for the challenge and taming those birds. The scrolls can wait until she reclaims her position."

"Understood."

"And bring some food with you; we'll be there most of the day. Gather a variety. Elaysia might have aversions to certain things. She—"

"I know. I've handled it. See you there shortly." Zavik offered a slight bow and hurried across the platform.

Konar descended the ramps in silence and arrived at a hillside overlooking the training grounds as the first streaks of light illuminated the clouds. Located a half hour walk north of the stables, the territory spanned to the Nipai River. It had seen little action since the international trade settlement spawned a peace treaty hundreds of years ago, but tales of the rigorous training previously expected of Neharem warriors often circulated during evening meals and fireside stories. Though the land's history was wrought with conflicts and battles, peacetime resulted in competitions between the tribes, which culminated in an annual tournament of skills. Dirt paths still bore treads from those who raced over them, and beyond the tracks, an archery field with static targets. Totems paying homage to past warriors surrounded the wrestling pits and climbing walls, but many were weathered beyond recognition.

"I've dreamed of competing here my whole life," a crisp voice said. *Yerakai.* The Apáasutai sat cross-legged beside him, staring off toward the grounds, stormbird nestled in his lap. "My mother was one of the victors in the final season of the trials. I like to think I inherited some of her skills."

"I remember her well." Konar dropped to a knee, ignoring the aches that accompanied it. He had a while still before he needed to replenish. "The arrows flew from her hand with such accuracy that many swore they *listened* to her. Though, I must say, the idea of you craving battle baffles me. You were an amicable boy and not such a different man now."

"You misunderstand me. I've never craved violence. I can't delight in the destruction of life." Yerakai secured his hair in two braids. "I do, however, love the thrill of a challenge. Our people were stronger, more attuned to the world back when we partook in the annual trials. The exercise of such skills lessens the need for violent inclinations."

"Some might argue it encourages violence and unrest instead of mediating it. Once you master a skill, you want to use it."

"And what do you believe, High Elder?"

Konar frowned. He'd been the driving force behind the elimination of the trials, but now he wasn't so sure he'd do it again. "I believe there will always be those who twist well-meaning intentions for personal gain. Whether we train or not, violence finds its way back into the world. The war between egoism and altruism is intertwined in our souls, and higher awareness through compassion and generosity is what creates the thin line separating an individual from one side to the other. Not that it's a finite line. I've danced between both most of my life. Only a fool would believe we can root out either side before its time."

"Which is?"

"The end of life as we know it."

Yerakai rubbed his jaw. "Some say that's nearer than we think. Mavet grows stronger in Haeshol with each passing day."

"Depends on your interpretation of the stories and few surviving texts. I don't think we're meant to know."

The sun peeked over the mountains, flooding the valley in a sea of golden splendor. Konar rose to welcome it. To his relief, Yerakai refrained from delving further into unnerving questions.

Elaysia appeared on the hill, a frown fixed to her face, the Stormriders and stormbirds trailing her. Zavik brought up the rear, stumbling under a basket of food. They looked an odd assortment, even as they laughed and prodded each other with inside jokes, but only the spirit mattered when it came to friends. It's what made a bond strong. Their diversity gave them strength, and Elaysia had foreseen it long before him.

"'I salute the light within your eyes where your spirit shines through,'" Konar called out, quoting the bit he'd memorized from the Shaktari scroll. "'For within it, I find my own.'" He wrung his hands as he strode toward them. "I appreciate you meeting me here. I haven't been a staunch supporter of your party, and for that I'm sorry."

Jakki yawned and rubbed her stormbird's curved beak. "And why the change of heart, High Elder? Things not working out for you with Rajar in command?"

"Jakki." Mardus shot her a glare.

Konar lifted his hand. "It's alright, Mardus. She's wise to question. We become stronger by addressing our doubts." He retrieved a hunk of venison from Zavik and extended it to Jakki's stormbird as a peace offering. "I, along with the elders, feared what path your venture might set Neharem on. We've savored peace for so long that we'd do anything to maintain it, even if all we cling to is an illusion. It's easier to pretend things are fine. Much harder to embrace change when you've been told the world just *is* a certain way."

Konar rested his chin atop steepled fingers as he paced. "I've been awakened. I can't remain blind to the escalating threat any longer. If we are to face it, we must prepare, and I can think of no better place to start than with this fine group."

"Do tell, High Elder, what you were awakened from." The question, cold and toneless, came from Elaysia.

"My High Chieftain—"

"I'm hardly that anymore. It's why we're gathered here, yes? Something about me competing for the right to lead? Apparently, this contest sifts out the worthiest." She clenched her fists. "Though, I hear there are other ways to remove leaders."

"I'm not certain what you're referencing." The sun had risen higher, bathing them in warmth, but a chill seized Konar's spine.

"I doubt that." Elaysia clucked at Onitus and stomped up the hillside. The rest of the group eyed him, a few of them glaring.

"I heard you've discovered the Prophets' Scrolls," Yerakai said, gentle voice drawing everyone's attention.

Zavik blushed. "Actually, I did, believe it or not. Two, anyway."

"Are they filled with life-altering magic?" Jakki asked, voice drenched in sarcasm. But there was a hunger in her eyes.

"More like well-meaning foresights." Konar slipped off his outer robe, exposing his arms to the sun's rays.

"Like what?" Jakki pried.

"Shaktari is difficult to translate verbatim." Konar searched his memory for a passage that wouldn't trigger panic. "It alludes to an unavoidable precipice of great consequence yet promises redemption and a time when all inhabitants of Quinaria will embrace unity and bring forth a new age."

"Essentially, a cleansing and rebirth," Zavik added.

Jakki snorted. "How wonderfully ambiguous of them."

"Didn't Kyas predict something similar?" Mardus asked.

"Igtheos," Zavik corrected, "long before Kyas, when Agaas was first founded. I wouldn't hold it close to heart, though."

"Perhaps we should," Konar said.

Zavik tilted his head. "We shouldn't presume—"

"I presume nothing. We must train and study, not only to return Elaysia to her rightful place, but also to plan for the inevitable war ahead. Your quest has all but confirmed it. We are neither ready for their numbers or new weapons."

A solemn hush fell over the group.

Konar cleared his throat and adopted a positive demeanor. "But the gods are with us. We still have time to prepare, and you can begin by getting these birds in the air. They should've been flying by now." He regarded Xaren's small, black stormbird and shook his head. "Now, if you'll excuse me."

Konar didn't wait for anyone to object and marched up the worn trail winding around the hillside. Perched on the tallest rockface overlooking the training ground sat Elaysia. Onitus stood watch beside her, his dark, fire-tipped feathers shimmering like sunlight breaking through storm clouds. The double-crest on his head raised as Konar approached.

"You don't care to train?" Konar gestured below as he took a seat beside her.

"Not convinced it's necessary." Her face scrunched up the way Elishon's used to when confronted with an unappealing task. "My Stormriders and I would be more useful outside the jurisdiction of Agaas. The people seem happy enough with Rajar."

"You know this from personal observation?"

"I don't have to." She rolled a blade of grass into a ball and flicked it over the edge. "I know how it works."

"The people fear Rajar, and those who don't are bloodthirsty." Unable to bear her expression, one of hatred tinged in sorrow, he closed his eyes. "Ellie, you've always searched for an alternative destiny, and maybe this is it. You're too complex to be defined by one moment. One achievement." Konar rested his hand on hers. "One failure. Your life and choices are your own. Things will transpire as they're meant to, but you can play a part if you assume your role as intended. Otherwise, find contentment in being a bystander, and deal with the effects of inaction like everyone else."

"You do put things so well, High Elder. Tell me, did my parents"—she curled her fingers into a fist and shook her head, eyes down—"another time, perhaps. Too many things to sort out right now like how in Haeshol I challenge Rajar to hoksanu when he bests me in both strength and knowledge. Wonderful tradition. Praise the ancients." She paced, muttering obscenities.

"Rajar lacks wisdom. You can master the rest." Konar offered her his waterskin.

She accepted. For a fleeting moment, she looked like the girl he'd raised. Uncertain but eager.

"Zav said Rajar will declare war within the next moon cycle. It would hardly be enough time if I wasn't..." She brushed a hand over her stomach and looked away. "This is hopeless."

"We do have our work cut out for us, but I'm willing to rise to the challenge if you are."

Elaysia returned the waterskin. The girl he'd raised was gone again, replaced by a woman he barely knew. Beautiful as the dawn, unruly as the sea, and jaded as a war veteran.

"I'll do it, but not for Neharem. I've already let our people down." She pointed at the group training below. "I owe it to them. And to my parents' namesake." She marched down the path, eyes glistening. Onitus stalked after her.

Konar couldn't shake the feeling there was something in her voice, in her eyes, that made her seem guarded around him. Perhaps she believed he was still angry with her. Judging. Condemning. She didn't trust him with her heart, and rightfully so. He needed to show her he'd changed, that he believed in her more than anyone.

He hurried after her. "You inspire me, Elaysia. Even now, your wisdom surpasses that of most elders. A true leader places others above self and knows success is unattainable without counsel. You've embraced this." He offered his arm. She refused.

"I'm not a true leader, if there is such a thing, but I agree one should often put others above self. Though, no counsel is better than ill counsel. Wouldn't you agree?"

Chest tight, Konar nodded and walked a few paces behind, giving her the space she so adamantly desired.

The evening of the trials bathed the training grounds in shades of fire and violet as the sun set. Steady thumps from the war drums echoed through the valley. A small gathering of Agaasians and representatives from each tribe murmured on the hillside, lounging on blankets and consuming smoked meats and anderberry wine. The air smelled of pine and kinawa smoke, but Konar neglected his pipe, inhaling his worries instead. The stormbirds screeched and flapped, drawing his attention to the hilltop. Their mother approached.

A hush fell over the crowd as Elaysia descended. He'd almost forgotten how she'd looked when she'd first returned: a slump-shouldered waif with dodgy eyes and brittle hair. She'd since gained back the weight she'd lost in Az Zar—and then some, thanks to the child growing within—resulting in a curved figure alongside new muscle earned through training. Tonight, outfitted for hoksanu with leather-wrapped braids, a stormbird headdress, and an embroidered tunic in a vibrant, forest green, she embodied a goddess. Judging from the expressions of others, many agreed.

Elaysia regarded him with a curt nod. "High Elder."

Konar resisted pulling her in for an embrace. Things still weren't right between them. She'd shown him decency when they trained but maintained her distance. Whenever he'd dared to pry, she assured him they'd speak earnestly after hoksanu. He told himself not to worry, that she simply wanted more independence after regaining her role. He'd comply, content to intervene only regarding issues of undeniable importance.

"Your parents would be proud," he said, noting the fragments of their ceremonial clothes sewn into her tunic. "And dare I say it, I'm even prouder." He reached to straighten her headdress, but she dodged him and fixed it herself.

"Let's see if I make myself proud." Onitus flutter-hopped to follow, but Elaysia halted him with the stern look of a mother. "Wait here," she told the stormbird, whose head now reached her waist. "I'll be back soon. I promise."

Sweat trickled down Konar's forehead as she marched into the clearing where Rajar strutted in a headdress half the size of his body. He joined the wall of elders with painted faces locked in solemn dispositions and hands clenching nevethium torches.

Seize your victory, Ellie.

Elaysia approached Rajar. "High Chieftain." Her rich voice silenced the spectators' murmurs. "I invoke hoksanu and challenge you for the right to lead our people again. With the chiefs and elders of all twelve tribes as witness, you shall not refuse my challenge or so forfeit your rule and live eternally without honor." She drove a spear into the ground.

Rajar advanced until his exposed chest was level with her face. "A unity proposal would've served Neharem, and my nights, well."

Some of the Lautei laughed and hollered. Konar forced his tongue to remain silent, though he was one crass comment away from intervening.

"But if it's death you seek, so be it. Were my shame so great, I don't know that I'd care to face another day either." He slammed his spear down beside hers. The drumbeat loudened and quickened in response. "I'll make it a quick death if I can help it."

Rajar spat and summoned High Elder Strong-spear to the center of the field. The ancient Lautei prayed over the challenge and announced the two trials that, if necessary, would be followed with a tiebreaker. People congregated, singing deep-throated vibrations as they moved in a way not entirely dancing or writhing.

"How much longer?" Zavik's voice startled Konar, but before he could scold him, the drums climaxed and stopped, silencing the crowd.

The trials had begun.

Rajar sprinted across the clearing and into the woods. Elaysia entered paces behind. The slight bulge in her stomach was easily masked by her tunic, but according to Maseeya, she already bore a heavy burden.

Jakki sauntered over, absently holding out a wineskin as she stared into the woods. "Apparently Rajar's been training so he's not all talk for once." She glared. "He's planning something."

Zavik shook his head and pulled a blanket tighter around his shoulders. "Elaysia's prepared for him."

"No one's prepared for this." Jakki brought the wineskin to her lips. "That's why it's the determinant."

"Rajar fights for himself; Elaysia for others." Konar grabbed their shoulders and squeezed them. "You both give her strength. Now, trust her to handle the rest."

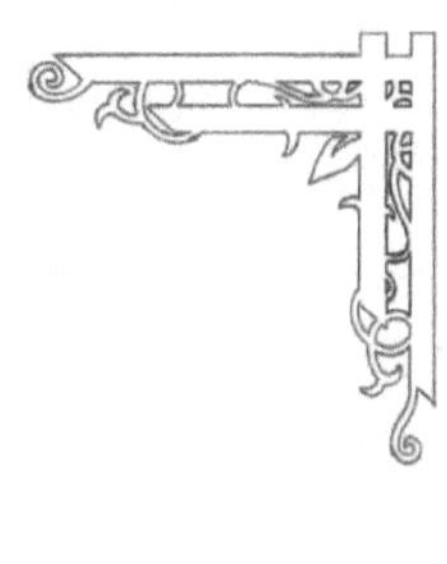

ELAYSIA

Moonlight streamed through the branches, bathing tree trunks in a cool, satin white. Elaysia attuned to every crunching leaf and snapping twig as she threaded through the forest. The first trial gave combatants two hours to track and kill a ryptan. If someone hadn't made the kill—or been killed—before the sand ran out and a horn signaled the end of the trial, they'd tie and confirm inclusion of the third trial. She tried to clear her mind of speculations, such as how many had died while attempting the hunt. Few invoked hoksanu due to the unlikelihood of survival. Few also got impregnated by their enemies willingly, and well, here she was.

She slowed to a jog, sucking in damp air while evading a thicket, and took care to raise her bow above the tangled branches. The trials allowed one weapon, leaving her with an obvious choice. She ran her thumb over the curve of her bow. Studied the soil. With Yerakai's guidance, she'd located ryptan tracks the day prior. Hopefully, it hadn't strayed far. The reptilian-avian hybrid stood two feet taller than the average man and crippled its prey with talons before shredding them with teeth sharp as daggers. She'd seen one before, but from a distance while cocooned in her father's arms. The stories said they once numbered the thousands, thriving in mated pairs throughout northern Neharem. Few survived now, and they lived secluded. They didn't tear into villages and rip children from their cots as fireside stories warned. But assuming one was lucky enough to find a ryptan and provoke an attack, the odds for beating it were—

Honestly, Elaysia, not helpful. Not now.

Fingers sinking into the soil, she crept through some ferns, searching for the tracks she'd traced earlier. They led to a concealed nest built out of branches and wrapped in a layer of thorns around the outside. Clever. Breathing slowed, she dropped into a meditative state and listened for nature's secrets. Wind. Insects chirping. Drumbeats from the trial grounds. She must've waited over an hour, until finally...

There.

Forest debris crackled. Elaysia tiptoed toward the sound and climbed a tree a short distance from where, she hoped, the ryptan waited.

Bark lodged underneath her nails as she pulled herself onto the perfect needle-shrouded lookout branch. Below, the ryptan strutted on two legs that, although thick and muscled, bent like a bird's heels. It froze and cocked its serpentine head as if it knew she was there. Fangs overlapped its jaw, and the scaling on its limbs transformed into feathers around its neck and back where flightless wings folded atop its arms. It took a few steps closer to her tree and cocked its head again. Elaysia retrieved a lyvium arrow and lined up her shot. As she let the arrow fly, Rajar burst into the clearing, racing toward the beast with his great obsidian-toothed club. The ryptan loosed a gut-wrenching screech. It crashed toward Rajar with gnashing teeth, dodging her headshot. They vanished into the foliage.

Elaysia cursed and grabbed a firm branch to lower herself down. As soon as her feet kissed the ground, Rajar screamed. She prowled after them, keeping to the ferns, until she found the skirmish near the nest. Rajar lunged with his club. The ryptan dodged the blow and lodged its teeth into his arm. It threw him into a tree. He crumpled on the ground, stunned. Maybe dead.

With the beast distracted, she had a chance. Two arrows drawn this time. A certain kill. But before she let go, the ryptan's eyes found hers. They reflected the night sky, black and speckled with flashes of silver and gold. It darted to the nest and nuzzled leaves around to expose a solitary egg. Rajar moaned, stirring behind her.

Elaysia looked at her stomach and back at the ryptan guarding its nest. It didn't want to play this game any more than she did.

Her father's voice struck her as if he stood beside her in the forest: *The ones meant to protect often abuse their power and become the ones we need protection from.*

"Not me, Edoja. I refuse to become that." Before reason took hold, she backed away from the nest and into the clearing where Rajar lay struggling.

"What're you doing?" he slurred, blood dripping from his lips. "Kill it before it kills us."

"She doesn't *want* to kill us. She wants to survive."

Elaysia grabbed a rock and drove it into his skull hard enough to render him unconscious for what would hopefully be the rest of the trial. Her blood ran warm as she watched him lie there, vulnerable as a babe. She traced the tip of her arrowhead over his neck and imagined slicing through the thin skin. No one would be the wiser if the chief met his demise in the woods. It's what he would do. But he hadn't given her cause. Not yet.

And if I end up killing you, I want you to know it was me.

Dragging his body a safe distance away from the ryptan took her the rest of the allotted time, and when the horn sounded, she collapsed, head swimming as though with the strongest of wine.

Rajar came to in a fury, spittle flying from his lips. "How dare you strike me, you cowardly"—he coughed up a spurt of blood and wiped it off his face in a smear. "You did this on purpose. I had you bested."

"I saved your life."

A war horn cut through the night. The second trial. She raced for the coastline.

"Don't worry, Ellie," Zavik shouted from the hill as she passed him and the Stormriders. "It's your best challenge."

Elaysia grimaced. It wasn't this trial she feared. It was the one now certain to follow. The wind ruffled feathers on her headdress as she ran, her mind focused on the task ahead and a hand on her belly. It jiggled the way her breasts did when not properly supported.

"Madness," she said after a burst of nervous laughter. Then, to her stomach, "I'm sure you're loving this."

When she reached the base of one of the gidmörni trees growing along the cliffside, she slung her bow over her shoulder and climbed. The second trial commanded her to harvest a flower that grew at the top. Legend said the trees thrived on ocean water by extracting nevethium fragments, which gave them immense height and greenish-blue bark. Elaysia, along with any decent climber, could easily scale such a tree with its abundance of branches, save for the last portion toward the top where the blossoms grew. There, it was dangerously thin and often snapped when a climber drew close.

The climb began easy enough. The branches were right where she needed them and not too slick from ocean mists. As she neared the halfway point, however, she caught sight of Rajar climbing a good distance above her the next tree over. She climbed faster, limbs aching from gripping and heart pounding from exertion. Carrying another life required twice the effort on her part to do anything she once deemed easy, and tonight already tested well past her limits. The further up she climbed, the more the wind hissed around her, chilling her bones and pulling at her body like a sail.

A cry mingled with the wind's howls. Elaysia stole a glance. Rajar had plummeted several branches and clutched onto one for survival, his legs flailing beneath him. A fall now would kill him. Or her. Elaysia reassured herself she was still lighter and the superior climber. She bit her lip and reached for the next branch, sap sliding down her hands and into her sleeves. The tree creaked and groaned beneath her, setting her heart aflutter. When the first blossom was less than a body's length away, something snapped. She panicked and lowered a branch.

Even a child would risk cracking the thin branches between her and the prize. Did she want it that badly? It could mean death to push on, but it would mean certain failure to retreat now.

No. She refused to let this all be for nothing.

Elaysia gritted her teeth and reached up, fingers trembling as everything in her body tensed. The branch cracked immediately. She cursed and leaned back to adjust her bow.

The bow. Of course.

Grabbing the bottom of her bow, she raised it toward the branch and hooked it over the base of the stem. The blossom came free with a tug. She shot out her hand and intercepted its fall, staring in awe at the iridescent petals. It was believed consuming the flower gave one visions of the future.

She didn't need to eat it to know what came next.

The high elders didn't hide their shocked expressions when Elaysia returned to the training grounds and dropped the blossom before them. Rajar was nowhere to be seen. Hope surged inside her. Maybe he'd fallen to his death, or at least sustained injuries rendering him incapable of a duel. She bowed and retreated to her Stormriders.

"You've won," Xaren cried, rushing up to her. "You've bested him one to nothing."

Elaysia didn't want to bear the bad news, nor was she certain she could speak it aloud. She averted her eyes.

"Not exactly," Zavik said timidly. He handed Elaysia water and a handful of anderberries, keeping his gaze on Xaren. "Even though she won the second trial, she still tied the first. Since she's the challenger and not the seated high chieftain, the last trial must be completed."

Elaysia's chest tightened. She forced down the berries without tasting them.

Xaren looked bewildered. "But if Rajar wins, they'd still be tied."

Jakki tossed aside her empty wineskin. "Idiot. Whoever wins the third trial *wins*. It's to the death."

"High Chieftain," Lumira said, pulling Elaysia aside. "You cannot best him in a duel, especially close combat with a bow. I'll go in your place."

Elaysia frowned and counted her arrows. "I know you mean well, but the participants must complete all trials alone."

Konar joined them with a grunt. She knew what he was thinking before he said it. "This is why I advised against a bow."

"Good thing you don't have to face the wrath of my terrible decision making. I'll figure it out." She gulped some water and marched to the arena, Zavik trailing quietly behind her.

When they reached the venue that would determine her fate, an oval-shaped pit encircled by ropes and posts, Rajar was already inside, swinging his club in mock blows.

"What's your plan?" Zavik asked as he strapped leather braces to Elaysia's forearms. They'd do little against Rajar's blows, but their illusion of protection seemed to ease Zavik's anxiety.

"Survive." Elaysia forced a laugh. All her strategies boiled down to exactly that.

Attendance had doubled since the trials began, and the crowd rumbled with anticipation. High Elder Sower raised a weathered hand to quiet everyone and explained the rules, eyeing Rajar all the while. Elaysia stepped into the ring. She avoided looking back at her Stormriders. They'd be there after she won, and if she didn't, she wouldn't have their apprehensive expressions be the last thing she saw.

Elaysia stood toe-to-toe with Rajar, the usual devious look in his eyes replaced with uncensored hatred. His club was half the length of her body. A direct hit meant death.

Rajar eyed her belly. "Two kills for one." The stench of alcohol rolled off his breath.

There's my advantage.

Elaysia flinched twice before the horn blew, tumbling out of the way moments before Rajar's first swing. Everything slowed. Rajar ripped the club's lodged teeth out of the ground and lunged for her. Another swing sailed over her head. She sidestepped, hurrying to string an arrow. He was on her before she let it fly. She dodged his club, scrambling for distance. His foot found her thigh with a *thud.* She gasped. Her legs buckled beneath her, the injured one warm and spasming. She crawled away from another swing. Landed a kick to his stomach. She needed space, but the arena hardly allowed for it. Lungs rasping, she darted around the pen. Rajar, though slower, especially with his club, never allowed her enough distance for a clean shot. She couldn't outrun him much longer.

No more running.

Wielding her bow like a staff, Elaysia charged Rajar. He hesitated, mouth agape. Elaysia struck his face. He screamed and rubbed his reddening cheek, then coughed a mixture of blood and teeth onto the ground. Not enough to kill him, but enough to enrage him to push past wisdom.

Blood trailed down the sides of Rajar's mouth as he lumbered toward her. "Time to join your family."

Elaysia backed against a pole. She planted her feet and closed her eyes. People screamed her name, Zavik's cry surpassing the others, but she tuned them out. She looked inward, gathering the pain, the lies, and the fear, redirecting it toward the man who, at this moment, embodied the cause of it all. She grabbed an arrow. He'd be on her in moments.

Three.

Two.

One.

Elaysia dove between his legs as he smashed the club down on the post where she'd stood. Its teeth caught in the wood. Before Rajar dislodged the weapon, she drove the arrow into his back with her bare hands. His cries filled the air as she sprinted back far enough to lose another in his leg. He limped toward her, dragging the club. She dropped him with an arrow in his good leg. Dawn crept over the mountains and spilled into the valley, lavishing the moment in ironic serenity. Bow–drawn, she crossed the arena to meet him. He regarded her with bloodshot eyes and snarled.

"You filthy, scheming mutt—" Rajar stopped short as Elaysia lowered the arrow to his head. "You lack the courage. You're a foolish, fearful child. Neharem deserves better, and I won't rest until she's mine." He spat in her face. A mixture of blood and bile.

Elaysia loosed the arrow. It lodged in Rajar's eye. His body twitched for a moment, then went lax. The bow fell from her hands, landing in the dirt with a *thud.* The crowd fell silent. A violent rush swirled Elaysia's stomach and crept up her throat. She heaved beside Rajar's body. On unsteady legs, she walked toward the high elders and thrust a trembling hand behind her.

"I've done all the challenge asks of me, and by the right granted to me through hoksanu, I ask to be reseated as high chieftain of Neharem."

With that, Elaysia strode away from the arena and locked herself in her loft for three days.

The ceremony commenced within a fortnight, nearly a year to the day since Elaysia's ill-fated induction. Fitting. This time, however, she opted for a less-traditional approach—or more traditional, depending how far back into the histories one looked. It would be held outside at sundown, sans speech and short one tribal representation; the Lautei fled after Rajar's death. The Banaxa remained to spite her, but the other tribes appeared neutral, if not supportive. Regardless, as she reclined against the steam hut wall, muscles shedding tension like a snakeskin, she found herself apathetic. A greater threat loomed, engorged as a storm cloud. Tonight, it would rain.

Maseeya poked her head inside and wrinkled her nose. "You've been in there too long. It's not good for the baby."

Elaysia peeled herself off the bench. After a quick dip in the stream, Maseeya wrapped her in a blanket and escorted her up the ramps to the High Tree, her arm linked in Elaysia's.

"You're showing." Maseeya patted Elaysia's belly. "I'll make you new clothes soon."

"Just cut a hole in my tunic. Should do the trick."

Maseeya rolled her eyes and *tsked*. Inside her loft, she retrieved a red gown of Az Zarian silk. Elaysia's eyes widened as she noted the low-cut back and exposed right arm.

"It's beautiful, but..." The words caught in her throat. A wave of disappointment surged through Maseeya's eyes. Elaysia chewed her lip. "I've never worn something that revealing."

Maseeya set the dress down and kneeled beside Elaysia, taking her hands in her own. "Our bodies are merely shells containing our souls, our true selves. Don't hide to appease the masses."

"But—"

"Make them deal with their prejudices head-on. If they don't evolve beyond it, that's their failing, not yours." Maseeya flashed a smile that Elaysia couldn't help but return. "Besides, you'll look radiant in this dress, and the other pieces were made here in Agaas."

Elaysia caressed the fabric. It was a beautiful dress. Gold-plated armor accented her hips, waist and shoulders, and someone had sculpted a pauldron opposite the cape into a stormbird's head. Onitus fluffed his feathers as if in approval. She slipped into the gown, silk clinging to her newly developed curves like a mist. After Elaysia dressed, Maseeya spread red tint on her lips and gestured to the door.

"Wait." Elaysia ran her fingers through her wavy hair. "Shouldn't we tame it or something?"

"You aren't rushing off to battle. It deserves to be free."

Elaysia hugged Maseeya, savoring the spiced smell of her hair, and with a cluck to Onitus, she started down the hall. She made it several paces before Maseeya called out.

"You're sure you don't want Konar to escort you?" She hovered in the doorway with an enormous grin and proud eyes.

"I need to escort myself this time." Elaysia took a step, then ran back for a final embrace. "Thank you for everything, Maseeya. You're a mother to me. I hope you know that."

Maseeya's eyes moistened. "I'll cherish it forever. Now go. I'll be watching."

Elaysia meandered through Agaas, relishing the stillness rarely found in the holy city. When she reached the beach, the soft murmur of a crowd greeted her amid flutes and drums. Onitus soared ahead, his midnight-blue plumage glimmering as vibrant as her armor in the blood-orange sunset. Elaysia wove through the crowd, waiting for any lingering mutters of disproval, but they never came. Or she chose to ignore them. Either way, she no longer cared. She was through with hiding. Instead, she cherished the gasps from people taking in Onitus's powerful elegance. Though he was smaller than the three females, his stature was nothing to mock, and he'd been the first stormbird to take flight.

At the head of the beach, where the waves kissed the sand, waited those she loved most. She approached Zavik first. He blushed.

"You look, um, ready to rule again." Zavik had initially refused to stand alongside the Stormriders, but his compliance only required so much prodding.

"If I look it, the confidence will follow, right?" She bumped her shoulder against his, exposed arm tingling in the briny breeze.

The Stormriders lined up beside Zavik along with their mostly behaved stormbirds; Shadow squawked in protest each time the waves dared to nip at his talons. Mardus, Yerakai, Jakki, and Grokhion wore ceremonial garments from their respective tribes, and Anahi, Xaren, and Lumira passed for Agaasian, thanks to Maseeya's handiwork. They greeted Elaysia with fists over their hearts and nods of approval. After the high elders restored their blessings to the second-time high chieftain, Jakki raised Elaysia's arm and pledged allegiance. The crowd responded with a thunderous cheer, chanting Elaysia's family name and shouting praises to Khiev-Tatamic.

A buzz akin to alcohol raced through Elaysia's body as she broke away from her Stormriders to address the people. Onitus followed, a deep screech erupting from his lungs. The people quieted. Elaysia closed her eyes. Inhaled the salty air. Tasted it on her tongue. The sun's warmth faded as the moons rose to supplant it. This time, it would be different. She'd fought for this. Earned this.

Elaysia opened her eyes, the bonds of shame and worry severed, at least for the moment. As she looked at her stormbird who shouldn't exist, the cheering people who'd hastened to unseat her, and her stomach where she carried a child from a love never meant to last, she found hope.

"Children of Neharem," she began, striving to find her own cadence instead of imitating Konar's. "Bound in blood are we, but there's more that unites us still: a deep love and respect for Quinaria and the life she so amply provides us. We understand life's cycle. You can't take without giving back. Quinaria's resources aren't infinite. But there are those who bleed her dry, repeatedly raping the land while we sit idle. I've seen what's become of Az Zar. The desolate patches they've sown dry. The factories they've built. The beasts they've annihilated. The people they've exploited. And now they move west. Trading with us is no longer enough. The All-Sovereign plots to enslave and absorb our people and do to Neharem what he's done to his land. We are either Quinaria's enemy or her ally. Which will you be? I'm not inciting violence. Not yet. But we must stand strong. For our culture. For our children. For our world. And when the time comes, if war is asked of us, we must fight. Are you with me?"

Neharem shouted in agreement, fists, children, and weapons raised high. Elaysia lifted her hand. The crowd fell silent.

"One voice is easily silenced. A hundred voices? Harder, but still weak. An idea, children of Neharem, an idea that's carried within the very bones of our nation cannot be silenced. Take a stand. For Neharem. For Quinaria. But most importantly, for yourselves. Only then will it inspire you to sacrifice everything. Now, shall we drink?" Elaysia bowed. The melody of flutes and drums filled the air, and people flocked back to Agaas.

Zavik ran up, beaming. "You couldn't have done better."

"I can always do better, but thank you. I'm happy they support us."

Elaysia's smile faded as she caught sight of Konar chattering with an elder. His violet eyes locked onto hers, flickering with awareness of what was about to transpire. He dismissed the elder and moved to an isolated section of the beach to await her.

Zavik squeezed her arm. "You must confront him. I'll gather the Stormriders."

"No. I'll do it myself. I don't want to cause a commotion tonight."

"Ellie..."

"Save me some smoked salmon. I won't be long."

Elaysia trudged barefoot through the sand toward Konar. She wasn't ready to let him go, to hear the confession tumble from his lips. But at least she was ready to stand on her own.

It was what he'd always wanted.

EPILOGUE

Rykahl grumbled all the way from the palace to the temple, occasionally drawing eyes from his escort of elite assassins. One looked his way now. Rykahl scowled until the soldier's gaze retreated. He raised a wine pouch to his lips. The journey wouldn't have been terrible in his prime, but he hadn't replenished in two moon cycles, and the shriveled carcass of his true age surfaced through aching limbs, wrinkled skin, and poor digestion. A thick fog rolled off the inlet, veiling the path ahead. When the sprawling archway of the temple emerged from the mist, and the roar of the waterfall drowned out all other sounds, he flicked his hand and broke free from the soldiers. They'd remain at the gate like the faithful dogs they were. He crossed the courtyard and hesitated outside the temple doors, letting his hand linger on the nevethium handle. This would not go well. She'd refused to return his letters, much less see him, since the petty band of savages swooped the girl away. But tonight, she'd sent a messenger boy to summon him. Her territory, of course.

He cracked the door open. His slippers made no sound as he shuffled across the great hall toward Karliah, but she sensed his presence and turned. She wore the simple cloak of her priests, fabric dyed nearly as dark as her skin. A scroll lay on the altar, and she returned to it, staring intently. She made no move to acknowledge him.

Rykahl moved to the opposite side of the altar and exaggerated a bow. "My lady."

"I have no patience for your formalities, genuine or not. You've lost my prize, and your means of making amends is a bow?" She refused to look up and scribbled something on a sliver of parchment.

"I've lost?" *Ungrateful wench.* Rykahl fought to control his tone. "You had her on the slaughter table."

"You've disappointed our Lord."

"And you let a dying girl and a handful of rogue warriors slip through your fingers."

"Who planted the weak link?"

"Zadel? He was as much your choice as mine."

"One task, I gave you. One. You failed."

"I never fail. I simply learn what not to do next time." Rykahl dared a few steps closer. "Besides, if your Lord is so powerful, why didn't he intervene? Perhaps he disapproved of your sacrifice. Or you."

Karliah lowered her hood. Her face contorted in a smile that made Rykahl's insides wriggle. She snapped her fingers, summoning two priests built like soldiers. One, a nyrian nearly as tall as a beridian, lumbered toward Rykahl and grabbed him by his throat.

Rykahl squirmed under his grasp, cheeks burning. "I'll have your head for this, you blundering fool." He searched for Karliah over the priest's shoulder. "You've gone too far, Karliah. Tell him to release me at once. I'm weakened in this, this—"

"Your natural form?" She crossed her arms and leaned against the table. If she cared for his well-being, she didn't show it. "I worried that if you went too long without being exposed to your true self, you might forget how much you need me and our Lord." She retrieved a small shieum from her robes, one she had custom made, and spun it on the table. "Losing their high chieftain is disappointing, but hardly your worst mistake."

Rykahl's arms grew weak from scrabbling at the hands around his neck. "The stormbirds," he gasped.

"Do you understand what's at stake if they reach sexual maturity? They would've been easier to work with as hatchlings, and you've lost us that chance." She snapped her fingers again. The priest lifted Rykahl higher, then slammed him to the ground.

Rykahl curled into a fetal position. Pain thudded into his elbow. Heavy bruising in his hip, if the way it throbbed was any sign. "I've done everything you've asked." His knees cracked as he struggled to rise. "I always have. What more do you want?"

"More than you can give." She glided to the altar. Two priests entered the room carrying an unconscious Neharem warrior. Apparently, she'd saved one of their wounded to inflict her twisted sense of justice upon.

Rykahl turned away. The sacrifices didn't unnerve him like the first had centuries ago, but the sight of blood still turned his stomach. He played no part in the rituals, and he intended to keep it that way. "What do you mean more than I can give? You can't do this without me."

"Can't I?"

The breath caught in his throat. He avoided her until his flesh was renewed.

After the Caman departed, Rykahl escaped into the courtyard. The fog still hung thick, and nevethium lamps glowed through the mist like wolf eyes. He extended his elbow. No pain. No aches.

No soul.

He clenched his fist and bit down on his lip until it drew blood.

Karliah joined him, gazing up through long eyelashes. "Don't worry. We still have need of you."

Rykahl choked on a laugh. "We? I wasn't aware you two were on such intimate terms."

"Jealous?" Her lips parted and curled up to one side, revealing a dimple.

A stirring of the longing he'd once felt tugged at him. *It's a trick, you fool. She outgrew you long ago.* He frowned.

Karliah feigned disappointment. "Lucky for you, Mavet used your failures to his advantage. Everything's going as planned. The young high chieftain may prove to be more useful on her throne than in the grave." A spark crept into Karliah's eyes. She traced the embroidery on Rykahl's robe. "Henceforth, I'll be moving into the palace and overseeing your daily affairs."

Rykahl stiffened. "We agreed long ago that scenario could be implicating."

"Long ago, we did." Karliah patted his chest then strolled about the temple courtyard as if she owned it. Theoretically she did, he supposed. "Your people are so crippled by fear they wouldn't dare say anything now, assuming they noticed. They're content to go about life with their heads buried in minuscule affairs. I suppose that's one thing you've succeeded at during your tenure."

The compliment, however coated in sarcasm, filled him with an air of confidence.

"I'll allow it." He strolled opposite her, hands clasped behind his back. "But our resources run dry. The skulmor won't steal nevethium for us any longer. Something to do with giants in the north and pushback from Neharem."

"Force them. They're mindless dogs."

"Cannot, I'm afraid. They've all but disappeared. Mavet knows where."

"Or Zahal, then."

"The river runs dry due east, and their diminishing croplands can't sustain further nevethium loss. Unless you want to deprive Cadar of her crystals, we need to go below."

"Not yet." Karliah bit the words. "We need more nevethium and time to develop a means of conveyance."

"Seems a conundrum, seeing as how that's why we need to go below."

"There are other surface nevethium stores."

"War is out of the question. Neharem poses a formidable challenge with the stormbirds, and they're no longer under the leadership you'd conspired for. No word from our ambassadors in Orillon, either. And"—he loosened a tangle in his hair, holding the ends up to examine it—"I have it on good authority the girl has come into possession of two scrolls."

"Impossible." There was worry in her voice, however faint.

"Apparently not." He closed the distance between them. "The Caverns exist after all."

"She couldn't have. We've had people searching for years."

"It wasn't her. One of her subordinates. Az Zarian descent." He regarded Karliah through the corner of his eye. "Would you like to rethink your plan?"

Whatever lapse in composure Karliah had, she regained it and slithered closer. "How do you destroy a nation willing to sacrifice the little they have?" Rykahl shrugged. "You break them from within."

Rykahl moved toward the archway. He could just make out the soldiers' forms in the fog. "Rajar is dead."

"Rajar served his purpose by overseeing the destruction of the living tree on the girl's induction day. That nevethium heart alone was worth his involvement. Besides, him staging the coup was only the first of many steps to weaken Neharem, and his death doesn't mean our options are exhausted. It's easy to find people willing to dissent. Spend a day undercover in your own city, Your Holiness. The stories you'd hear." She paused, waiting, presumably, for him to react.

For once, he didn't.

She grabbed his arm and spun him to face her. "It's time to remind our people they must serve their country and their god if they wish to live in peace. Draft all males sixteen and older unless elderly or invalid. Effective immediately, all slaves work double shifts. Anyone who refuses or is caught conspiring with the enemy will be made a public example of. And"—she jerked her thumb toward his guards—"it's time to replace your palace servants and officials again. They'll be suspicious now if they weren't already."

"As you wish." He needed a drink. Badly.

Karliah twisted her nevethium necklace. "I know Neharem's next move, and we'll be several steps ahead of them. We may have to lose some to win it all, but that's a sacrifice I'm willing to make."

"We have another angle to work with as well." Rykahl wrapped his arm around her waist and guided her across the path, the heat of her body warm against his. "The high chieftain will soon find herself at odds with an old advisor's dubious past, if she hasn't already. It will devastate her fragile, naïve spirit."

Karliah halted. "He's alive? You're sure it's him?"

"She confirmed it."

"And she believed you?"

"Not at first, but doubt is like a tree. The transition from sapling is subtle. Once you realize how great it's grown, it's too late to stop it."

"Oh, Konar, what have you gotten yourself into?" Karliah cracked a smile, revealing two rows of spotless teeth. "This only serves to strengthen us. I'll approach him with an offer he can't refuse."

"And what makes you think he won't?"

"How could he refuse me? He's my brother, after all."

AUTHOR'S NOTE

Thank you for reading *Of Thieves and Shadows*. I hope it provided you an escape while giving you some thought-provoking moments to dwell on. If you can spare a few minutes, I'd be ever so honored if you could leave a review on Goodreads and on Amazon (or wherever you purchased the book from). Aside from purchasing a book, leaving a rating and review is one of the best ways to support an author. Your feedback is important to me and will help other readers both find the book and decide whether to read it.

If you'd like to stay up to date on my writing journey, upcoming releases, and be the first to receive exciting news, please sign up for my newsletter at bshgarcia.com/subscribe. When you sign up, you'll also receive exclusive access to a **free** prequel novelette, *From the Ashes*. Set over two thousand years prior to the events in *Of Thieves and Shadows*, this story follows Igtheos amid the Nyzarian civil war and the deadly Siege of Cadar.

Note: if you're having difficulties navigating to the subscribe link via your e-reader, it may be easiest to just type the website into your phone or computer. Not all of the e-reader browsers are up to date.

You can also interact with me on Instagram and Twitter (@bshgarcia), and follow me for important updates on Facebook, Goodreads, and Threads (same handle).

Finally, I'd like to note that the fictional lands of Quinaria are inspired by events and legends from all over the world. None is intended as a faithful representation of any one country or culture at any point in history.

Thank you again for your support. I can't wait to thrust you into the next installment of this epic saga.

-B. S. H. Garcia

THE
INHABITANTS
OF
QUINARIA

The Inhabitants of Quinaria

The Tribes of Neharem

AGAAS {UH-GAHS}: *the capital of Neharem was founded long after the tribes evolved and was key in unifying them—located in Apáasutai territory*

- **Elaysia {ee-lay-zhuh}**: *nyman.* Surviving heir to the high chieftain and recently inducted leader of the twelve tribes of Neharem.

- **Konar {ko-nar}**: *nyrian.* High elder of Neharem and acting high chieftain until Elaysia came of age. Co-guardian of Elaysia after the death of her parents.

- **Jakki {juh-key}**: *nyrian.* Close friend of Elaysia's and next in line to become chief of the Yustano.

- **Maseeya {ma-see-uh}**: *human.* Once a handmaid to Annalee, Elaysia's mother, she now oversees food acquisition and distribution in Agaas. Co-guardian to Elaysia.

- **Zavik {zav-ick}**: *human.* A refugee from Orillon, he is a dear friend of Elaysia's and apprenticed to Konar to become a high elder.

- **Lumira {loo-meer-uh}**: *beridian.* A mercenary with no ties who finds herself seeking work of the unethical sort in Neharem.

- **Elishon {ee-lye-shun}—(deceased):** *nyrian.* Father of Elaysia and former high chieftain of Neharem.

- **Annalee {ann-uh-lee}—(deceased):** *human.* Mother of Elaysia and former citizen of Az Zar.

- **Annonitus {an-non-eye-tis}—(deceased):** *nyman.* Elder brother of Elaysia.

- **High Elder Strong-spear:** *nyrian:* The eldest of the three high elders overseeing Agaas and Neharem alongside the high chieftain.

- **High Elder Sower {so-er}:** *human.* The youngest of the three high elders overseeing Agaas and Neharem alongside the high chieftain.

- **Kayrune {kay-roon}—(deceased):** *nyrian.* Son of Konar.

APÁASUTAI {AH-PAW-SOO-TIE}: *a medium-sized tribe occupying the forests on the west coast, the Apáasutai are known for their hunting skills and bold-colored artforms.*

- **Yerakai {yer-uh-kye:** *nyrian.* A skilled tracker and well-respected among his people with close ties to Elaysia and Konar.

- **Arkuun {ar-koon}:** *nyrian.* Chief of the Apáasutai.

ATSUKUT {AT-SOO-CUUT}: *a small-sized tribe in the north, the Atsukut are said to have giants' blood giving them larger statures.*

BANAXA {BUH-NOX-UH}: *the largest tribe in Neharem known for their predominantly human population, they occupy a large plains territory.*

DARUK {DUH-RUUK}: *known for their fierce warriors and inclination toward farming, this small northern tribe shares a border with the formidable Skulmor.*

. **Jörd {yerd}:** *human.* One of the Daruk's best warriors.

. **Gibrund {jib-rund}:** *nyrian.* Chief of the Daruk.

KAHALOÁN {KAH-HUH-LOW-UHN}: *a small coastal tribe reliant on fishing and weaving textiles for trade.*

. **Raenais {ruh-nayz}:** *nyrian.* Chief of the Kahaloán.

LAUTEI {L-OW-TAY}: *second only to the Banaxa in population and to the Atsukut in stature, they have a history of aggression and were the last to join Agaas in a united Neharem.*

. **Rajar {ruh-zhar}:** *nyrian.* Chief of the Lautei.

MOÁKUN {MO-AH-KUN}: *a coastal tribe key to Neharem's trade alliance with Az Zar, they are skilled seafarers and boat-builders.*

. **Mardus {mar-dus}:** *human.* Son of the chief and frequent envoy to Agaas.

- **Orandus {oh-ran-dus}**: *human.* Chief of the Moákun and father of Mardus.

Moatiwe {MO-AH-TEE-WAY}: *exclusively nyrian, they are known for their ice-white eyes and aloof, taciturn natures.*

- **Unleto {uhn-leht-o}**: *nyrian.* A warrior.

- **Eeshta {ee-shta}**: *nyrian.* A warrior.

Morotôk {MO-ROH-TOKE}: *the smallest and northernmost tribe is comprised of hard-working individuals well acclimated to harsh weather and scarce resources.*

- **Amkah {ahm-kah}**: *human.* Chief of the Morotôk.

Ni'anko {NEE-ON-KOH}: *pacifist and philosophical, this west coast tribe welcomes anyone who honors their ways, native or not.*

- **Grokhion {grow-key-uhn}**: *beridian.* A transplant from The Beridian Isles who keeps his past shrouded.

- **Kelsia {kel-see-uh}**: *nyrian.* Chief of the Ni'anko.

Tangeesh {TANG-EESH}: *the southernmost tribe has merged the neighboring nation of Orillon's lifestyle with their own, including interbreeding with them.*

- **Anahi {uh-naw-hee}**: *human.* An Orillon native, she's

lived amongst the Tangeesh trading for several years.

YUSTANO {YOO-STAHN-OH}: *located on an island just off the southeastern coast of Neharem, they cultivate rare crops and place great value in artistic expression.*

. **Jattai {juh-tye}**: *nyrian.* Chief of the Yustano and mother of Jakki.

Neighboring Nations

ORILLON {OH-RILL-UHN}: *a short sail from Neharem, Orillon revels in luxury and consists of small oases scattered amid a desert landscape.*

. **Lanston {lan-stun}**: *human.* A successful merchant working in Orillon's capital, Munskahan.

. **T'Vak {t-vaak}**: *human.* A backhander for hire.

AZ ZAR {UHZ-ZAR}: *an empire with a long and bloody history, Az Zar boasts the strongest army in Quinaria.*

. **Davier {daav-ee-air}**: *human.* A decorated captain in the All-Sovereign's army.

. **Xaren {zah-ren}**: *human.* A soldier in the All-Sovereign's army.

. **The All-Sovereign**: *nyrian.* The supreme ruler of Az

Zar and believed by many to be a god.

- **The Lord Priestess:** *nyrian.* The head of the Mavist order and right hand to the All-Sovereign.

- **Dalgus {dal-gus}:** *nyrian.* Servant to the All-Sovereign.

- **Zhia {zee-uh}:** *nyrian.* A decorated general in the All-Sovereign's army.

- **Xianna {zee-ah-na}:** *human.* Davier's sister, a girl of six.

- **Kiska {kiss-kah}:** *human.* Davier's sister, a girl of ten.

- **Dynah {dye-nah}:** *human.* Davier's sister, a girl of fifteen.

- **Kyreena {kye-ree-na}:** *human.* Davier's mother.

- **Davkahl {daav-call}:** *human.* Davier's father, a war veteran.

- **Rykahl {rye-call}:** *nyrian.* A part of the ruling line of Zal Drusa. Next in line to become the emperor of Az Zar.

- **Karliah {kar-lye-uh}:** *nyrian.* Advisor to Rykahl.

- **Ryman {rye-mun}:** *nyrian.* A part of the ruling line of Zal Drusa. Son of Rykahl.

- **Ireena {eye-ree-na}—(deceased):** *nyrian.* Wife of Rykahl.

- **Ashaat the Victor {uh-shaat}—(deceased):** *nyrian.* The first emperor of Az Zar and ancestor of House Zal

Drusa.

- **Igtheos** {ig-thee-ohs}—(deceased): *nyrian*. The leader of the ancient Nyzarian rebellion and co-founder of Agaas.

THE BERIDIAN ISLES (THE ISLES): *home to the fierce beridians, a mighty seafaring people who prefer minimal contact with the mainlanders of Quinaria.*

- **Lumira:** *beridian*. (See under Agaas).

- **Grokhion:** *beridian*. (See under Ni'anko).

Other Important Figures

STORMBIRDS:

- **Onitus** {o-nigh-tus}: Largest of the males, reserved in demeanor but fiercely loyal and impulsive. Bonded to Elaysia.

- **Anadu** {uh-nah-doo}: Second only in size to Siren, she's the boldest of the bunch. Bonded with Lumira.

- **Siren** {sigh-ren}: The largest of the stormbirds, she's standoffish around outsiders and prone to aggression. Bonded to Jakki.

- **Wind Chaser:** Per his namesake, he's the fastest and

quite intelligent. Bonded to Yerakai.

- **Shadow:** The smallest of the bunch, he's unnoticed (as stormbirds go) and sleek. Bonded to Xaren.

- **Keera {key-ruh}:** Looks intimidating but she's actually the kindest of the birds. Bonded to Mardus.

- **Corvax:** He's an excellent judge of character with a strong memory. Bonded to Anahi.

- **Roth:** He's the wisest and not easily triggered but will do anything to protect his own. Bonded to Grokhion.

DIVINITY:

- **Khiev-Tatamic {khey-ev-ta-tah-mec}:** The great Creator. Commonly worshiped in Neharem.

- **Mavet/The Son {mah-vet}:** The son of Khiev-Tatamic. Worshiped in Az Zar, demonized in Neharem.

- **Chai'Tik/The Daughter {shy-teek}:** The daughter of Khiev-Tatamic. Worshiped in Neharem, demonized in Az Zar.

- **Rayanti {ray-ahn-tee}:** The god of war. Worshiped by the Lautei.

- **Itaso {ee-taas-oh}:** The mother of water. Worshiped by the Yustano.

- **Minara {mee-nar-uh}:** The goddess of love. Worshiped by the Kahaloán.

- **Rash-Yaanah {raash-yah-nuh}:** The god of the harvest. Worshiped by the Daruk.

- **Moartea {mo-ar-tee}:** The goddess of death. Worshiped by the Moatiwe.

THE
RACES
OF
QUINARIA

The Races of Quinaria

Beridians {bur-rid-ee-in}
- Physical features: Feline-esque beings covered in fur instead of skin with the tails and ears of great cats, they stand six to eight feet tall and walk upright

- Lifespan: Average of 300 years

- Traits: Poisonous claws, nocturnal vision

- Location: Predominately their isles with the exception of a few backhanders and explorers

Humans
- Physical features: Standard human variations

- Lifespan: Average of 75 years

- Traits: Skilled with tools and weapons

- Location: Some in eastern Az Zar and Neharem, but Orillon consists predominantly of humans

Myrem {meer-rem} (*also classified as Vysilliam in some belief systems, one of the three original races comprising a trinity of beings suited for sky, water, and land*)
- Physical features: Unknown, but rumored to be amphibious

- Lifespan: Rumored to be 1000 years

- Traits: The ability to breathe underwater

- Location: Unknown as they've not surfaced in generations

Nazrath {naz–wrath}

- Physical features: Giants rumored to have been three
times the size of a nyrian while still resembling their
basic features

- Lifespan: Unknown

- Traits: Immense strength and intelligence

- Location: Once northern Az Zar, but rumored to have
retreated to the Uncharted North where they died off

Nymans {nigh–men}

- Physical features: These rarely conceived human–nyrian hybrids tend to result in dual to tri–toned skin, hair,
and eyes while retaining the nyrian pointed ears and
luminescent eyes

- Lifespan: Average of 200 years

- Traits: While they tend to carry the superior health
and intellect of the nyrian parent, most nymans struggle
with infertility

- Location: Neharem and Orillon

Nyrians {neer-ree-in} *(also classified as Vysilliam in some belief systems, one of the three original races comprising a trinity of beings suited for sky, water, and land)*

- Physical features: Slightly taller than humans on average, white hair, pointed ears, and luminescent eyes

- Lifespan: Average of 500 years

- Traits: Strong immune systems, superior intelligence (due in part to the extended lifespan), better vision

- Location: Az Zar, Neharem (rarely found in Orillon)

Shaktar {shack-tar} *(also classified as Vysilliam in some belief systems, one of the three original races comprising a trinity of beings suited for sky, water, and land)*

- Physical features: Unknown, but legend says they could fly

- Lifespan: Rumored to have been eternal

- Traits: Unknown

- Location: Unknown, but legend says they occupy caverns in eastern Orillon

Skulmor {skull-mor}

- Physical features: Canine-esque beings covered in fur instead of skin with the tails and ears of wolves, they are roughly eight feet tall and prefer to move on all fours (though they can walk upright)

- Lifespan: Average of 40 years

- Traits: Hulking strength and powerful fangs

- Location: The Skulmor territory (nomadic)

GLOSSARY

Glossary

Agaas {uh-gaas}- the capital of Neharem.

anderberries- a sweet and salty berry that grows in the forest near Apáasutai coastline. Commonly used in baking and for wines.

arkthanax {arc-thuh-nax}- an Az Zarian invention capable of performing the work of a hundred men, much faster, and with little to no breaks. Production includes textile weaving, mining, etc.

aspar {as-per}- the basic monetary unit of Az Zar, and commonly used in Orillon. Made from lyvium (see definition) and casted into coins of varying size and shape to denote value.

awskada {aw-ska-duh}- the Zarith word for "witch."

backhander- someone for hire, usually for dangerous and/or illegitimate work, such as brute force, smuggling, body guarding, assassinating, etc.

belzaith {bell-zay-uth}- the Hispen word for "underworld spirit." Also, the name of Grokhion's ax.

Beridian Moonlight- a strong, sweet, fortified wine made from a rare fruit and a potent plant native to the Beridian Isles. It is highly alcoholic yet surprisingly palatable, and the secret plant added during fermentation creates a unique high for the consumer. (Also called Moonlight).

Cadar {cay-dar}- the capital of Az Zar.

Caman {cay-men}- immortal beings loyal to Mavet. Depending on one's belief system, they are said to be angels, demons, or myth.

Chai'Tik {shy-teek}– a goddess of great power, she is revered, demonized, or considered farce, depending on one's belief system. Also called The Daughter.

deathstalker– giant insects equipped with stingers that release a deadly venom. One of the three orders of The Great Beasts of Old.

Dzro Jiazin {zhro-jye-zin}– (also called The Cleansing) an Az Zarian holiday celebrating the foundation of Az Zar.

dzvadra {zhvah-dra}– the Zarith word for "deathstalker."

edoja {ee-doh-juh}– the Nyrinian word for "father."

endei {en-dye}– an Apáasutai phrase for "a bad omen."

eudna {yood-nuh}– the Zarith word for "father."

eumma {yuum-muh}– the Zarith word for "mother."

Everworld– an eternal paradise that is key to the belief system of some tribes and peoples.

Feasting Moons– summer. Contains the months Gryphar, sub-Gryphar, and Phoenal.

Gathering Moons– fall. Contains the months sub-Phoenal, Mavalar, and sub-Mavalar.

gidmörni tree {gid-meeorn-ee}– a tree species that grows on the cliffs of the western Neharem coastline and produces rare blossoms that provide extreme clarity when consumed.

Great Beasts of Old– the first of the beasts, wise as the Vysilliam (see definition) and blessed with long life and special abilities. Includes stormbirds, seaserpents, and deathstalkers.

groundshakes– a sudden and violent shaking of the ground, sometimes causing great destruction, as a result of movements within the land's crust or volcanic action.

hal-eudna {haal-yood-nuh}– the Zarith word for "grandfather."

Haeshol {hay-sholl}– a torturous, eternal holding place that is key to the belief system of some tribes and peoples.

helgin {hell-gin}- a monstrous boar with four tusks.

Hispen {hiss-pen}- the official language of The Beridian Isles.

hoksanu {hoke-saw-noo}- an ancient Neharem tradition allowing one to challenge a chief or the high chieftain for the right to lead. It consists of two to three trials between the leader and the challenger.

Khiev-Tatamic {khey-ev-ta-tah-mec}- the first god, the creator or discoverer of the world, he is revered, demonized, or considered farce based on the belief system of the character.

kinawa {key-naw-wah}- a stout, aromatic, erect annual herb native to Neharem. When smoked, its leaves release a psychoactive substance. It's believed to have therapeutic properties and enlighten one's mind.

kuba {koob-uh}- a nutrient-dense grain native to Az Zar. It has a nutty aroma and is most often steamed.

kuza {koo-zuh}- private military used by the great houses in Orillon.

lightbursts- contraptions that light up the sky with bursts of greenish-yellow light for celebrations. Commonly found in Az Zar and Orillon.

living trees- giant trees found in northwestern Neharem. The city of Agaas lives in them, and they are nurtured by large nevethium (see definition) crystals referred to as "hearts."

love-giver- a person who engages in sexual activity for payment. Commonly found in Orillon and considered an honorable profession, unlike the whores of Az Zar who are often slaves.

lyda {lye-duh}- the Nyrinian word for "demon."

lyvium {lye-vee-um}- native to Az Zar, it is stronger than any other metal, yet light and flexible, making it ideal for weapons.

Mavet {mah-vet}- a god of great power, he is revered, demonized, or considered farce, depending on one's belief system. Also called The Son.

Mavism {mah-viz-um}- the official religion of Az Zar, it contains rigid practices surrounding penance and the giving of one's self to Mavet, the savior, and the government.

mizol {mye-zoll}- a crustacean that produces a fluorescent, waterproof ink.

moon cycle- roughly a month's time on Quorath.

Munskahan {moon-ska-haan}- the capital of Orillon.

Myremese {meer-rem-eez}- a lost language once spoken by the myrem and retained by a handful of scholars.

nazrath- giants descended of the nyrian bloodline.

nevethium {nuh-veth-ee-um}- radiant green crystals whose absence, when overharvested and misused, renders the surrounding land inhospitable. Also referred to as "the heart of Quinaria."

Novitae {no-vee-tay}- a Neharem holiday celebrating the story of creation.

Nyrinian {nee-rin-ee-in}- the ancient tongue once spoken by all nyrians is the official language of Agaas. It is also spoken by upper-class citizens in Az Zar who choose to honor the ancient ways.

nytak {nigh-tack}- a deer-like creature native to Neharem with scaled hooves and long, furry tails.

pocoaon tree {poh-co-uhn}- a tree species found throughout Quinaria in generally cool areas. Most grow near rivers, lakes, or swamps, and have limber, dangling branches.

populum {pop-yoo-lum}- a hallucination-inducing root native to Orillon.

Prophets, the- a sacred order coinciding with Az Zar's foundation. They studied the natural world, kept records, explored alternate histories, and some believe they learned the powers of gods.

Prophets' Scrolls, the– parchments containing years of research, history, and philosophy, penned by the Prophets. Rumored to contain magic spells unlocking the power of gods.

Quinaria {quee-narr-ee-uh}– the central landmass on which the story unfolds. Includes Neharem, Az Zar, and Orillon. See map for details.

Quorath {cor-rath}– the planet in which Quinaria resides. Includes all of the known and unknown world.

ravager bird {rav-uh-jer}– a carrion bird species with brilliant red feathers found throughout Quinaria.

Resting Moons– winter. Contains the months Onelar, sub-Onelar, Vynar, and sub-Vynar.

ryptan {rip-tin}– a large avian-reptilian hybrid with feathers and scales. They rely on large talons and fangs to hunt and defend. Native to Neharem.

sandcat– large felines with long fangs. Native to Az Zar.

seahawk– birds that are both aerial and aquatic.

seaserpent– giant serpents that live in the sea. One of the three orders of The Great Beasts of Old.

sedare {suh-dare}– a mushroom native to Az Zar and known for its medicinal properties, specifically pain relief.

seers {see-ers}– a contraption worn over the eyes to enhance poor eyesight.

Shaktari {shack-tar-ee}– a lost language once spoken by the shaktar and retained by a handful of scholars.

shieum {shee-um}– new weapons made of lyvium and nevethium that launch far deadlier projectiles than arrows and make a booming sound when used. (Also called thunder-makers).

snatcher– a thief.

Sowing Moons: spring. Contains the months Chailar, sub-Chailar, Tiknal, and sub-Tiknal.

spirit walkers- angels or demons, or lesser gods and goddesses, depending on one's belief system.

stormbird- giant birds of prey capable of manipulating/channeling the weather. One of the three orders of The Great Beasts of Old.

Stormrider- an individual who has bonded with a stormbird and gained the privilege of approaching it, maintaining physical and emotional contact, and riding on its back.

sun-blood tree- a tree species found in Az Zar that produces small, tangy citrus fruits. They have vibrant crimson blossoms and are found in much of Az Zar's architecture and general imagery.

toi {toy}- a fermented plant drink with fruity undertones common among the southern tribes of Neharem.

tulek bear {too-lek}- giant bears of the north.

tungata root {toon-gah-tuh}- an earthy root located in northern Neharem that is often ground up into a powder and put in teas for energy.

tuross {ter-ross}- flying lizards bred from ancient times when messages needed to transcend water, land, and sky. They are still a primary form of long-distance communication.

Vysilliam {vye-sill-ee-um}- believed by some to be the three original races of Quinaria comprising a trinity of beings suited for sky, water, and land. Includes the shaktar, myrem, and nyrians.

watcher- someone who helps patrol or guard in Neharem.

Westmun {west-mun}- the official language of Orillon.

zaka-zaka {zah-kuh-zah-kuh}- a large marsupial serving as the primary form of transportation in Orillon deserts.

Zarith {zare-rith}- the official language of Az Zar.

ACKNOWLEDGMENTS

I used to think of writing as a solitary pursuit, and while the initial draft is, the journey to publication, like any epic quest, requires many allies.

Foremost, I want to thank my husband, Jared. You've been my muse, given me insight even when I didn't want (but desperately needed) it, picked apart my character motivations and plot holes, hand-drew beautiful art, created a hell of a map, and forced me to bring this book to print. I wanted to quit so many times, but you kept me going. Thanks for being the Sam to my Frodo.

To my children, Björn and Éowyn. You did everything in your power to stop this book, yet motivated me all the more. I hope this makes you proud one day.

Thank you, Piña Colada, Sake Bomb, and Mimosa. You've been there through many late night writing sessions, snuggling me, gazing at me, and occasionally getting fur caught in my keyboard. Pretty sure Piña deleted at least one draft.

My betas provided invaluable insight. Kelsey, Keira, Jacqueline, Kaela, Abbi, and Jessa, thank you for sacrificing your time and energy to make this story better. I'm forever indebted to you. Special thanks to Kelsey for letting me pick her brain all hours of the day and for comforting me when the slightest insecurity arises. Also special thanks to Kaela for creating some beautiful character art.

To my critique partner, Kaylea, who helped fine-tune this story and tolerated all my long-winded emails, thank you. I'm so lucky to have you on this journey with me. And to my international support team, Sarah, Ruth, Elin, Rebecca, Katharine, Elena, Alla, and Sindy—really, the whole writing community on Instagram—thank you. Our discussions have changed how I view story and my author journey, and your critiques have strengthened my craft. You're all brilliant writers. I'm honored to be acquainted with you.

Thanks to my talented cover designer, Jeff. The art is breathtaking. To my editors Claire and Jon, thank you for making the final product polished and professional.

Dad and Mom, this book may not be what you expected, but I still want to thank you for always encouraging my creative pursuits and for getting me hooked on books as a kid. Dad, I'll always cherish our bedtime Poe sessions. Mom, all those hours you spent on me instead of yourself mattered.

Tyler, Ryan, and Kensey: Siblings have many purposes, but one of the most influential periods of my childhood arose from you all allowing me to dictate our playacting epics in the backyard of a small coastal town. It was through play I learned story, and I couldn't have experimented with proper character and plot development without willing pawns—er, partners. I promise I will bring Boris and Josh to the page one day.

To Wardruna, thank you. I drafted much of my story while listening to you on repeat, and damn, do you set a scene.

Finally, thanks to you, dear reader. I know how hard it is to choose a book when social media and streaming services are vying for your attention, but you did just that, and I'm forever grateful.

ABOUT THE AUTHOR

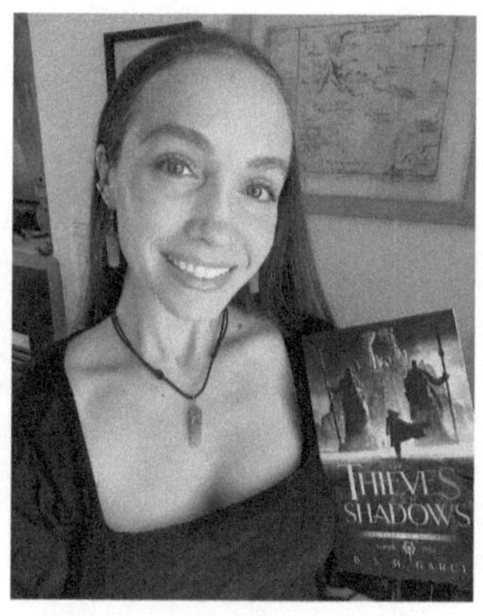

B. S. H. Garcia is the author of the epic fantasy series, *The Heart of Quinaria*. A household manager by day, writer by night, she graduated with honors from The University of Colorado with a bachelor's degree in English Writing. To get into character for her stories, she trudges through the woods in cosplay with a mead-filled drinking horn and has traveled from Oregon to New Zealand seeking inspiration. Visit her online at www.bshgarcia.com. There, you can get your hands on a FREE copy of *The Heart of Quinaria* prequel novelette, *From the Ashes*. All she asks for in exchange is your soul.

www.ingramcontent.com/pod-product-compliance
Lightning Source LLC
Chambersburg PA
CBHW061033310726
48969CB00004B/934